THE WORLDS OF SCIENCE FICTION

"A COLLECTION TO MAKE THE S-F READER PROUD OF HIS TASTE, AND TO LEAD THE GENERAL READER TO WONDER WHAT OTHER WEALTH HE'S MISSED."—*Fort Wayne News Sentinel*

The stories in this collection are by some of today's best known s-f writers, who provide an illuminating note on the background of their stories. Ranging in time from the present to the far future, and in settings from this world to outer space, their backgrounds are sometimes familiar and sometimes new. Alien monster, robots, creatures of the far future crowd their exciting pages. They tell of man as he is, as he was, and as he may be —in space travel, mind travel, time travel and in dimensions of existence full of wonder and danger.

". . . TOPNOTCH ANTHOLOGY . . . A DISTINGUISHED COLLECTION."—*Madison Capital Times*

THE WORLDS OF
SCIENCE FICTION

Edited and with an introduction by

Robert P. Mills

PAPERBACK LIBRARY, Inc.
New York

PAPERBACK LIBRARY EDITION

First Printing: July, 1965

For James H. Silberman

Library of Congress Catalog Card Number: 63-12175

This Paperback Library Edition is published by
arrangement with The Dial Press.

*Paperback Library books are published by Paperback Library, Inc. Its
trademark, consisting of the words "Paperback Library" and associated
distinctive design, is registered in the United States Patent Office.
Paperback Library, Inc., 260 Park Avenue South, New York, N.Y. 10010.*

ACKNOWLEDGMENTS

The First Men by Howard Fast
© 1960 by Mercury Press, Inc.; reprinted by permission of Paul R. Reynolds.

A Work of Art by James Blish
© 1956 by James Blish; originally entitled "Art Work"; reprinted by permission of Kenneth S. White.

Evening Primrose by John Collier
© 1941 by John Collier; reprinted by permission of Harold Matson Co., Inc.

Memento Homo by Walter M. Miller, Jr.
© 1954 by Ziff Davis Pub. Co.; reprinted by permission of Harold Matson Co., Inc.

A Miracle of Rare Device by Ray Bradbury
© 1961 by Ray Bradbury; originally appeared in Playboy; reprinted by permission of Harold Matson Co., Inc.

"All You Zombies—" by Robert A. Heinlein
© 1960 by Mercury Press, Inc.; reprinted by permission of Lurton Blassingame.

Faq' by George P. Elliott
© 1952 by George P. Elliott; originally appeared in The Hudson Review; reprinted by permission of Russell & Volkening.

Babel II by Damon Knight
© 1953 by Galaxy Publishing Corp.; reprinted by permission of author.

A Saucer of Loneliness by Theodore Sturgeon
© 1953 by Theodore Sturgeon; originally appeared in Galaxy; reprinted by permission of author.

Night Piece by Poul Anderson
© 1961 by Mercury Press, Inc.; reprinted by permission of Scott Meredith Literary Agency, Inc.

Now Let Us Sleep by Avram Davidson
© 1957 by Mercury Press, Inc.; reprinted by permission of the author.

The Strange Girl
© 1962 by Mark Van Doren; reprinted by permission of Nannine Joseph.

The Quest for Saint Aquin by Anthony Boucher
© 1951 by Henry Holt & Co.; reprinted by permission of Willis Kingsley Wing.

The War in the Air by R. V. Cassill
© 1952 by Epoch; reprinted by permission of Russell & Volkening, Inc.

The Ugly Little Boy
© 1958 by Galaxy Publishing Corp.; reprinted by permission of the author.

INTRODUCTION

A large proportion of the freshest, most stimulating fiction of our times is being done in the taboo-free field of science fantasy, and this anthology's purpose is to offer prime examples of that statement. The selections come from the pens of a clutch of distinguished writers who have occasionally or often investigated the vistas which are opened up when the fences of reality are levelled.

As a bonus—each story is a favorite, on one count or another, of its author, and the author in each instance has attached a note explaining why. And the epilogue, from Alfred Bester, looks into the problems of an author asked to name his favorites among his own works . . . in the course of which he tells a multitude of stories.

The stories here are not exclusively pure science fiction, though there are some examples present—the intention is to offer a wide variety of stories which will be intriguing and intelligible to the general reader as well as to the fan of science fiction (which last, in its more specialized forms, requires, for understanding, a scientific bent and some knowledge of what has been done in the field).

The range in time is from the distant past to the far future, and in setting, from this world to outer space. There are familiar social backgrounds, and new ones that man may come to one day, or strive toward, or strive to avoid; there are aliens and robots and the people who live next door; there is man as he was, as he is, and as he may be. There is space travel, and mind travel and time travel and stasis; there is hope, and there is despair.

There is one constant—man. And what all these stories attempt to do in one way or another is find a new vantage point from which to look at that curious beast in his endlessly various, noble and ignoble aspects.

—ROBERT P. MILLS

CONTENTS

The handful of science-fiction stories that I have written were done for the simple pleasure of doing them. I would think of something I wanted to say, and a science fiction story would be the only way of saying it, and mostly it was more fun than effort. *The First Men* was the hardest of the lot, because I was trying to say something very important to my own thinking; and when I finished, I found myself half-believing what I had written. That is a disconcerting position for a writer of fantasy to find himself in; but my doubts were eased when all sorts of people, friends and strangers, also began to half-believe it. I have received an astonishing amount of correspondence and comment on this story, much of it from psychologists and sociologists who have been thinking in the same directions. For myself, I like it best of my stories in that vein.

HOWARD FAST

THE FIRST MEN

by HOWARD FAST

By Airmail:

Calcutta, India
Nov. 4th, 1945

Mrs. Jean Arbalaid
Washington, D.C.

My dear sister:

I found it. I saw it with my own eyes, and thereby I am convinced that I have a useful purpose in life—overseas investigator for the anthropological whims of my sister. That, in any case, is better than boredom. I have no desire to return home; I will not go into any further explanations or reasons. I am neurotic, unsettled and adrift. I got my discharge in Karachi, as you know. I am very happy to be an ex-GI and a tourist, but it took me only a few weeks to become bored to distraction. So I was quite pleased to have a mission from you. The mission is completed.

It could have been more exciting. The plain fact of the matter is that the small Associated Press item you sent me was quite accurate in all of its details. The little village of Chunga is in Assam. I got there by plane, narrow gauge train and ox-cart—a fairly pleasant trip at this time of the year, with the back of the heat broken; and there I saw the child, who is now fourteen years old.

I am sure you know enough about India to realize that fourteen is very much an adult age for a girl in these parts—the majority of them are married by then. And there is no question about the age. I spoke at length to the mother and father, who identified the child by two very distinctive birthmarks. The identification was substantiated by relatives and other villagers—all of whom remembered the birthmarks. A circumstance not unusual or remarkable in these small villages.

9

The child was lost as an infant—at eight months, a common story, the parents working in the field, the child set down, and then the child gone. Whether it crawled at that age or not, I can't say; at any rate, it was a healthy, alert and curious infant. They all agree on that point.

How the child came to the wolves is something we will never know. Possibly a bitch who had lost her own cubs carried the infant off. That is the most likely story, isn't it? This is not *lupus,* the European variety, but *pallipes,* its local cousin, nevertheless a respectable animal in size and disposition, and not something to stumble over on a dark night. Eighteen days ago, when the child was found, the villagers had to kill five wolves to take her, and she herself fought like a devil out of hell. She had lived as a wolf for thirteen years.

Will the story of her life among the wolves ever emerge? I don't know. To all effects and purposes, she is a wolf. She cannot stand upright—the curvature of her spine being beyond correction. She runs on all fours and her knuckles are covered with heavy callus. They are trying to teach her to use her hands for grasping and holding, but so far unsuccessfully. Any clothes they dress her in, she tears off, and as yet she has not been able to grasp the meaning of speech, much less talk. The Indian anthropologist, Sumil Gojee, has been working with her for a week now, and he has little hope that any real communication will ever be possible. In our terms and by our measurements, she is a total idiot, an infantile imbecile, and it is likely that she will remain so for the rest of her life.

On the other hand, both Professor Gojee and Dr. Chalmers, a government health service man, who came up from Calcutta to examine the child, agree that there are no physical or hereditary elements to account for the child's mental condition, no malformation of the cranial area and no history of imbecilism in her background. Everyone in the village attests to the normalcy—indeed, alertness and brightness—of the infant; and Professor Gojee makes a point of the alertness and adaptability she must have required to survive for thirteen years among the wolves. The child responds excellently to reflex tests, and neurologically, she appears to be sound. She is strong—beyond the strength of a thirteen-year-old—wiry, quick in her movements, and possesses an uncanny sense of smell and hearing.

Professor Gojee has examined records of eighteen similar cases recorded in India over the past hundred years, and in every case, he says, the recovered child was an idiot in our terms—or a wolf in objective terms. He points out that it would be incorrect to call this child an idiot or an imbecile—any more than we would call a wolf an idiot or an imbecile. The child is a wolf, perhaps a very superior wolf, but a wolf nevertheless.

I am preparing a much fuller report on the whole business. Meanwhile, this letter contains the pertinent facts. As for money—I am very well heeled indeed, with eleven hundred dollars I won in a crap game. Take care of yourself and your brilliant husband and the public health service.

Love and kisses,
Harry

By cable:

```
HARRY FELTON
HOTEL EMPIRE
CALCUTTA, INDIA.
NOVEMBER 10, 1945
THIS IS NO WHIM, HARRY, BUT VERY SERIOUS
INDEED. YOU DID NOBLY. SIMILAR CASE IN
PRETORIA. GENERAL HOSPITAL, DR. FELIX VAN-
OTT. WE HAVE MADE ALL ARRANGEMENTS WITH
AIR TRANSPORT.
```

JEAN ARBALAID

By Airmail:

Pretoria, Union of South Africa
November 15, 1945

Mrs. Jean Arbalaid
Washington, D.C.

My dear sister:

You are evidently a very big wheel, you and your husband, and I wish I knew what your current silly season adds up to. I suppose in due time you'll see fit to tell me. But in any case, your priorities command respect. A full colonel was bumped, and I was promptly whisked to South Africa, a beautiful country of pleasant climate and, I am sure, great promise.

I saw the child, who is still being kept in the General Hospital here, and I spent an evening with Dr. Vanott and a young and reasonably attractive Quaker lady, Miss Gloria Oland, an anthropologist working among the Bantu people for her Doctorate. So, you see, I will be able to provide a certain amount of background material—more as I develop my acquaintance with Miss Oland.

Superficially, this case is remarkably like the incident in Assam. There it was a girl of fourteen; here we have a Bantu boy of eleven. The girl was reared by the wolves; the boy, in this case, was reared by the baboons—and rescued from them by a White Hunter, name of Archway, strong, silent type, right out of Hemingway. Unfortunately, Archway has a nasty temper and doesn't like children, so when the boy understandably bit him, he whipped the child to within an inch of its life. "Tamed him," as he puts it.

At the hospital, however, the child has been receiving the best of care and reasonable if scientific affection. There is no way of tracing him back to his parents, for these Basuto- land baboons are great travelers and there is no telling where they picked him up. His age is a medical guess, but reasonable. That he is of Bantu origin, there is no doubt. He is handsome, long-limbed, exceedingly strong, and with no indication of any cranial injury. But like the girl in Assam, he is —in our terms—an idiot and an imbecile.

That is to say, he is a baboon. His vocalization is that of a baboon. He differs from the girl in that he is able to use his hands to hold things and to examine things, and he has a more active curiosity; but that, I am assured by Miss Oland, is the difference between a wolf and a baboon.

He too has a permanent curvature of the spine; he goes on all fours as the baboons do, and the back of his fingers and hands are heavily callused. After tearing off his clothes the first time, he accepted them, but that too is a baboon trait. In this case, Miss Oland has hope for his learning at least rudimentary speech, but Dr. Vanott doubts that he ever will. Incidentally, I must take note that in those eighteen cases Professor Gojee referred to, there was no evidence of human speech being learned beyond its most basic elements.

So goes my childhood hero, Tarzan of the Apes, and all the noble beasts along with him. But the most terrifying thought is this—what is the substance of man himself, if this can happen to him? The learned folk here have been trying to explain to me that man is a creature of his thought and that his thought is to a very large extent shaped by his environment; and that this thought process—or mentation as they call it—is based on words. Without words, thought becomes a process of pictures, which is on the animal level and rules out all, even the most primitive, abstract concepts. In other words, man cannot become man by himself: he is the result of other men and of the totality of human society and experience.

The man raised by the wolves is a wolf, by the baboons a baboon—and this is implacable, isn't it? My head has been swimming with all sorts of notions, some of them not at all pleasant. My dear sister, what are you and your husband up to? Isn't it time you broke down and told old Harry? Or do you want me to pop off to Tibet? Anything to please you, but preferably something that adds up.

Your ever-loving Harry

By Airmail:

Washington, D.C.
November 27, 1945

Mr. Harry Felton
Pretoria, Union of South Africa

Dear Harry:

You are a noble and sweet brother, and quite sharp too. You are also a dear. Mark and I want you to do a job for us, which will enable you to run here and there across the face of the earth, and be paid for it too. In order to convince you, we must spill out the dark secrets of our work—which we have decided to do, considering you an upright and trustworthy character. But the mail, it would seem, is less trustworthy; and since we are working with the Army, which has a constitutional dedication to *top-secret* and similar nonsense, the information goes to you via diplomatic pouch. As of receiving this, consider yourself employed; your expenses will be paid, within reason, and an additional eight thousand a year for less work than indulgence.

So please stay put at your hotel in Pretoria until the pouch arrives. Not more than ten days. Of course, you will be notified.

Love, affection and respect,
Jean

By diplomatic pouch:

Washington, D.C.
December 5, 1945

Mr. Harry Felton
Pretoria, Union of South Africa

Dear Harry:

Consider this letter the joint effort of Mark and myself. The conclusions are also shared. Also, consider it a very serious document indeed.

You know that for the past twenty years, we have both been deeply concerned with child psychology and child development. There is no need to review our careers or our experience in the Public Health Service. Our work during the war, as part of the Child Reclamation Program, led to an interesting theory, which we decided to pursue. We were given leave by the head of the service to make this our own project, and recently we were granted a substantial amount of army funds to work with.

Now down to the theory, which is not entirely untested, as you know. Briefly—but with two decades of practical work as a background—it is this: Mark and I have come to the conclusion that within the rank and file of Homo Sapiens is the leavening of a new race. Call them man-plus—call them what you will. They are not of recent arrival; they have been cropping up for hundreds, perhaps thousands of years. But they are trapped in and molded by human environment as certainly and implacably as your Assamese girl was trapped among the wolves or your Bantu boy among the baboons.

By the way, your two cases are not the only attested ones we have. By sworn witness, we have records of seven similar cases, one in Russia, two in Canada, two in South America, one in West Africa, and, just to cut us down to size, one in the United States. We also have hearsay and folklore of three hundred and eleven parallel cases over a period of fourteen centuries. We have in fourteenth century Germany, in the folio MS of the monk, Hubercus, five case histories which he claims to have observed. In all of these cases, in the seven cases witnessed by people alive today, and in all but sixteen of the hearsay cases, the result is more or less precisely what you have seen and described yourself: the child reared by the wolf is a wolf.

14

Our own work adds up to the parallel conclusion: the child reared by a man is a man. If man-plus exists, he is trapped and caged as certainly as any human child reared by animals. Our proposition is that he exists.

Why do we think this super-child exists? Well, there are many reasons, and neither the time nor the space to go into all in detail. But here are two very telling reasons. Firstly, we have case histories of several hundred men and women, who as children had IQs of 150 or above. In spite of their enormous intellectual promise as children, less than 10 per cent have succeeded in their chosen careers. Roughly another 10 per cent have been institutionalized as mental cases beyond recovery. About 14 per cent have had or require therapy in terms of mental health problems. Six per cent have been suicides, 1 per cent are in prison, 27 per cent have had one or more divorces, 19 per cent are chronic failures at whatever they attempt—and the rest are undistinguished in any important manner. All of the IQs have dwindled—almost in the sense of a smooth graph line in relation to age.

Since society has never provided the full potential for such a mentality, we are uncertain as to what it might be. But we can guess that against it, they have been reduced to a sort of idiocy—an idiocy that we call normalcy.

The second reason we put forward is this: we know that man uses only a tiny fraction of his brain. What blocks him from the rest of it? Why has nature given him equipment that he cannot put to use? Or has society prevented him from breaking the barriers around his own potential?

There, in brief, are two reasons. Believe me, Harry, there are many more—enough for us to have convinced some very hard-headed and unimaginative government people that we deserve a chance to release *superman*. Of course, history helps —in its own mean manner. It would appear that we are beginning another war—with Russia this time, a cold war, as some have already taken to calling it. And among other things, it will be a war of intelligence—a commodity in rather short supply, as some of our local mental giants have been frank enough to admit. They look upon our man-plus as a secret weapon, little devils who will come up with death rays and superatom bombs when the time is ripe. Well, let them. It is inconceivable to imagine a project like this under benign sponsorship. The important thing is that Mark and I have been placed in full charge of the venture—millions of dollars,

15

top priority—the whole works. But nevertheless, *secret to the ultimate*. I cannot stress this enough.

Now, as to your own job—if you want it. It develops step by step. First step: in Berlin, in 1937, there was a Professor Hans Goldbaum. Half Jewish. The head of the Institute of Child Therapy. He published a small monograph on intelligence testing in children, and he put forward claims—which we are inclined to believe—that he could determine a child's IQ during its first year of life, in its pre-speech period. He presented some impressive tables of estimations and subsequent checked results, but we do not know enough of his method to practice it ourselves. In other words, we need the professor's help.

In 1937, he vanished from Berlin. In 1943, he was reported to be living in Cape Town—the last address we have for him. I enclose the address. Go to Cape Town, Harry darling. (Myself talking, not Mark.) If he has left, follow him and find him. If he is dead, inform us immediately.

Of course you will take the job. We love you and we need your help.

Jean

By Airmail:

Cape Town, South Africa
December 20, 1945

Mrs. Jean Arbalaid
Washington, D.C.

My dear sister:

Of all the hairbrained ideas! If this is our secret weapon, I am prepared to throw in the sponge right now. But a job is a job.

It took me a week to follow the Professor's meandering through Cape Town—only to find out that he took off for London in 1944. Evidently, they needed him there. I am off to London.

Love,
Harry

By diplomatic pouch:

Washington, D.C.
December 26, 1945

Mr. Harry Felton
London, England

Dear Harry:

This is dead serious. By now, you must have found the professor. We believe that despite protestations of your own idiocy, you have enough sense to gauge his method. Sell him this venture. Sell him! We will give him whatever he asks—and we want him to work with us as long as he will.

Briefly, here is what we are up to. We have been allocated a tract of eight thousand acres in northern California. We intend to establish an environment there—under military guard and security. In the beginning, the outside world will be entirely excluded. The environment will be controlled and exclusive.

Within this environment, we intend to bring forty children to maturity—to a maturity that will result in man-plus.

As to the details of this environment—well that can wait. The immediate problem is the children. Out of forty, ten will be found in the United States; the other thirty will be found by the professor and yourself—outside of the United States.

Half are to be boys; we want an even boy-girl balance. They are to be between the ages of six months and nine months, and all are to show indications of an exceedingly high IQ—that is, if the professor's method is any good at all.

We want five racial groupings: Caucasian, Indian, Chinese, Malayan and Bantu. Of course, we are sensible of the vagueness of these groupings, and you have some latitude within them. The six so-called *Caucasian* infants are to be found in European types, and two Mediterranean types. A similar breakdown might be followed in other areas.

Now understand this—no cops and robbers stuff, no OSS, no kidnapping. Unfortunately, the world abounds in war orphans—and in parents poor and desperate enough to sell their children. When you want a child and such a situation arises, buy! Price is no object. I will have no maudlin sentimentality or scruples. These children will be loved and cherished—and if you should acquire any by purchase, you will be giving a child life and hope.

17

When you find a child, inform us immediately. Air transport will be at your disposal—and we are making all arrangements for wet nurses and other details of child care. We shall also have medical aid at your immediate disposal. On the other hand, we want healthy children—within the general conditions of health within any given area.

Now good luck to you. We are depending on you and we love you. And a merry Christmas.

Jean

By diplomatic pouch:

Copenhagen, Denmark
February 4, 1946

Mrs. Jean Arbalaid
Washington, D.C.

Dear Jean:

I seem to have caught your silly *top-secret* and *classified* disease, and I have been waiting for a free day and a diplomatic pouch to sum up my various adventures. From my "guarded" cables, you know that the professor and I have been doing a Cook's Tour of the baby market. My dear sister, this kind of shopping spree does not sit at all well with me. However, I gave my word, and there you are. I will complete and deliver.

By the way, I suppose I continue to send these along to Washington, even though your "environment," as you call it, has been established. I'll do so until otherwise instructed.

There was no great difficulty in finding the professor. Being in uniform—I have since acquired an excellent British wardrobe—and having all the fancy credentials you were kind enough to supply, I went to the War Office. As they say, every courtesy was shown to Major Harry Felton, but I feel better in civilian clothes. Anyway, the professor had been working with a child reclamation project, living among the ruins of the East End, which is pretty badly shattered. He is an astonishing little man, and I have become quite fond of him. On his part, he is learning to tolerate me.

I took him to dinner—you were the lever that moved him, my dear sister. I had no idea how famous you are in certain circles. He looked at me in awe, simply because we share a mother and father.

Then I said my piece, all of it, no holds barred. I had expected your reputation to crumble into dust there on the spot, but no such thing. Goldbaum listened with his mouth and his ears and every fiber of his being. The only time he interrupted me was to question me on the Assamese girl and the Bantu boy; and very pointed and meticulous questions they were. When I had finished, he simply shook his head—not in disagreement but with sheer excitement and delight. I then asked him what his reaction to all this was.

"I need time," he said. "This is something to digest. But the concept is wonderful—daring and wonderful. Not that the reasoning behind it is so novel. I have thought of this— so many anthropologists have. But to put it into practice, young man—ah, your sister is a wonderful and remarkable woman!"

There you are, my sister. I struck while the iron was hot, and told him then and there that you wanted and needed his help, first to find the children and then to work in the environment.

"The environment," he said; "you understand that is everything, everything. But how can she change the environment? The environment is total, the whole fabric of human society, self-deluded and superstitious and sick and irrational and clinging to legends and phantasies and ghosts. Who can change that?"

So it went. My anthropology is passable at best, but I have read all your books. If my answers were weak in that department, he did manage to draw out of me a more or less complete picture of Mark and yourself. He then said he would think about the whole matter. We made an appointment for the following day, when he would explain his method of intelligence determination in infants.

We met the next day, and he explained his methods. He made a great point of the fact that he did not test but rather determined, within a wide margin for error. Years before, in Germany, he had worked out a list of fifty characteristics which he noted in infants. As these infants matured, they were tested regularly by normal methods—and the results were checked against his original observations. Thereby, he began to draw certain conclusions, which he tested again and again over the next fifteen years. I am enclosing an unpublished article of his which goes into greater detail. Sufficient to say that he convinced me of the validity of his methods. Subsequently, I watched him examine a hundred and four

19

British infants—to come up with our first choice. Jean, this is a remarkable and brilliant man.

On the third day after I had met him, he agreed to join the project. But he said this to me, very gravely, and afterwards I put it down exactly as he said it:

"You must tell your sister that I have not come to this decision lightly. We are tampering with human souls—and perhaps even with human destiny. This experiment may fail, but if it succeeds it can be the most important event of our time—even more important and consequential than this war we have just fought. And you must tell her something else. I had a wife and three children, and they were put to death because a nation of men turned into beasts. I watched that, and I could not have lived through it unless I believed, always, that what can turn into a beast can also turn into a man. We are neither. But if we go to create man, we must be humble. We are the tool, not the craftsman, and if we succeed, we will be less than the result of our work."

There is your man, Jean, and as I said, a good deal of a man. Those words are verbatim. He also dwells a great deal on the question of environment, and the wisdom and judgment and love necessary to create this environment. I think it would be helpful if you could send me a few words at least concerning this environment you are establishing.

We have now sent you four infants. Tomorrow, we leave for Rome—and from Rome to Casablanca.

But we will be in Rome at least two weeks, and a communication should reach me there.

More seriously—
And not untroubled,
Harry

By diplomatic pouch:

Via Washington, D.C.
February 11, 1946

Mr. Harry Felton
Rome, Italy

Dear Harry:

Just a few facts here. We are tremendously impressed by

your reactions to Professor Goldbaum, and we look forward eagerly to his joining us. Meanwhile, Mark and I have been working night and day on the environment. In the most general terms, this is what we plan.

The entire reservation—all eight thousand acres—will be surrounded by a wire fence and will be under army guard. Within it, we shall establish a home. There will be between thirty and forty teachers—or group parents. We are accepting only married couples who love children and who will dedicate themselves to this venture. That they must have additional qualifications goes without saying.

Within the proposition that somewhere in man's civilized development, something went wrong, we are returning to the prehistory form of group marriage. That is not to say that we will cohabit indiscriminately—but the children will be given to understand that parentage is a whole, that we are all their mothers and fathers, not by blood but by love.

We shall teach them the truth, and where we do not know the truth, we shall not teach. There will be no myths, no legends, no lies, superstitions, no premises and no religions. We shall teach love and cooperation and we shall give love and security in full measure. We shall also teach them the knowledge of mankind.

During the first nine years, we shall command the environment entirely. We shall write the books they read, and shape the history and circumstances they require. Only then, will we begin to relate the children to the world as it is.

Does it sound too simple or too presumptuous? It is all we can do, Harry, and I think Professor Goldbaum will understand that full well. It is also more than has ever been done for children before.

So good luck to both of you. Your letters sound as if you are changing, Harry—and we feel a curious process of change within us. When I put down what we are doing, it seems almost too obvious to be meaningful. We are simply taking a group of very gifted children and giving them knowledge and love. Is this enough to break through to that part of man which is unused and unknown? Well, we shall see. Bring us the children, Harry, and we shall see.

With love,
Jean

In the early spring of 1965, Harry Felton arrived in Washington and went directly to the White House. Felton had just

21

turned fifty; he was a tall and pleasant-looking man, rather lean, with graying hair. As President of the Board of Shipways, Inc.—one of the largest import and export houses in America —he commanded a certain amount of deference and respect from Eggerton, who was then Secretary of Defense. In any case, Eggerton, who was nobody's fool, did not make the mistake of trying to intimidate Felton.

Instead, he greeted him pleasantly; and the two of them, with no others present, sat down in a small room in the White House, drank each other's good health, and talked about things.

Eggerton proposed that Felton might know why he had been asked to Washington.

"I can't say that I do know," Felton said.

"You have a remarkable sister."

"I have been aware of that for a long time," Felton smiled.

"You are also very close-mouthed, Mr. Felton," the secretary observed. "So far as we know, not even your immediate family has ever heard of man-plus. That's a commendable trait."

"Possibly and possibly not. It's been a long time."

"Has it? Then you haven't heard from your sister lately?"

"Almost a year," Felton answered.

"It didn't alarm you?"

"Should it? No, it didn't alarm me. My sister and I are very close, but this project of hers is not the sort of thing that allows for social relations. There have been long periods before when I have not heard from her. We are poor letter writers."

"I see," nodded Eggerton.

"I am to conclude that she is the reason for my visit here?"

"Yes."

"She's well?"

"As far as we know," Eggerton said quietly.

"Then what can I do for you?"

"Help us, if you will," Eggerton said, just as quietly. "I am going to tell you what has happened, Mr. Felton, and then perhaps you can help us."

"Perhaps," Felton agreed.

"About the project, you know as much as any of us; more, perhaps, since you were in at the inception. So you realize that such a project must be taken very seriously or laughed off entirely. To date, it has cost the government eleven million dollars, and that is not something you laugh off. Now you understand that the unique part of this project was its exclusiveness. That word is used advisedly and specifically. Its success depended upon the creation of a unique and exclusive environment, and in terms of that environment, we agreed not to send any observers into the reservation for a period of fifteen years. Of course, during those fifteen years, there have been many conferences with Mr. and Mrs. Arbalaid and with certain of their associates, including Dr. Goldbaum.

"But out of these conferences, there was no progress report that dealt with anything more than general progress. We were given to understand that the results were rewarding and exciting, but very little more. We honored our part of the agreement, and at the end of the fifteen-year period, we told your sister and her husband that we would have to send in a team of observers. They pleaded for an extension of time—maintaining that it was critical to the success of the entire program —and they pleaded persuasively enough to win a three-year extension. Some months ago, the three-year period was over. Mrs. Arbalaid came to Washington and begged a further extension. When we refused, she agreed that our team could come into the reservation in ten days. Then she returned to California."

Eggerton paused and looked at Felton searchingly.

"And what did you find?" Felton asked.

"You don't know?"

"I'm afraid not."

"Well—" the Secretary said slowly, "I feel like a damn fool when I think of this, and also a little afraid. When I say it, the fool end predominates. We went there and we found nothing."

"Oh?"

"You don't appear too surprised, Mr. Felton?"

"Nothing my sister does has ever really surprised me. You mean the reservation was empty—no sign of anything?"

"I don't mean that, Mr. Felton. I wish I did mean that. I wish it was so pleasantly human and down to earth. I wish we thought that your sister and her husband were two clever and unscrupulous swindlers who had taken the government for eleven million. That would warm the cockles of our hearts compared to what we do have. You see, we don't know whether the reservation is empty or not, Mr. Felton, because the reservation is not there."

"What?"

"Precisely. The reservation is not there."

"Come now," Felton smiled. "My sister is a remarkable

woman, but she doesn't make off with eight thousand acres of land. It isn't like her."

"I don't find your humor entertaining, Mr. Felton."

"No. No, of course not. I'm sorry. Only when a thing makes no sense at all—how could an eight-thousand-acre stretch of land not be where it was? Doesn't it leave a large hole?"

"If the newspapers get hold of it, they could do even better than that, Mr. Felton."

"Why not explain," Felton said.

"Let me try to—not to explain but to describe. This stretch of land is in the Fulton National Forest, rolling country, some hills, a good stand of redwood—a kidney-shaped area. It was wire-fenced, with army guards at every approach. I went there with our inspection team, General Meyers, two army physicians, Gorman, the psychiatrist, Senator Totenwell of the Armed Services Committee, and Lydia Gentry, the educator. We crossed the country by plane and drove the final sixty miles to the reservation in two government cars. A dirt road leads into it. The guard on this road halted us. The reservation was directly before us. As the guard approached the first car, the reservation disappeared."

"Just like that?" Felton whispered. "No noise—no explosion?"

"No noise, no explosion. One moment, a forest of redwoods in front of us—then a gray area of nothing."

"Nothing? That's just a word. Did you try to go in?"

"Yes—we tried. The best scientists in America have tried. I myself am not a very brave man, Mr. Felton, but I got up enough courage to walk up to this gray edge and touch it. It was very cold and very hard—so cold that it blistered these three fingers."

He held out his hand for Felton to see.

"I became afraid then. I have not stopped being afraid." Felton nodded. "Fear—such fear," Eggerton sighed.

"I need not ask you if you tried this or that?"

"We tried everything, Mr. Felton, even—I am ashamed to say—a very small atomic bomb. We tried the sensible things and the foolish things. We went into panic and out of panic, and we tried everything."

"Yet you've kept it secret?"

"So far, Mr. Felton."

"Airplanes?"

"You see nothing from above. It looks like mist lying in the valley."

"What do your people think it is?"

Eggerton smiled and shook his head. "They don't know. There you are. At first, some of them thought it was some kind of force field. But the mathematics won't work, and of course it's cold. Terribly cold. I am mumbling. I am not a scientist and not a mathematician, but they also mumble, Mr. Felton. I am tired of that kind of thing. That is why I asked you to come to Washington and talk with us. I thought you might know."

"I might," Felton nodded.

For the first time, Eggerton became alive, excited, impatient. He mixed Felton another drink. Then he leaned forward eagerly and waited. Felton took a letter out of his pocket.

"This came from my sister," he said.

"You told me you had no letter from her in almost a year!"

"I've had this almost a year," Felton replied, a note of sadness in his voice. "I haven't opened it. She enclosed this sealed envelope with a short letter, which only said that she was well and quite happy, and that I was to open and read the other letter when it was absolutely necessary to do so. My sister is like that; we think the same way. Now, I suppose it's necessary, don't you?"

The Secretary nodded slowly but said nothing. Felton opened the letter and began to read aloud.

June 12, 1964

My dear Harry:

As I write this, it is twenty-two years since I have seen you or spoken to you. How very long for two people who have such love and regard for each other as we do! And now that you have found it necessary to open this letter and read it, we must face the fact that in all probability we will never see each other again. I hear that you have a wife and three children— all wonderful people. I think it is hardest to know that I will not see them or know them.

Only this saddens me. Otherwise, Mark and I are very happy—and I think you will understand why.

About the barrier—which now exists or you would not

25

have opened the letter—tell them that there is no harm to it and no one will be hurt by it. It cannot be broken into because it is a negative power rather than a positive one, an absence instead of a presence. I will have more to say about it later, but possibly explain it no better. Some of the children could likely put it into intelligible words, but I want this to be my report, not theirs.

Strange that I still call them children and think of them as children—when in all fact we are the children and they are adults. But they still have the quality of children that we know best, the strange innocence and purity that vanishes so quickly in the outside world.

And now I must tell you what came of our experiment—or some of it. Some of it, for how could I ever put down the story of the strangest two decades that men ever lived through? It is all incredible and it is all commonplace. We took a group of wonderful children, and we gave them an abundance of love, security and truth—but I think it was the factor of love that mattered most. During the first year, we weeded out each couple that showed less than a desire to love these children. They were easy to love. And as the years passed, they became our children—in every way. The children who were born to the couples in residence here simply joined the group. No one had *a father* or *a mother;* we were a living functioning group in which all men were the fathers of all children and all women the mothers of all children.

No, this was not easy, Harry—among ourselves, the adults, we had to fight and work and examine and turn ourselves inside out again and again, and tear our guts and hearts out, so that we could present an environment that had never been before, a quality of sanity and truth and security that exists nowhere else in all this world.

How shall I tell you of an American Indian boy, five years old, composing a splendid symphony? Or of the two children, one Bantu, one Italian, one a boy, one a girl, who at the age of six built a machine to measure the speed of light? Will you believe that we, the adults, sat quietly and listened to these six-year-olds explain to us that since the speed of light is a constant everywhere, regardless of the motion of material bodies, the distance between the stars cannot be mentioned in terms of light, since that is not distance on our plane of being? Then believe also that I put it poorly. In all of these matters, I have the sensations of an uneducated immigrant whose child is exposed to all the wonders of school and knowledge. I understand a little, but very little.

If I were to repeat instance after instance, wonder after wonder—at the age of six and seven and eight and nine, would you think of the poor, tortured, nervous creatures whose parents boast that they have an IQ of 160, and in the same breath bemoan the fate that did not give them normal children? Well, ours were and are *normal* children. Perhaps the first normal children this world has seen in a long time. If you heard them laugh or sing only once, you would know that. If you could see how tall and strong they are, how fine of body and movement. They have a quality that I have never seen in children before.

Yes, I suppose, dear Harry, that much about them would shock you. Most of the time, they wear no clothes. Sex has always been a joy and a good thing to them, and they face it and enjoy it as naturally as we eat and drink—more naturally, for we have no gluttons in sex or food, no ulcers of the belly or the soul. They kiss and caress each other and do many other things that the world has specified as shocking, nasty, etc.—but whatever they do, they do with grace and joy. Is all this possible? I tell you that it has been my life for almost twenty years now. I live with boys and girls who are without evil or sickness, who are like pagans or gods—however you would look at it.

But the story of the children and of their day-to-day life is one that will be told properly and in its own time and place. All the indications I have put down here add up only to great gifts and abilities. Mark and I never had any doubts about these results; we knew that if we controlled an environment that was predicated on the future, the children would learn more than any children do on the outside. In their seventh year of life they were dealing easily and naturally with scientific problems normally taught on the college level, or higher, outside. This was to be expected, and we would have been very disappointed if something of this sort had not developed. But it was the unexpected that we hoped for and watched for—the flowering of the mind of man that is blocked in every single human being on the outside.

And it came. Originally, it began with a Chinese child in the fifth year of our work. The second was an American child, then a Burmese. Most strangely, it was not thought of as anything very unusual, nor did we realize what was happen-

27

ing until the seventh year, when there were already five of them.

Mark and I were taking a walk that day—I remember it so well, lovely, cool and clear California day—when we came on a group of children in a meadow. There were about a dozen children there. Five of them sat in a little circle, with a sixth in the center of the circle. Their heads were almost touching. They were full of little giggles, ripples of mirth and satisfaction. The rest of the children sat in a group about ten feet away—watching intently.

As we came to the scene, the children in the second group put their fingers to their lips, indicating that we should be quiet. So we stood and watched without speaking. After we were there about ten minutes, the little girl in the center of the circle of five, leaped to her feet, crying ecstatically.

"I heard you! I heard you! I heard you!"

There was a kind of achievement and delight in her voice that we had not heard before, not even from our children. Then all of the children there rushed together to kiss her and embrace her, and they did a sort of dance of play and delight around her. All this we watched with no indication of surprise or even very great curiosity. For even though this was the first time anything like this—beyond our guesses or comprehension—had ever happened, we had worked out our own reaction to it.

When the children rushed to us for our congratulations, we nodded and smiled and agreed that it was all very wonderful. "Now, it's my turn, mother," a Senegalese boy told me. "I can almost do it already. Now there are six to help me, and it will be easier."

"Aren't you proud of us?" another cried.

We agreed that we were very proud, and we skirted the rest of the questions. Then, at our staff meeting that evening, Mark described what had happened.

"I noticed that last week," Mary Hengel, our semantics teacher nodded. "I watched them, but they didn't see me."

"How many were there?" Professor Goldbaum asked intently.

"Three. A fourth in the center—their heads together. I thought it was one of their games and I walked away."

"They make no secret of it," someone observed.

"Yes," I said, "they took it for granted that we knew what they were doing."

"No one spoke," Mark said. "I can vouch for that."

"Yet they were listening," I said. "They giggled and laughed as if some great joke was taking place—or the way children laugh about a game that delights them."

It was Dr. Goldbaum who put his finger on it. He said, very gravely, "Do you know, Jean—you always said that we might open that great area of the mind that is closed and blocked in us. I think that they have opened it. I think they are teaching and learning to listen to thoughts."

There was a silence after that, and then Atwater, one of our psychologists, said uneasily, "I don't think I believe it. I've investigated every test and report on telepathy ever published in this country—the Duke stuff and all the rest of it. We know how tiny and feeble brain waves are—it is fantastic to imagine that they can be a means of communication."

"There is also a statistical factor," Rhoda Lannon, a mathematician, observed. "If this faculty existed even as a potential in mankind, is it conceivable that there would be no recorded instance of it?"

"Maybe it has been recorded," said Fleming, one of our historians. "Can you take all the whippings, burnings and hangings of history and determine which were telepaths?"

"I think I agree with Dr. Goldbaum," Mark said. "The children are becoming telepaths. I am not moved by a historical argument, or by a statistical argument, because our obsession here is environment. There is no record in history of a similar group of unusual children being raised in such an environment. Also, this may be—and probably is—a faculty which must be released in childhood or remain permanently blocked. I believe Dr. Haenigson will bear me out when I say that mental blocks imposed during childhood are not uncommon."

"More than that." Dr. Haenigson, our chief psychiatrist, nodded. "No child in our society escapes the need to erect some mental block in his mind. Whole areas of every human being's mind are blocked in early childhood. This is an absolute of human society."

Dr. Goldbaum was looking at us strangely. I was going to say something—but I stopped. I waited and Dr. Goldbaum said:

"I wonder whether we have begun to realize what we may have done. What is a human being? He is the sum of his memories, which are locked in his brain, and every moment of experience simply builds up the structure of those memories. We don't know as yet what is the extent or power of

29

the gift these children of ours appear to be developing, but suppose they reach a point where they can share the totality of memory? Is it not simply that among themselves there can be no lies, no deceit, no rationalization, no secrets, no guilts—it is more than that."

Then he looked from face to face, around the whole circle of our staff. We were beginning to comprehend him. I remember my own reactions at that moment, a sense of wonder and discovery and joy and heartbreak too; a feeling so poignant that it brought tears to my eyes.

"You know, I see," Dr. Goldbaum nodded. "Perhaps it would be best for me to speak about it. I am much older than any of you—and I have been through, lived through the worst years of horror and bestiality that mankind ever knew. When I saw what I saw, I asked myself a thousand times: What is the meaning of mankind—if it has any meaning at all, if it is not simply a haphazard accident, an unusual complexity of molecular structure? I know you have all asked yourselves the same thing. Who are we? What are we destined for? What is our purpose? Where is sanity or reason in these bits of struggling, clawing, sick fish? We kill, we torture, we hurt and destroy as no other species does. We ennoble murder and falsehood and hypocrisy and superstition; we destroy our own bodies with drugs and poisonous food; we deceive ourselves as well as others—and we hate and hate and hate.

"Now something has happened. If these children can go into each other's minds completely—then they will have a single memory, which is the memory of all of them. All experience will be common to all of them, all knowledge, all dreams—and they will be immortal. For as one dies, another child is linked to the whole, and another and another. Death will lose all meaning, all of its dark horror. Mankind will begin, here in this place, to fulfill a part of its intended destiny—to become a single, wonderful unit, a whole—almost in the old words of your poet, John Donne, who sensed what we have all sensed at one time, that no man is an island unto himself. Has any thoughtful man lived without having a sense of that singleness of mankind? I don't think so. We have been living in darkness, in the night, struggling each of us with his own poor brain and then dying with all the memories of a lifetime. It is no wonder that we have achieved so little. The wonder is that we have achieved so much. Yet all that we know, all that we have done will be nothing compared to what these children will know and do and create—"

So the old man spelled it out, Harry—and saw almost all of it from the beginning. That was the beginning. Within the next twelve months, each one of our children was linked to all of the others telepathically. And in the years that followed, every child born in our reservation was shown the way into that linkage by the children. Only we, the adults, were forever barred from joining it. We were of the old, they of the new; their way was closed to us forever—although they could go into our minds, and did. But never could we feel them there or see them there, as they did each other.

I don't know how to tell you of the years that followed, Harry. In our little, guarded reservation, man became what he was always destined to be, but I can explain it only imperfectly. I can hardly comprehend, much less explain, what it means to inhabit forty bodies simultaneously, or what it means to each of the children to have the other personalities within them, a part of them—what it means to live as man and woman always and together. Could the children explain it to us? Hardly, for this is a transformation that must take place, from all we can learn, before puberty—and as it happens, the children accept it as normal and natural—indeed as the most natural thing in the world. We were the unnatural ones—and one thing they never truly comprehended is how we could bear to live in our aloneness, how we could bear to live with the knowledge of death as extinction.

We are happy that this knowledge of us did not come at once. In the beginning, the children could merge their thoughts only when their heads were almost touching. Bit by bit, their command of distance grew—but not until they were in their fifteenth year did they have the power to reach out and probe with their thoughts anywhere on earth. We thank God for this. By then the children were ready for what they found. Earlier, it might have destroyed them.

I must mention that two of our children met accidental death—in the ninth and the eleventh year. But it made no difference to the others, a little regret, but no grief, no sense of great loss, no tears or weeping. Death is totally different to them than to us; a loss of flesh; the personality itself is immortal and lives consciously in the others. When we spoke of a marked grave or a tombstone, they smiled and said that we could make it if it would give us any comfort. Yet later, when Dr. Goldbaum died, their grief was deep and terrible, for his was the old kind of death.

Outwardly, they remained individuals—each with his or

31

her own set of characteristics, mannerisms, personality. The boys and the girls make love in a normal sexual manner—though all of them share the experience. Can you comprehend that? I cannot—but for them everything is different. Only the unspoiled devotion of mother for helpless child can approximate the love that binds them together—yet here it is also different, deeper even than that.

Before the transformation took place, there was sufficient of children's petulance and anger and annoyance—but after it took place, we never again heard a voice raised in anger or annoyance. As they themselves put it, when there was trouble among them, they washed it out—when there was sickness, they healed it; and after the ninth year, there was no more sickness—even three or four of them, when they merged their minds, could go into a body and cure it.

I use these words and phrases because I have no others, but they don't describe. Even after all these years of living with the children, day and night, I can only vaguely comprehend the manner of their existence. What they are outwardly, I know, free and healthy and happy as no men were before, but what their inner life is remains beyond me.

I spoke to one of them about it once, Arlene, a tall, lovely child whom we found in an orphanage in Idaho. She was fourteen then. We were discussing personality, and I told her that I could not understand how she could live and work as an individual, when she was also a part of so many others, and they were a part of her.

"But I remain myself, Jean. I could not stop being myself."

"But aren't the others also yourself?"

"Yes. But I am also them."

"But who controls your body?"

"I do. Of course."

"But if they should want to control it instead of you?"

"Why?"

"If you did something they disapproved of," I said lamely.

"How could I?" she asked. "Can you do something you disapprove of?"

"I am afraid I can. And do."

"I don't understand. Then why do you do it?"

So these discussions always ended. We, the adults, had only words for communication. By their tenth year, the children had developed methods of communication as far beyond words as words are beyond the dumb motions of animals. If one of them watched something, there was no necessity for it to be described; the others could see it through his eyes. Even in sleep, they dreamed together.

I could go on for hours attempting to describe something utterly beyond my understanding, but that would not help, would it, Harry? You will have your own problems, and I must try to make you understand what happened, what had to happen. You see, by the tenth year, the children had learned all we knew, all we had among us as material for teaching. In effect, we were teaching a single mind, a mind composed of the unblocked, unfettered talent of forty superb children; a mind so rational and pure and agile that to them we could only be objects of loving pity.

We have among us Axel Cromwell, whose name you will recognize. He is one of the greatest physicists on earth, and it was he who was mainly responsible for the first atom bomb. After that, he came to us as one would go into a monastery —an act of personal expiation. He and his wife taught the children physics, but by the eighth year, the children were teaching Cromwell. A year later, Cromwell could follow neither their mathematics nor their reasoning; and their symbolism, of course, was out of the structure of their own thoughts.

Let me give you an example. In the far outfield of our baseball diamond, there was a boulder of perhaps ten tons. (I must remark that the athletic skill, the physical reactions of the children, was in its own way almost as extraordinary as their mental powers. They have broken every track and field record in existence—often cutting world records by one third. I have watched them run down our horses. Their movements can be so quick as to make us appear sluggards by comparison. And they love baseball—among other games.)

We had spoken of either blasting the boulder apart or rolling it out of the way with one of our heavy bulldozers, but it was something we had never gotten to. Then, one day, we discovered that the boulder was gone—in its place a pile of thick red dust that the wind was fast leveling. We asked the children what had happened, and they told us that they had reduced the boulder to dust—as if it was no more than kicking a small stone out of one's path. How? Well, they had loosened the molecular structure and it had become dust. They explained, but we could not understand. They tried to explain to Cromwell how their thoughts could do this, but he could no more comprehend it than the rest of us.

I mention one thing. They built an atomic fusion power

plant, out of which we derive an unlimited store of power. They built what they call free fields into all our trucks and cars, so that they rise and travel through the air with the same facility they have on the ground. With the power of thought, they can go into atoms, rearrange electrons, build one element out of another—and all this is elementary to them, as if they were doing tricks to amuse us and amaze us.

So you see something of what the children are, and now I shall tell you what you must know.

In the fifteenth year of the children, our entire staff met with them. There were fifty-two of them now, for all the children born to us were taken into their body of singleness —and flourished in their company, I should add, despite their initially lower IQs. A very formal and serious meeting, for in thirty days the team of observers were scheduled to enter the reservation. Michael, who was born in Italy, spoke for them; they needed only one voice.

He began by telling us how much they loved and cherished us, the adults who were once their teachers. "All that we have, all that we are, you have given us," he said. "You are our fathers and mothers and teachers—and we love you beyond our power to say. For years now, we have wondered at your patience and self-giving, for we have gone into your minds and we know what pain and doubt and fear and confusion you all live with. We have also gone into the minds of the soldiers who guard the reservation. More and more, our power to probe grew—until now there is no mind anywhere on earth that we cannot seek out and read.

"From our seventh year, we knew all the details of this experiment, why we were here and what you were attempting—and from then until now, we have pondered over what out future must be. We have also tried to help you, whom we love so much, and perhaps we have been a little help in easing your discontents, in keeping you as healthy as possible, and in easing your troubled nights in that maze of fear and nightmare that you call sleep.

"We did what we could, but all our efforts to join you with us have failed. Unless that area of the mind is opened before puberty, the tissues change, the brain cells lose all potential of development, and it is closed forever. Of all things, this saddens us most—for you have given us the most precious heritage of mankind, and in return we have given you nothing."

"That isn't so," I said. "You have given us more than we gave you."

"Perhaps," Michael nodded. "You are very good and kind people. But now the fifteen years are over, and the team will be here in thirty days—"

I shook my head. "No. They must be stopped."

"And all of you?" Michael asked, looking from one to another of the adults.

Some of us were weeping. Cromwell said:

"We are your teachers and your fathers and mothers, but you must tell us what to do. You know that."

Michael nodded, and then he told us what they had decided. The reservation must be maintained. I was to go to Washington with Mark and Dr. Goldbaum—and somehow get an extension of time. Then new infants would be brought into the reservation by teams of the children, and educated here.

"But why must they be brought here?" Mark asked. "You can reach them wherever they are—go into their minds, make them a part of you?"

"But they can't reach us," Michael said. "Not for a long time. They would be alone—and their minds would be shattered. What would the people of your world outside do to such children? What happened to people in the past who were possessed of devils, who heard voices? Some became saints, but more were burned at the stake."

"Can't you protect them?" someone asked.

"Some day—yes. Now, no—there are not enough of us. First, we must help move children here, hundreds and hundreds more. Then there must be other places like this one. It will take a long time. The world is a large place and there are a great many children. And we must work carefully. You see, people are so filled with fear—and this would be the worst fear of all. They would go mad with fear and all that they would think of is to kill us."

"And our children could not fight back," Dr. Goldbaum said quietly. "They cannot hurt any human being, much less kill one. Cattle, our old dogs and cats, they are one thing—"

(Here Dr. Goldbaum referred to the fact that we no longer slaughtered our cattle in the old way. We had pet dogs and cats, and when they became very old and sick, the children caused them peacefully to go to sleep—from which they never awakened. Then the children asked us if we might do the same with the cattle we butchered for food.)

35

"—but not people," Dr. Goldbaum went on. "They cannot hurt people or kill people. We are able to do things that we know are wrong, but that is one power we have that the children lack. They cannot kill and they cannot hurt. Am I right, Michael?"

"Yes—you are right." Michael nodded. "We must do it slowly and patiently—and the world must not know what we are doing until we have taken certain measures. We think we need three years more. Can you get us three years, Jean?"

"I will get it," I said.

"And we need all of you to help us. Of course we will not keep any of you here if you wish to go. But we need you —as we have always needed you. We love you and value you, and we beg you to remain with us . . ."

Do you wonder that we all remained, Harry—that no one of us could leave our children—or will ever leave them, except when death takes us away? There is not so much more that I must tell now.

We got the three years we needed, and as for the gray barrier that surrounds us, the children tell me that it is a simple device indeed. As nearly as I can understand, they altered the time sequence of the entire reservation. Not much —by less than one ten-thousandth of a second. But the result is that your world outside exists this tiny fraction of a second in the future. The same sun shines on us, the same winds blow, and from inside the barrier, we see your world unaltered. But you cannot see us. When you look at us, the present of our existence has not yet come into being—and instead there is nothing, no space, no heat, no light, only the impenetrable wall of nonexistence.

From inside, we can go outside—from the past into the future. I have done this during the moments when we experimented with the barrier. You feel a shudder, a moment of cold—but no more.

There is also a way in which we return, but understandably, I cannot spell it out.

So there is the situation, Harry. We will never see each other again, but I assure you that Mark and I are happier than we have ever been. Man will change, and he will become what he was intended to be, and he will reach out with love and knowledge to all the universes of the firmament. Isn't that what man has always dreamt of, no war or hatred or hunger or sickness or death? We are fortunate to be alive while this is happening, Harry—we should ask no more.

With all my love,
Jean

Felton finished reading, and then there was a long, long silence while the two men looked at each other. Finally, the Secretary spoke:

"You know we shall have to keep knocking at that barrier—trying to find a way to break through?"

"I know."

"It will be easier, now that your sister has explained it."

"I don't think it will be easier," Felton said tiredly. "I do not think that she has explained it."

"Not to you and me, perhaps. But we'll put the eggheads to work on it. They'll figure it out. They always do."

"Perhaps not this time."

"Oh, yes," the Secretary nodded. "You see, we've got to stop it. We can't have this kind of thing—immoral, godless, and a threat to every human being on earth. The kids were right. We would have to kill them, you know. It's a disease. The only way to stop a disease is to kill the bugs that cause it. The only way. I wish there was another way, but there isn't."

Ostensibly this is a story about the future of serious music, but actually it proposes no novelties in that field. Its real subject is the creative process itself; I chose a composer for my hero because I dislike stories about writers, but I might have used any art. The story adopts a radical scientific assumption in order to make a philosophical and emotional point that could have been made in no other way—which is the highest form of science-fiction and the most difficult to bring off. This sample so satisfies me that I regard it as a testament; and, also, as *A Work of Art*.

JAMES BLISH

A WORK OF ART

by JAMES BLISH

Instantly, he remembered dying. He remembered it, however, as if at two removes—as though he were remembering
a memory rather than an actual event, as though he himself
had not actually been there when he had died.

Yet the memory was all from his own point of view, not
that of some detached and disembodied observer which might
have been his soul. He had been most conscious of the rasp-
ing, unevenly-drawn movements of the air in his chest. The
doctor's face, blurring rapidly, had bent over him, loomed,
come closer still, and then had vanished as the head, turned
sideways to listen to his lungs, had passed below his cone of
vision.

It had become rapidly darker, and then, only then, had he
realized that these were to be his last minutes. He had tried
dutifully to say Pauline's name, but his memory contained no
record of that sound: only of the rattling breath, and of the
film of sootiness thickening in the air, blotting out everything
for an instant.

Only an instant . . . and then the memory was over. The
room was bright again, and the ceiling, he noticed with
wonder, had turned a soft green. The doctor's head lifted
again and looked down at him.

It was not the same doctor. This one was a far younger
man, with an ascetic face and gleaming, almost fey eyes.
There was no doubt about it. One of the last conscious
thoughts that he had had was that of gratitude that the attending physician, there at the end, had not been the one of
the three who obviously hated him for his one-time associations with the Nazi hierarchy. The attending doctor, instead,
had worn an expression amusingly proper for that of a Swiss
expert called to the deathbed of an eminent man: a mixture of
worry at the prospect of losing so famous a patient and com-
placency at the thought that at the old man's age nobody

could blame his doctor if he died. Pneumonia after all is a serious matter at 85, penicillin or no.

But this man was none of the three.

"You're all right now," the new doctor said, freeing his patient's head of a whole series of little silvery rods which had been clinging to it by a sort of fish-net cap. "Rest a minute and try to be calm. Do you know your name?"

He drew a cautious breath. There seemed to be nothing at all the matter with his lungs now. Indeed, he felt positively healthy.

"Certainly," he said, a little nettled. "Do you know yours?"

The doctor smiled crookedly. "You're in character, it appears," he said. "My name is Barkun Kris; I am a mind sculptor. Yours?"

"Richard Strauss. Composer."

"Very good," Dr. Kris said, and turned away. Strauss, however, had already been diverted by a new singularity. *Strauss* is a word as well as a name in German; it has many meanings—an ostrich, for instance, or bouquet—von Wolzogen had had a high old time working all the possible puns into the libretto of *Fire-Famine*. And it happened to be the first German word to be spoken either by himself or by Dr. Kris since that twice-removed moment of death. The language was not French or Italian, either. It was most like English, but not the English Strauss knew; nevertheless, he was having no trouble speaking it and even thinking in it.

Well, he thought, I'll be able to conduct *The Loves of Danae* after all. It isn't every composer who can premier his own last opera posthumously. Still, there was something queer about all this—the queerest part of all being that conviction, which would not go away, that he had actually been dead for just a short time. Of course medicine was making great strides, everyone knew that, but—

"Explain all this," he said, lifting himself to one elbow. The bed was different, too, and not nearly as comfortable as the one he had died in. (It was astonishing how easily that word came to him.) As for the room, it looked more like a dynamo shed than a sickroom. Had modern medicine taken to reviving its corpses on the floor of the Siemens-Schuckert plant?

"In a moment," Dr. Kris said. He finished rolling some machine back into what Strauss impatiently supposed to be its place, and crossed to the pallet. "Now. There are many things you'll have to take for granted without understanding

40

them, Dr. Strauss, or even attempting to. Not everything in the world today is explicable in terms of your assumptions. Please bear that in mind."

"Very well. Proceed, please."

"The date," Dr. Kris said, "is 2161, or in other words, it is now two hundred and twelve years after your death. Naturally you'll realize that by this time nothing remains of your body but some bones, which we have not disturbed. The body you have now was born in our own time and was volunteered for your use. It resembles your old one only vaguely. Before you look in a mirror to see what it's like, remember that its physical difference from the one you were used to is all in your favor. It's in perfect health, not unpleasant for other people to look at, and its physiological age is about fifty —which in these times is late youth."

A miracle? No, not in this new age, surely. It was simply a work of medicine. But what medicine! This was Nietzsche's eternal recurrence and the immortality of the *Uebermensch* combined into one.

"And where is this?" the composer said.

"In Port York, part of the state of Manhattan, in the United States. You will find the country less changed in some respects than I imagine you anticipate. Other changes, of course, will seem radical to you, but it's hard for me to predict which ones will strike you that way. A certain resilience on your part will bear cultivating."

"I understand," Strauss said, sitting up. "One question, please. Is it still possible for a composer to make a living in this century?"

"Indeed it is," Dr. Kris said, smiling. "As we expect you to do. That is one of the purposes for which we've—brought you back."

"I gather, then," Strauss said somewhat dryly, "that there is still a demand for my music. Some of the critics in the old days—"

"That's not quite how it is," Dr. Kris said. "I understand that some of your work is still played, but frankly I know very little about that side of the matter. My interest is rather in—"

A door opened somewhere and another man came in. He was older and more ponderous than Kris and had a certain air of the academic about him, but he too was wearing the oddly-tailored surgeon's gown and looked upon Kris' patient with the glowing eyes of an artist.

41

"A success again, Kris?" he said. "Congratulations."

"They're not in order yet," Dr. Kris said. "The final proof is what counts. Dr. Strauss, if you feel strong enough, Dr. Seirds and I would like to ask you some questions. We'd like to make sure your memory is clear."

"Certainly. Go ahead."

"According to our records," Kris said, "you once knew a man whose initials were R.K.L.; this was while you were conducting at the Vienna Staatsoper." He made the double "a" at least twice too long, as though German were a dead language he was striving to pronounce with the classical accent. "What was his name, and who was he?"

"That would be Kurt List—his first name was Richard, but he didn't use it. He was the assistant stage manager. Also he had talent; he was a pupil of that terrible young man, Berg—Alban Berg."

The two doctors looked at each other, but some iron rule seemed to forbid them any expression.

"Why did you offer to write an overture for *The Woman without a Shadow* and give the manuscript to the city of Vienna?"

"So I wouldn't have to pay the garbage-removal tax on the Maria Therese villa the city'd given me."

"In the back yard of your estate at Garmish-Partenkirchen there was a tombstone. What was carved on it?"

Strauss frowned. That was a question he would have been happy to be unable to answer. If one is to play childish jokes on one's self, it's best not to carve them in stone and put the carving where you can't help seeing it every time you go out back to tinker with the Mercedes.

"It says," he replied wearily, " 'Sacred to the memory of Guntram, Minnesinger, slain in a horrible way by his father's own symphony orchestra.' "

"When was *Guntram* premièred?"

"In—let me see—1894, I think."

"Where?"

"In Weimar?"

"Yes. Who was the leading lady?"

"Pauline de Ahna."

"And then—?"

"I married her." Strauss leaned forward anxiously. "Is she—"

"No," Dr. Kris said. "I'm sorry, Dr. Strauss; but we lack

42

the data to reconstruct more or less ordinary people. You must forgive us that."

The composer sighed. He did not know whether to be sorry or glad. He had loved Pauline, to be sure. On the other hand, this was a new life. It would be pleasant not to have to take off one's shoes every time one entered the house, so as not to scratch the polished hardwood floors. And also pleasant, perhaps, to have two o'clock in the afternoon come by without hearing Pauline's magic formula for dismissing guests: "Richard—*jetzt Komponiert!*"

"Next question," he said.

For reasons which Strauss did not understand, but was content to take for granted, he was separated from Drs. Kris and Seirds as soon as both were satisfied that the composer's memory was reliable, his health stable. His estate, he was given to understand, had long since been broken up—a sorry end for what had once been one of the major fortunes of Europe—but he was handed sufficient money to set up lodgings and resume an active life. He was provided, too, with introductions which proved valuable.

It took even longer than his realist's mind had expected to become adjusted to the changes that had taken place in music alone. It was, he quickly began to suspect, now a dying art, which would soon have a status not much above that which had been enjoyed by flower arranging, back in what he thought of as his own time. The trend toward fragmentation, which had been noticeable enough during his first life, had in 2161 proceeded almost to completion.

He paid no more attention to current American popular tunes than he had bothered to pay in his previous life, yet it was evident that their assembly-line production methods—all the ballad composers now frankly used a slide-rule-like device called a Hit Machine—now had their counterparts almost throughout serious music.

The conservatives these days, for instance, were the 12-tone composers—always, in Strauss' opinion, a dryly mechanical lot, but never as much so as now. Their gods—Schoenberg, Berg, Webern, the late Stravinsky—were looked upon by the listening public as great masters, on the abstruse side perhaps, but as worthy of reverence as any of the Three B's.

There was one wing of the conservatives, however, which had gone the 12-tone procedure one better. These men com-

43

posed what was called "stochastic music," put together by choosing each individual note by consultation with tables of random numbers. Their bible, their basic text, was a volume called *Operational Aesthetics,* which in turn derived from a discipline called information theory, and not one word of it seemed to touch upon any of the techniques and customs of composition known to Strauss. The ideal of this group was to produce music which would be "universal"—that is, wholly devoid of any trace of the composer's individuality, wholly a musical expression of the universal Laws of Chance. The Laws of Chance seemed to have a style of their own, all right, but to Strauss it seemed the style of an idiot child being taught to hammer a flat piano to keep him from getting into trouble.

By far the largest body of work being produced, however, fell into a category misleadingly called "science music." The term reflected nothing but the titles of the works, which dealt with space flight, time travel, and other subjects of a romantic or an unlikely nature. There was nothing in the least scientific about the music, which consisted of a mélange of clichés, imitations, and recordings of natural sounds (often so distorted that it was impossible to guess their origin), and stylistic tricks—in many of which Strauss was horrified to see his own time-warped and shopworn image.

The most popular form of science music was a nine-minute composition called a concerto, though it bore no resemblance at all to the classical concerto form; it was instead a sort of free rhapsody after Rachmaninoff—long after. A typical one—"Song of the Rings," it was called, by somebody named H. Valerion Krafft—began with a loud assault on the tam-tam, after which all the strings rushed up the scale in unison, followed at a respectful distance by the harp and one clarinet in parallel 6/4's. At the top of the scale cymbals were bashed together, *forte possible,* and the whole orchestra launched itself into a major-minor, wailing sort of melody; the whole orchestra, that is, except for the French horns, which were plodding back down the scale again in what was evidently supposed to be a countermelody. The second phrase of the theme was picked up by a solo trumpet with a suggestion of tremolo, the orchestra died back to its roots to await the next flash flood, and at this point, to the astonishment of every four-year-old child in the audience, the piano entered with the second theme.

Behind the orchestra stood a group of thirty women,
44

ready to come in with a wordless chorus intended to suggest the eeriness of Deep Space; but at this point, too, Strauss had already learned to get up and leave. After a few such experiences he could also count upon meeting in the lobby Sindi Noness, the agent to whom Dr. Kris had introduced him, and who was handling the reborn composer's output (what there was of it thus far). Sindi had come to expect these walkouts on the part of his client and patiently awaited them, standing beneath a bust of Gian-Carlo Menotti; but he liked them less and less, and lately had been greeting them by turning alternately red and white like a totipotent barber pole.

"You shouldn't have done it," he burst out after the Krafft incident. "You can't just walk out on a new Krafft concerto. The man's the president of the Interplanetary Society for Contemporary Music. How am I ever going to persuade them that you're a contemporary if you keep snubbing them?"

"What does it matter?' Strauss said. "They don't know me by sight."

"You're wrong. They know you very well, and they're watching every move you make. You're the first major composer the mind sculptors ever tackled, and the ISCM would be glad to turn you back with a rejection slip."

"Why?"

"Oh," said Sindi, "there are lots of reasons. The sculptors are snobs. So are the ISCM boys. Each of them wants to prove to the other that their own art is the king of them all. And then there's the competition; it would be easier to flunk you than to let you into the market. I really think you'd better go back in. I could make up some excuse—"

"No," Strauss said shortly. "I have work to do."

"But that's just the point, Richard. How are we going to get an opera produced without the ISCM? It isn't as though you wrote theremin solos or something that didn't cost so—"

"I have work to do," he said, and left.

And he did: work which absorbed him as had no other project during the last twenty years of his former life. He had scarcely touched pen to music paper—both had been astonishingly hard to find—when he realized that nothing in his long career had provided him with touchstones by which to judge what music he should write *now*.

The old tricks came swarming back by the thousands, to be sure: the sudden, unexpected key changes at the crest of a

45

melody; the interval stretching; the piling of divided strings, playing in the high harmonics, upon the already tottering top of a climax; the scurry and bustle as phrases were passed like lightning from one choir of the orchestra to another; the flashing runs in the brass, the chuckling of the clarinets, the snarling mixtures of color to emphasize dramatic tension—all of them.

But none of them satisfied him now. He had been content with them for most of a lifetime and had made them do an astonishing amount of work. But now it was time to strike out afresh. Some of the tricks, indeed, actively repelled him: where had he gotten the notion, clung to for decades, that violins screaming out in unison somewhere in the stratosphere was a sound interesting enough to be worth repeating inside a single composition, let alone in all of them?

And nobody, he reflected contentedly, ever approached such a new beginning better equipped. In addition to the past lying available in his memory, he had always had a technical armamentarium second to none; even the hostile critics had granted him that. Now that he was, in a sense, composing his first opera—his first after more than a score of them!—he had every opportunity to make it a masterpiece.

And every such intention.

There were, of course, many minor distractions. One of them had been that search for old-fashioned score paper, and a pen and ink with which to write on it. Very few of the modern composers, it developed, wrote down their music at all. A large bloc of them used tape, patching together snippets of tone and sounds snipped from other tapes, superimposing one tape on another, and varying the results by twirling an elaborate array of knobs this way or that. Almost all the composers of 3-V scores, on the other hand, wrote on the sound track itself, rapidly scribbling jagged wiggly lines which, when passed through a photocell-audio circuit, produced a noise reasonably like an orchestra playing music, overtones and all.

The last-ditch conservatives who still wrote notes on paper did so with the aid of a musical typewriter. The device, Strauss had to admit, semed perfected at last; it had manuals and stops like an organ, but it was not much more than twice as large as a standard letter-writing typewriter and produced a neat page. But he was satisfied with his own spidery, highly legible manuscript and refused to abandon it, badly through the one pen-nib he had been able to buy coarsened it. It helped to tie him to his past.

Joining the ISCM had also caused him some bad moments, even after Sindi had worked him around the political road-blocks. The Society man who examined his qualifications as a member had run through the questions with no more interest than might have been shown by a veterinarian examining his four thousandth sick calf.

"Had anything published?"

"Yes, nine tone poems, about three hundred songs, an—"

"Not when you were alive," the examiner said, somewhat disquietingly. "I mean since the sculptors turned you out again."

"Since the sculptors—oh, I understand. Yes, a string quartet, two song cycles—"

"Good. Alfie, write down 'songs'. Play an instrument?"

"Piano."

"Hm." The examiner studied his fingernails. "Oh, well. Do you read music? Or do you use a Scriber or tape clips? Or a Machine?"

"I read."

"Here." The examiner sat Strauss down in front of a viewing lectern, over the lit surface of which an endless belt of translucent paper was traveling. On the paper was an immensely magnified sound track. "Whistle me the tune of that, and name the instruments it sounds like."

"I don't read that *Musiksticheln,*" Strauss said frostily. "Or write it, either. I use standard notation, on music paper."

"Alfie, write down 'Reads notes only.'" He laid a sheet of grayly-printed music on the lectern above the ground glass. "Whistle me that."

"That" proved to be a popular tune called "Vangs, Snifters, and Store-Credit Snooky" which had been written on a Hit Machine in 2159 by a guitar-faking politician who sang it at campaign rallies. (In some respects, Strauss reflected, the United States had indeed not changed very much.) It had become so popular that anybody could have whistled it from the title alone, whether he could read the music or not. Strauss whistled it, and to prove his bona fides added, "It's in the key of B-flat."

The examiner went over to the green-painted upright piano and hit one greasy black key. The instrument was horribly out of tune—the note was much nearer to the standard 440/cps A than it was to B-flat—but the examiner said, "So

it is. Alfie, write down 'Also reads flats'. All right, son, you're
a member. Nice to have you with us. Not many people can
read that old-style notation any more. A lot of them think
they're too good for it.'

"Thank you," Strauss said.

"My feeling is, if it was good enough for the old masters,
it's good enough for us. We don't have people like them
with us these days, it seems to me. Except for Dr. Krafft,
of course. They were *great* back in the old days—men like
Shilkrit, Steiner, Tiomkin, Pearl . . . Wilder, Janssen . . .
Real goffin."

"Doch gewiss," Strauss said politely.

But the work went forward. He was making a little in-
come now, from small works. People seemed to feel a special
interest in a composer who had come out of the mind sculptors' laboratories; and in addition, the material itself, Strauss
was quite certain, had merits of its own to help sell it.

It was the opera which counted, however. That grew and
grew under his pen, as fresh and new as his new life, as
founded in knowledge and ripeness as his long full memory.
Finding a libretto had been troublesome at first. While it
was possible that something existed which might have served
among the literature for 3-V—though he doubted it—he
found himself unable to tell the good from the bad through
the fog cast over both by incomprehensibly technical production directions. Eventually, and for only the third time in
his whole career, he had fallen back upon a play written
in a language other than his own; and, for the first time,
decided to set it in that language.

The play was Christoper Fry's *Venus Observed,* in all
ways a perfect Strauss opera libretto, as he came gradually to
realize. Though nominally a comedy, with a complex farcical
plot, it was a verse play with considerable depth to it, and a
number of characters who cried out to be brought by music
into three dimensions; plus a strong undercurrent of autumnal
tragedy, of leaf-fall and apple-fall—precisely the kind of
contradictory dramatic mixture which von Hofmannsthal had
supplied him in *The Knight of the Rose,* in *Ariadne on Naxos,*
and in *Arabella.*

Alas for von Hofmannsthal; but here was another long
dead playwright who seemed nearly as gifted. And the musical
opportunities were immense. There was, for instance, the
fire which ended act two; what a *donneé* for a composer to
whom orchestration and counterpoint were as important as air

and water! Or take the moment where Perpetua shoots the apple from the Duke's hand; in that one moment a single passing reference could add Rossini's marmoreal *William Tell* to the texture as nothing but an ironic footnote! And the Duke's great curtain speech, beginning:

> Shall I be sorry for myself? In mortality's name
> I'll be sorry for myself. Branches and boughs,
> Brown hills, the valleys faint with brume,
> A burnish on the lake . . .

There was a speech for a great tragic comedian, in the spirit of Falstaff; the final union of laughter and tears, punctuated by the sleepy comments of Reedbeck, to whose sonorous snores (trombones, no less than four of them, *con sordini?*) the opera would greatly end . . .

What could be better? And yet he had come upon the play only by the unlikeliest series of accidents. At first he had planned to do a straight knockabout farce, in the idiom of *The Silent Woman,* just to warm himself up. Remembering that Zweig had adapted that libretto for him, in the old days, from a play by Ben Jonson, Strauss had begun to search out English plays of the period just after Jonson's, and had promptly run aground on an awful specimen in heroic couplets called *Venice Preserv'd,* by one William Atwe. The Fry play had directly followed the Atwe in the memory bank, and he had sent down for it out of curiosity; why should a twentieth-century playwright be punning on a title from the 18th?

After ten pages of the Fry play, the minor puzzle of the pun disappeared entirely from his concern. His Muse was smiling again; he had an opera.

Sindi worked miracles in arranging for the performance. The date of the première was set even before the score was finished, reminding Strauss pleasantly of those heady days when Fuerstner had been snatching the conclusion of *Elektra* off his worktable a page at a time, before the ink was even dry, to rush it to the engraver before publication deadline. The situation now, however, was even more complicated, for some of the score had to be scribed, some of it taped, some of it engraved in the old way, to meet the new techniques of performance; there were moments when Sindi seemed to be turning quite gray.

But *Venus Observed* was, as usual, forthcoming complete for Strauss' pen in plenty of time. Writing the music in first draft had been hellishly hard work, much more like being reborn than had been that confused awakening in Barkun Kris' laboratory, with its overtones of being dead instead; but Strauss found that he still retained his old ability to score from the draft almost effortlessly, as undisturbed by Sindi's half-audible worrying in the room with him as he was by the terrifying supersonic bangs of the rockets that bulleted invisibly over the city.

When he was finished, he had two days still to spare before the beginning of rehearsals. With those, furthermore, he would have nothing to do. The techniques of performance in this age were so completely bound up with the electronic arts as to reduce his own experience—he, the master Kapellmeister of them all!—to the hopelessly primitive.

He did not mind. The music, as written, would speak for itself. In the meantime he found it grateful to forget the year-long preoccupation with the stage for a while. He went back to the library and browsed rather unselectively through old poems, vaguely seeking texts for a song or two. He knew better than to bother with recent poets; they could not speak to him and he knew it. The Americans of his own age, he thought, might give him a clue toward understanding this America of 2161, and if some such poem gave birth to a song, so much the better.

The search was relaxing and he gave himself up to enjoying it. Finally he struck a tape that he liked: a tape read in a cracked old voice that twanged of Idaho of 1900. The poet's name was Pound; he said:

> . . . the souls of all men great
> At times pass through us,
> And we are melted into them, and are not
> Save reflexions of their souls.
> Thus I am Dante for a space and am
> One François Villon, ballard-lord and thief
> Or am such holy ones I may not write,
> Lest blasphemy be writ against my name;
> This for an instant and the flame is gone . . .

> So cease we from all being for the time,
> And these, the Masters of the Soul, live on.

He smiled. That lesson had been written again and again, from Plato onward. Yet the poem was a history of his own case, a sort of theory for the metempsychosis he had undergone, and in its formal way it was moving. It would be fitting to make a little hymn of it, in honor of his own rebirth and of the poet's insight.

A series of solemn, breathless chords framed themselves in his inner ear, against which the words might be intoned in a high, gently bending hush at the beginning . . . and then a dramatic passage in which the great names of Dante and Villon would enter ringing like challenges to Time . . . He wrote for a while in his notebook before he returned the reel to the stacks.

These, he thought, are good auspices.

And so the night of the première arrived, the audience pouring into the hall, the 3-V cameras riding on no visible supports through the air, and Sindi calculating his share of his client's earnings by a complicated game he played on his fingers, the basic law of which seemed to be that one plus one equaled ten. The hall filled to the roof with people from every class, as though what was to come would be a circus rather than an opera.

There were, surprisingly, nearly fifty of the aloof and aristocratic mind sculptors, clad in formal clothes which were exaggerated black and scarlet versions of their surgeon's gowns. They had bought a bloc of seats near the front of the auditorium, where the gigantic 3-V figures which would shortly fill the "stage" before them (the real singers would perform on a small stage in the basement) could not but seem monstrously out of proportion, but Strauss supposed that they had taken this into account in advance and dismissed it.

There was a tide of whispering in the audience as the sculptors began to trickle in, and with it an undercurrent of excitement the meaning of which was unknown to Strauss. He did not attempt to fathom it, however; he was coping with his own mounting tide of opening-night tension, which despite all the years he had never quite been able to shake.

The sourceless, gentle light in the auditorium dimmed, and Strauss mounted the podium. There was a score before him, but he doubted that he would need it. Directly before him, poking up from among the musicians and the microphones, were the inevitable 3-V snouts, waiting to carry his image to the singers in the basement.

The audience was quiet now. This was the moment. His baton swept up, and then decisively down, and the first theme came surging out of the pit. The stage came alight, revealing the Duke's housetop observatory with its phallic telescope, and there began that reminiscent introductory scene which had served so well in lieu of a prelude, since it allowed almost all of the important leitmotivs to be exposed.

For a while he was deeply immersed in the always tricky business of keeping the large orchestra together and sensitive to the flexing of the musical web beneath his hand. As his control firmed and became more secure, however, the task became slightly less demanding, and he was able to pay more attention to what the whole sounded like.

There, there was something amiss. Of course there were the expectable occasional surprises as some bit of orchestral color emerged with a different *klang* than he had calculated; that happened to every composer, even after a lifetime of experience. And there were moments when the singers, entering upon a phrase more difficult to handle than he had expected, sounded like someone about to fall off a tightrope (though none of them had actually fluffed once thus far; they were as fine a group of voices as he had ever had to work with).

But those were details. It was the over-all sound that was wrong. He was losing not only the excitement of the première —after all, that couldn't last at the same pitch all evening— but also his very interest in what was coming from the stage and the pit. He was tiring gradually, too, his baton arm becoming heavier and heavier. As the first act mounted to what should have been an impassioned outpouring of shining tone, he discovered that he was bored—so bored as to wish he could go back to his desk to work on that song.

Then the first act was over; only two more to go. He scarcely heard the applause. The twenty minutes' rest in his dressing room was just barely enough to give him the necessary strength. He was baffled. It was as though the music had been written by another person, though he could plainly remember having put down every note of it.

And suddenly, in the middle of the last act, he understood.

There was nothing new here. It was the old Strauss all over again—but weaker, more dilute than ever, as though someone had magically turned him into that tired, failing old man which had been the critical caricature of him during his ripest years. Compared with the output of composers like

52

Krafft, *Venus Observed* doubtless sounded like a masterpiece to this audience. But he knew, as he would have known in the old days had the critics been right. Then they had been wrong; but now, the resolutions, the determination to abandon the old clichés and mannerisms, the striving for something new—they had all come to nothing against the force of habit. Being brought to life again had meant bringing back to life as well all those deeply graven reflexes of his style. He had only to pick up his pen and they had overpowered him with easy automatism, no more under his control than the perk of a finger away from a flame, and so devoid of real life as to call into question whether he had ever had even a drop of the divine ichor in his veins . . .

His eyes filled. His body was young, but he was an old man . . . an old man. Another thirty-five years of this? Never, never. He had said all this before, centuries before. Nearly half a century condemned to saying it all over again, in a weaker and still weaker voice, aware that even this debased century would come to recognize in him only the burnt husk of greatness? No, never, never!

He was aware, dully, that the opera was over. The audience was screaming its joy. He knew that sound. They had screamed that way when *Day of Peace* had been premièred, because the Party had commanded them to scream. Here they were cheering the man he had been, not the man that *Venus Observed* showed with cruel clarity that he had become, had they ears to hear that. Cheers of ignorance—is the long travail only for these? No. Never.

He turned slowly toward the audience. With a subdued shock, and with a surprising sense of relief, he saw that the cheers were not, after all, for him.

They were for Dr. Barkun Kris.

Kris was standing in the middle of the bloc of mind sculptors, bowing to the audience. The sculptors nearest him were struggling with each other to shake his hand. More hands grasped his as he made his way to the aisle and walked forward to the podium. When he mounted the rostrum and took the composer's limp hand in his, the cheering became delirious.

Kris lifted his arm. Instantly, there was an intent hush in the house.

"Thank you," he said clearly. "Ladies and gentlemen, before we take leave of Dr. Strauss, let us again tell him what a privilege it has been for us to hear this fresh example of his mastery. I am sure no farewell could be more fitting."

The ovation lasted five minutes, and would have gone on another five if Kris had not cut it off.

"Dr. Strauss," he said, "in a moment, when I speak a certain formulation to you, you will realize that your name is Jerom Bosch, a man born in our century and with a life in it all his own. The superimposed memories which have made you assume the mask, the *persona*, of a great composer will be gone. We would like to keep Richard Strauss with us for another full lifetime, but the laws governing mind sculpture do not permit us so to extinguish forever the donor of your body, who has his own right to a long life. I tell you this so that you may understand why these people here share your applause with me."

A wave of assenting sound.

"The art of mind sculpture—the creation of artificial personalities for aesthetic enjoyment—may never reach such a pinnacle again. For you should understand that as Jerom Bosch you had no talent for music at all; indeed, we searched a long time to find a donor who was utterly unable to carry even the simplest tune. Yet we were able to impose upon such unpromising material not only the personality but the genius of a great composer. That genius belongs entirely to you, to the *persona* that thinks of itself as Richard Strauss. None of the credit goes to the man who volunteered for the scultpure. That is your triumph, and we salute you for it."

Now the ovation could no longer be contained. Strauss, with a crooked smile, watched Dr. Kris bow. This mind sculpturing was a suitably sophisticated kind of cruelty for this age; but the impulse, of course, had always existed. It was the same impulse that had made Rembrandt and Leonardo turn cadavers into art works.

It deserved a suitably sophisticated payment under the *lex talionis:* an eye for an eye, a tooth for a tooth—and a failure for a failure.

No, he need not tell Dr. Kris that the Richard Strauss he had created was as empty of genius as a dry gourd. The joke would always be on the sculptor who had been capable of producing a counterfeit of a great composer but might never hear the hollowness of the music now preserved on the 3-V tapes. Kris had done his homework in the critics well, but in the music badly; and for his pains, he had a critics' Strauss. He was welcome to it.

But for an instant a surge of revolt poured through his bloodstream. I am I, he thought. I am Richard Strauss until I die, and will never be Jerom Bosch, who was utterly unable to carry even the simplest tune. His hand, still holding the baton, came sharply up, though whether to deliver or to ward off a blow he could not tell.

He let it fall again, and instead bowed—not to the audience, but to Dr. Kris.

He was sorry for nothing, as Kris turned to him to say the word that would plunge him back into death, except that he would now have no chance to set that poem to music.

The stories I want to write are very different from those I like to read. I should like to put down something resembling a dream; a sort of collage of banalities, of improbable landscapes with two-dimensional figures, of arbitrary situations and haphazard denouements. But, as in dreams, all this should add up to rather more than the sum of its parts. Most of my stories fail in this important respect, but *Evening Primrose* fails less conspicuously than the rest; therefore it is my favorite. If I had written it in these days, I think I should call it *The Best Equipped Bomb-Shelter in the World.*

JOHN COLLIER

EVENING PRIMROSE

by JOHN COLLIER

In a pad of Highlife Bond, bought by
Miss Sadie Brodribb at Bracey's for 25¢

MARCH 21 Today I made my decision. I would turn my back for good and all upon the *bourgeois* world that hates a poet. I would leave, get out, break away—

And I have done it. I am free! Free as the mote that dances in the sunbeam! Free as a house-fly crossing first-class in the largest of luxury liners! Free as my verse! Free as the food I shall eat, the paper I write upon, the lamb's-wool-lined softly slithering slippers I shall wear.

This morning I had not so much as a car-fare. Now I am here, on velvet. You are itching to learn of this haven; you would like to organize trips here, spoil it, send your relations-in-law, perhaps even come yourself. After all, this journal will hardly fall into your hands till I am dead. I'll tell you.

I am at Bracey's Giant Emporium, as happy as a mouse in the middle of an immense cheese, and the world shall know me no more.

Merrily, merrily shall I live now, secure behind a towering pile of carpets, in a corner-nook which I propose to line with eiderdowns, angora vestments, and the Cleopatræan tops in pillows. I shall be cosy.

I nipped into this sanctuary late this afternoon, and soon heard the dying footfalls of closing time. From now on, my only effort will be to dodge the night-watchman. Poets can dodge.

I have already made my first mouse-like exploration. I tiptoed as far as the stationery department, and, timid, darted back with only these writing materials, the poet's first need. Now I shall lay them aside, and seek other necessities: food, wine, the soft furniture of my couch, and a natty smoking-jacket. This place stimulates me. I shall write here.

57

DAWN, NEXT DAY I suppose no one in the world was ever more astonished and overwhelmed than I have been tonight. It is unbelievable. Yet I believe it. How interesting life is when things get like that!

I crept out, as I said I would, and found the great shop in mingled light and gloom. The central well was half illuminated; the circling galleries towered in a pansy Piranesi of toppling light and shade. The spidery stairways and flying bridges had passed from purpose into fantasy. Silks and velvets glimmered like ghosts, a hundred pantie-clad models offered simpers and embraces to the desert air. Rings, clips, and bracelets glittered frostily in a desolate absence of Honey and Daddy.

Creeping along the transverse aisles, which were in deeper darkness, I felt like a wandering thought in the dreaming brain of a chorus girl down on her luck. Only, of course, their brains are not so big as Bracey's Giant Emporium. And there was no man there.

None, that is, except the night-watchman. I had forgotten him. As I crossed an open space on the mezzanine floor, hugging the lee of a display of sultry shawls, I became aware of a regular thudding, which might almost have been that of my own heart. Suddenly it burst upon me that it came from outside. It was footsteps, and they were only a few paces away. Quick as a flash I seized a flamboyant mantilla, whirled it about me and stood with one arm outflung, like a Carmen petrified in a gesture of disdain.

I was successful. He passed me, jingling his little machine on its chain, humming his little tune, his eyes scaled with refractions of the blaring day. "Go, worldling!" I whispered, and permitted myself a soundless laugh.

It froze on my lips. My heart faltered. A new fear seized me.

I was afraid to move. I was afraid to look around. I felt I was being watched, by something that could see right through me. This was a very different feeling from the ordinary emergency caused by the very ordinary night-watchman. My conscious impulse was the obvious one: to glance behind me. But my eyes knew better. I remained absolutely petrified, staring straight ahead.

My eyes were trying to tell me something that my brain refused to believe. They made their point. I was looking straight into another pair of eyes, human eyes, but large, flat, luminous. I have seen such eyes among the nocturnal crea-

58

tures, which creep out under the artificial blue moonlight in the zoo.

The owner was only a dozen feet away from me. The watchman had passed between us, nearer him than me. Yet he had not seen him. I must have been looking straight at him for several minutes at a stretch. I had not seen him either.

He was half reclining against a low dais where, on a floor of russet leaves, and flanked by billows of glowing home-spun, the fresh-faced waxen girls modeled spectator sports suits in herringbones, checks, and plaids. He leaned against the skirt of one of these Dianas; its folds concealed perhaps his ear, his shoulder, and a little of his right side. He, himself, was clad in dim but large-patterned Shetland tweeds of the latest cut, suède shoes, a shirt of a rather broad *motif* in olive, pink and gray. He was as pale as a creature found under a stone. His long thin arms ended in hands that hung floatingly, more like trailing, transparent fins, or wisps of chiffon, than ordinary hands.

He spoke. His voice was not a voice; it was a mere whistling under the tongue. "Not bad, for a beginner!"

I grasped that he was complimenting me, rather satirically, on my own, more amateurish, feat of camouflage. I stuttered. I said, "I'm sorry. I didn't know anyone else lived here." I noticed, even as I spoke, that I was imitating his own whistling sibilant utterance.

"Oh, yes," he said. *"We* live here. It's delightful."

"We?"

"Yes, all of us. Look!"

We were near the edge of the first gallery. He swept his long hand round, indicating the whole well of the shop. I looked. I saw nothing. I could hear nothing, except the watchman's thudding step receding infinitely far along some basement aisle.

"Don't you see?"

You know the sensation one has, peering into the half-light of a vivarium? One sees bark, pebbles, a few leaves, nothing more. And then, suddenly, a stone breathes—it is a toad; there is a chameleon, another, a coiled adder, a mantis among the leaves. The whole case seems crepitant with life. Perhaps the whole world is. One glances at one's sleeve, one's feet.

So it was with the shop. I looked, and it was empty. I looked, and there was an old lady, clambering out from behind the monstrous clock. There were three girls, elderly

59

ingénues, incredibly emaciated, simpering at the entrance of the perfumery. Their hair was a fine floss, pale as gossamer. Equally brittle and colorless was a man with the appearance of a colonel of southern extraction, who stood regarding me while he caressed mustachios that would have done credit to a crystal shrimp. A chintzy woman, possibly of literary tastes, swam forward from the curtains and drapes.

They came thick about me, fluttering, whistling, like a waving of gauze in the wind. Their eyes were wide and flatly bright. I saw there was no color to the iris.

"How raw he looks!"

"A detective! Send for the Dark Men!"

"I'm not a detective. I am a poet. I have renounced the world."

"He is a poet. He has come over to us. Mr. Roscoe found him."

"He admires us."

"He must meet Mrs. Vanderpant."

I was taken to meet Mrs. Vanderpant. She proved to be the Grand Old Lady of the store, almost entirely transparent.

"So you are a poet, Mr. Snell? You will find inspiration here. I am quite the oldest inhabitant. Three mergers and a complete rebuilding, but they didn't get rid of me!"

"Tell how you went out by daylight, dear Mrs. Vanderpant, and nearly got bought for Whistler's *Mother.*"

"That was in pre-war days. I was more robust then. But at the cash desk they suddenly remembered there was no frame. And when they came back to look at me—"

"—She was gone."

Their laughter was like the stridulation of the ghosts of grasshoppers.

"Where is Ella? Where is my broth?"

"She is bringing it, Mrs. Vanderpant. It will come."

"Tiresome little creature! She is our foundling, Mr. Snell. She is not quite our sort."

"Is that so, Mrs. Vanderpant? Dear, dear!"

"I lived alone here, Mr. Snell, for many years. I took refuge here in the terrible times in the eighties. I was a young girl then, a beauty, people were kind enough to say, but poor Papa lost his money. Bracey's meant a lot to a young girl, in the New York of those days, Mr. Snell. It seemed to me terrible that I should not be able to come here in the ordinary way. So I came here for good. I was quite alarmed when others began to come in, after the crash of 1907. But it was the dear Judge, the Colonel, Mrs. Bilbee—"

I bowed. I was being introduced.

"Mrs. Bilbee writes plays. *And* of a very old Philadelphia family. You will find us quite *nice* here, Mr. Snell."

"I feel it a great privilege, Mrs. Vanderpant."

"And of course, all our dear *young* people came in '29. *Their* poor papas jumped from skyscrapers."

I did a great deal of bowing and whistling. The introductions took a long time. Who would have thought so many people lived in Bracey's?

"And here at last is Ella with my broth."

It was then I noticed that the young people were not so young after all, in spite of their smiles, their little ways, their *ingénue* dress. Ella was in her teens. Clad only in something from the shop-soiled counter, she nevertheless had the appearance of a living flower in a French cemetery, or a mermaid among polyps.

"Come, you stupid thing!"

"Mrs. Vanderpant is waiting."

Her pallor was not like theirs; not like the pallor of something that glistens or scuttles when you turn over a stone. Hers was that of a pearl.

Ella! Pearl of this remotest, most fantastic cave! Little mermaid, brushed over, pressed down by objects of a deadlier white—tentacles—! I can write no more.

MARCH 28 Well, I am rapidly becoming used to my new and half-lit world, to my strange company. I am learning the intricate laws of silence and camouflage which dominate the apparently casual strollings and gatherings of the midnight clan. How they detest the night-watchman, whose existence imposes these laws on their idle festivals!

"Odious, vulgar creature! He reeks of the coarse sun!"

Actually, he is quite a personable young man, very young for a night-watchman, so young that I think he must have been wounded in the war. But they would like to tear him to pieces.

They are very pleasant to me, though. They are pleased that a poet should have come among them. Yet I cannot like them entirely. My blood is a little chilled by the uncanny ease with which even the old ladies can clamber spider-like from balcony to balcony. Or is it because they are unkind to Ella?

Yesterday we had a bridge party. Tonight, Mrs. Bilbee's little play, *Love in Shadowland,* is going to be presented. Would you believe it?—another colony, from Wanamaker's, is coming over *en masse* to attend. Apparently people live in all the great stores. This visit is considered a great honor, for there is an intense snobbery in these creatures. They speak with horror of a social outcast who left a high-class Madison Avenue establishment, and now leads a wallowing, beach-comberish life in a delicatessen. And they relate with tragic emotion the story of the man in Altman's, who conceived such a passion for a model plaid dressing jacket that he emerged and wrested it from the hands of a purchaser. It seems that all the Altman colony, dreading an investigation, were forced to remove beyond the social pale, into a five-and-dime. Well, I must get ready to attend the play.

APRIL 14   I have found an opportunity to speak to Ella. I dared not before; here one has a sense always of pale eyes secretly watching. But last night, at the play, I developed a fit of hiccups. I was somewhat sternly told to go and secrete myself in the basement, among the garbage cans, where the watchman never comes.

There, in the rat-haunted darkness, I heard a stifled sob, "What's that? Is it you? Is it Ella? What ails you, child? Why do you cry?"

"They wouldn't even let me see the play."

"Is that all? Let me console you."

"I am so unhappy."

She told me her tragic little story. What do you think? When she was a child, a little tiny child of only six, she strayed away and fell asleep behind a counter, while her mother tried on a new hat. When she woke, the store was in darkness.

"And I cried, and they all came around, and took hold of me. 'She will tell, if we let her go,' they said. Some said, 'Call in the Dark Men.' 'Let her stay here,' said Mrs. Vanderpant. 'She will make me a nice little maid.' "

"Who are these Dark Men, Ella? They spoke of them when I came here."

"Don't you know? Oh, it's horrible! It's horrible!"

"Tell me, Ella. Let us share it."

She trembled. "You know the morticians, 'Journey's End,' who go to houses when people die?"

"Yes, Ella."

"Well, in that shop, just like here, and at Gimbel's, and at Bloomingdale's, there are people living, people like these."

"How disgusting! But what can they live upon, Ella, in a funeral home?"

"Don't ask me! Dead people are sent there, to be embalmed. Oh, they are terrible creatures! Even the people here are terrified of them. But if anyone dies, or if some poor burglar breaks in, and sees these people, and might tell—"

"Yes? Go on."

"Then they send for the others, the Dark Men."

"Good heavens!"

"Yes, and they put the body in Surgical Supplies—or the burglar, all tied up, if it's a burglar—and they send for these others, and then they all hide, and in they come, the others —Oh! they're like pieces of blackness. I saw them once. It was terrible."

"And then?"

"They go in, to where the dead person is, or the poor burglar. And they have wax there—and all sorts of things. And when they're gone there's just one of these wax models left, on the table. And then our people put a dress on it, or a bathing suit, and they mix it up with all the others, and nobody ever knows."

"But aren't they heavier than the others, these wax models? You would think they'd be heavier."

"No. They're not heavier. I think there's a lot of them— gone."

"Oh, dear! So they were going to do that to you, when you were a little child?"

"Yes, only Mrs. Vanderpant said I was to be her maid."

"I don't like these people, Ella."

"Nor do I. I wish I could see a bird."

"Why don't you go into the pet-shop?"

"It wouldn't be the same. I want to see it on a twig, with leaves."

"Ella, let us meet often. Let us creep away down here and meet. I will tell you about birds, and twigs and leaves."

MAY 1   For the last few nights the store has been feverish with the shivering whisper of a huge crush at Bloomingdale's. Tonight was the night.

"Not changed yet? We leave on the stroke of two." Roscoe has appointed himself, or been appointed, my guide or my guard.

"Roscoe, I am still a greenhorn. I dread the streets."

"Nonsense! There's nothing to it. We slip out by two's and three's, stand on the sidewalk, pick up a taxi. Were you never out late in the old days? If so, you must have seen us, many a time."

"Good heavens, I believe I have! And often wondered where you came from. And it was from here! But, Roscoe, my brow is burning. I find it hard to breathe. I fear a cold."

"In that case you must certainly remain behind. Our whole party would be disgraced in the unfortunate event of a sneeze."

I had relied on their rigid etiquette, so largely based on fear of discovery, and I was right. Soon they were gone, drifting out like leaves aslant on the wind. At once I dressed in flannel slacks, canvas shoes, and a tasteful sport shirt, all new in stock today. I found a quiet spot, safely off the track beaten by the night-watchman. There, in a model's lifted hand, I set a wide fern frond culled from the florist's shop, and at once had a young, spring tree. The carpet was sandy, sandy as a lake-side beach. A snowy napkin; two cakes, each with a cherry on it; I had only to imagine the lake and to find Ella.

"Why, Charles, what's this?"

"I'm a poet, Ella, and when a poet meets a girl like you he thinks of a day in the country. Do you see this tree? Let's call it *our* tree. There's the lake—the prettiest lake imaginable. Here is grass, and there are flowers. There are birds, too, Ella. You told me you like birds."

"Oh, Charles, you're so sweet. I feel I hear them singing."

"And here's our lunch. But before we eat, go behind the rock there, and see what you find."

I heard her cry out in delight when she saw the summer dress I had put there for her. When she came back the spring day smiled to see her, and the lake shone brighter than before. "Ella, let us have lunch. Let us have fun. Let us have a swim. I can just imagine you in one of those new bathing suits."

"Let's just sit here, Charles, and talk."

So we sat and talked, and the time was gone like a dream. We might have stayed there, forgetful of everything, had it not been for the spider.

"Charles, what are you doing?"

"Nothing, my dear. Just a naughty little spider, crawling over your knee. Purely imaginary, of course, but that sort are sometimes the worst. I had to try to catch him."

"Don't, Charles! It's late. It's terribly late. They'll be back any minute. I'd better go home."

I took her home to the kitchenware on the sub-ground floor, and kissed her good-day. She offered me her cheek. This troubles me.

MAY 10   "Ella, I love you."

I said it to her just like that. We have met many times. I have dreamt of her by day. I have not even kept up my journal. Verse has been out of the question.

"Ella, I love you. Let us move into the trousseau department. Don't look so dismayed, darling. If you like, we will go right away from here. We will live in that little restaurant in Central Park. There are thousands of birds there."

"Please—please don't talk like that!"

"But I love you with all my heart."

"You mustn't."

"But I find I must. I can't help it. Ella, you don't love another?"

She wept a little. "Oh, Charles, I do."

"Love another, Ella? One of these? I thought you dreaded them all. It must be Roscoe. He is the only one that's any way human. We talk of art, life, and such things. And he has stolen your heart!"

"No, Charles, no. He's just like the rest, really. I hate them all. They make me shudder."

"Who is it, then?"

"It's him."

"Who?"

"The night-watchman."

"Impossible!"

"No. He smells of the sun."

"Oh, Ella, you have broken my heart."

"Be my friend, though."

"I will. I'll be your brother. How did you fall in love with him?"

"Oh, Charles, it was so wonderful. I was thinking of birds, and I was careless. Don't tell on me, Charles. They'll punish me."

"No. No. Go on."

"I was careless, and there he was, coming round the corner. And there was no place for me; I had this blue dress on. There were only some wax models in their underthings."

"Please go on."

"I couldn't help it. I slipped off my dress, and stood still."

"I see."

"And he stopped just by me, Charles. And he looked at me. And he touched my cheek.

"Did he notice nothing?"

"No. It was cold. But Charles, he said—he said—'Say, honey, I wish they made 'em like you on Eighth Avenue.' Charles, wasn't that a lovely thing to say?"

"Personally, I should have said Park Avenue."

"Oh, Charles, don't get like these people here. Sometimes I think you're getting like them. It doesn't matter what street, Charles; it was a lovely thing to say."

"Yes, but my heart's broken. And what can you do about him? Ella, he belongs to another world."

"Yes, Charles, Eighth Avenue. I want to go there. Charles, are you truly my friend?"

"I'm your brother, only my heart's broken."

"I'll tell you. I will. I'm going to stand there again. So he'll see me."

"And then?"

"Perhaps he'll speak to me again."

"My dearest Ella, you are torturing yourself. You are making it worse."

"No, Charles. Because I shall answer him. He will take me away."

"Ella, I can't bear it."

"Ssh! There is someone coming. I shall see birds—real birds, Charles—and flowers growing. They're coming. You must go."

MAY 13   The last three days have been torture. This evening I broke. Roscoe had joined me. He sat eyeing me for a long time. He put his hand on my shoulder.

He said, "You're looking seedy, old fellow. Why don't you go over to Wanamaker's for some skiing?"

His kindness compelled a frank response. "It's deeper than that, Roscoe. I'm done for. I can't eat, I can't sleep. I can't write, man, I can't even write."

"What is it? Day starvation?"

"Roscoe—it's love."

"Not one of the staff, Charles, or the customers? That's absolutely forbidden."

"No, it's not that, Roscoe. But just as hopeless."

"My dear fellow, I can't bear to see you like this. Let me help you. Let me share your trouble."

Then it all came out. It burst out. I trusted him. I think I trusted him. I really think I had no intention of betraying Ella, of spoiling her escape, of keeping her here till her heart turned towards me. If I had, it was subconscious. I swear it.

But I told him all. All! He was sympathetic, but I detected a sly reserve in his sympathy. "You will respect my confidence, Roscoe? This is to be a secret between us."

"As secret as the grave, old chap."

And he must have gone straight to Mrs. Vanderpant. This evening the atmosphere has changed. People flicker to and fro, smiling nervously, horribly, with a sort of frightened sadistic exaltation. When I speak to them they answer evasively, fidget, and disappear. An informal dance has been called off. I cannot find Ella. I will creep out. I will look for her again.

LATER Heaven! It has happened. I went in desperation to the manager's office, whose glass front overlooks the whole shop. I watched till midnight. Then I saw a little group of them, like ants bearing a victim. They were carrying Ella. They took her to the surgical department. They took other things.

And, coming back here, I was passed by a flittering, whispering horde of them, glancing over their shoulders in a thrilled ecstasy of panic, making for their hiding places. I, too, hid myself. How can I describe the dark inhuman creatures that passed me, silent as shadows? They went there—where Ella is.

What can I do? There is only one thing. I will find the watchman. I will tell him. He and I will save her. And if we are overpowered—Well, I will leave this on a counter. To-morrow, if we live, I can recover it.

If not, look in the windows. Look for three new figures: two men, one rather sensitive-looking, and a girl. She has blue eyes, like periwinkle flowers, and her upper lip is lifted a little.

Look for us.

Smoke them out! Obliterate them! Avenge us!

I knew and loved Old Donegal, who used a different name, and whose mistress was not a thundering rocket, but a thundering steam locomotive and who died long ago. I suppose it is that love that makes this story a favorite, in spite of its flaws, its corn, and its obvious obsolescence as science fiction.

WALTER M. MILLER, JR.

MEMENTO HOMO

by WALTER M. MILLER, JR.

. . . quia pulvis es et in pulverem reverteris.

Old Donegal was dying. They had all known it was coming, and they watched it come—his haggard wife, his daughter, and now his grandson, home on emergency leave from the pre-astronautics academy. Old Donegal knew it too, and had known it from the beginning, when he had begun to lose control of his legs and was forced to walk with a cane. But most of the time, he pretended to let them keep the secret they shared with the doctors—that the operations had all been failures, and that the cancer that fed at his spine would gnaw its way brainward until the paralysis engulfed vital organs, and then Old Donegal would cease to be. It would be cruel to let them know that he knew. Once, weeks ago, he had joked about the approaching shadows.

"Buy the plot back where people won't walk over it, Martha," he said. "Get it way back under the cedars—next to the fence. There aren't many graves back there yet. I want to be alone."

"Don't *talk* that way, Donny!" his wife had choked. "You're not dying."

His eyes twinkled maliciously. "Listen, Martha, I want to be buried face-down. I want to be buried with my back to space, understand? Don't let them lay me out like a lily."

"Donny, *please!*"

"They oughta face a man the way he's headed," Donegal grunted. "I been up—*way* up. Now I'm going straight down."

Martha had fled from the room in tears. He had never done it again, except to the interns and nurses, who, while they insisted that he was going to get well, didn't mind joking with him about it.

Martha can bear my death, he thought, can bear pre-knowledge of it. But she couldn't bear thinking that he might take it calmly. If he accepted death gracefully, it would be like

69

deliberately leaving her, and Old Donegal had decided to help her believe whatever would be comforting to her in such a troublesome moment.

"When'll they let me out of this bed again?" he complained.

"Be patient, Donny," she sighed. "It won't be long. You'll be up and around before you know it."

"Back on the moon-run, maybe?" he offered. "Listen, Martha, I been planet-bound too long. I'm not too old for the moon-run, am I? Sixty-three's not so old."

That had been carrying things too far. She knew he was hoaxing, and dabbed at her eyes again. The dead must humor the mourners, he thought, and the sick must comfort the visitors. It was always so.

But it was harder, now that the end was near. His eyes were hazy, and his thoughts unclear. He could move his arms a little, clumsily, but feeling was gone from them. The rest of his body was lost to him. Sometimes he seemed to feel his stomach and his hips, but the sensation was mostly an illusion offered by higher nervous centers, like the "ghost-arm" that an amputee continues to feel. The wires were down, and he was cut off from himself.

He lay wheezing on the hospital bed, in his own room, in his own rented flat. Gaunt and unshaven, gray as winter twilight, he lay staring at the white net curtains that billowed gently in the breeze from the open window. There was no sound in the room but the sound of breathing and the loud ticking of an alarm clock. Occasionally he heard a chair scraping on the stone terrace next door, and the low mutter of voices, sometimes laughter, as the servants of the Keith mansion arranged the terrace for late afternoon guests.

With considerable effort, he rolled his head toward Martha who sat beside the bed, pinchfaced and weary.

"You ought to get some sleep," he said.

"I slept yesterday. Don't talk, Donny. It tires you."

"You ought to get more sleep. You never sleep enough. Are you afraid I'll get up and run away if you go to sleep for awhile?"

She managed a brittle smile. "There'll be plenty of time for sleep when . . . when you're well again." The brittle smile fled and she swallowed hard, like swallowing a fishbone. He glanced down, and noticed that she was squeezing his hand spasmodically.

There wasn't much left of the hand, he thought. Bones and ugly tight-stretched hide spotted with brown. Bulging knuckles

70

with yellow cigarette stains. My hand. He tried to tighten it, tried to squeeze Martha's thin one in return. He watched it open and contract a little, but it was like operating a remote-control mechanism. Goodbye, hand, you're leaving me the way my legs did, he told it. I'll see you again in hell. How hammy can you get, Old Donegal? You maudlin ass.

"Requiescat," he muttered over the hand, and let it lie in peace.

Perhaps she heard him. "Donny," she whispered, leaning closer, "won't you let me call the priest now? Please."

He rattled a sigh and rolled his head toward the window again. "Are the Keiths having a party today?" he asked. "Sounds like they're moving chairs out on the terrace."

"Please, Donny, the priest?"

He let his head roll aside and closed his eyes, as if asleep. The bed shook slightly as she quickly caught at his wrist to feel for a pulse.

"If I'm not dying, I don't need a priest," he said sleepily.

"That's not right," she scolded softly. "You know that's not right, Donny. You know better."

Maybe I'm being too rough on her? he wondered. He hadn't minded getting baptized her way, and married her way, and occasionally priest-handled the way she wanted him to when he was home from a space-run, but when it came to dying, Old Donegal wanted to do it his own way.

He opened his eyes at the sound of a bench being dragged across the stone terrace. "Martha, what kind of a party are the Keiths having today?"

"I wouldn't know," she said stiffly. "You'd think they'd have a little more respect. You'd think they'd put it off a few days."

"Until—?"

"Until you feel better."

"I feel fine, Martha. I like parties. I'm glad they're having one. Pour me a drink, will you? I can't reach the bottle anymore."

"It's empty."

"No it isn't, Martha, it's still a quarter full. I know. I've been watching it."

"You shouldn't have it, Donny. Please don't."

"But this is a party, Martha. Besides, the doctor says I can have whatever I want. Whatever I want, you hear? That means I'm getting well, doesn't it?"

"Sure, Donny, sure. Getting well."

"The whiskey, Martha. Just a finger in a tumbler, no more. I want to feel like it's a party."

Her throat was rigid as she poured it. She helped him get the tumbler to his mouth. The liquor seared his throat, and he gagged a little as the fumes clogged his nose. Good whiskey, the best—but he couldn't take it any more. He eyed the green stamp on the neck of the bottle on the bedtable and grinned. He hadn't had whiskey like that since his spacedays. Couldn't afford it now, not on a blastman's pension.

He remembered how he and Caid used to smuggle a couple of fifths aboard for the moon-run. If they caught you, it meant suspension, but there was no harm in it, not for the blastroom men who had nothing much to do from the time the ship acquired enough velocity for the long, long coaster ride until they started the rockets again for lunar landing. You could drink a fifth, jettison the bottle through the trash lock, and sober up before you were needed again. It was the only way to pass the time in the cramped cubicle, unless you ruined your eyes trying to read by the glow-lamps. Old Donegal chuckled. If he and Caid had stayed on the run, Earth would have a ring by now, like Saturn—a ring of Old Granddad bottles.

"You said it, Donny-boy," said the misty man by the billowing curtains. "Who else knows the Gegenschein is broken glass?"

Donegal laughed. Then he wondered what the man was doing there. The man was lounging against the window, and his unzipped space rig draped about him in an old familiar way. Loose plug-in connections and hose-ends dangled about his lean body. He was freckled and grinning.

"Caid," Old Donegal breathed softly.

"What did you say, Donny?" Martha answered.

Old Donegal blinked hard and shook his head. Something let go with a soggy snap, and the misty man was gone. I'd better take it easy on the whiskey, he thought. You got to wait, Donegal, old lush, until Nora and Ken get here. You can't get drunk until they're gone, or you might get them mixed up with memories like Caid's.

Car doors slammed in the street below. Martha glanced toward the window.

"Think it's them? I wish they'd get here. I wish they'd hurry."

Martha arose and tiptoed to the window. She peered down

72

toward the sidewalk, put on a sharp frown. He heard a distant mutter of voices and occasional laughter, with group-footsteps milling about on the sidewalk. Martha murmured her disapproval and closed the window.

"Leave it open," he said.

"But the Keiths' guests are starting to come. There'll be such a racket." She looked at him hopefully, the way she did when she prompted his manners before company came.

Maybe it wasn't decent to listen in on a party when you were dying, he thought. But that wasn't the reason. Donegal, your chamber-pressure's dropping off. Your brains are in your butt-end, where a spacer's brains belong, but your butt-end died last month. She wants the window closed for her own sake, not yours.

"Leave it closed," he grunted. "But open it again before the moon-run blasts off. I want to listen."

She smiled and nodded, glancing at the clock. "It'll be an hour and a half yet. I'll watch the time."

"I hate that clock. I wish you'd throw it out. It's loud."

"It's your medicine-clock, Donny." She came back to sit down at his bedside again. She sat in silence. The clock filled the room with its clicking pulse.

"What time are they coming?" he asked.

"Nora and Ken? They'll be here soon. Don't fret."

"Why should I fret?" He chuckled. "That boy—he'll be a good spacer, won't he, Martha?"

Martha said nothing, fanned at a fly that crawled across his pillow. The fly buzzed up in an angry spiral and alighted on the ceiling. Donegal watched it for a time. The fly had natural-born space-legs. I know your tricks, he told it with a smile, and I learned to walk on the bottomside of things before you were a maggot. You stand there with your magnasoles hanging to the hull, and the rest of you's in free fall. You jerk a sole lose, and your knee flies up to your belly, and reaction spins you half-around and near throws your other hip out of joint if you don't jam the foot down fast and jerk up the other. It's worse'n trying to run through knee-deep mud with snow-shoes, and a man'll go nuts trying to keep his arms and legs from taking off in odd directions. I know your tricks, fly. But the fly was born with his magnasoles, and he trotted across the ceiling like Donegal never could.

"That boy Ken—he ought to make a damn good space-engineer," wheezed the old man.

Her silence was long, and he rolled his head toward her

73

again. Her lips tight, she stared down at the palm of his hand, unfolded his bony fingers, felt the cracked calluses that still welted the shrunken skin, calluses worn there by the linings of space gauntlets and the handles of fuel valves, and the rungs of get-about ladders during free fall.

"I don't know if I should tell you," she said.

"Tell me what, Martha?"

She looked up slowly, scrutinizing his face. "Ken's changed his mind, Nora says. Ken doesn't like the academy. She says he wants to go to medical school."

Old Donegal thought it over, nodded absently. "That's fine. Space medics get good pay." He watched her carefully.

She lowered her eyes, rubbed at his calluses again. She shook her head slowly. "He doesn't want to go to space."

The clock clicked loudly in the closed room.

"I thought I ought to tell you, so you won't say anything to him about it," she added.

Old Donegal looked grayer than before. After a long silence, he rolled his head away and looked toward the limp curtains.

"Open the window, Martha," he said.

Her tongue clucked faintly as she started to protest, but she said nothing. After frozen seconds, she sighed and went to open it. The curtains billowed, and a babble of conversation blew in from the terrace of the Keith mansion. With the sound came the occasional brassy discord of a musician tuning his instrument. She clutched the window-sash as if she wished to slam it closed again.

"Well! Music!" grunted Old Donegal. "That's good. This is some shebang. Good whiskey and good music and you." He chuckled, but it choked off into a fit of coughing.

"Donny, about Ken—"

"No matter, Martha," he said hastily. "Space-medic's pay is good."

"But Donny—" She turned from the window, stared at him briefly, then said, "Sure, Donny, sure," and came back to sit down by his bed.

He smiled at her affectionately. She was a man's woman, was Martha—always had been, still was. He had married her the year he had gone to space—a lissome, wistful, old-fashioned lass, with big violet eyes and gentle hands and gentle thoughts—and she had never complained about the long and lonely weeks between blast-off and glide-down, when most spacers' wives listened to the psychiatrists and soap-

74

operas and soon developed the symptoms that were expected of them, either because the symptoms were *chic,* or because they felt they should do something to earn the pity that was extended to them. "It's not so bad," Martha had assured him. "The house keeps me busy till Nora's home from school, and then there's a flock of kids around till dinner. Nights are a little empty, but if there's a moon, I can always go out on the porch and look at it and know where you are. And Nora gets out the telescope you built her, and we make a game of it. 'Seeing if Daddy's still at the office' she calls it."

"Those were the days," he muttered.
"What, Donny?"
"Do you remember that Steve Farran song?"
She paused, frowning thoughtfully. There were a lot of Steve Farran songs, but after a moment she picked the right one, and sang it softly . . .

> "O moon whereo'er the clouds fly,
> Beyond the willow tree,
> There is a ramblin' space guy
> I wish you'd save for me."
> *Mare Tranquilitatis,*
> O dark and tranquil sea,
> Until he drops from heaven,
> Rest him there with thee . . ."

Her voice cracked, and she laughed. Old Donegal chuckled weakly.
"Fried mush," he said. "That one made the cats wilt their ears and wail at the moon."
"I feel real crazy," he added. "Hand me the king kong, fluffmuff."
"Keep cool, Daddy-O, you've had enough." Martha reddened and patted his arm, looking pleased. Neither of them had talked that way, even in the old days, but the out-dated slang brought back memories—school parties, dances at the Rocketport Club, the early years of the war when Donegal had jockeyed an R-43 fighter in the close-space assaults against the Soviet satellite project. The memories were good.
A brassy blare of modern "slide" arose suddenly from the Keith terrace as the small orchestra launched into its first number. Martha caught an angry breath and started toward the window.

"Leave it," he said. "It's a party. Whiskey, Martha. Please —just a small one."

She gave him a hurtful glance.

"Whiskey. Then you can call the priest."

"Donny, it's not right. You know it's not right—to bargain for such as that."

"All right. Whiskey. Forget the priest."

She poured it for him, and helped him get it down, and then went out to make the phone-call. Old Donegal lay shuddering over the whiskey taste and savoring the burn in his throat. Jesus, but it was good.

You old bastard, he thought, you got no right to enjoy life when nine-tenths of you is dead already, and the rest is foggy as a thermal dust-rise on the lunar *mare* at hell-dawn. But it wasn't a bad way to die. It ate your consciousness away from the feet up; it gnawed away the Present, but it let you keep the Past, until everything faded and blended. Maybe that's what Eternity was, he thought—one man's subjective Past, all wrapped up and packaged for shipment, a single space-time entity, a one-man microcosm of memories, when nothing else remains.

"If I've got a soul, I made it myself," he told the gray nun at the foot of his bed.

The nun held out a pie pan, rattled a few coins in it. "Contribute to the Radiation Victims' Relief?" the nun purred softly.

"I know you," he said. "You're my conscience. You hang around the officer's mess, and when we get back from a sortie, you make us pay for the damage we did. But that was forty years ago."

The nun smiled, and her luminous eyes were on him softly. "Mother of God!" he breathed, and reached for the whiskey. His arm obeyed. The last drink had done him good. He had to watch his hand to see where it was going, and squeezed the neck until his fingers whitened so that he knew that he had it, but he got it off the table and onto his chest, and he got the cork out with his teeth. He had a long pull at the bottle, and it made his eyes water and his hands grow weak. But he got it back to the table without spilling a bit, and he was proud of himself.

The room was spinning like the cabin of a gyro-gravved ship. By the time he wrestled it to a standstill, the nun was gone. The blare of music from the Keith terrace was louder, and laughing voices blended with it. Chairs scraping and

76

glasses rattling. A fine party, Keith, I'm glad you picked today. This shebang would be the younger Keith's affair. Ronald Tonwyler Keith, III, scion of Orbital Engineering and Construction Company—builders of the moonshuttle ships that made the run from the satellite station to Luna and back.

It's good to have such important neighbors, he thought. He wished he had been able to meet them while he was still up and about. But the Keiths' place was walled-in, and when a Keith came out, he charged out in a limousine with a chauffeur at the wheel, and the iron gate closed again. The Keiths built the wall when the surrounding neighborhood began to grow shabby with age. It had once been the best of neighborhoods, but that was before Old Donegal lived in it. Now it consisted of sooty old houses and rented flats, and the Keith place was really not a part of it anymore. Nevertheless, it was really something when a pensioned blastman could say, "I live out close to the Keiths—you know, the *Ronald* Keiths." At least, that's what Martha always told him.

The music was so loud that he never heard the doorbell ring, but when a lull came, he heard Nora's voice downstairs, and listened hopefully for Ken's. But when they came up, the boy was not with them.

"Hello, skinny-britches," he greeted his daughter.

Nora grinned and came over to kiss him. Her hair dangled about his face, and he noticed that it was blacker than usual, with the gray streaks gone from it again.

"You smell good," he said.

"You don't, Pops. You smell like a sot. Naughty!"

"Where's Ken?"

She moistened her lips nervously and looked away. "He couldn't come. He had to take a driver's lesson. He really couldn't help it. If he didn't go, he'd lose his turn, and then he wouldn't finish before he goes back to the academy." She looked at him apologetically.

"It's all right, Nora."

"If he missed it, he wouldn't get his copter license until summer."

"It's okay. Copters! Hell, the boy should be in jets by now!"

Several breaths passed in silence. She gazed absently toward the window and shook her head. "No jets, Pop. Not for Ken."

He glowered at her. "Listen! How'll he get into space? He's got to get his jet licenses first. Can't get in rockets without 'em."

Nora shot a quick glance at her mother. Martha rolled her

77

eyes as if sighing patiently. Nora went to the window to stare down toward the Keith terrace. She tucked a cigarette between scarlet lips, lit it, blew nervous smoke against the pane.

"Mom, can't you call them and have that racket stopped?"

"Donny says he likes it."

Nora's eyes flitted over the scene below. "Female butterflies and puppy-dogs in sport jackets. And the cadets." She snorted. "Cadets! Imagine Ron Keith the Third ever going to space. The old man buys his way into the academy, and they throw a brawl as if Ronny passed the Compets."

"Maybe he did," growled Old Donegal.

"Hah!"

"They live in a different world, I guess," Martha sighed. "If it weren't for men like Pops, they'd never've made their fortune."

"I like the music, I tell you," grumbled the old man.

"I'm half-a-mind to go over there and tell them off," Nora murmured.

"Let them alone. Just so they'll stop the racket for blast-away."

"Look at them!—polite little pattern-cuts, all alike. They take pre-space, because it's the thing to do. Then they quit before the pay-off comes."

"How do you know they'll quit?"

"That party—I bet it cost six months' pay, spacer's pay," she went on, ignoring him. "And what do real spacers get? Oley gets killed, and Pop's pension wouldn't feed the Keiths' cat."

"You don't understand, girl."

"I lost Oley. I understand enough."

He watched her silently for a moment, then closed his eyes. It was no good trying to explain, no good trying to tell her the dough didn't mean a damn thing. She'd been a spacer's wife, and that was bad enough, but now she was a spacer's widow. And Oley? Oley's tomb revolved around the sun in an eccentric orbit that spun-in close to Mercury, then reached out into the asteroid belt, once every 725 days. When it came within rocket radius of Earth, it whizzed past at close to fifteen miles a second.

You don't rescue a ship like that, skinny-britches, my darling daughter. Nor do you salvage it after the crew stops screaming for help. If you use enough fuel to catch it, you won't get back. You just leave such a ship there forever, like an asteroid, and it's a damn shame about the men trapped aboard. Heroes all, no doubt—but the smallness of the widow's monthly check failed to confirm the heroism, and Nora was bitter about the price of Oley's memory, perhaps.

Ouch! Old Donegal, you know she's not like that. It's just that she can't understand about space. You ought to make her understand.

But did he really understand himself? You ride hot in a roaring blast-room, hands tense on the mixer controls and the pumps, eyes glued to instruments, body sucked down in a four-gravity thrust, and wait for the command to choke it off. Then you float free and weightless in a long nightmare as the beast coasts moonward, a flung javelin.

The "romance" of space—drivel written in the old days. When you're not blasting, you float in a cramped hotbox, crawl through dirty mazes of greasy pipe and cable to tighten a lug, scratch your arms and bark your shins, get sick and choked up because no gravity helps your gullet get the food down. Liquid is worse, but you gag your whiskey down because you have to.

Stars?—you see stars by squinting through a viewing lens, and it's like a photo-transparency, and if you aren't careful, you'll get an eyeful of Old Blinder and back off with a punch-drunk retina.

Adventure?—unless the skipper calls for course-correction, you float around in the blast-cubicle with damn little to do between blast-away and moon-down, except sweat out the omniscient accident statistics. If the beast blows up or gets gutted in space, a statistic had your name on it, that's all, and there's no fighting back. You stay outwardly sane because you're a hog for punishment; if you weren't, you'd never get past the psychologists.

"Did you like horror movies when you were a kid?" asked the psych. And you'd damn well better answer "yes," if you want to go to space.

Tell her, old man, you're her pop. Tell her why it's worth it, if you know. You jail yourself in a coffin-size cubicle, and a crazy beast thunders berserk for uncontrollable seconds, and then you soar in ominous silence for the long long hours. Grow sweaty, filthy, sick, miserable, idle—somewhere out in Big Empty, where Man's got no business except the trouble he always makes for himself wherever he goes. Tell her why it's worth it, for pay less than a good bricklayer's. Tell her why Oley would do it again.

79

"It's a sucker's run, Nora," he said. "You go looking for kicks, but the only kicks you get to keep is what Oley got. God knows why—but it's worth it."

Nora said nothing. He opened his eyes slowly. Nora was gone. Had she been there at all?

He blinked around at the fuzzy room, and dissolved the shifting shadows that sometimes emerged as old friendly faces, grinning at him. He found Martha.

"You went to sleep," said Martha. "She had to go. Kennie called. He'll be over later, if you're not too tired."

"I'm not tired. I'm all head. There's nothing much to get tired."

"I love you, Old Donegal."

"Hold my hand again."

"I'm holding it, old man."

"Then hold me where I can feel it."

She slid a thin arm under his neck, and bent over his face to kiss him. She was crying a little, and he was glad she could do it now without fleeing the room.

"Can I talk about dying now?" he wondered aloud.

She pinched her lips together and shook her head.

"I lie to myself, Martha. You know how much I lie to myself?"

She nodded slowly and stroked his gray temples.

"I lie to myself about Ken, and about dying. If Ken turned spacer, I wouldn't die—that's what I told myself. You know?"

She shook her head. "Don't talk, Donny, please."

"A man makes his own soul, Martha."

"That's not true. You shouldn't say things like that."

"A man makes his own soul, but it dies with him, unless he can pour it into his kids and his grandchildren before he goes. I lied to myself. Ken's a yellow-belly. Nora made him one, and the boots won't fit."

"Don't, Donny. You'll excite yourself again."

"I was going to give him the boots—the over-boots with magnasoles. But they won't fit him. They won't ever fit him. He's a lily-livered lap-dog, and he whines. Bring me my boots, woman."

"Donny!"

"The boots, they're in my locker in the attic. I want them."

"What on earth!"

"Bring me my goddam space boots and put them on my feet. I'm going to wear them."

"You can't; the priest's coming."

80

"Well, get them anyway. What time is it? You didn't let me sleep through the moon-run blast, did you?"

She shook her head. "It's half an hour yet . . . I'll get the boots if you promise not to make me put them on you."

"I want them on."

"You can't, until Father Paul's finished."

"Do I have to get my feet buttered?"

She sighed. "I wish you wouldn't say things like that. I wish you wouldn't, Donny. It's sacrilege, you know it is."

"All right—'anointed'," he corrected wearily.

"Yes, you do."

"The boots, woman, the boots."

She went to get them. While she was gone, the doorbell rang, and he heard her quick footsteps on the stairs, and then Father Paul's voice asking about the patient. Old Donegal groaned inwardly. After the priest, the doctor would come, at the usual time, to see if he were dead yet. The doctor had let him come home from the hospital to die, and the doctor was getting impatient. Why don't they let me alone? he growled. Why don't they let me handle it in my own way, and stop making a fuss over it? I can die and do a good job of it without a lot of outside interference, and I wish they'd quit picking at me with syringes and sacraments and enemas. All he wanted was a chance to listen to the orchestra on the Keith terrace, to drink the rest of his whiskey, and to hear the beast blast-away for the satellite on the first lap of the run to Luna.

It's going to be my last day, he thought. My eyes are going fuzzy, and I can't breathe right, and the throbbing's hurting my head. Whether he lived through the night wouldn't matter, because delirium was coming over him, and then there would be the coma, and the symbolic fight to keep him pumping and panting. I'd rather die tonight and get it over with, he thought, but they probably won't let me go.

He heard their voices coming up the stairs . . .

"Nora tried to get them to stop it, Father, but she couldn't get in to see anybody but the butler. He told her he'd tell Mrs. Keith, but nothing happened. It's just as loud as before."

"Well, as long as Donny doesn't mind—"

"He just says that. You know how he is."

"What're they celebrating, Martha?"

"Young Ronald's leaving—for pre-space training. It's a going-away affair." They paused in the doorway. The small priest

81

smiled in at Donegal and nodded. He set his black bag on the floor inside, winked solemnly at the patient.

"I'll leave you two alone," said Martha. She closed the door and her footsteps wandered off down the hall.

Donegal and the young priest eyed each other warily.

"You look like hell, Donegal," the padre offered jovially. "Feeling nasty?"

"Skip the small talk. Let's get this routine over with."

The priest humphed thoughtfully, sauntered across to the bed, gazed down at the old man disinterestedly. "What's the matter? Don't want the 'routine'? Rather play it tough?"

"What's the difference?" he growled. "Hurry up and get out. I want to hear the beast blast off."

"You won't be able to," said the priest, glancing at the window, now closed again. "That's quite a racket next door."

"They'd better stop for it. They'd better quiet down for it. They'll have to turn it off for five minutes or so."

"Maybe they won't."

It was a new idea, and it frightened him. He liked the music, and the party's gaiety, the nearness of youth and good times—but it hadn't occurred to him that it wouldn't stop so he could hear the beast.

"Don't get upset, Donegal. You know what a blast-off sounds like."

"But it's the last one. The last time. I want to hear."

"How do you know it's the last time?"

"Hell, don't I know when I'm kicking off?"

"Maybe, maybe not. It's hardly your decision."

"It's not, eh?" Old Donegal fumed. "Well, bigawd you'd think it wasn't. You'd think it was Martha's and yours and that damfool medic's. You'd think I got no say-so. Who's doing it anyway?"

"I would guess," Father Paul grunted sourly, "that Providence might appreciate His fair share of the credit."

Old Donegal made a surly noise and hunched his head back into the pillow to glower.

"You want me?" the priest asked. "Or is this just a case of wifely conscience?"

"What's the difference? Give me the business and scram."

"No soap. Do you want the sacrament, or are you just being kind to your wife? If it's for Martha, I'll go *now*."

Old Donegal glared at him for a time, then wilted. The priest brought his bag to the bedside.

"Bless me, father, for I have sinned."

"Bless you, son."

"I accuse myself . . ."

Tension, anger, helplessness—they had piled up on him, and now he was feeling the after-effects. Vertigo, nausea, and the black confetti—a bad spell. The whiskey—if he could only reach the whiskey. Then he remembered he was receiving a Sacrament, and struggled to get on with it. Tell him, old man, tell him of your various rottennesses and vile transgressions, if you can remember some. A sin is whatever you're sorry for, maybe. But Old Donegal, you're sorry for the wrong things, and this young jesuitical gadget wouldn't like listening to it. I'm sorry I didn't get it instead of Oley, and I'm sorry I fought in the war, and I'm sorry I can't get out of this bed and take a belt to my daughter's backside for making a puny whelp out of Ken, and I'm sorry I gave Martha such a rough time all these years—and wound up dying in a cheap flat, instead of giving her things like the Keiths had. I wish I had been a sharpster, contractor, or thief . . . instead of a common laboring spacer, whose species lost its glamor after the war.

Listen, old man, you made your soul yourself, and it's yours. This young dispenser of oils, Substances, and mysteries wishes only to help you scrape off the rough edges and gouge out the bad spots. He will not steal it, nor distort it with his supernatural chisels, nor make fun of it. He can take nothing away, but only cauterize and neutralize, he says, so why not let him try? Tell him the rotten messes.

"Are you finished, my son?"

Old Donegal nodded wearily, and said what he was asked to say, and heard the soft mutter of Latin that washed him inside and behind his ghostly ears . . . *ego te absolvo in Nomine Patris* . . . and he accepted the rest of it lying quietly in the candlelight and the red glow of the sunset through the window, while the priest anointed him and gave him Bread, and read the words of the soul in greeting its Spouse: "I was asleep, but my heart waked; it is the voice of my beloved calling: come to me my love, my dove, my undefiled . . ." and from beyond the closed window came the sarcastic wail of a clarinet painting hot slides against a rhythmic background.

It wasn't so bad, Old Donegal thought when the priest was done. He felt like a schoolboy in a starched shirt on Sunday morning, and it wasn't a bad feeling, though it left him weak.

The priest opened the window for him again, and re-packed his bag. "Ten minutes till blast-off," he said. "I'll see what I can do about the racket next door."

When he was gone, Martha came back in, and he looked at her face and was glad. She was smiling when she kissed him, and she looked less tired.

"Is it all right for me to die now?" he grunted.

"Donny, don't start that again."

"Where's the boots? You promised to bring them?"

"They're in the hall. Donny, you don't want them."

"I want them, and I want a drink of whiskey, and I want to hear them fire the beast." He said it slow and hard, and he left no room for argument.

When she had got the huge boots over his shrunken feet, the magnasoles clanged against the iron bed-frame and clung there, and she rolled him up so that he could look at them, and Old Donegal chuckled inside. He felt warm and clean and pleasantly dizzy.

"The whiskey, Martha, and for God's sake, make them stop the noise till after the firing. Please!"

She went to the window and looked out for a long time. Then she came back and poured him an insignificant drink.

"Well?"

"I don't know," she said. "I saw Father Paul on the terrace, talking to somebody."

"Is it time?"

She glanced at the clock, looked at him doubtfully, and nodded. "Nearly time."

The orchestra finished a number, but the babble of laughing voices continued. Old Donegal sagged. "They won't do it. They're the Keiths, Martha. Why should I ruin their party?"

She turned to stare at him, slowly shook her head. He heard someone shouting, but then a trumpet started softly, introducing a new number. Martha sucked in a hurt breath, pressed her hands together, and hurried from the room.

"It's too late," he said after her.

Her footsteps stopped on the stairs. The trumpet was alone. Donegal listened; and there was no babble of voices, and the rest of the orchestra was silent. Only the trumpet sang —and it puzzled him, hearing the same slow bugle-notes of the call played at the lowering of the colors.

The trumpet stopped suddenly. Then he knew it had been for him.

A brief hush—then thunder came from the blast-station

84

two miles to the west. First the low reverberation, rattling the windows, then the rising growl as the sleek beast knifed skyward on a column of bluewhite hell. It grew and grew until it drowned the distant traffic sounds and dominated the silence outside.

Quit crying, you old fool, you maudlin ass . . .

"My boots," he whispered, "my boots . . . please . . ."

"You've got them on, Donny."

He sank quietly then. He closed his eyes and let his heart go up with the beast, and he sank into the gravity padding of the blastroom, and Caid was with him, and Oley. And when Ronald Keith, III, instructed the orchestra to play Blastroom Man, after the beast's rumble had waned, Old Donegal was on his last moon-run, and he was grinning. He'd had a good day.

Martha went to the window to stare out at the thin black trail that curled starward above the blast station through the twilight sky. Guests on the terrace were watching it too.

The doorbell rang. That would be Ken, too late. She closed the window against the chill breeze, and went back to the bed. The boots, the heavy, clumsy boots—they clung to the bedframe, with his feet half out of them. She took them off gently and set them out of company's sight. Then she went to answer the door.

When I was a boy I crossed the United States on many occasions with my brother and my parents, in an old Buick. I lived for a time in Tucson, Arizona, and Roswell, New Mexico, and it was while moving around in those states that I saw my first mirage. It was a "permanent" mirage, one that could be seen almost every clear day in the year. It was so permanent, in fact, that the state had marked its position with a small enscribed stone. I have long since forgotten the name of the mirage—probably something like Mirage View or Mirage Point—but I have not forgotten the fabulous town that lay buried in the shimmering silver depths of the strange warm water lake that was the center of the illusion. I have carried that memory with me from my 12th year. The more I thought about it, over the years, the more I wanted to find a way to write a story about it. And the way to write a story about anything is to bring on several characters who have need, one way or another, for the thing you wish to write about. So I finally sat down and put two needful characters into an old car and ran them over the desert and onto the scene and then sat back and typed and let the characters speak and live and write the story for me. What resulted was *A Miracle of Rare Device*. I am happy I had enough sense to relax and let my characters take over and live in wonder for a moment with an old love of mine. When I write this way, trusting my characters, trusting my idea, which means trusting my subconscious, I write best and easily. I can only hope the reader will trust my characters, my idea, and my subconscious the way I do. Here is the desert, then, here are the needful wanderers, here is the well-remembered trick of incredible light, here is *A Miracle of Rare Device*.

RAY BRADBURY

A MIRACLE OF RARE DEVICE

by RAY BRADBURY

On a day neither too mellow nor too tart, too hot nor too cold, the ancient tin lizzie came over the desert hill traveling at commotion speed. The vibration of the various armored parts of the car caused road-runners to spurt up in floury bursts of dust. Gila monsters, lazy displays of Indian jewelry, took themselves out of the way. Like an infestation, the Ford clamored and dinned away into the deeps of the wilderness.

In the front seat, squinting back, Old Will Bantlin shouted, "Turn off!"

Bob Greenhill spun-swung the lizzie off behind a billboard. Instantly, both men turned. Both peered over the crumpled top of their car, praying to the dust they had wheeled up on the air.

"Lay down! Lay low! Please . . ."

And the dust blew slowly down.

Just in time.

"Duck!"

A motorcycle, looking as if it had burnt through all nine rings of Hell, thundered by. Hunched over its oily handle bars, a hurricane figure, a man with a creased and most unpleasant face, goggled and sun-deviled, leaned on the wind. Roaring bike and man flung away down the road.

The two old men sat up in their lizzie, exhaling.

"So long, Ned Hopper," said Bob Greenhill.

"Why?" said Will Bantlin, "why's he always tailing us?"

"Willy-William, talk sense," said Greenhill. "We're his luck, his Judas goats. Why should he let us go, when trailing us around the land makes him rich and happy and us poor and wise?"

The two men looked at each other, half-in, half-out of their smiles. What the world hadn't done to them, thinking about it had. They had enjoyed 30 years of nonviolence together, in their case meaning nonwork. "I feel a harvest coming on," Will would say, and they'd clear out of town before the wheat ripened. Or, "Those apples are ready to fall!" So they'd stand back about 300 miles so as not to get hit on the head.

Now Bob Greenhill slowly let the car, in a magnificent controlled avalanche, drift back out on the road.

"Willy, friend, don't be discouraged."

"I've been through 'discouraged,'" said Will. "I'm knee-deep in 'accepting.'"

"Accepting what?"

"Finding a treasure chest of canned beans one day and no can opener. Finding a thousand can openers next day and no beans."

Bob Greenhill listened to the motor talking to itself like an old man under the hood, sounding like sleepless nights and rusty bones and well-worn dreams.

"Our bad luck can't last forever, Willy."

"No, but it sure tries. You and me sell ties and who's across the street ten cents cheaper?"

"Ned Hopper."

"We strike gold in Tonopah and who registers the claim first?"

"Old Ned."

"Haven't we done him a lifetime of favors? Aren't we overdue for something just ours, that never winds up his?"

"Time's ripe, Willy," said Robert, driving calmly. "Trouble is, you, me, Ned never really decided what we wanted. We've run through all the ghost towns, see something, grab. Ned sees and grabs, too. He don't want it, he just wants it because *we* want it. He keeps it till we're out of sight, then tears it up and hangdogs after us for more litter. The day we really know what we want is the day Ned gets scared of us and runs off forever. Ah, hell." Bob Greenhill breathed the clear fresh-water air running in morning streams over the windshield. "It's good anyway. That sky. Those hills. The desert and—"

His voice faded.

Will Bantlin glanced over. "What's wrong?"

"For some reason . . ." Bob Greenhill's eyes rolled, his leathery hands turned the wheel slow, ". . . we got to . . . pull off . . . the road . . ."

The lizzie bumped on the dirt shoulder. They drove down in a dusty wash and up out and suddenly along a dry peninsula of land overlooking the desert. Bob Greenhill, looking hypnotized, put out his hand to turn the ignition key. The

88

old man under the hood stopped complaining about insomnia and slept.

"Now, why did you do *that?!*" asked Will Bantlin.

Bob Greenhill gazed at the wheel in his suddenly intuitive hands. "Seemed as if I had to. Why?" He blinked up. He let his bones settle and his eyes grow lazy. "Maybe only to look at the land out there. Good. All of it been here a billion years."

"Except for that city," said Will Bantlin.

"City?" said Bob.

He turned to look and the desert was there and the distant hills the color of lions and far out beyond, suspended in a sea of warm morning sand and light, was a kind of floating image, a hasty sketch of a city.

"That can't be Phoenix," said Bob Greenhill. "Phoenix is ninety miles off. No other big place around . . ."

Will Bantlin rumpled the map on his knees, searching.

"No . . . no other town."

"It's coming clearer!" cried Bob Greenhill, suddenly.

They both stood absolutely straight up in the car and stared over the dusty windshield, the wind whining softly over their craggy faces.

"Why, you know what that is, Bob? A mirage! Sure, that's it! Light rays just right, atmosphere, sky, temperature. City's the other side of the horizon somewhere. Look how it jumps, fades in and out. It's reflected against that sky up there like a mirror and comes down here where we can see it! A mirage, by gosh!"

"That *big?*"

Will Bantlin measured the city as it grew taller, clearer in a shift of wind, a soft far whirlabout of sand.

"The granddaddy of them all! That's not Phoenix. Not Santa Fe or Alamogordo, no. Let's see. It's not Kansas City—"

"That's too far off, anway—"

"Yeah, but look at those buildings. Big! Tallest in the world. Only one place like that in the world."

"You don't mean—New York?"

Will Bantlin nodded slowly and they both stood in the silence looking out at the mirage. And the city was tall and shining now and almost perfect, in the early morning light.

"Oh, my," said Bob, after a long while. "That's fine."

"It is," said Will.

"But," said Will, a moment later, whispering, as if afraid

89

the city might hear, "what's it doing three thousand miles from home, here in the middle of Nowhere, Arizona?"

Bob Greenhill gazed and spoke. "Willy, friend, never question nature. It just sits there and minds its knitting. Radio waves, rainbows, northern lights, all that, heck, let's just say a great big picture got took of New York City and is being developed here, three thousand miles away on a morn when we need cheering, just for us."

"Not just us." Will peered over the side of the car. "Look!"

There in the floury dust lay cross-hatchings, diagonals, fascinating symbols printed out in a quiet river of traveling.

"Tire marks," said Bob Greenhill. "Lots of cars pulled off here."

"For what, Bob?" Will Bantlin leaped from the car, landed on the earth, tromped it, turned on it, knelt to touch it with a swiftly and suddenly trembling hand. "For what, for what? To see the mirage? Yes, sir! To see the mirage!"

"So?"

"Boy Howdy!" Will stood up, thrummed his voice like a motor. "Brrrummm!" He turned an imaginary wheel. He ran along a tire track. "Brrrummm! Eeeee! Brakes on! Robert-Bob, you know what we *got* here?! Look East! Look West! This is the only point in miles you can pull off the highway and sit and stare your eyes out!"

"Sure, it's nice people have an eye for beauty—"

"Beauty, my socks! Who *owns* this land?"

"The state, I reckon . . ."

"You reckon wrong! You and me! We set up camp, register a claim, improve the property and the law reads it's *ours* . . . right?"

"Hold on!" Bob Greenhill was staring out at the desert, and the strange city there. "You mean you want to . . . *homestead a mirage?!*"

"Right, by zingo! Homestead a mirage!"

Robert Greenhill stepped down and wandered around the car looking at the tire-treaded earth.

"Can we *do* that?"

"*Do* it? Excuse my dust!"

In an instant, Will Bantlin was pounding tent pegs in the soil, stringing twine.

"From here to here, and here to here, it's a gold mine, we pan it; it's a cow, we milk it; it's a lakeful of money, we swim in it!"

Rummaging in the car, he heaved out cases and brought

forth a large cardboard which had once advertised cheap cravats. This, reversed, he painted over with a brush and began lettering.

"Willy," said his friend, "nobody's going to pay to see any darned old——"

"Mirage? Put up a fence, tell folks they can't see a thing, and that's just their itch. There!"

He held up the sign:

SECRET VIEW MIRAGE.
THE MYSTERIOUS CITY.
25¢ per car. Motor bikes a dime.

"Here comes a car. Watch!"

"William——"

But Will, running, lifted the sign.

"Hey! Look! Hey!"

The car roared past, a bull ignoring the matador.

Bob shut his eyes so as not to see Will's smile wiped away.

But then——a marvelous sound.

The squeal of brakes.

The car was backing up! Will was leaping forward, waving, pointing.

"Yes, sir! Yes, ma'am! Secret View Mirage! The Mysterious City! Drive right in!"

The tread marks in the simple dirt became numerous, and then, quite suddenly, innumerable.

A great boll of heat-wafted dust hung over the dry peninsula where in a vast sound of arrivals, with braked wheels, slammed doors, stilled engines, the cars of many kinds from many places came and took their places in a line. And the people in the cars were as different as people can be who come from four directions but are drawn in a single moment by a single thing, all talking at first. but growing still at last at what they saw out in the desert. The wind blew softly about their faces, fluttering the hair of the women, the open shirt collars of the men. They sat in their cars for a long time, or they stood on the rim of the earth, saying nothing, and at last one by one turned to go.

As the first car drove back out past Bob and Will, the woman in it nodded happily.

"Thanks! Why, it *is* just like Rome!"

"Did she say 'Rome' or 'home'?" asked Will.

91

Another car wheeled toward the exit.

"Yes, sir!" The driver reached out to shake Bob's hand. "Just looking made me feel I could speak French!"

"French!?" cried Bob.

Both stepped forward swiftly as the third car made to leave. An old man sat at the wheel, shaking his head.

"Never seen the like. I mean to say, fog and all, Westminster Bridge, better than a postcard, and Big Ben off there in the distance. How do you *do* it? God bless. Much obliged."

Both men, disquieted, let the old man drive away, then slowly wheeled to look out along their small thrust of land toward the growing simmer of noon.

"Big Ben?" said Will Bantlin. "Westminster Bridge? Fog?"

Faintly, faintly, they thought they heard, they could not be sure, they cupped their ears, wasn't that a vast clock striking three times off there beyond land's rim? Weren't foghorns calling after boats and boat horns calling back on some lost river?

"Almost speak French?" whispered Robert. "Big Ben? Home? Rome? *Is* that Rome out there, Will?"

The wind shifted. A broiling surge of warm air tumbled up plucking changes on an invisible harp. The fog almost solidified into gray stone monuments. The sun almost built a golden statue on top of a breasted mount of fresh-cut snow marble.

"How—" said William Bantlin, "how could it change? How could it be four, five cities? Did we *tell* anyone what city they'd see? No. Well, then, Bob, *well!*"

Now they fixed their gaze on their last customer who stood alone at the rim of the dry peninsula. Gesturing his friend to silence, Robert moved silently to stand to one side and behind their paying visitor.

He was a man in his late 40s with a vital, sunburned face, good, warm, clear-water eyes, fine cheekbones, a receptive mouth. He looked as if he had traveled a long way around in his life, over many deserts, in search of a particular oasis. He resembled those architects found wandering the rubbled streets below their buildings as the iron, steel and glass go soaring high to block out, fill an empty piece of sky. His face was that of such builders who suddenly see reared up before them on the instant, from horizon to horizon, the perfect implementation of an old, old dream. Now, only half-aware of William and Robert beside him, the stranger spoke at last in a quiet, an easy, a wondrous voice, saying what he saw, telling what he felt:

"...In Xanadu ..."

"What?" asked William.

The stranger half-smiled, kept his eyes on the mirage, and quietly, from memory, recited:

> "In Xanadu did Kubla Khan
> A stately pleasure-dome decree:
> Where Alph, the sacred river, ran
> Through caverns measureless to man
> Down to a sunless sea ..."

His voice spelled the weather and the weather blew about the other two men and made them more still.

> "So twice five miles of fertile ground
> With walls and towers were girdled round ...
> And there were gardens bright with sinuous rills,
> Where blossomed many an incense-bearing tree;
> And here were forests ancient as the hills,
> Enfolding sunny spots of greenery ..."

William and Robert looked off at the mirage and what the stranger said was there, in the golden dust, some fabled Middle East or Far East clustering of minarets, domes, frail towers risen up in a magnificent sift of pollen from the Gobi, a spread of river stone baked bright by the fertile Euphrates, Palmyra not yet ruins, only just begun, newly minted, then abandoned by the departing years, now shimmered by heat, now threatening to blow away forever.

The stranger, his face transformed, beatified by his vision, finished it out:

"It was a miracle of rare device,

A sunny pleasure-dome with caves of ice ..."

And the stranger grew silent.

Which made the silence in Bob and Will all the deeper.

The stranger fumbled with his wallet, his eyes wet.

"Thank you, thank you."

"You already paid us," said William.

"If I had more, you'd get it all."

He gripped William's hand, left a five-dollar bill in it, got in his car, looked for a last time out at the mirage, then sat down, started the car, idled it with wonderful ease, and, face glowing, eyes peaceful, drove away.

Robert walked a few steps after the car, stunned.

Then William suddenly exploded, flung his arms up, whooped, kicked his feet, wheeled around.

"Hallelujah! Fat of the land! Full dinner pails! New squeaky shoes! Look at my fistfuls!"

But Robert said, "I don't think we should take it."

William stopped dancing. "What?"

Robert looked steadily at the desert.

"We can't ever really own it. It's way out there. Sure, we can homestead the land, but . . . We don't even know what *that* thing is."

"Why, it's New York and—"

"Ever *been* to New York?"

"Always wanted. Never did."

"Always wanted, never did." Robert nodded slowly. "Same as them. You heard: Paris. Rome. London. And this last man. Xanadu. Willy, Willy, we got hold of something strange and big here. I'm scared we won't do right by it."

"Well, we're not keeping anyone out, are we?"

"Who knows? Might be a quarter's too much for some. It don't seem right, a natural thing handled by unnatural rules. Look and tell me I'm wrong."

William looked.

And the city was there like the first city he had seen as a boy when his mother took him on a train across a long meadow of grass early one morning and the city rose up head by head, tower by tower to look at him, to watch him coming near. It was that fresh, that new, that old, that frightening, that wonderful.

"I think," said Robert, "we should take just enough to buy gas for a week, put the rest of the money in the first poor box we come to. That mirage is a clear river running, and people coming by thirsty. If we're wise, we dip one cup, drink it cool in the heat of the day and go. If we stop, build dams, try to own the whole river . . ."

William, peering out through the whispering dust wind, tried to relax, accept.

"If you say so."

"I don't. The wilderness all around says."

"Well, I say *different!*"

Both men jumped and spun about.

Half up the slope stood a motorcycle. Sitting it, rainbowed with oil, eyes goggled, grease masking his stubbly cheeks, was a man of familiar arrogance and free-running contempt.

"Ned Hopper!"

Ned Hopper smiled his most evilly benevolent smile, un-braked the cycle and glided the rest of the way down to halt by his old friends.

"You—" said Robert.

"Me! Me! Me!" Ned Hopper honked his cycle horn three times, laughing loud, head back. "Me!"

"Shut up!" cried Robert. "Bust it like a mirror."

"Bust *what* like a mirror?"

William, catching Robert's concern, glanced apprehensive-ly out beyond at the desert.

The mirage flurried, trembled, misted away, then hung itself like a tapestry once more, on the air.

"Nothing out there! What you guys up to?" Ned peered down at the tread-marked earth. "I was twenty miles on, to-day, when I realized you boys was hiding back behind. Says to myself, that ain't like my buddies who led me to that gold mine in '47, lent me this cycle with a dice roll in '55. All those years we help each other and now you got secrets from friend Ned. So I come back. Been up on that hill half the day, spying." Ned lifted binoculars from his greasy jacket front. "You know I can read lips? Sure! Saw all the cars zip in here, the cash. Quite a show you're running!"

"Keep your voice down," warned Robert. "So long."

Ned smiled sweetly. "Sorry to see you go. But I surely respect your getting off my property."

"Yours!" Robert and William cried, caught themselves, and said, in a trembling whisper, "yours?"

Ned laughed. "When I saw what you was up to, I just cycled into Phoenix. See this little-bitty Government paper sticking out my back pocket?"

The paper was there, neatly folded.

William put out his hand.

"Don't give him the pleasure," said Robert.

William pulled his hand back. "You want us to believe you filed a homestead claim?"

Ned shut up the smile inside his eyes. "I do. I don't. Even if I was lying, I could still make Phoenix on my bike quick-er'n your jalopy." Ned surveyed the land with his binoculars. "So just put down all the money you earned from two this afternoon, when I filed my claim, from which time on you was trespassing my land."

Robert flung the coins in the dust. Ned Hopper glanced casually at the bright litter.

"The U.S. Government Mint! Hot dog, nothing out there, but dumb bunnies willing to pay for it!"

Robert turned slowly to look at the desert.

"You don't see anything?"

Ned snorted. "Nothing and you *know* it!"

"But we do!" cried William. "We—"

"Will," said Robert.

"But, Bob!"

"Nothing out there. Like he said." Bob winked.

More cars were driving up now in a great thrum of engines.

"Excuse, gents, got to mind the box office!" Ned strode off, waving. "Yes, sir, ma'am! This way! Cash in advance!"

"Why?" William watched Ned Hopper run off, yelling. "Why are we letting him do this?"

"Wait," said Robert, almost serenely. "You'll see."

They got out of the way as a Ford, a Buick and an ancient Moon motored in.

Twilight. On a hill about 200 yards above the Mysterious City Mirage viewpoint, William Bantlin and Robert Greenhill fried and picked at a small supper, hardly bacon, mostly beans. From time to time, Robert used some battered opera glasses on the scene below.

"Had thirty customers since we left this afternoon," he observed. "Got to shut down soon, though. Only ten minutes of sun left."

William stared at a single bean on the end of his fork. "Tell me again: why? Why every time our luck is good, Ned Hopper jumps out of the earth?"

Robert sighed on the opera-glass lenses and wiped them on his cuff. "Because, friend Will, we are the pure in heart. We shine with a light. And the villains of the world they see that light beyond the hills and say, 'Why, now, there's some innocent, some sweet all-day sucker.' And the villains come to warm their hands at us. I don't know what we can do about it, except maybe put out the light."

"I wouldn't want to do that." William brooded gently, his palms to the fire. "It's just, I was hoping this time was comeuppance time. A man like Ned Hopper, living his white underbelly life, ain't he about due for a bolt of lightning?"

"Due?" Robert screwed the opera glasses tighter into his eyes. "Why, it just struck! Oh, ye of little faith!" William jumped up beside him. They shared the glasses, one lens each, peering down. "Look!"

And William, looking, cried:

"Peduncle Q. Mackinaw!"

"Also: Gullable M. Crackers!"

For far below, Ned Hopper was stomping around outside a car. People gesticulated at him. He handed them some money. The car drove off. Faintly, you could hear Ned's anguished cries.

William gasped. "He's giving money back! Now he almost hit that man there. The man shook his fist at him! Ned's paid him back, too! Look—more fond farewells!"

"Yah-hee!" whooped Robert, happy with his half of the glasses.

Below, all the cars were dusting away now. Old Ned did a violent kicking dance, threw his goggles in the dust, tore down the sign, let forth a terrible oath.

"Dear me," mused Robert. "I'm glad I can't hear them words. Come on, Willy!"

As William Bantlin and Robert Greenhill drove back up to the Mysterious City turnoff, Ned Hopper rocketed out in a screaming fury. Braying, roaring on his cycle, he hurled the painted cardboard through the air. The sign whistled up, a boomerang. It hissed, narrowly missing Bob. Long after Ned was gone in his banging thunder, the sign sank down and lay on the earth where William picked it up and brushed it off.

It was twilight indeed now and the sun touching the far hills and the land quiet and hushed and Ned Hopper gone away, and the two men alone in the abandoned territory in the thousand-treaded dust, looking out at the sand and the strange air.

"Oh, no . . ." said William.

"I'm afraid . . . yes," said Robert.

The desert was empty in the pink gold light of the setting sun. The mirage was gone. A few dust devils whirled and fell apart, way out on the horizon, but that was all.

William let out a huge groan of bereavement.

"*He* did it! Ned! Ned Hopper, come back, you! Oh, damnit, Ned, you spoiled it all! Blast you to Perdition!"

He stopped. "Bob, how can you *stand* there!?"

Robert smiled sadly. "Right now, I'm feeling sorry for Ned Hopper."

"Sorry!"

"He never saw what we saw. He never saw what anybody saw. He never believed for one second. And you know what? Disbelief is catching. It rubs off on people."

97

William searched the disinhabited land.

"Is *that* what happened?"

"Who knows?" Robert shook his head. "One thing sure: when folks drove in here, the city, the cities, the mirage, whatever, was there. But it's awful hard to see when people stand in your way. Without so much as moving, Ned Hopper put his big hand across the sun. First thing you know, theater's closed for good."

"Can't we—" William hesitated, "can't we open it up again? How? How do you bring a thing like that back?"

They let their eyes play over the sand, the hills, the few lone clouds, the sky emptied of wind and very still.

"Maybe if we just look out the sides of our eyes, not direct at it, relax, take it easy . . ."

They both looked down at their shoes, their hands, the rocks at their feet, anything. But at last William mourned. "*Are* we? Are we the pure in heart?"

Robert laughed just a little bit.

"Oh, not like the kids who came through here today, and saw anything they wanted to see, and not like the big simple people born in the wheat fields and by God's grace wandering the world and will never grow up. We're neither the little children nor the big children of the world, Willy, but we are one thing: glad to be alive. We know the air mornings on the road, how the stars go up and then down the sky. Old Ned, he stopped being glad a long time ago. I hate to think of him driving his cycle on the road the rest of the night, the rest of the year . . ."

As he finished this, Robert noticed that William was sliding his eyes carefully to one side, toward the desert.

Robert whispered, carefully, *"See* anything . . . ?"

William sighed. "No. Maybe . . . tomorrow . . ."

A single car came down the highway.

The two men glanced at each other. A wild look of hope flashed in their eyes. But they could not quite bring themselves to fling up their hands and yell. They simply stood with the painted sign held in their arms.

The car roared by.

The two men followed it with their wishful eyes.

The car braked. It backed up. In it were a man, a woman, a boy, a girl. The man called out:

"You closed for the night?!"

William said, "It's no use—"

Robert cut in. "He means, 'No use giving us money!' Last customer of the day, and family. Free! On the house!"

"Thank you, neighbor, thank you!"

The car roared out onto the viewpoint.

William seized Robert's elbow. "Bob, what ails you? Disappoint those kids, that nice family?"

"Hush up," said Robert, gently. "Come on."

The kids piled out of the car. The man and his wife climbed slowly out into the sunset. The sky was all gold and blue now, and a bird sang somewhere in the fields of sand.

"Watch," said Robert.

And they moved up to stand behind the family where it lined up now to look out over the desert.

William held his breath.

The man and wife squinted into the twilight, uneasily.

The kids said nothing. Their eyes flexed and filled with a distillation of late sunlight.

William cleared his throat. "It's late. Uh—can't see too well—"

The man was going to reply, when the boy said, "Oh, we can see—fine!"

"Sure!" The girl pointed. "There!"

The mother and father followed her gesture, as if it might help, and it did.

"Lord," said the woman, "for a moment I thought—but now—yes—there it is!"

The man read his wife's face, saw a thing there, borrowed it, and placed it on the land and in the air.

"Yes," he said, at last. "Oh, yes."

William stared at them, the desert, and then at Robert, who smiled and nodded.

The faces of the father, the mother, the daughter, the son were glowing now, looking off at the desert.

"Oh," murmured the girl, "is it *really* there?"

And the father nodded, his face bright with what he saw that was just within seeing and just beyond knowing. He spoke as if he stood alone in a great forest church.

"Yes. And, Lord . . . it's beautiful."

William started to lift his head, but Robert whispered, "Easy. It's coming. Don't try. Easy, Will."

And then William knew what to do.

"I," he said, "I'm going to go stand with the kids."

And he walked slowly over and stood right behind the boy and the girl. He stood for a long time there, like a man

99

between two warm fires on a cool evening, and they warmed him and he breathed soft and at last let his eyes drift up, let his attention wander easy out toward the twilight desert and the hoped-for city in the dusk.

And there in the dust softly blown high from the land, reassembled on the wind into half-shapes of towers and spires, and minarets, was the mirage.

He felt Robert's breath on his neck, close, whispering, half-talking to himself:

"It was . . . a miracle of rare device . . .
A sunny pleasure-dome with caves of ice . . ."

And the city was there.

And the sun set and the first stars came out.

And the city was very clear, as William heard himself repeat, aloud or perhaps for only his secret pleasure:

"It was a miracle of rare device . . ."

And they stood in the dark until they could not see.

Mark Twain invented the time travel story, six years later H. G. Wells perfected it and revealed its paradoxes. Between them they left little for latecomers to do. But they are still fun to write. Some stories are chores, some are fun—this is one I enjoyed writing.

ROBERT A. HEINLEIN

"ALL YOU ZOMBIES—"

by ROBERT A. HEINLEIN

2217 Time Zone V (EST) 7 Nov 1970 NYC—"Pop's Place": I was polishing a brandy snifter when the Unmarried Mother came in. I noted the time—10:17 p.m. zone five, or eastern time, November 7th, 1970. Temporal agents always notice time and date; we must.

The Unmarried Mother was a man twenty-five years old, no taller than I am, childish features and a touchy temper. I didn't like his looks—I never had—but he was a lad I was here to recruit, he was my boy. I gave him my best barkeep's smile.

Maybe I'm too critical. He wasn't swish; his nickname came from what he always said when some nosy type asked him his line: "I'm an unmarried mother." If he felt less than murderous he would add: "—at four cents a word. I write confession stories."

If he felt nasty, he would wait for somebody to make something of it. He had a lethal style of infighting, like a female cop—one reason I wanted him. Not the only one.

He had a load on and his face showed that he despised people more than usual. Silently I poured a double shot of Old Underwear and left the bottle. He drank it, poured another.

I wiped the bar top. "How's the 'Unmarried Mother' racket?"

His fingers tightened on the glass and he seemed about to throw it at me; I felt for the sap under the bar. In temporal manipulation you try to figure everything, but there are so many factors that you never take needless risks.

I saw him relax that tiny amount they teach you to watch for in the Bureau's training school. "Sorry," I said. "Just asking, 'How's business?' Make it 'How's the weather?' "

He looked sour. "Business is okay. I write 'em, they print 'em, I eat."

I poured myself one, leaned toward him. "Matter of fact,"

103

I said, "you write a nice stick—I've sampled a few. You have an amazingly sure touch with the woman's angle."

It was a slip I had to risk; he never admitted what pen-names he used. But he was boiled enough to pick up only the last: " 'Woman's angle!' " he repeated with a snort. "Yeah, I know the woman's angle. I should."

"So?" I said doubtfully. "Sisters?"

"No. You wouldn't believe me if I told you."

"Now, now," I answered mildly, "bartenders and psychiatrists learn that nothing is stranger than truth. Why, son, if you heard the stories I do—well, you'd make yourself rich. Incredible."

"You don't know what 'incredible' means!"

"So? Nothing astonishes me. I've always heard worse."

He snorted again. "Want to bet the rest of the bottle?"

"I'll bet a full bottle." I placed one cn the bar.

"Well—" I signaled my other bartender to handle the trade. We were at the far end, a single-stool space that I kept private by loading the bar top by it with jars of pickled eggs and other clutter. A few were at the other end watching the fights and somebody was playing the juke box—private as a bed where we were.

"Okay," he began, "to start with, I'm a bastard."

"No distinction around here," I said.

"I mean it," he snapped. "My parents weren't married."

"Still no distinction," I insisted. "Neither were mine."

"When—" He stopped, gave me the first warm look I ever saw on him. "You mean that?"

"I do. A one-hundred-percent bastard. "In fact," I added, "No one in my family ever marries. All bastards."

"Oh, that." I showed it to him. "It just looks like a wedding ring; I wear it to keep women off." It is an antique I bought in 1985 from a fellow operative—he had fetched it from pre-Christian Crete. "The Worm Ouroboros . . . the World Snake that eats its own tail, forever without end. A symbol of the Great Paradox."

He barely glanced at it. "If you're really a bastard, you know how it feels. When I was a little girl—"

"Wups!" I said. "Did I hear you correctly?"

"Who's telling this story? When I was a little girl—Look, ever hear of Christine Jorgenson? Or Roberta Cowell?"

"Uh, sex-change cases? You're trying to tell me—"

"Don't interrupt or swelp me, I won't talk. I was a foundling, left at an orphanage in Cleveland in 1945 when I was a month old. When I was a little girl, I envied kids with parents. Then, when I learned about sex—and, believe me, Pop, you learn fast in an orphanage—"

"I know."

"—I made a solemn vow that any kid of mine would have both a pop and a mom. It kept me 'pure,' quite a feat in that vicinity—I had to learn to fight to manage it. Then I got older and realized I stood darn little chance of getting married —for the same reason I hadn't been adopted." He scowled. "I was horse-faced and buck-toothed, flat-chested and straight-haired."

"You don't look any worse than I do."

"Who cares how a barkeep looks? Or a writer? But people wanting to adopt pick little blue-eyed golden-haired morons. Later on, the boys want bulging breasts, a cute face, and an Oh-you-wonderful-male manner." He shrugged. "I couldn't compete. So I decided to join the W.E.N.C.H.E.S."

"Eh?"

"Women's Emergency National Corps, Hospitality & Entertainment Section, what they now call 'Space Angels'— Auxiliary Nursing Group, Extraterrestrial Legions."

I knew both terms, once I had them chronized. We use still a third name, it's that elite military service corps: Women's Hospitality Order Refortifying & Encouraging Spacemen. Vocabulary shift is the worst hurdle in time-jumps—did you know that "service station" once meant a dispensary for petroleum fractions? Once on an assignment in the Churchill Era, a woman said to me, "Meet me at the service station next door"—which is not what it sounds; a "service station" (then) wouldn't have a bed in it.

He went on: "It was when they first admitted you can't send men into space for months and years and not relieve the tension. You remember how the wowsers screamed?—that improved my chance, since volunteers were scarce. A gal had to be respectable, preferably virgin (they liked to train them from scratch), above average mentally, and stable emotionally. But most volunteers were old hookers, or neurotics who would crack up ten days off Earth. So I didn't need looks; if they accepted me, they would fix my buck teeth, put a wave in my hair, teach me to walk and dance and how to listen to a man pleasingly, and everything else—plus training for the prime duties. They would even use plastic surgery if it would help—nothing too good for Our Boys.

"Best yet, they made sure you didn't get pregnant during

your enlistment—and you were almost certain to marry at the end of your hitch. Same way today, A.N.G.E.L.S. marry spacers—they talk the language.

"When I was eighteen I was placed as a 'mother's helper.' This family simply wanted a cheap servant but I didn't mind as I couldn't enlist till I was twenty-one. I did housework and went to night school—pretending to continue my high school typing and shorthand but going to a charm class instead, to better my chances for enlistment.

"Then I met this city slicker with his hundred-dollar bills." He scowled. "The no-good actually did have a wad of hundred-dollar bills. He showed me one night, told me to help myself.

"But I didn't. I liked him. He was the first man I ever met who was nice to me without trying games with me. I quit night school to see him oftener. It was the happiest time of my life.

"Then one night in the park the games began."

He stopped. I said, "And then?"

"And then *nothing!* I never saw him again. He walked me home and told me he loved me—and kissed me good-night and never came back." He looked grim. "If I could find him, I'd kill him!"

"Well," I sympathized, "I know how you feel. But killing him—just for doing what comes naturally—hmm . . . Did you struggle?"

"Huh? What's that got to do with it?"

"Quite a bit. Maybe he deserves a couple of broken arms for running out on you, but—"

"He deserves worse than that! Wait till you hear. Somehow I kept anyone from suspecting and decided it was all for the best. I hadn't really loved him and probably would never love anybody—and I was more eager to join the W.E.N.C.H.E.S. than ever. I wasn't disqualified, they didn't insist on virgins. I cheered up.

"It wasn't until my skirts got tight that I realized."

"Pregnant?"

"He had me higher 'n a kite! Those skinflints I lived with ignored it as long as I could work—then kicked me out and the orphanage wouldn't take me back. I landed in a charity ward surrounded by other big bellies and trotted bedpans until my time came.

"One night I found myself on an operating table, with a nurse saying, 'Relax. Now breathe deeply.'

106

"I woke up in bed, numb from the chest down. My surgeon came in. 'How do you feel?" he says cheerfully.

" 'Like a mummy.'

" 'Naturally. You're wrapped like one and full of dope to keep you numb. You'll get well—but a Caesarian isn't a hangnail.'

" 'Caesarian' I said. 'Doc—*did I lose the baby?*'

" 'Oh, no. Your baby's fine.'

" 'Oh. Boy or girl?'

" 'A healthy little girl. Five pounds, three ounces.'

"I relaxed. It's something, to have made a baby. I told myself I would go somewhere and tack 'Mrs.' on my name and let the kid think her papa was dead—no orphanage for *my* kid!

"But the surgeon was talking. 'Tell me, uh—' He avoided my name. '—did you ever think your glandular setup was odd?'

"I said, 'Huh? Of course not. What are you driving at?'

"He hesitated. 'I'll give you this in one dose, then a hypo to let you sleep off your jitters. You'll have 'em.'

" 'Why?' I demanded.

" 'Ever hear of that Scottish physician who was female until she was thirty-five?—then had surgery and became legally and medically a man? Got married. All okay.'

" 'What's that got to do with me?'

" 'That's what I'm saying. You're a man.'

"I tried to sit up. '*What?*'

" 'Take it easy. When I opened you, I found a mess. I sent for the Chief of Surgery while I got the baby out, then we held a consultation with you on the table—and worked for hours to salvage what we could. You had two full sets of organs, both immature, but with the female set well enough developed for you to have a baby. They could never be any use to you again, so we took them out and rearranged things so that you can develop properly as a man.' He put a hand on me. 'Don't worry. You're young, your bones will readjust, we'll watch your glandular balance—and make a fine young man out of you.'

"I started to cry. 'What about my *baby?*'

" 'Well, you can't nurse her, you haven't milk enough for a kitten. If I were you, I wouldn't see her—put her up for adoption.'

" '*No!*'

"He shrugged. 'The choice is yours; you're her mother— well, her parent. But don't worry now; we'll get you well first.'

"Next day they let me see the kid and I saw her daily—trying to get used to her. I had never seen a brand-new baby and had no idea how awful they look—my daughter looked like an orange monkey. My feelings changed to cold determination to do right by her. But four weeks later that didn't mean anything."

"Eh?"

"She was snatched."

" 'Snatched?' "

The Unmarried Mother almost knocked over the bottle we had bet. "Kidnapped—stolen from the hospital nursery!" He breathed hard. "How's that for taking the last a man's got to live for?"

"A bad deal," I agreed. "Let's pour you another. No clues?"

"Nothing the police could trace. Somebody came to see her, claimed to be her uncle. While the nurse had her back turned, he walked out with her."

"Description?"

"Just a man, with a face-shaped face, like yours or mine." He frowned. "I think it was the baby's father. The nurse swore it was an older man but he probably used makeup. Who else would swipe my baby? Childless women pull such stunts—but whoever heard of a man doing it?"

"What happened to you then?"

"Eleven more months of that grim place and three operations. In four months I started to grow a beard; before I was out I was shaving regularly . . . and no longer doubted that I was male." He grinned wryly. "I was staring down nurses' necklines."

"Well," I said, "seems to me you came through okay. Here you are, a normal man, making good money, no real troubles. And the life of a female is not an easy one."

He glared at me. "A lot you know about it!"

"So?"

"Ever hear the expression 'a ruined woman'?"

"Mmm, years ago. Doesn't mean much today."

"I was as ruined as a woman can be; that bum *really* ruined me—I was no longer a woman . . . and I didn't know *how* to be a man."

"Takes getting used to, I suppose."

"You have no idea. I don't mean learning how to dress, or not walking into the wrong rest room; I learned those in the hospital. But how could I *live*? What job could I get? Hell,

108

I couldn't even drive a car. I didn't know a trade; I couldn't do manual labor—too much scare tissu, too tender.

"I hated him for having ruined me for the W.E.N.C.H.E.S., too, but I didn't know how much until I tried to join the Space Corps instead. One look at my belly and I was marked unfit or military service. The medical officer spent time on me just from curiosity; he had read about my case.

"So I changed my name and came to New York. I got by as a fry cook, then rented a typewriter and set myself up as a public stenographer—what a laugh! In four months I typed four letters and one manuscript. The manuscript was for *Real Life Tales* and a waste of paper, but the goof who wrote it, sold it. Which gave me an idea; I bought a stack of confession magazines and studied them." He looked cynical. "Now you know how I get the authentic woman's angle on an unmarried-mother story . . . through the only version I haven't sold— the true one. Do I win the bottle?"

I pushed it toward him. I was upset myself, but there was work to do. I said, "Son, you still want to lay hands on that so-and-so?"

His eyes lighted up—a feral gleam.

"Hold it!" I said. "You wouldn't kill him?"

He chuckled nastily. "Try me."

"Take it easy. I know more about it than you think I do. I can help you. I know where he is."

He reached across the bar. *"Where is he?"*

I said softly, "Let go my shirt, sonny—or you'll land in the alley and we'll tell the cops you fainted." I showed him the sap.

He let go. "Sorry. But where is he?" He looked at me. "And how do you know so much?"

"All in good time. There are records—hospital records, orphanage records, medical records. The matron of your orphanage was Mrs. Fetherage—right? She was followed by Mrs. Gruenstein—right? Your name, as a girl, was 'Jane'— right? And you didn't tell me any of this—right?"

I had him baffled and a bit scared. "What's this? You trying to make trouble for me?"

"No indeed. I've your welfare at heart. I can put this character in your lap. You do to him as you see fit—and I guarantee that you'll get away with it. But I don't think you'll kill him. You'd be nuts to—and you aren't nuts. Not quite."

He brushed it aside. "Cut the noise. *Where is he?*"

I poured him a short one; he was drunk but anger was

offsetting it. "Not so fast. I do something for you—you do something for me."

"Uh . . . what?"

"You don't like your work. What would you say to high pay, steady work, unlimited expense account, your own boss on the job, and lots of variety and adventure?"

He stared. "I'd say, 'Get those goddam reindeer off my roof!' Shove it, Pop—there's no such job."

"Okay, put it this way: I hand him to you, you settle with him, then try my job. If it's not all I claim—well, I can't hold you."

He was wavering; the last drink did it. "When d'yuh d'liver 'im?" he said thickly.

"If it's a deal—*right now!*"

He shoved out his hand. "It's a deal!"

I nodded to my assistant to watch both ends, noted the time —2300—started to duck through the gate under the bar— when the juke box blared out: "I'm My Own Grandpaw!" The service man had orders to load it with Americana and classics because I couldn't stomach the "music" of 1970, but I hadn't known that tape was in it. I called out, "Shut that off! Give the customer his money back." I added, "Storeroom, back in a moment," and headed there with my Unmarried Mother following.

It was down the passage across from the johns, a steel door to which no one but my day manager and myself had a key; inside was a door to an inner room to which only I had a key. We went there.

He looked blearily around at windowless walls. "Where is 'e?"

"Right away." I opened a case, the only thing in the room; it was a U.S.F.F. Co-ordinates Transformer Field Kit, series 1992, Mod. II—a beauty, no moving parts, weight twenty-three kilos fully charged, and shaped to pass as a suitcase. I had adjusted it precisely earlier that day; all I had to do was to shake out the metal net which limits the transformation field.

Which I did. "Wha's that?" he demanded.

"Time machine," I said and tossed the net over us.

"Hey!" he yelled and stepped back. There is a technique to this; the net has to be thrown so that the subject will instinctively step back *onto* the metal mesh, then you close the net with both of you inside completely—else you might leave shoe soles behind or a piece of foot, or scoop up a slice of floor. But that's all the skill it takes. Some agents con a sub-

110

ject into the net; I tell the truth and use that instant of utter astonishment to flip the switch. Which I did.

1030-VI-3 April 1963 - Cleveland, Ohio-Apex Bldg.: "Hey!" he repeated. "Take this damn thing off!"

"Sorry," I apologized and did so, stuffed the net into the case, closed it. "You said you wanted to find him."

"But—you said that was a time machine!"

I pointed out a window. "Does that look like November? Or New York?" While he was gawking at new buds and spring weather, I reopened the case, took out a packet of hundred-dollar bills, checked that the numbers and signatures were compatible with 1963. The Temporal Bureau doesn't care how much you spend (it costs nothing) but they don't like unnecessary anachronisms. Too many mistakes, and a general court martial will exile you for a year in a nasty period, say 1974 with its strict rationing and forced labor. I never make such mistakes; the money was okay.

He turned around and said, "What happened?"

"He's here. Go outside and take him. Here's expense money." I shoved it at him and added, "Settle him, then I'll pick you up."

Hundred-dollar bills have a hypnotic effect on a person not used to them. He was thumbing them unbelievingly as I eased him into the hall, locked him out. The next jump was easy, a small shift in era.

7100-VI-10 March 1964 - Cleveland-Apex Bldg.: There was a notice under the door saying that my lease expired next week; otherwise the room looked as it had a moment before. Outside, trees were bare and snow threatened; I hurried, stopping only for contemporary money and a coat, hat, and topcoat I had left there when I leased the room. I hired a car, went to the hospital. It took twenty minutes to bore the nursery attendant to the point where I could swipe the baby without being noticed. We went back to the Apex Building. This dial setting was more involved as the building did not yet exist in 1945. But I had precalculated it.

0100-VI-20 Sept 1945 - Cleveland-Skyview Motel: Field kit, baby, and I arrived in a motel outside town. Earlier I had registered as "Gregory Johnson, Warren, Ohio," so we arrived in a room with curtains closed, windows locked, and

111

doors bolted, and the floor cleared to allow for waver as the machine hunts. You can get a nasty bruise from a chair where it shouldn't be—not the chair of course, but backlash from the field.

No trouble. Jane was sleeping soundly; I carried her out, put her in a grocery box on the seat of a car I had provided earlier, drove to the orphanage, put her on the steps, drove two blocks to a "service station" (the petroleum products sort) and phoned the orphanage, drove back in time to see them taking the box inside, kept going and abandoned the car near the motel—walked to it and jumped forward to the Apex Building in 1963.

2200-VI-24 April 1963 - Cleveland-Apex Bldg.: I had cut the time rather fine—temporal accuracy depends on span, except on return to zero. If I had it right, Jane was discovering, out in the park this balmy spring night, that she wasn't quite as "nice" a girl as she had thought. I grabbed a taxi to the home of those skinflints, had the hackie wait around a corner while I lurked in shadows.

Presently I spotted them down the street, arms around each other. He took her up on the porch and made a long job of kissing her good-night—longer than I thought. Then she went in and he came down the walk, turned away. I slid into step and hooked an arm in his. "That's all, son," I announced quietly. "I'm back to pick you up."

"You!" He gasped and caught his breath.

"Me. Now you know who *he* is—and after you think it over you'll know who you are . . . and if you think hard enough, you'll figure out who the baby is . . . and who *I* am."

He didn't answer, he was badly shaken. It's a shock to have it proved to you that you can't resist seducing yourself. I took him to the Apex Building and we jumped again.

2300-VIII-12 Aug 1985 - Sub Rockies Base: I woke the duty sergeant, showed my I.D., told the sergeant to bed my companion down with a happy pill and recruit him in the morning. The sergeant looked sour, but rank is rank, regardless of era; he did what I said—thinking, no doubt, that the next time we met he might be the colonel and I the sergeant. Which can happen in our corps. "What name?" he asked.

I wrote it out. He raised his eyebrows. "Like so, eh? *Hmm—*"

"You just do your job, Sergeant." I turned to my companion.

"Son, your troubles are over. You're about to start the best job a man ever held—and you'll do well. *I know.*"

"That you will!" agreed the sergeant. "Look at me—born in 1917—still around, still young, still enjoying life." I went back to the jump room, set everything on pre-selected zero.

2301-V-7 Nov 1970-NYC - "Pop's Place": I came out of the storeroom carrying a fifth of Drambuie to account for the minute I had been gone. My assistant was arguing with the customer who had been playing "I'm My Own Grandpaw!" I said, "Oh, let him play it, then unplug it." I was very tired.

It's rough, but somebody must do it and it's very hard to recruit anyone in the later years, since the Mistake of 1972. Can you think of a better source than to pick people all fouled up where they are and give them well-paid, interesting (even though dangerous) work in a necessary cause? Everybody knows now why the Fizzle War of 1963 fizzled. The bomb with New York's number on it didn't go off, a hundred other things didn't go as planned—all arranged by the likes of me.

But not the Mistake of '72; that one is not our fault—and can't be undone; there's no paradox to resolve. A thing either is, or it isn't, now and forever amen. But there won't be another like it; an order dated "1992" takes precedence any year.

I closed five minutes early, leaving a letter in the cash register telling my day manager that I was accepting his offer to buy me out, so see my lawyer as I was leaving on a long vacation. The Bureau might or might not pick up his payments, but they want things left tidy. I went to the room back of the storeroom and forward to 1993.

2200-VII-12 Jan 1993 - Sub Rockies Annex-HQ Temporal DOL: I checked in with the duty officer and went to my quarters, intending to sleep for a week. I had fetched the bottle we bet (after all, I won it) and took a drink before I wrote my report. It tasted foul and I wondered why I had ever liked Old Underwear. But it was better than nothing; I don't like to be cold sober, I think too much. But I don't really hit the bottle either; other people have snakes—I have people.

I dictated my report; forty recruitments all okayed by the Psych Bureau—counting my own, which I knew would be okayed. I was here, wasn't I? Then I taped a request for

113

assignment to operations; I was sick of recruiting. I dropped both in the slot and headed for bed.

My eye fell on "The By-Laws of Time," over my bed:

Never Do Yesterday What Should Be Done Tomorrow.
If At Last You Do Succeed, Never Try Again.
A Stitch in Time Saves Nine Billion.
A Paradox May Be Paradoctored.
It Is Earlier When You Think.
Ancestors Are Just People.
Even Jove Nods.

They didn't inspire me the way they had when I was a recruit; thirty subjective-years of time-jumping wears you down. I undressed and when I got down to the hide I looked at my belly. A Caesarian leaves a big scar but I'm so hairy now that I don't notice it unless I look for it.

Then I glanced at the ring on my finger.

The Snake That Eats Its Own Tail, Forever and Ever . . . I *know* where *I* came from—but *where did all you zombies come from?*

I felt a headache coming on, but a headache powder is one thing I do not take. I did once—and you all went away.

So I crawled into bed and whistled out the light.

You aren't really there at all. There isn't anybody but me —Jane—here alone in the dark.

I miss you dreadfully!

I especially like *Faq'* because I think it to be the most success-ful fable I have ever written. Personality, character, realistic setting, psychology, social institutions—this story takes a complete vacation from them all, and yet manages to be about something that matters. I enjoy reading and writing moral fables, and this one seems to me the clearest and best shaped one I have done; also, it has a moral that I think important.

GEORGE P. ELLIOTT

FAQ'

by GEORGE P. ELLIOTT

During the war my geographer was a lieutenant in the Air Corps. On one of his trips to North Africa his plane flew over the lower edge of the Atlas Mountains, where they meet the Sahara. For long stretches the range was a desolation, as he had expected, relieved only by a few ribbons of green. No doubt rivers from melting snows came down these valleys and squandered themselves in the desert, supplying just enough water to keep a strip of trees and grasses alive on their banks. All this was what he had learned in his studies. But he had also been taught that no one lived on the south side of the mountains, and yet he was quite certain that in one of the valleys he had seen a cluster of huts and some smoke weaving up through the trees. The smoke could have been mist— though it was a hot clear day—but the huts were certainly human dwellings. His curiosity was aroused. He resolved to satisfy it as soon as he was able.

After the war, when he was able to investigate, he discovered only two references to anything that could possibly be identified as his special valley. The first was in a book written in 1837 by one Benjamin Huntley, *Exploring the Atlas Mountains*. Huntley mentions hearing of the existence of a village somewhere south of Mount Tizi, but he says he doubts if his informants were reliable. The other reference was in a twelfth-century Arabic manuscript now in the Royal Library in Madrid, a report on revenues from slave trading in Spain and Northwest Africa. On a map in this manuscript a spot considerably south and west of Mount Tizi is identified as Faq'. There is nothing in the text to explain Faq'; there was nothing but the word itself on the old parchment map. There was nothing else at all anywhere. What was he to do?

If he sought the assistance of one of the learned societies, he would certainly lose much or all of the credit for the discovery—if discovery there was to be. But the expenses would probably come to more than his purse could bear, unless he risked making the explorations quite alone and with no further reconnaissance by air. And it was a risk—the region was a true wilderness, mountainous, arid, huge, and inhospitable even to plants. But he was young and a good mountaineer and he could speak Arabic, and for years he had been risking his life for a lesser cause—to him—than this. His is the sort that wants every place to be given its right name; for him the words terra incognita signify an admission of defeat or a region of impenetrable cold; error is his evil. It was clear what he must do: discover Faq'.

I will not tell you much about the adventures he had before he reached his goal, the delays caused by the suspicion and incredulity of small officials, the hostility of the hill people, the grandeur of that wilderness in which he wandered for weeks not even sure of the existence of his goal, the privation and fatigue and load of bad doubt which only his pride could support, the great good fortune by which he was saved from starvation by a wounded eagle dropping from the skies near to him—too weak to kill it outright, he had to suck its blood. But finally he stood at the brink of a fertile valley, a valley flat and broad for these mountains, but inaccessible from above because of the sheer rise of the range and from the sides because of the steep cliffs and, as he found, uninviting from below because it narrowed to a gorge that emptied the river out precipitously; but people lived here—it was Faq'. It took him three days to discover the tortuous route of access into the valley, and one whole day to get to the floor. Among rushes at the edge of the river he collapsed, one hand trailing in the water, flat on his belly, sunk at last into that weariness which his pride no longer needed to deny. He lay there for at least one day and perhaps two, he had no way of knowing. When he awoke he could scarcely roll over, and the hand which had fallen into the water was wrinkled white and seemed to be paralyzed. It was lucky for him that he was not discovered, for the women of Faq' would have killed him if they had found him asleep.

He finally rolled onto his back, and lay wondering whether he would ever be able to get up. But as he lay there in the soft rushes in the warmth of afternoon he began to notice, as though for the first time, that vast clean sky under which he had so long labored; and in his fatigue he could not resist the sudden fancy that the sky was not *over* him—he was not *below* its perfection, but rather he was a part of it. "For is not the blueness of the sky," he said to himself, "achieved only by the refraction of light on innumerable particles, which are about me here as well as out there, and maybe in me for all I know?" The longer he lay, looking not up but out, into, among, the more it seemed to him that the sky was not so absolute a blue as it had been on the days before. Yet there could be no mist, not here on this side of these mountains. He lay wondering whether so much blandness had deceived his senses, but he was swimming in that perfection all the same; and then suddenly an explanation for the seeming mistiness occurred to him. It was a light smoke haze. He remembered the curls of smoke he had seen from the airplane, and he observed that there was no wind. No doubt a nearly imperceptible film of smoke obscured his perfect vision. This saddened him for a moment, but then he thought, "Why is it not as absolute a perfection, the sky with this faint and even haze in it, as a clean sky? These smoke particles had been added, but thinly like the blue particles, perfectly distributed. They are not an adulteration, but a version of that other perfection, a part of it, distributed differently now than before; if it hadn't been for that tiny difference I would never have noticed the whole, huge sublimity, and who can say that one of these versions is truer than the other?" Full of these reflections he arose and went down the riverside in search of friends.

He had not gone far when he heard children's laughter in the woods across the river. The stream was neither very wide nor fast-flowing, and at its deepest it did not come over his chest; yet he thought he would never get across it alive. When he was ten yards from the opposite shore he fell in exhaustion into the stream, and floated on the current more dead than alive. But he was caught in an eddy where he lay with his nose and eyes just sticking above water, slowly revolving under the green shade of an hospitable tree like a log in the pool. All he had to do to save himself was to crawl up under the tree onto a pleasant bank. But it didn't seem worth the trouble. It was too lovely there to move, looking up into the twining imperfections of this tree, cool and still and spread out and wet, slowly going about in the eddy, finally without will, only a thing that once had been able to think and now was at peace in the enveloping water, in one complete embrace happy. He does not yet understand why he ever climbed out of the water. He was not conscious of making a decision. All of a sudden it came to him that the sun had gone down and it was time to come home; before he could reflect on this odd notion (where was home?) he found himself climbing out on the bank, a live man again. Never since then has he felt anything out of the ordinary about floating in a river or looking at the sky, and he doesn't know exactly how to explain the experiences of that day—his fatigue perhaps, or the special air and water there, or his relief at finding his goal. What he is sure of is this: while he didn't know what to expect from the people of Faq', he was prepared for it when it came.

It was dusk when he approached the huts. They were long and thin, and all of them pointed up the valley toward the mountains. There were no windows in them. They were interspersed among trees. At some distance he could see a large hut in which there were fire, cooking, noise, children. He crept up to the closest hut, and crouched on the dark side of it listening to the mutter coming from within. The muttering was fast and monotonous, in a man's voice. It seemed to be a praying in some Arabic dialect. He could make out some of the words, or thought he could; they seemed to be numerals. As he listened to that unflagging drone it occurred to him that this must be a machine, no man could do it; but then he heard a clearing of the throat and a slight pause, and he realized it was a man all right, but a man imitating a machine. A praying machine. He thought of hermits.

Footsteps approached. He glued himself to the wall. He heard a woman murmuring, a slight altercation, a moment of laughter, stirring sounds, and then footsteps going away. He looked carefully around the edge of the building and saw a well-built young man, not an old one as he had expected, and a young woman. Side by side they were approaching the building of light and noise. Others were coming to it also. There were no dogs around; at least none had smelled him out, none were barking. He crept nearer the communal house. The odor of cooking food nearly made him faint it was so pleasant. Nevertheless, he lay low a while, trying to understand what was going on. Everything about the scene appeared to be unexceptional and happy. There were several men and many more women and a good many children. Three old women came out into the darkness and on the way to their huts began singing quietly a song the like of which he had never heard. He saw a young man catch and embrace a struggling young woman at the door to the hut, to the general merriment, all with an openness which he had never so much as heard of among Mohammedans. He had no idea what would be best for him to do.

What he finally did was to walk straight toward the doorway crying as loud as he could, which was not very loud, "Food in the name of Allah!"

Well, they took care of him, fed him, and nursed him back to strength again. He learned later that he was the only outsider who had ever been allowed to live in Faq'—to stay alive, I mean, not just abide there. I think it was more than a matter of whim that he was allowed to stay. He was completely at their mercy and they could understand something of what he said, so much was in his favor; but mostly he helped himself with his own honest pride.

After he had eaten some of the vegetable stew which is their chief food, watched intently by a hundred dark, silent faces, the chief, Alfaleen, asked him in their dialect who he was. Now my geographer had noticed that no one had mentioned Allah and that the chief's style was very plain for Arabic, with none of those honorific courtesies universal among Mohammedans. He had noticed this, but hadn't known what to make of it. He answered, "Destroyer of boundaries." There was no response. Either they had not understood his accent or else they were not at all impressed. "Foe of all ignorance," he said. No response. "Seeker of truth."

Then Alfaleen said to him, "What must be?"

"What has always been will always be."

"What must be?"

"So long as there are hills the rain will flow down them in streams."

Alfaleen repeated, "What must be?"

"Each number will always have two neighbors."

But Alfaleen asked again, "What must be?"

And this time he gave the answer he would never before in his life have given: "Nothing." It saved him.

He was wondered a thousand times why he gave that unlikely answer. He had of course heard of the indeterminacy principle; he had heard, with fascination, that law is a matter of statistical probability and that truth is finally a matter of whichever of the many geometries best suits your needs. But since he had never been able to imagine such things he had not believed in them, and he certainly had never asked himself whether or not a stone *must* fall, two plus two *must* equal four. Yet had said to Alfaleen, that black, cool, impersonal man, that nothing must be. He attributes this answer of his to the power of Alfaleen's mind. He was concentrating hard on understanding what was being said to him and on choosing the correct Arabic words for his answers, he was weak with fatigue, he sensed that much depended upon his answer, and he was alerted by the very strangeness of the question. Even so, he thinks it was the power of that other mind which put the answer into his mouth. He learned to respect that power.

For a week he convalesced. The women and children, among whom he stayed, treated him with all the friendliness in the world. Alfaleen had commanded him to tell them nothing about the place from which he had come, and had also commanded them not to ask him about it. He had nothing to do but to lie about listening to them, learning what their customs were and how they thought and what they were afraid of—not learning it so much as taking it in like the food and water and bright air. He observed that none of the mature men did any of the ordinary tasks, like gathering fuel, fishing, repairing the huts, irrigating the fields; they seemed to have some other work. The women did not resent this state of affairs; it had not occurred to them, apparently, that things could be otherwise arranged. The children were amazingly unrestricted and happy. There were at least twice as many girls as boys for some reason, but the women did not seem to treat the boys with any great reverence. The children were not allowed to go near the huts at the other end of the village (where he had heard the man praying like a machine). Every morning Alfaleen would take the boys over five off to school. The girls learned from the women. Boys were punished for being too rough, too "manly"; girls were punished for using a number over one hundred. The children had a game which they loved to play, with innumerable variations: a boy would sit in a special position and begin to count in a low regular voice, and a girl or perhaps two or three of them would try to distract him. They would use every means imaginable except hurting: shout in his ear, caress him, throw cold water on him, count backwards in his same rhythm, put food in his mouth. Some of the boys had developed amazing powers of concentration, but the wiles of the girls were irresistible. No boy could hold out for more than a quarter of an hour—but no ordinary boy would have held out against those girls for two minutes, whatever he was doing. One little girl, about eight or nine who was particularly attached to him—a quiet thing with a clumsy, strong body, rather deliberate, rather grave—told him one morning that she had had a nightmare about the end of the world. She had dreamed, she said, that "they came to the end of the counting and I was one of the ones left over." A little boy who got angry with him once called him a "slow counter." From the awed silence and snickers with which the other children greeted this, he concluded that it was a serious insult. The women and children were the happiest he had ever seen; yet there was nothing intense about what they did. They seemed never to have suffered. He was too feeble, too contented to feel any strangeness about all this; while it lasted it seemed exactly the way things should be. But when he was strong again at the end of a week and Alfaleen removed him from his idyl he was glad it was over.

At first Alfaleen asked him questions about the world from which he had come. 'Which men are most revered? Which have the greatest power? For what is a man put to death? What is God nowadays?' But the questioning did not go on for long. Alfaleen was feeling him out, determining just how to introduce him to the life which he was entering. To one who lives with beauty hourly, as to a man in love, the various semblances of beauty to which he may be exposed are all imperfect and not in the least interesting; he wants to be with the true beauty. Alfaleen's was the beauty of truth, and he wanted to share it. He tried tricks and deceptions in his questionings, but he was hopelessly honest; it was clear that no one had lied in Faq' for a long time.

Well, the upshot of it all was that he was deemed worthy to become a bearer of the mystery of the truth, a participant in it. He was taken to a hut of his own in the men's section of the village—a bare, dark, quiet hut—and there taught to count. One sat in a certain manner—the way the boys had sat in their game—weaved in a certain rhythm, closed one's senses to the outside world, thought only of the perfection of one's technique, and counted in a steady voice. He was given a block of numbers very high in the series, told certain permissible abbreviations and short cuts, and left each morning to his counting. Alfaleen instructed him each afternoon in the history and aims of Faq'. He understood it all in a way. He was quite good at counting. But then he had to be; anyone who fell below a certain monthly quota was put to death. So was any cheater. Alfaleen would prowl about outside the huts listening to the voices of the counters—two or three times a day he came by, so keen and trained that he could tell by the very cadences of the murmuring count whether the counter was in danger of falling behind. There were no cheaters.

In the tenth century, when the Arabs were conquerors of

North Africa and Spain and were also developing advanced mathematical theories, a nobleman-mathematician named Alfaleen stopped in the province of Maraq' while en route to Spain to enter the faculty of the new college of mathematics. But he fell out with the theologians of Maraq' and was condemned for his heresy. Alfaleen had maintained that pure reason, and only pure reason, could ever achieve the truth, and that since thought was the greatest power in the universe then Allah must be thought. According to the theologians this was as much as to say that the Koran wasn't worth a couple of quadratic equations and that if God is idea then idea is God. To rescue the youth of Spain from such notions they recommended to the govenor of Maraq' that he execute Alfaleen. But the governor was an old friend of Alfaleen's father; instead of executing him, he had him and all his party driven off into the granite wilderness to perish for heresy. And that would have been that; but by some hook or crook they fell in with a band of native blacks, founded Faq', and established a colony. Their descendants have lived there in peace ever since. They had no animals or tools, but none were needed. The outside world forgot they were there, and any stranger who happened to come to Faq' was put to death.

So far as their traditions tell, the constitution of Faq' has remained unaltered since its founding—the laws of reason are ageless. There is Alfaleen, the chief, the philosopher, the king; there are the men, who count; and there are the women, who do the work and tend to the men. The original Alfaleen, to whose genius Faq' owes its peace and its purpose, had by the exercise of pure reason seen the folly of racial distinctions; blacks and Arabs had intermingled as they desired, the third Alfaleen was himself pure black, and by now the blend of races is complete. He had seen the problem of keeping down the population; defectives, women who can no longer work, innovators, are all put to death. The ratio of women to men had been kept fairly constant at three to one. Though the women, having no souls, cannot be entrusted with the high mission of Faq', yet the actual survival of the colony has come more and more to rest upon them—they weed out the unfit, they maintain everyone physically, and they keep watch on the men. Indeed, though Alfaleen is the governor, it is the women who actually make and execute all the rules and customs—except, of course, those having to do with the only thing that matters, the exercise of pure reason, the counting.

For Alfaleen has set his people reason's purest problem:

number. And each Alfaleen, chosen solely for his ability, spends his life in the contemplation of number and the attributes of number in the confidence that the penetration of this mystery, the final conquering of it, will lay bare the secret to all power. But not many men are capable of such true and ultimate endeavor; hence, as soon as the colony had stabilized itself, Alfaleen, like a good philosopher-king, had set his subjects to the accomplishment of a communal task, one which in its very nature surpasses any other that men have set themselves: counting. By hypothesis the highest nameable number is as far from the end as one is, and there is no end to counting. It is the function of Faq' to test this hypothesis in the only statistically verifiable fashion, actually by counting forever.

The women may not use a number greater than one hundred; the life of Faq' does not make larger numbers necessary and woman's reason would sully truth. Originally there was much defection from the strict regime, and at one time had the insurrectionists banded together they could have overthrown the rule of this godless theocracy, but Alfaleen won out. They have reached a very high number; they expect in our lifetime to reach the number beyond which numbers have no name. Into that darkness Alafleen will shed the light of reason.

More and more in the past few centuries Alfaleen has come to believe that the core of the problem of number lies in its oneness-endlessness and that the original impulse which set the men of Faq' to telling the rosary of reason's mystery was by no means an expedient but rather an attempt to mechanize the mystery itself. For this, says Alfaleen, is not only the activity of reason, it is reason pure, this counting, because only incidentally does it correspond to anything outside man's mind. It becomes clearer and clearer that without this endless and exact demonstration of reason's truth all reason would be subverted and mankind go back to what it had been before.

Alfaleen said, and certainly he believes it, that there is a sense in which man's destiny hangs upon those counters in Faq', for that they do not reach the end of counting is the demonstration of all hypothesis. If they should reach the end, reason would have done what is impossible to it and the rest would be chess, for then they would have proved that reason too has its law—absolute positive correlation. But if they should quit counting—weary, exhausted, rebellious, defeated —then would you and I have succumbed at last to our weariness and rebellion and defeat, and the women would take over.

At first he was exhilarated by the novelty of the life and what seemed to be the importance of the counting. At the outset boredom was the dread at the back of his mind, but in fact he was never bored. The counting seemed to hypnotize him into a state of strange tranquility. He was tranced, as it were, into reason's realm. So much so, indeed, that it was not many weeks before he quite lost interest in exercise and food and the evening conviviality. Then girls taunted and seduced him, with an innocent artfulness and a voluptuous naïveté which he found (as had the boys in the game) irresistible. One night he counted in his sleep, and all the next day he was required to play with children and make love to young women and lie in the sun. Everything was communal in Faq', property and love as well as the great task. It was a world of reason and sense and trance, and he found it far happier than the world of mystery and strong feeling from which he had come. But eventually he began to think.

Or perhaps not to think so much as to remember. He remembered the anxiety and injustice and despair and the huge splendors of this world—the poverty, the right and wrong, the power, the pain. Especially the pain. He told himself again and again that ten thousand sink that one may rise, that whole cities stink in ugliness that fifty men may make and enjoy only a little beauty. But not all the reasonableness he could muster, nor horror at his memories, nor the truth and high pleasantness of Faq' could drive the thought of pain from his mind. For it was pain, suffering, moral agony, that his memories revolved about. It became clearer and clearer to him that he could not live without pain, not even thus happily, not even thus participating in the great task of man's noblest faculty. He tried hurting himself physically; he had a large rock balanced precariously once, ready to roll onto his arm and smash it. But the absurdity of such an act here in this equable valley stopped him from doing it. And afterwards the indignity he felt at not having been able to prepare a pain for himself than this which any accident might provide, not having been able to go through with even this little thing made him resolve to leave Faq' as soon as he could. For a long time he had been dissembling at his counting, with great anxiety and guiltiness. Now that he had resolved to leave, it suddenly seemed silly to him, and he dissembled without a qualm.

He sat day after day in his hut making the sounds of counting, and often actually tranced into it—it had its own

126

power. But most of the time he was planning his escape. It was necessarily an escape too, for anyone guilty of any defection, from bad health to rebelliousness, was without mercy or remorse killed. He collected food and water and made himself a substitute for shoes. He walked on rocky ground till his feet were horny. He played and swam very hard till he was strong and supple. He had no human ties to break; four of the women were pregnant at the time, one perhaps with his child, perhaps all four, perhaps none, he did not care. He would miss Alfaleen's cold, pure speculations, but never, he knew, so much as he now missed the pain of this world of ours. He lay in the sun till he was nearly as black as they, and in the middle of one stormy night he left. He was not pursued.

He returned to us after much difficulty. He is suffering with us now, and looking back at the bland perfection of Faq' with a sometimes acute nostalgia. But my geographer is determined never to go there again, for he is sure that though he does not know what is right for men ordered perfection is wrong, and that though suffering is bad the lack of suffering is much worse.

I'm fond of this story because I remember it as easy to write. This may sound like a hell of a reason, but if you had suffered with me through *Stranger Station* or *What Rough Beast*, it wouldn't. When I wrote *Babel II*, I was not trying to lift myself by my bootstraps, or dredge up some inaccesible portion of my id for examination: I was having fun. I trust you will, too.

DAMON KNIGHT

BABEL II

by DAMON KNIGHT

From the front he looked a little like Happy Hooligan, if you remember that far back. From the side, where you got a better view of that silver-white crest, he looked more like a cross between George Arliss and a cockatoo.

He stood just under four feet tall, big head, crest and all. He had a wrinkled violet-gray skin, curious S-whorled ears, and a Tweedledum tummy; he was dressed in an electric-blue jacket and small-clothes of some crinkly material that glittered when he moved, with jackboots on his stubby legs and a white-metal disk, a quarter as big as he was, slung by a baldrick from one narrow shoulder.

Lloyd Cavanaugh saw the apparition first, at eleven o'clock on a Wednesday morning in May, in the living room of his studio apartment on East 50th Street in Manhattan. It stepped into view, seemingly, from behind the drawing table at the far end of the room.

Which was nonsense. The drawing table, with its top horizontal and the breakfast dishes still on it, was shoved back against the closed drapes of the window. On the right, between the table and the record cabinet, there was about six inches clearance; on the left, between the table and the keg he kept his ink and brushes on, even less.

Cavanaugh, a bad-tempered young man with a long morose face casually connected to a knobby, loose-jointed body, scowled across the pool of brilliance on the model table and said, "What the hell?" He switched off the floods and turned on the room lights.

Suddenly illuminated, the Hooligan-thing blazed at him like a Christmas tree ornament. Its eyes blinked rapidly; then the long upper lip curled up in an astonishing crescent-shaped bucktoothed smile. It made a sound like *"Khakh-ptui!"* and nodded its head several times.

Cavanaugh's first thought was for the Hasselblad. He picked it up, tripod and all, carried it crabwise backward to safety behind the armchair, then crossed the room and took a poker out of the fireplace rack. Gripping this weapon, he advanced on the Hooligan.

The thing came to meet him, grinning and nodding. When they were two strides apart it stopped, bowed jerkily, and lifted the white disk at the end of the baldrick, holding it at the top, with one of the flat sides toward Cavanaugh.

A picture formed in the disk.

In stereo and full color, it showed a ten-inch Cavanaugh bending over something on a tripod. The hands moved swiftly, fitting pieces together; then the figure stepped back and stared with evident approval at an oblong box shape at the top of the tripod, with a chromed cylinder projecting from the front of it. The Hasselblad.

Cavanaugh lowered the poker. Jaw unhinged, he stared at the disk, which was now blank, then at the Hooligan's violet face and the silvery growth above it, which was neither hair nor feathers, but something in between. . . . "How did you do that?" he demanded.

"Szu szat," said the Hooligan alertly. He jiggled the disk at Cavanaugh, pointed to his head, then to the disk, then to Cavanaugh's head, then to the disk again. Then he held the thing out at arm's length, cocking his head to one side.

Cavanaugh took the disk gingerly. Gooseflesh was prickling along his arms. "You want to know if I made the camera?" he said tentatively. "Is that it?"

"Szat it," said the Hooligan. He bowed again, nodded twice, and opened his eyes very wide.

Cavanaugh reflected. Staring at the disk, he imagined an enormous machine with a great many drive belts and moving parts, all whirling furiously. There it was, a little blurred, but not bad. He put a hopper on one side of it, made a man walk up and pour in a bucketful of scrap metal, and then showed a stream of cameras coming out the other side.

The Hooligan, who had been peering intently at the other side of the disk, straightened up and took the disk back with another bow. Then he whirled around rapidly three times, holding his nose with one hand and making violent gestures with the other.

Cavanaugh fell back a step, gripping his poker more firmly.

The Hooligan darted past him, moving so fast his legs twinkled, and fetched up with his chin on the edge of the model table, staring at the setup in the middle of the tabletop.

"Hey!' said Cavanaugh angrily, and followed him. The

130

Hooligan turned and held out the disk again. Another picture formed: Cavanaugh bending over the table, this time, putting tiny figures together and arranging them in front of a painted backdrop.

. . . Which was substantially what had happened. Cavanaugh was, by profession, a comic-book artist. He was indifferent to the work itself; it was automatic; it paid him well; but it had ruined him as a draftsman. He couldn't draw, paint or etch for fun any more. So he had taken up photography —specifically, tabletop photography.

He built his models out of clay and papier-mâché and wire and beads and bits of wood and a thousand other things; he painted or dyed them, composed them, lighted them—and then, with the Hasselblad and a special, very expensive shallow-focus lens, he photographed them. The results, after the first year, had begun to be surprising.

The setup on the table now was a deceptively simple one. Background and middle distance were a tangle of fir and mountain laurel, scaled half an inch to a foot. In the foreground were three figures grouped around the remains of a campfire. They were not human; they were attenuated, gray, hairless creatures with big mild eyes, dressed in oddly cut hiking clothes.

Two, with their backs to a block of crumbling masonry half sunken in the ground, were leaning together over a sheet of paper unrolled from a metal cylinder. The third was seated on a stone, nearer the camera, with a shank of meat in its hand. The shape of the half-gnawed bones was disturbingly familiar; and when you looked more closely you would begin to wonder if those projections at the end could be fingers, all but concealed by the eater's hand. As a matter of fact, they were; but no matter how long you looked at the photograph you would never be quite sure.

The Hooligan was thrusting the disk at him again, grinning and winking and teetering on his heels. Cavanaugh, suppressed annoyance in favor of curiosity, accepted it and ran through the same sequence the Hooligan had shown him.

"That's right," he said. "I made it. So what?"

"Szo khvat!" The Hooligan's hand made a gesture, too swift to follow, and suddenly contained what looked like a large fruit, like a purple pear with warts. Seeing Cavanaugh's uncomprehending expression, he put it back wherever it had come from and produced a wadded mass of translucent pink threads. Cavanaugh scowled irritably. "Look—" he began.

The Hooligan tried again. This time he came up with a brilliant, faceted white stone about the size of a cherry.

Cavanaugh felt his eyes bulging. If that was a diamond . . .

"Khoi-ptoo!" said the Hooligan emphatically. He pointed to the stone and to Cavanaugh, then to himself and the model setup. His meaning was clear: he wanted to trade.

It was a diamond, all right; at least, it scribed a neat line in the glass of an empty beer bottle. It was also brilliant, pure white and, so far as Cavanaugh could tell, flawless. He put it on his postage scale; it weighed a little less than an ounce. Say twenty grams, and a carat was two hundred milligrams. . . . It worked out to a preposterous one hundred carats, a little less than the Hope diamond in its prime.

He stared at the thing suspiciously. There *had* to be a catch in it, but with the best will in the world he couldn't see any. The models were a means to an end; once he was finished with them, they simply took up room. So what could he lose?

The Hooligan was gazing at him, owl-eyed. Cavanaugh picked up the disk and gave him his answer: a series of pictures that showed Cavanaugh photographing the models, processing the film, and then ceremoniously accepting the diamond and handing the models over.

The Hooligan bowed repeatedly, capered, stood briefly on his hands, and patted Cavanaugh's sleeve, grinning. Taking this for consent, Cavanaugh put the Hasselblad back in place, turned on the floods, and began where he had left off. He took half a dozen color shots, then reloaded with black-and-white film and took half a dozen more.

The Hooligan watched everything with quivering attention. He followed Cavanaugh into the darkroom and goggled over the edge of the workbench while Cavanaugh developed the black-and-white film, fixed it, washed and dried it, cut it apart and printed it.

And as soon as the first print came out of the frame, the Hooligan made urgent gestures and held out another diamond, about half the size of the first. He wanted the prints, too!

Sweating, Cavanaugh dug into his files and brought up color prints and transparencies of his other work: the Hansel and Gretel series, Cavor and the Grand Lunar, *Walpurgisnacht*, Gulliver extinguishing the palace fire in Lilliput, the Head of the N.I.C.E. The Hooligan bought them all. As each bargain was struck, he picked up his purchase and put it away wherever it was that he got the diamonds. Cavanaugh watched him closely, but couldn't figure out where they went.

For that matter, where had the Hooligan come from?

Assured that Cavanaugh had no more pictures, the Hooligan was darting around the room, peering into corners, bending to look into bookshelves, standing on tiptoe to see what was on the mantlepiece. He pointed at a five-inch wooden figurine a squatting, hatchet-faced man-shape with its arms crossed, elbows on knees—an Ifugao carving that Cavanaugh had brought hom from the Philippines. In the disk, a copy of the Goldberg machine Cavanaugh had used, to explain cameras, appeared for an instant. The Hooligan cocked his head at him.

"No," said Cavanaugh. "Handmade." He took the disk and gave the Hooligan a view of a brown-skinned man gouging splinters out of a block of mahogany. Then, for kicks, he made the man shrink to a dot on an island on a globe that slowly turned, with Asia and Australia vanishing around one limb while the Americas rolled into sight from the other. He made a red dot for New York, and pointed at himself.

"Khrrrzt," said the Hooligan thoughtfully. He turned away from the Ifugao and pointed to a bright diamond-patterned rug that hung on the wall over the couch. "Khandmate?"

Cavanaugh, who had just made up his mind to give up the Ifugao for another diamond, was nonplused. "Wait a minute," he said, and made another moving picture in the disk: himself handing over the Ifugao for the standard emolument.

The Hooligan leaped back, ears flapping, crest aquiver. Recovering somewhat, he advanced again and showed Cavanaugh a revised version: the Hooligan receiving a wood carving from, and handing a diamond to, the brown-skinned man Cavanaugh had pictured as its creator.

"Khand-mate?" he said again, pointing to the rug.

Somewhat sourly, Cavanaugh showed him the rug being woven by a straw-hatted Mexican. Still more sourly, he answered the Hooligan's pictographed "Where?" with a map of Mexico; and more sourly still, he identified and located the artists responsible for a Swedish silver pitcher, a Malay kris, an Indian brass hubble-bubble, and a pair of loafers hand-cobbled in Greenwich Village.

The Hooligan, it appeared, bought only at the source.

At any rate, if he wasn't going to get any more diamonds, he could get some information. Cavanaugh took the disk and projected a view of the Hooligan popping into sight and moving forward across the room. Then he ran it backward and looked inquiringly at the Hooligan.

For answer, he got a picture of a twilit depthless space where crested little creatures like the Hooligan walked among tall fungoid growths that looked like tiers of doughnuts on a stick. Another planet? Cavanaugh touched the disk and made the viewpoint tilt upward; the Hooligan obligingly filled in more of the featureless violet haze. No sun, no moon, no stars.

Cavanaugh tried again: a picture of himself, standing on the globe of the earth and peering at the night sky. Suddenly a tiny Hooligan-figure appeared, uncomfortably perched on a star.

The Hooligan countered with a picture that left Cavanaugh more confused than before. There were two globes, swinging in emptiness. One was solid-looking, and standing on it was a tiny man-shape; the other was violet mist, with the tubby, crested figure of a Hooligan inside it. The two spheres revolved very slowly around each other, coming a little nearer with each circuit, while the solid globe flickered light-dark, light-dark. Eventually they touched, clung, and the Hooligan-figure darted across. The solid globe flickered once more, the Hooligan shot back to the misty one, and the spheres separated, moving very gradually apart as they circled.

Cavanaugh gave up.

The Hooligan, after waiting a moment to be sure that Cavanaugh had no more questions, made his deepest bow to date and conjured up a final diamond: a beauty, larger than all but one or two that Cavanaugh already had.

Picture of Cavanaugh accepting the diamond and handing over something blurred: *What for?*

Picture of the Hooligan rejecting the blur: *For nothing.* Picture of the Hooligan patting Cavanaugh's sleeve: *For friendship.*

Feeling ashamed of himself, Cavanaugh got a bottle of May wine and two glasses out of the bookshelf. He explained to the Hooligan, via the disk, what the stuff was and—sketchily —what it was supposed to do to you.

This was a mistake.

The Hooligan, beaming enormously between sips, drank the wine with every sign of enjoyment. Then, with an impressive flourish, he put a smallish green and white doodad on the table. It had a green crystalline base with a slender knob-

134

tipped metal shaft sprouting upright from the center of it. That was all.

Feeling abnormally open-minded and expectant, Cavanaugh studied the Hooligan's pictograph explanation. The gadget, apparently, was the Hooligan equivalent of alcoholic beverages. (Picture of Cavanaugh and the Hooligan, with enormous smiles on their faces, while colored lights flashed on and off inside their transparent skulls.) He nodded when the little man glanced at him for permission. With one thick finger, the Hooligan carefully tapped the doodad's projecting knob. Knob and shaft vibrated rapidly.

Cavanaugh had the odd sensation that someone was stirring his brains with a swizzle stick. It tickled. It was invigorating. It was delightful. "Ha!" he said.

"Kho!" said the Hooligan, grinning happily. He picked up the doodad, put it away—Cavanaugh *almost* saw where it went—and stood up. Cavanaugh accompanied him to the door. He patted Cavanaugh's sleeve; Cavanaugh pumped his hand. Then, cheerfuly bouncing three steps at a time, he disappeared down the stairwell.

From the window, a few minutes later, Cavanaugh saw him riding by—atop a Second Avenue bus.

II

The euphoric feeling diminished after a few minutes, leaving Cavanaugh in a relaxed but bewildered state of mind. To reassure himself, he emptied his bulging trousers pockets onto the table. Diamonds—solid, cool, sharp-edged, glowingly beautiful. He counted them; there were twenty-seven, ranging from over a hundred carats to about thirty; worth, altogether—how much?

Steady, he warned himself. There may be a catch in it yet. The thing to do was to get downtown to an appraiser's and find out. Conveniently, he knew where there was one—in the French Building, across the hall from Patriotic Comics. He picked out two of the stones, a big one and a little one, and zipped them into the inner compartment of his wallet. Jittering a little with excitement, he dumped the rest into a paper bag and hid them under the kitchen sink.

A yellow cab was cruising down the avenue. Cavanaugh hailed it and got in. "Forty-fifth and Fifth," he said.

"Boo?" said the driver, twisting to look at him.

Cavanaugh glowered. "Forty-fifth Street," he said distinctly, "and Fifth Avenue. Let's go."

"Zawss," said the driver, pushing his cap up, "owuh kelg trace wooj'l, fook. Bnog nood ig ye nolik?"

Cavanaugh got out of the cab. "Pokuth *chowig'w!*" said the driver, and zoomed away, grinding his gears.

Jaw unhinged, Cavanaugh stared after him. He felt his ears getting hot. "Why didn't I get his license number?" he said aloud. "Why didn't I stay upstairs where it was safe? Why do I live in this idiotic goddamn city?"

He stepped back onto the sidewalk. "Lowly, badny?" said a voice in his ear.

Cavanaugh whirled. It was an urchin with a newspaper in his hand, a stack of them under his arm. "Will you kindly mind your own business?" Cavanaugh said. He turned, took two steps toward the corner, then froze, faced around again, and marched back.

It was as he had thought: the headline of the paper in the boy's hand read, MOTN LNIUL IMAP QYFRAT.

The name of the paper, which otherwise looked like the *News*, was *Pionu Vajl*.

The newsboy was backing away from him, with a wary look in his eyes.

"Wait," said Cavanaugh hastily. He clutched in his pocket for change, found none, and got a bill out of his wallet with trembling fingers. He thrust it at the child. "I'll take a paper."

The boy took the bill, glanced at it, threw it on the pavement at Cavanaugh's feet, and ran like sixty.

Cavanaugh picked up the bill. In each corner of it was a large figure 4. Over the familiar engraving of G. Washington were the words FRA EVOFAP LFIFAL YK IQATOZI. Under it, the legend read, YVA PYNNIT.

He clutched his collar, which was throttling him. That vibrating gadget— But that couldn't be it; it was the world that was scrambled, not Cavanaugh. And *that* was impossible, because . . .

A dirty little man in a derby rushed at him, grabbing for his lapels. "Poz'k," he gabbled, "fend gihekn, fend gihekn? Fwuz eeb l' mwukd sahtz'kn?"

Cavanaugh pushed him away and retreated.

The little man burst into tears. "FWUH!" he wailed. "Fwuh vekn r' NAHP shaoo?"

Cavanaugh stopped thinking. Out of the corner of his eye,

he saw that a crosstown bus had just pulled up down at the end of the block. He ran for it.

The red-faced driver was half out of his seat, bellowing gibberish at a fat woman who was shrieking back at him, brandishing a dangerous parasol. Beyond them the narrow aisle was packed full of bewildered faces, annoyed faces, shouting faces. The air bristled with dislocated consonants.

Farther down, somebody shrieked and hammered on the rear door. Cursing, the driver turned around to open it. The fat woman seized this opportunity to clout him on the head, and when the resulting melee was over, Cavanaugh found himself halfway down the bus, well wedged in, without having paid his fare.

The bus moved. Hysterical passengers got off at every stop, but the ones that crowded on were in no better shape. Nobody, Cavanaugh realized numbly, could understand anybody; nobody could read anything written.

The din was increasing; Cavanaugh could hear the driver's bellowing voice getting steadily hoarser and weaker. Up ahead, horns were blowing furiously. Concentrating with the greatest difficulty, he managed: *How far?* That was the crucial point— had whatever it was happened simultaneously all over New York . . . or all over the world? Or, horrid thought, was it a sort of infection that he was carrying with him?

He had to find out.

The traffic got thicker. At Sixth Avenue the bus, which had been moving by inches, stopped altogether and the doors slammed open. Peering forward, Cavanaugh saw the driver climb down, hurl his uniform cap to the street and disappear, shoulders hunched, into the crowd.

Cavanaugh got out and walked west into bedlam. Auto horns were howling, sirens shrieking; there was a fight every fifteen yards and a cop for every tenth fight. After a while it became obvious that he would never get to Broadway; he battled his way back to Sixth and turned south.

The loudspeaker over a record store was blaring a song Cavanaugh knew and detested; but instead of the all-too-familiar words, the raucous female voice was chanting:

"Kee-*ee* tho-*iv* i-*if* zeg*mlit Podn mawgeth oo-ooguaatch . . ."

It sounded just as good.

The street sign directly ahead of him read, 13FR. LF. Even the *numbers* were cockeyed.

Cavanaugh's head hurt. He went into a bar.

It was well patronized. Nobody in a white coat was in evidence, but about a third of the customers were behind the bar, serving the rest—a bottle at a time.

Cavanaugh elbowed his way into the first tier and hesitated between two bottles labeled respectively CIF 05 and ZITLFIOTL. Neither sounded particularly appetizing, but the amber liquid in each looked to be what he needed. He settled for the Zitlfiotl. After his second swallow, feeling more alert, he scanned the backbar and located a radio.

It was, he found when he reached it, already turned on, but nothing was coming out but a power hum. He twiddled with the knobs. At the right of the dial—which was eccentrically numbered from 77 to 408—he picked up an orchestra playing *Pictures at an Exhibition;* otherwise, nothing.

That, he decided, settled it. WQXR, with an all-music program, was on the air; the others were off. That meant that speech was coming out double-talk, not only in New York and New Jersey broadcasts, but in network programs from the West Coast. Or—wait a minute—even if a radio performer in Hollywood were able to speak straight English, wouldn't it be nonsense to an engineer in Manhattan?

This led him by easy stages to the next problem. Selecting an unfrequented table in the rear, and carrying his Zitlfiotl with him, he seated himself with circumspection and carefully laid out on the table the following important articles:

A partially used envelope.

A fountain pen.

A one-dollar bill.

His social-security card.

A salvaged newspaper.

Now, the question was, did any order remain in the patterns of human speech, or was all reduced to utter chaos? Scientific method, encouraged by Zitlfiotl, would discover the answer.

As a preliminary gambit, he wrote the letters of the alphabet, in a severely vertical line, on the unused surface of the envelope.

Next, after reflection, he copied down the text of the one-dollar bill. Thusly:

FRA EVOFAP LFIFAL YK IQATOZI YVA PYNNIT

138

Under each line, letter by letter, he added what *ought* to be the text of the one-dollar bill.

This gave him fifteen letters, which he wrote down in their proper places opposite the already established letters of the alphabet. Following the identical procedure with the *Pionu Vajl*, or *Daily News*, and, with his own signature, which appeared on the card as *Nnyup Ziciviemr*, gave him four letters more, with the result:

A E	H	O I	V N
B	I A	P D	W
C V	J W	Q M	X
D	K F	R H	Y O
E U	L S	S	Z C
F T	M G	T R	
G	N L	U Y	

Now came the supreme test. He copied down the *Vajl's* puzzling headline and transliterated it according to his findings:

MOTN LNIUL
GIRL SLAYS
IMAP QYFRAT
AGED MOTHER

A triumphant success. He could now communicate.

The point is, he told himself lucidly, when I think I am saying "Listen to me," in actuality I am saying "Nolfav fy qa," and this is why nobody understands anyone else. And therefore, if I were to think I am saying "Nolfav fy qa," I would actually be saying "Listen to me." And in this way will we build the Revolution.

But it didn't work.

Some time later he found himself in a disused classroom with an unruly student body consisting of three men with spectacles and beards and a woman with hair in her eyes; he was attempting to teach them by means of blackboard exercises a new alphabet which began E, blank, V, blank, U, T, blank. The blanks, he explained, were most important.

At a later period he was standing on the first landing of the left-hand staircase in the lobby of the Forty-second Street Branch of the New York Public Library shouting to an assembled crowd, over and over, "Myp-piqvap opoyfl! Myp-piqvap opoyfl!"

And at a still later time he woke up, cold sober, leaning on an imitation-marble-topped table in a partially wrecked cafeteria. Sunlight was slanting through the plate glass onto the wall to his left; it must be either late afternoon or early morning.

Cavanaugh groaned. He had gone into that bar, he remembered, because his head hurt: about like taking a mickey finn for nausea.

And as for the rest of it—before *and* after . . . how much of that had he imagined?

He raised his head and stared hopefully at the lettering on the windows. Even back-to-front he could tell that it wasn't in English. The first letter was a Z.

He groaned again and propped his chin up with his hands, carefully, so as not to slosh. He tried to stay that way, not moving, not looking, not noticing, but eventually an insistent thought brought him upright again.

How long?

How long was this going to last? How long could it last before the whole world went to hell in a hand basket? Not very long.

Without language, how could you buy anything, sell anything, order anything? And if you could, what would you use for money—four-dollar bills marked YVA PYNNIT?

. . . Or, he amended bitterly, something equally outlandish. Because that was the point he had overlooked a few drunken hours ago—everybody's alphabet was different. To Cavanaugh, YVA PYNNIT. To somebody else, AGU MATTEK, or ENY ZEBBAL, or . . .

Twenty-six letters in the alphabet. Possible combinations, 26 x 25 x 24 x 23 x 22 and so on down to x 1 . . . figure roughly one decimal place for each operation . . .

Something in the *septillions*.

Not as many if vowels were traded for vowels, consonants for consonants, as seemed to have happened in his case, but still plenty. More than the number of people alive in the world.

That was for the written word. For speech, he realized suddenly, it would be just about twenty-five decimal places worse. Not letters, phonemes—forty of them in ordinary spoken English.

A swizzle stick that stirred up your brains—that switched

the reflex arcs around at random, connecting the receptor pattern for *K* with the response pattern for *H*, or *D* or anything. . . .

Cavanaugh traced a letter with his forefinger on the table-top, frowning at it. Hadn't he always made an A like that—a vertical stroke and three horizontal ones?

But, damn it, that was the fiendish thing about it—memory didn't mean a thing, because all the memories were still there but they were scrambled. As if you had ripped out all the connections in a telephone switchboard and put them back differently.

Of course; it *had* to be that way—nobody had gone around repainting all the signs or reprinting all the newspapers or forging a phony signature on Cavanaugh's social-security card. That half-circle first letter of his name, even though it looked like a Z to him, was still a C.

Or was it? If a tree falls with nobody to hear it, is there a sound? And if beauty is in the eye of the beholder, then which way is up? Or, rather, thought Cavanaugh, repressing a tendency toward hysteria, *which way is out?*

First things first.

The Hooligan.

He came from some place that wasn't exactly a place, across a distance that wasn't exactly a distance. But it must be a difficult journey, because there was no record of any previous appearances of little cockatoo-crested art collectors. . . .

He bought the local handicrafts with stones that were priceless on this planet, and very likely dirt-common where he came from. Pretty beads for the natives. In politeness, you offered him a drink. And being polite right back at you, he gave you a shot of swizzle-sticks-in-the-head.

Firewater. A mild stimulant to the Hooligan, hell on wheels to the aborigines. Instead of getting two people mildly confused, it turned a whole planet pole over equator . . . and, communicating by pictures as he did, it was probable that the Hooligan *still* didn't know what damage he had done. He would finish his tour and go happily back home with his prizes, and then a few thousand years from now, maybe, when the human race had put itself together again into half-acre nations and two-for-a-nickel empires, another Hooligan would come along. . . .

Cavanaugh upset his chair.

Icicles were forming along his spine.

141

This wasn't the first time. It had happened at least once before, a few thousand years ago, in the valley of the Euphrates. Not Bedlam—Babel.

III

The sun was quartering down toward the west, gilding a deserted Forty-second Street with the heartbreaking false promise of spring in New York. Leaning dizzily against the door frame, Cavanaugh saw broken display windows and dark interiors. He heard a confused roaring from somewhere uptown, but the few people who passed him were silent, bewildered.

There was a nasty wreck at the corner of Seventh Avenue, and another at Eighth; that accounted, he saw with relief, for the lack of traffic in this block. Holding the top of his head down with one hand, he scuttled across the street and dived into the black maw of the IRT subway.

The arcade and the station itself were empty, echoing. Nobody behind the newsstands, nobody playing the pinball machines, nobody in the change booth. Swallowing hard, Cavanaugh went through the open gate and clattered down the stairs to the downtown platform.

A train was standing in the express lane, doors open, lights burning, motor chuffing quietly. Cavanaugh ran down to the first car and went across the vestibule to the motorman's cubicle.

The control lever was missing.

Cursing, Cavanaugh climbed back to the street. He had to find the Hooligan; he had one chance in a million of doing it, and one wasted minute now might be the one minute that mattered.

The little man could be anywhere on the planet by now. But he'd expressed interest in objects in Cavanaugh's apartment that came variously from the Philippines, Mexico, Malaya, Sweden, India—and Greenwich Village. If, improbably, he hadn't got around to the Village yet, then Cavanaugh might be able to catch him there; it was the only hope he had.

On Eighth Avenue south of Forty-first, he came upon a yellow cab parked at the curb. The driver was leaning against the wall under a Zyzi-Zyni sign, talking to himself, with gestures.

Cavanaugh clutched him by the sleeve and made urgent

motions southward. The driver looked at him vaguely, cleared his throat, moved two feet farther down the wall and resumed his interrupted discourse.

Fuming, Cavanaugh hesitated for a moment, then fumbled in his pockets for pen and paper. He found the envelope with his world-saving alphabet on it, tore it open to get a blank space, and sketched rapidly:

The driver looked at it boredly, then with a faint gleam of intelligence. Cavanaugh pointed to the first picture and looked at him interrogatively.

"Oweh?" said the driver.

"That's right," said Cavanaugh, nodding violently. "Now the next—"

The driver hesitated. "Mtshell?"

That couldn't be right, with a consonant at the end of it. Cavanaugh shook his head and pointed to the blacked-in circle.

"Vcode," said the driver.

Cavanaugh moved his finger to the white circle.

"Mah."

"Right!" said Cavanaugh. "Oweh mah—" He pointed to the third picture.

That was the tough one; the driver couldn't get it. "Vnakjaw?" he hazarded.

Not enough syllables. Cavanaugh shook his head and passed on to the fourth picture.

"Vbzyetch."

Cavanaugh nodded, and they started through the sequence again.

"Oweh—mah—vbzyetch." A look of enlightenment spread over the driver's face. *"Jickagl! Jickagl!* Vbzyetch!"

"You've got it," Cavanaugh told him. "Sheridan Square. *Jickagl* Vbzyetch."

Halfway to the cab, the driver stopped short, with a remembering look on his face, and held out his hand insinuatingly.

Cavanaugh took the bills out of his wallet and fanned them

at him. The driver shook his head. "Ngup-joke," he said sadly, and turned back toward his wall.

Twenty minutes later Cavanaugh was poorer by one thirty-carat diamond, and the cab driver, with a smile on his honest face, was opening the door for him at the western corner of Sheridan Square (which is triangular), a few yards from the bullet-colored statue of the General.

Cavanaugh made signs to him to wait, got a happy grin and a nod in reply, and ran down the block.

He passed Janigian's shop once without recognizing it, and for an excellent reason: there was not a shoe or a slipper visible anywhere in the big, bare work- and sales-room.

The door was ajar. Cavanaugh went in, stared suspiciously at the empty shelves and then at the door to the back room, which was closed by a hasp and the largest, heaviest padlock he had ever seen in his life. This was odd (a) because Janigian did not believe in locking his doors, and this one, in fact, had never even had a latch, and (b) because Janigian never went anywhere—having been permanently startled, some years ago, by E. B. White's commentary on the way the pavement comes up to meet your foot when you lift it.

Cavanaugh stepped forward, got his fingernails into the crack between the door and the jamb, and pulled.

The hasp, being attached to the jamb only by the sawed-off heads of two screws, came free; the door swung open.

Inside was Janigian.

He was sitting cross-legged on a small wooden chest, looking moderately wild-eyed. He had a rusty shotgun across his thighs, and two ten-inch butcher knives were stuck into the floor in front of him.

When he saw Cavanaugh he raised the gun, then lowered it a trifle. "Odeh!" he said. Cavanaugh translated this as "Aha!" which was Janigian's standard greeting.

"Odeh yourself," he said. He took out his wallet, removed his other diamond—the big one—and held it up.

Janigian nodded solemnly. He stood up, holding the shotgun carefully under one arm, and with the other, without looking down, opened the lid of the chest. He pulled aside a half-dozen dirty shirts, probed deeper, and scrabbled up a handful of something.

He showed it to Cavanaugh.

Diamonds.

He let them pour back into the chest, dropped the shirts

back on top, closed the lid and sat down again. "Odeh!" he said.

This time it meant "Good-by." Cavanaugh went away.

His headache, which had left him imperceptibly somewhere on Forty-second Street, was making itself felt again. Cursing without inspiration, Cavanaugh walked back up to the corner.

Now what? Was he supposed to pursue the Hooligan to the Philippines, or Sweden, or Mexico?

Well, why not?

If I don't get him, Cavanaugh told himself, I'll be living in a cave a year from now. I'll make a lousy caveman. Grubs for dinner *again* . . .

The cabman was still waiting on the corner. Cavanaugh snarled at him and went into the cigar store across the street. From an ankle-deep layer of neckties, pocketbooks and mashed candy bars he picked out a five-borough map. He trudged back across the street and got into the cab.

The driver looked at him expectantly. "Your mother has hairy ears," Cavanaugh told him.

"Zee kwa?" said the driver.

"Three of them," Cavanaugh said. He opened the map to the Queens-Long Island section, managed to locate Flushing Bay, and drew an X—which, on second thought, he scribbled into a dot—where La Guardia Field ought to be.

The driver looked at it, nodded—and held out his meaty hand.

Cavanaugh controlled an impulse to spit. Indignantly, he drew a picture of the diamond he had already given the man, pointed to it, then to the cabman, then to the map.

The driver shrugged and gestured outside with his thumb.

Cavanaugh gritted his teeth, shut his eyes tight, and counted to twenty. Eventually, when he thought he could trust himself to hold anything with a sharp point, he picked up the pen, found the Manhattan section of the map, and made a dot at Fiftieth and Second Avenue. He drew another picture of a diamond, with an arrow pointing to the dot.

The driver studied it. He leaned farther over the seat and put a stubby finger on the dot. "Fa mack alaha gur'l hih?" he demanded suspiciously.

"Your father comes from a long line of orangutans with loathsome diseases," said Cavanaugh, crossing his heart.

Reassured by the polysyllables, the driver put his machine into motion.

At the apartment, while the driver lurked heavily in the

145

living room, Cavanaugh picked out the very smallest diamond to pay his fare, and twelve others, from middling to big, for further emergencies. He also took two cans of hash, a can of tamales, an opener, a spoon, and a bottle of tomato juice in a paper bag; the thought of food revolted him at the moment, but he would have to eat sometime. Better than grubs, anyway. . . .

All the main arteries out of New York, Cavanaugh discovered, were choked—everybody who was on the island was apparently trying to get off, and vice versa. Nobody was paying much attention to traffic signals, and the battered results were visible at nearly every intersection.

It took them two hours to get to La Guardia.

Some sort of a struggle was going on around a car parked in front of the terminal building. As Cavanaugh's cab pulled up, the crowd broke and surged toward them; Cavanaugh had barely time to open the door and leap out. When he had bounced off the hood, tripped over somebody's feet, butted someone else in the stomach, and finally regained his balance a few seconds later, he saw the cab turning on two wheels, with one rear door hanging open, and a packed mass of passengers bulging out like a bee swarm. The cab's taillights wavered off down the road, a few stragglers running frantically after it.

Cavanaugh walked carefully around the diminished mob, still focused on the remaining car, and went into the building. He fought his way through the waiting room, losing his paper bag, several buttons from his shirt and nine tenths of his temper, and found an open gate onto the field.

The huge, floodlighted area was one inextricable confusion of people, dogs and airplanes—more planes than Cavanaugh had ever seen in one place before; forests of them—liners, transports, private planes of every size and shape.

The dogs were harder to account for. There seemed to be several dozen of them in his immediate vicinity, all large and vociferous. One especially active Dalmatian, about the size of a cougar, circled Cavanaugh twice and then reared up to put two tremendous forepaws on his chest. Cavanaugh fell like a tree. Man and dog stared at each other, eye to eye, for one poignant moment; then the beast whirled, thumping Cavanaugh soundly in the ribs, and was gone.

Raging, Cavanaugh arose and stalked forth onto the field. Somebody grabbed his sleeve and shouted in his ear; Cavanaugh swung at him, whirled completely around, and cannoned into somebody else, who hit him with a valise. Some time later, confused in mind and bruised of body, he found himself approaching a small, fragile-looking monoplane on whose wing sat an expressionless man in a leather jacket.

Cavanaugh climbed up beside him, panting. The other looked at him thoughtfully and raised his left hand, previously concealed by his body. There was a spanner in it.

Cavanaugh sighed. Raising one hand for attention, he opened his wallet and took out one of the larger gems.

The other man lowered the spanner a trifle.

Cavanaugh felt for his fountain pen; it was gone. Dipping one finger in the blood that was trickling from his nose, he drew a wobbly outline map of North America on the surface of the wing.

The other winced slightly, but watched with interest.

Cavanaugh drew the United States—Mexico border, and put a large dot, or blob, south of it. He pointed to the plane, to the dot, and held up the diamond.

The man shook his head.

Cavanaugh added a second.

The man shook his head again. He pointed to the plane, made motions as if putting earphones on his head, cocked his head in a listening attitude, and shook his head once more. *No radio.*

With one flattened hand, he made a zooming motion upward; with the other, he drew a swift line across his throat. *Suicide.*

Then he sketched an unmilitary salute. *Thanks just the same.*

Cavanaugh climbed down the wing. The next pilot he found gave him the same answer; and the next; and the next. There wasn't any fifth, because, in taking a shortcut under a low wing, he tripped over two silently struggling gentlemen who promptly transferred their quarrel to him. When he recovered from a momentary inattention, they were gone, and so was the wallet with the diamonds.

Cavanaugh walked back to Manhattan.

Counting the time he spent asleep under a trestle somewhere in Queens, it took him twelve hours. Even an Oregonian can find his way around in Manhattan, but a Manhattanite gets lost anywhere away from his island. Cavanaugh missed the Queensboro Bridge somehow, wandered south into Brooklyn without realizing it (he would rather have died), and wound up some sixty blocks off his course at the Williamsburg Bridge; this led him via Delancey Street into the Lower East Side, which was not much improvement.

Following the line of least resistance, and yearning for civilization (i.e., midtown New York), Cavanaugh moved northwestward along that erstwhile cowpath variously named the Bowery, Fourth Avenue and Broadway. Pausing only to rummage in a Union Square fruit-drink stand for cold frankfurters, he reached Forty-second Street at half-past ten, twenty-three and one half hours after his introduction to the Hooligan.

Times Square, never a very inspiring sight in the morning, was very sad and strange. Traffic, a thin trickle, was moving spasmodically. Every car had its windows closed tight, and Cavanaugh saw more than one passenger holding a rifle. The crowds on the littered sidewalks did not seem to be going anywhere, or even thinking about going anywhere. They were huddling.

Bookstores were empty and their contents scattered over the pavement; novelty shops, cafeterias, drugstores . . . the astonishing thing was that, here and there, trade was still going on. Money would still buy you a bottle of liquor, or a pack of cigarettes, or a can of food—the necessities. Pricing was a problem, but it was being solved in a forthright manner: above each counter, the main items of the store's stock in trade were displayed, each with one or two bills pasted to it. Cigarettes—George Washington. A fifth of whisky—Alexander Hamilton and Abraham Lincoln. A can of ersatzized meat—Andrew Jackson.

There was even one movie house open for business. It was showing a Charlie Chaplin Festival.

Cavanaugh was feeling extremely lightheaded and unsubstantial. Babylon, that great city! he thought; and Somewhere, parently, in the ginnandgo gap between antediluvious and annadominant the copyist must have fled with his scroll. . . .

The human race had now, in effect, Had It. New York was no longer a city; it was simply the raw material for an archaeologist's puzzle—a midden heap. And thinking of *Finnegan* again, he remembered, What a mnice old mness it all mnakes!

He looked at the faces around him, blank with a new misery, the misery of silence. That's what hits them the hardest, he thought. The speechlessness. They don't care about not being able to read—it's a minor annoyance. But they like to talk.

148

And yet, the human race could have survived if only the spoken word had been bollixed up, not the written word. It would have been easy enough to work out universal sound symbols for the few situations where speech was really vital. Nothing could replace the textbooks, the records, the libraries, the business letters.

By now, Cavanaugh thought bitterly, the Hooligan was trading shiny beads for grass skirts in Honolulu, or carved walrus tusks in Alaska, or . . .

Or was he? Cavanaugh stopped short. He had, he realized, been thinking of the Hooligan popping into view all over the globe the way he had appeared in his apartment—and, when he was through, popping back to where he belonged, from wherever he happened to be.

But, if he could travel that way, *why had he left Cavanaugh's place on a Second Avenue bus?*

Cavanaugh scrabbled frantically through his memory. His knees sagged.

The Hooligan had showed him, in the disk, that the two—universes, call them—came together rarely, and when they did, touched at one point only. Last time, the plain of Shinar. This time, Cavanaugh's living room.

And that one flicker, light-dark-light, before the pictured Hooligan moved back to its own sphere . . .

Twenty-four hours.

Cavanaugh looked at his watch. It was 10:37.

He ran.

Lead-footed, three quarters dead, and cursing himself, the Hooligan, the human race, God the Creator and the entire imaginable cosmos with the last breath in his body, Cavanaugh reached the corner of Forty-ninth and Second just in time to see the Hooligan pedaling briskly up the avenue on a bicycle.

He shouted, or tried to; nothing but a wheeze came out.

Whistling with agony, he lurched around the corner and ran to keep from falling on his face. He almost caught up with the Hooligan at the entrance to the building, but he couldn't stop to get the breath to make a noise. The Hooligan darted inside and up the stairs; Cavanaugh followed.

He can't open the door, he thought, halfway up. But when he reached the third-floor landing, the door was open.

Cavanaugh made one last effort, leaped like a salmon,

tripped over the doorsill, and spread-eagled himself on the floor in the middle of the room.

The Hooligan, one step away from the drawing table, turned with a startled "Chaya-dnih?"

Seeing Cavanaugh, he came forward with an expression of pop-eyed concern. Cavanaugh couldn't move.

Muttering excitedly to himself, the Hooligan produced the green-and-white doodad from somewhere—much, presumably, as a human being might have gone for the medicinal brandy—and set it on the floor near Cavanaugh's head.

"Urgh!" said Cavanaugh. With one hand, he clutched the Hooligan's disk.

The pictures formed without any conscious planning: the doodad, the lights flashing off and on in a skull—dozens, hundreds of skulls—then buildings falling, trains crashing, volcanoes erupting. . . .

The Hooligan's eyes bulged half out of their sockets. "Hakdaz!" he said, clapping his hands to his ears. He seized the disk and made conciliatory pictures—the doodad and a glass of wine melting into each other.

"I know that," said Cavanaugh hoarsely, struggling up to one elbow. "But *can you fix it?*" He made a picture of the Hooligan gesturing at the flashing lights, which promptly vanished.

"Deech, deech," said the Hooligan, nodding violently. He picked up the doodad and somehow broke the green base of it into dozens of tiny cubes, which he began to reassemble, apparently in a different order, with great care.

Cavanaugh hauled himself up into an armchair and let himself go limp as a glove. He watched the Hooligan, telling himself drowsily that if he wasn't careful, he'd be asleep in another minute. There was something odd about the room, something extraordinarily soothing. . . . After a moment he realized what it was.

The silence.

The two fishwives who infested the floor below were not screaming pleasantries across the coutryard at each other. Nobody was playing moron music on a radio tuned six times too loud for normal hearing.

The landlady was not shouting instructions from the top floor to the janitor in the basement.

Silence. Peace.

For some reason, Cavanaugh's mind turned to the subject of silent films: Chaplin, the Keystone Cops, Douglas Fair-

150

banks, Garbo . . . they would have to bring them out of the cans again, he thought, for everybody, not just the patrons of the Museum of Modern Art Film Library. . . .

Congress would have to rig up some sort of Telautograph system, with a screen above the Speaker's desk, perhaps.

Television. Television, thought Cavanaugh dreamily, would have to shut up and put up.

No more campaign oratory.

No more banquet speeches.

No more singing commercials.

Cavanaugh sat up. "Listen," he said tensely. "Could you fix just the writing—not the speech?"

The Hooligan goggled at him and held out the disk.

Cavanaugh took it and slowly began putting the idea into careful pictures. . . .

The Hooligan was gone—vanished like a burst soap bubble at the end of a headfirst dive across Cavanaugh's drawing table.

Cavanaugh sat where he was, listening. From outside, after a moment, came a confused, distance-muted roar. All over the city—all over the world, Cavanaugh supposed—people were discovering that they could read again; that the signs meant what they said; that each man's sudden island had been rejoined to the main.

It lasted twenty minutes and then faded slowly. In his mind's eye, Cavanaugh saw the orgy of scribbling that must be beginning now. He sat, and listened to the blessed silence.

In a little while a growing twinge forced itself upon his attention, like a forgotten toothache. After a moment, Cavanaugh identified it as his conscience. Just who are you, conscience was saying, to take away the gift of speech—the thing that once was all that distinguished man from the apes?

Cavanaugh dutifully tried to feel repentant, but it didn't work. Who said it was a gift? he asked his conscience. What did we use it for?

I'll tell you, he said. In the cigar store: Hey, waddya think of them Yankees? Yeah, that was som'n, wasn't it? Sure was! I tell you . . .

At home: So, how was the office t'day? Aa. Same goddamn madhouse. How'd it go with you? Awright. I can't complain. Kids okay? Yaa. Uh-huh. What's f-dinner?

At a party: Hello, Harry! Whattaya say, boy! How are ya? That's good. How's the . . . so I said to him, you can't tell me

151

what I'm gonna . . . like to, but it don't agree with me. It's my stummick; th' doctor says . . . organdy, with little gold buttons . . . Oh, yeah? Well, how would you like a poke in the snoot?

On the street corners: Lebensraum . . . Nordische Blut . . .

I, said Cavanaugh, rest my case.

Conscience did not reply.

In the silence, Cavanaugh walked across the room to the record cabinet and pulled out an album. He could read the lettering on its spine: MAHLER, *The Song of the Earth.*

He picked out one of the disks and put it on the machine— the "Drunkard's Song" in the fifth movement.

Cavanaugh smiled beatifically, listening. It was an artificial remedy, he was thinking; from the Hooligan's point of view, the human race was now permanently a little tipsy. And so what?

The words the tenor was singing were gibberish to Cavanaugh—but then they always had been; Cavanaugh spoke no German. He knew what the words meant.

> *Was geht mich denn der Frühling an!?*
> *Lasst mich betrunken sein!*
> "What then is the spring to me?
> . . . Let me be drunk!"

"Not one writer in twenty thousand," a knowledgeable agent once told me, "is competent to judge his own product." This may well be true; could I judge him and his sweeping statements? . . . Be that as it may, I have good and sufficient reasons for my special fondness for *Saucer*.

It was written in about four hours, one of those profoundly satisfying creations, which simply lays itself out, word after word, "feeling" right all the way. In addition, it is one of the stories which bears out something that I have been formulating for some time, namely, that good fiction is good to the extent that it is *fable;* that is, stories about foxes and grapes are not dubious accounts of improbably herbivorous foxes impossibly making spoken conclusions; they mean other things in other contexts. As such, *Saucer* is a fable, an explication of that endemic disease called loneliness. Finally, the story pleases me with its opening; few things I have ever done have so exploded onto the page.

THEODORE STURGEON

A SAUCER OF LONELINESS

by THEODORE STURGEON

If she's dead, I thought, I'll never find her in this white flood of moonlight on the white sea, with the surf seething in and over the pale, pale sand like a great shampoo. Almost always, suicides who stab themselves or shoot themselves in the heart carefully bare their chests; the same strange impulse generally makes the sea-suicide go naked.

A little earlier, I thought, or later, and there would be shadows for the dunes and the breathing toss of the foam. Now the only real shadow was mine, a tiny thing just under me, but black enough to feed the blackness of the shadow of a blimp.

A little earlier, I thought, and I might have seen her plodding up the silver shore, seeking a place lonely enough to die in. A little later and my legs would rebel against this shuffling trot through sand, the maddening sand that could not hold and would not help a hurrying man.

My legs did give way then and I knelt suddenly, sobbing—not for her; not yet—just for air. There was such a rush about me: wind, and tangled spray, and colors upon colors and shades of colors that were not colors at all but shifts of white and silver. If light like that were sound, it would sound like the sea on sand, and if my ears were eyes, they would see such a light.

I crouched there, gasping in the swirl of it, and a flood struck me, shallow and swift, turning up and outward like flower petals where it touched my knees, then soaking me to the waist in its bubble and crash. I pressed my knuckles to my eyes so they would open again. The sea was on my lips with the taste of tears and the whole white night shouted and wept aloud.

And there she was.

Her white shoulders were a taller curve in the sloping foam. She must have sensed me—perhaps I yelled—for she turned and saw me kneeling there. She put her fists to her temples and her face twisted, and she uttered a piercing wail of despair and fury, and then plunged seaward and sank.

I kicked off my shoes and ran into the breakers, shouting, hunting, grasping at flashes of white that turned to sea-salt and coldness in my fingers. I plunged right past her, and her body struck my side as a wave whipped my face and tumbled both of us. I gasped in solid water, opened my eyes beneath the surface and saw a greenish-white distorted moon hurtle as I spun. Then there was sucking sand under my feet again and my left hand was tangled in her hair.

The receding wave towed her away and for a moment she streamed out from my hand like steam from a whistle. In that moment I was sure she was dead, but as she settled to the sand, she fought and scrambled to her feet.

She hit my ear, wet, hard, and a huge, pointed pain lanced into my head. She pulled, she lunged away from me, and all the while my hand was caught in her hair. I couldn't have freed her if I had wanted to. She spun to me with the next wave, battered and clawed at me, and we went into deeper water.

"Don't . . . don't . . . I can't swim!" I shouted, so she clawed me again.

"Leave me alone," she shrieked. "Oh, dear God, why can't you *leave*" (said her fingernails) "*me* . . ." (said her fingernails) "*alone!*" (said her small hard fist).

So by her hair I pulled her head down tight to her white shoulder; and with the edge of my free hand I hit her neck twice. She floated again, and I brought her ashore.

I carried her to where a dune was between us and the sea's broad noisy tongue, and the wind was above us somewhere. But the light was as bright. I rubbed her wrists and stroked her face and said, "It's all right," and, "There!" and some names I used to have for a dream I had long, long before I ever heard of her.

She lay still on her back with the breath hissing between her teeth, with her lips in a smile which her twisted-tight, wrinkled-sealed eyes made not a smile but a torture. She was well, and conscious for many moments and still her breath hissed and her closed eyes twisted.

"Why couldn't you leave me alone?" she asked at last. She opened her eyes and looked at me. She had so much misery that there was no room for fear. She shut her eyes again and said, "You know who I am."

"I know," I said.

She began to cry.

I waited, and when she stopped crying, there were shadows among the dunes. A long time.

She said, "You don't know who I am. Nobody knows who I am."

I said, "It was in all the papers."

"That!" She opened her eyes slowly and her gaze traveled over my face, my shoulders, stopped at my mouth, touched my eyes for the briefest second. She curled her lips and turned away her head. "Nobody knows who I am."

I waited for her to move or speak, and finally I said, "Tell *me*."

"Who are you?" she asked, with her head still turned away.

"Someone who . . ."

"Well?"

"Not now," I said. "Later, maybe."

She sat up suddenly and tried to hide herself. "Where are my clothes?"

"I didn't see them."

"Oh," she said. "I remember. I put them down and kicked sand over them, just where a dune would come and smooth them over, hide them as if they never were . . . I hate sand. I wanted to drown in the sand, but it wouldn't let me . . . You mustn't look at me!" she shouted. "I hate to have you looking at me!" She threw her head from side to side, seeking. "I can't stay here like this! What can I do? Where can I go?"

"Here," I said.

She let me help her up and then snatched her hand away, half-turned from me. "Don't touch me. Get away from me."

"Here," I said again, and walked down the dune where it curved in the moonlight, tipped back into the wind and down and became not dune but beach. "Here," I pointed behind the dune.

At last she followed me. She peered over the dune where it was chest-high, and again where it was knee-high. "Back there?"

I nodded.

"So dark . . ." She stepped over the low dune and into the aching black of those moon-shadows. She moved away cautiously, feeling tenderly with her feet, back to where the dune was higher. She sank down into the blackness and disappeared there. I sat on the sand in the light. "Stay away from me," she spat.

I rose and stepped back. Invisible in the shadows, she breathed, "Don't go away." I waited, then saw her hand press out of the clean-cut shadows. "There," she said, "over there. In the dark. Just be a . . . Stay away from me now . . . Be a—voice."

I did as she asked, and sat in the shadows perhaps six feet from her.

She told me about it. Not the way it was in the papers.

She was perhaps seventeen when it happened. She was in Central Park in New York. It was too warm for such an early spring day, and the hammered brown slopes had a dusting of green of precisely the consistency of that morning's hoar frost on the rocks. But the frost was gone and the grass was brave and tempted some hundreds of pairs of feet from the asphalt and concrete to tread on it.

Hers were among them. The sprouting soil was a surprise to her feet, as the air was to her lungs. Her feet ceased to be shoes as she walked, her body was consciously more than clothes. It was the only kind of day which in itself can make a city-bred person raise his eyes. She did.

For a moment she felt separated from the life she lived, in which there was no fragrance, no silence, in which nothing ever quite fit nor was quite filled. In that moment the ordered disapproval of the buildings around the pallid park could not reach her; for two, three clean breaths it no longer mattered that the whole wide world really belonged to images projected on a screen; to gently groomed goddesses in these steel and glass towers; that it belonged, in short, always, always to someone else.

So she raised her eyes, and there above her was the saucer.

It was beautiful. It was golden, with a dusty finish like that of an unripe Concord grape. It made a faint sound, a chord composed of two tones and a blunted hiss like the wind in tall wheat. It was darting about like a swallow, soaring and dropping. It circled and dropped and hovered like a fish, shimmering. It was like all these living things, but with that beauty it had all the loveliness of things turned and burnished, measured, machined, and metrical.

At first she felt no astonishment, for this was so different from anything she had ever seen before that it had to be a trick of the eye, a false evaluation of size and speed and distance that in a moment would resolve itself into a sun-flash on an airplane or the lingering glare of a welding arc.

She looked away from it and abruptly realized that many other people saw it—saw *something*—too. People all around her had stopped moving and speaking and were craning upward. Around her was a globe of silent astonishment, and outside it she was aware of the life-noise of the city, the hard-breathing giant who never inhales.

She looked up again, and at last began to realize how large and how far away the saucer was. No: rather, how small and how very near it was. It was just the size of the largest circle she might make with her two hands, and it floated not quite eighteen inches over her head.

Fear came then. She drew back and raised a forearm, but the saucer simply hung there. She bent far sideways, twisted away, leaped forward, looked back and upward to see if she had escaped it. At first she couldn't see it; then as she looked up and up, there it was, close and gleaming, quivering and crooning, right over her head.

She bit her tongue.

From the corner of her eye, she saw a man cross himself. *He did that because he saw me standing here with a halo over my head, she thought.* And that was the greatest single thing that had ever happened to her. No one had ever looked at her and made a respectful gesture before, not once, not ever. Through terror, through panic and wonderment, the comfort of that thought nestled into her, to wait to be taken out and looked at again in lonely times.

The terror was uppermost now, however. She backed away, staring upward, stepping a ludicrous cakewalk. She should have collided with people. There were plenty of people there, gasping and craning, but she reached none. She spun around and discovered to her horror that she was the center of a pointing, pressing crowd. Its mosaic of eyes all bulged and its inner circle braced its many legs to press back and away from her.

The saucer's gentle note deepened. It tilted, dropped an inch or so. Someone screamed, and the crowd broke away from her in all directions, milled about, and settled again in a new dynamic balance, a much larger ring, as more and more people raced to thicken it against the efforts of the inner circle to escape.

The saucer hummed and tilted, tilted . . .

She opened her mouth to scream, fell to her knees, and the saucer struck.

It dropped against her forehead and clung there. It seemed almost to lift her. She came erect on her knees, made one effort to raise her hands against it, and then her arms stiffened down and back, her hands not reaching the ground. For perhaps a second and a half the saucer held her rigid, and then it passed a single ecstatic quiver to her body and dropped it. She plumped to the ground, the backs of her thighs heavy and painful on her heels and ankles.

The saucer dropped beside her, rolled once in a small circle, one just around its edge, and lay still. It lay still and dull and metallic, different and dead.

Hazily, she lay and gazed at the gray-shrouded blue of the good spring sky, and hazily she heard whistles.

And some tardy screams.

And a great stupid voice bellowing "Give her air!" which made everyone press closer.

Then there wasn't so much sky because of the blueclad bulk with its metal buttons and its leatherette notebook. "Okay, okay, what's happened here stand back figods sake."

And the widening ripples of observation, interpretation and comment: "It knocked her down." "Some guy knocked her down." "He knocked her down." "Some guy knocked her down and—" "Right in broad daylight this guy . . ." "The park's gettin' to be . . ." onward and outward, the adulteration of fact until it was lost altogether because excitement is so much more important.

Somebody with a harder shoulder than the rest bulling close, a notebook here, too, a witnessing eye over it, ready to change ". . . a beautiful brunette . . ." to "an attractive brunette" for the afternoon editions, because "attractive" is as dowdy as any woman is allowed to get if she is a victim in the news.

The glittering shield and the florid face bending close: "You hurt bad, sister?" And the echoes, back and back through the crowd, Hurt bad, hurt bad, badly injured, he beat the hell out of her, broad daylight . . ."

And still another man, slim and purposeful, tan gabardine, cleft chin and beard-shadow: "Flyin' saucer, hm? Okay, Officer, I'll take over here."

"And who the hell might you be, takin' over?"

The flash of a brown leather wallet, a face so close behind that its chin was pressed into the gabardine shoulder. The face said, awed: "F.B.I." and that rippled outward, too. The policeman nodded—the entire policeman nodded in one single bobbing genuflection.

"Get some help and clear this area," said the gabardine.

"Yes, *sir!*" said the policeman.

"F.B.I., F.B.I.," the crowd murmured and there was more sky to look at above her.

She sat up and there was glory in her face. "The saucer talked to me," she sang.

"You shut up," said the gabardine. "You'll have lots of chance to talk later."

"Yeah, sister," said the policeman. "My God, this mob could be full of Communists."

"You shut up, too," said the gabardine.

Someone in the crowd told someone else a Communist beat up this girl, while someone else was saying she got beat up because she was a Communist.

She started to rise, but solicitous hands forced her down again. There were thirty police there by that time.

"I can walk," she said.

"Now you just take it easy," they told her.

They put a stretcher down beside her and lifted her onto it and covered her with a big blanket.

"I can walk," she said as they carried her through the crowd.

A woman went white and turned away moaning, "Oh, my God, how awful!"

A small man with round eyes stared and stared at her and licked and licked his lips.

The ambulance. They slid her in. The gabardine was already there.

A white-coated man with very clean hands: "How did it happen, miss?"

"No questions," said the gabardine. "Security."

The hospital.

She said, "I got to get back to work."

"Take your clothes off," they told her.

She had a bedroom to herself then for the first time in her life. Whenever the door opened, she could see a policeman outside. It opened very often to admit the kind of civilians who were very polite to military people, and the kind of mili-

161

tary people who were even more polite to certain civilians. She did not know what they all did nor what they wanted. Every single day they asked her four million, five hundred thousand questions. Apparently they never talked to each other because each of them asked her the same questions over and over.

"What is your name?"

"How old are you?"

"What year were you born?"

Sometimes they would push her down strange paths with their questions.

"Now your uncle. Married a woman from Middle Europe, did he? Where in Middle Europe?"

"What clubs or fraternal organizations did you belong to? Ah! Now about that Rinkeydinks gang on 63rd Street. Who was *really* behind it?"

But over and over again, "What did you mean when you said the saucer talked to you?"

And she would say, "It talked to me."

And they would say, "And it said—"

And she would shake her head.

There would be a lot of shouting ones, and then a lot of kind ones. No one had ever been so kind to her before, but she soon learned that no one was being kind to *her*. They were just getting her to relax, to think of other things, so they could suddenly shoot that question at her: "What do you mean it talked to you?"

Pretty soon it was just like Mom's or school or any place, and she used to sit with her mouth closed and let them yell. Once they sat her on a hard chair for hours and hours with a light in her eyes and let her get thirsty. Home, there was a transom over the bedroom door and Mom used to leave the kitchen light glaring through it all night, every night, so she wouldn't get the horrors. So the light didn't bother her at all.

They took her out of the hospital and put her in jail. Some ways it was good. The food. The bed was all right, too. Through the window she could see lots of women exercising in the yard. It was explained to her that they all had much harder beds.

"You are a very important young lady, you know."

That was nice at first, but as usual it turned out they didn't mean her at all. They kept working on her. Once they brought the saucer in to her. It was inside a big wooden crate with a

162

padlock, and a steel box inside that with a Yale lock. It only weighed a couple of pounds, the saucer, but by the time they got it packed, it took two men to carry it and four men with guns to watch them.

They made her act out the whole thing just the way it happened with some soldiers holding the saucer over her head. It wasn't the same. They'd cut a lot of chips and pieces out of the saucer and, besides, it was that dead gray color. They asked her if she knew anything about that and for once she told them.

"It's empty now," she said.

The only one she would ever talk to was a little man with a fat belly who said to her the first time he was alone with her, "Listen, I think the way they've been treating you stinks. Now get this: I have a job to do. My job is to find out *why* you won't tell what the saucer said. I don't want to know what it said and I'll never ask you. I don't even want you to tell me. Let's just find out why you're keeping it a secret."

Finding out why turned out to be hours of just talking about having pneumonia and the flower pot she made in second grade that Mom threw down the fire escape and getting left back in school and the dream about holding a wine glass in both hands and peeping over it at some man.

And one day she told him why she wouldn't say about the saucer, just the way it came to her: "Because it was talking to *me,* and it's just nobody else's business."

She even told him about the man crossing himself that day. It was the only other thing she had of her own.

He was nice. He was the one who warned her about the trial. "I have no business saying this, but they're going to give you the full dress treatment. Judge and jury and all. You just say what you want to say, no less and no more, hear? And don't let 'em get your goat. You have a right to own something."

He got up and swore and left.

First a man came and talked to her for a long time about how maybe this Earth would be attacked from outer space by beings much stronger and cleverer than we are, and maybe she had the key to a defense. So she owed it to the whole world. And then even if the Earth wasn't attacked, just think of what an advantage she might give this country over its enemies. Then he shook his finger in her face and said that what she was doing amounted to working *for* the enemies of

163

her country. And he turned out to be the man that was defending her at the trial.

The jury found her guilty of contempt of court and the judge recited a long list of penalties he could give her. He gave her one of them and suspended it. They put her back in jail for a few more days, and one fine day they turned her loose.

That was wonderful at first. She got a job in a restaurant, and a furnished room. She had been in the papers so much that Mom didn't want her back home. Mom was drunk most of the time and sometimes used to tear up the whole neighborhood, but all the same she had very special ideas about being respectable, and being in the papers all the time for spying was not her idea of being decent. So she put her maiden name on the mailbox downstairs and told her daughter not to live there any more.

At the restaurant she met a man who asked her for a date. The first time. She spent every cent she had on a red handbag to go with her red shoes. They weren't the same shade, but anyway they were both red. They went to the movies and afterward he didn't try to kiss her or anything, he just tried to find out what the flying saucer told her. She didn't say anything. She went home and cried all night.

Then some men sat in a booth talking and they shut up and glared at her every time she came past. They spoke to the boss, and he came and told her that they were electronics engineers working for the government and they were afraid to talk shop while she was around—wasn't she some sort of spy or something? So she got fired.

Once she saw her name on a juke box. She put in a nickel and punched that number, and the record was all about "the flyin' saucer came down one day, and taught her a brand new way to play, and what it was I will not say, but she took me out of this world." And while she was listening to it, someone in the juke-joint recognized her and called her by name. Four of them followed her home and she had to block the door shut.

Sometimes she'd be all right for months on end, and then someone would ask for a date. Three times out of five, she and the date were followed. Once the man she was with arrested the man who was tailing them. Twice the man who was tailing them arrested the man she was with. Five times out of five, the date would try to find out about the saucer.

Sometimes she would go out with someone and pretend that it was a real date, but she wasn't very good at it.

So she moved to the shore and got a job cleaning at night in offices and stores. There weren't many to clean, but that just meant there weren't many people to remember her face from the papers. Like clockwork, every eighteen months, some feature writer would drag it all out again in a magazine or a Sunday supplement; and every time anyone saw a headlight on a mountain or a light on a weather balloon it had to be a flying saucer, and there had to be some tired quip about the saucer wanting to tell secrets. Then for two or three weeks she'd stay off the streets in the daytime.

Once she thought she had it whipped. People didn't want her, so she began reading. The novels were all right for a while until she found out that most of them were like the movies—all about the pretty ones who really own the world. So she learned things—animals, trees. A lousy little chipmunk caught in a wire fence bit her. The animals didn't want her. The trees didn't care.

Then she hit on the idea of the bottles. She got all the bottles she could and wrote on papers which she corked into the bottles. She'd tramp miles up and down the beaches and throw the bottles out as far as she could. She knew that if the right person found one, it would give that person the only thing in the world that would help. Those bottles kept her going for three solid years. Everyone's got to have a secret little something he does.

And at last the time came when it was no use any more. You can go on trying to help someone who *maybe* exists; but soon you can't pretend there is such a person any more. And that's it. The end.

"Are you cold?" I asked when she was through telling me. The surf was quieter and the shadows longer.

"No," she answered from the shadows. Suddenly she said, "Did you think I was mad at you because you saw me without my clothes?"

"Why shouldn't you be?"

"You know, I don't care? I wouldn't have wanted . . . wanted you to see me even in a ball gown or overalls. You can't cover up my carcass. It shows; it's there whatever. I just didn't want you to *see* me. At all."

"Me, or anyone?"

She hesitated. "You."

165

I got up and stretched and walked a little, thinking. "Didn't the F.B.I. try to stop you throwing those bottles?"

"Oh, sure. They spent I don't know how much taxpayers' money gathering 'em up. They still make a spot check every once in a while. They're getting tired of it, though. All the writing in the bottles is the same." She laughed. I didn't know she could.

"What's funny?"

"All of 'em—judges, jailers, juke-boxes—people. Do you know it wouldn't have saved me a minute's trouble if I'd told 'em the whole thing at the very beginning?"

"No?"

"No. They wouldn't have believed me. What they wanted was a new weapon. Super-science from a super-race, to slap hell out of the super-race if they ever got a chance, or out of our own if they don't. All those brains," she breathed, with more wonder than scorn, "all that brass. They think 'super-race' and it comes out 'super-science.' Don't they ever imagine a super-race has super-feelings, too—super-laughter, maybe, or super-hunger?" She paused. "Isn't it time you asked me what the saucer said?"

"I'll tell you," I blurted.

> *"There is in certain living souls*
> *A quality of loneliness unspeakable,*
> *So great it must be shared*
> *As company is shared by lesser beings.*
> *Such a loneliness is mine; so know by this*
> *That in immensity*
> *There is one lonelier than you."*

"Dear Jesus," she said devoutly, and began to weep. "And how is it addressed?"

"To the loneliest one . . ."

"How did you know?" she whispered.

"It's what you put in the bottles, isn't it?"

"Yes," she said. "Whenever it gets to be too much, that no one cares, that no one ever did . . . you throw a bottle into the sea, and out goes a part of your own loneliness. You sit and think of someone somewhere finding it . . . learning for the first time that the worst there is can be understood."

The moon was setting and the surf was hushed. We looked up and out to the stars. She said, "We don't know what loneliness is like. People thought the saucer was a saucer, but it

166

wasn't. It was a bottle with a message inside. It had a bigger ocean to cross—all of space—and not much chance of finding anybody. Loneliness? We don't know loneliness."

When I could, I asked her why she had tried to kill herself.

"I've had it good," she said, "with what the saucer told me. I wanted to . . . pay back. I was bad enough to be helped; I had to know I was good enough to help. No one wants me? Fine. But don't tell me no one, anywhere, wants my help. I can't stand that."

I took a deep breath. "I found one of your bottles two years ago. I've been looking for you ever since. Tide charts, current tables, maps and . . . wandering. I heard some talk about you and the bottles hereabouts. Someone told me you'd quit doing it, you'd taken to wandering the dunes at night. I knew why. I ran all the way."

I needed another breath now. "I got a club foot. I think right, but the words don't come out of my mouth the way they're inside my head. I have this nose. I never had a woman. Nobody ever wanted to hire me to work where they'd have to look at me. You're beautiful," I said. "You're beautiful."

She said nothing, but it was as if a light came from her, more light and far less shadow than ever the practiced moon could cast. Among the many things it meant was that even to loneliness there is an end, for those who are lonely enough, long enough.

167

Although highly appreciative of the honor, I can't help feeling that asking me to pick my favorite among my own stories is like inquiring whether I like Maine lobster, Moselle wine, or Dutch cigars best. Such things may all be found at the dinner table, but aren't really commensurable. In the same way, the works of a writer who tries his hand at a variety of motifs and approaches, both in and out of science fiction, can't fall into a single file of preference for him. The choice is further confused by all the subjective factors involved, the degree of his personal interest in a theme, private associations which may lend an extra flavor to some particular item, perhaps merely the good or bad mood he was in when he wrote it.

Still, an author obviously prefers *some* stories to some others, whatever may be his reasons for doing so. I've stuck my neck out by choosing *Night Piece* for this collection. It's quite unlike anything else I've done. But that's precisely why I'm fond of it. The basic idea of the story, the problem which arises as a consequence of that assumption, and the resolution of the problem, could have been handled in a straightforward narrative fashion. That didn't seem very challenging, though, nor very rewarding in this case, where the significant action takes place entirely within a man's mind. I have no pretensions to being a Kafka or a Capek, but it did seem to me it would be interesting to use, or attempt to use, some of their techniques. By going at the job sideways, perhaps I could suggest what it would actually feel like to be caught in a situation such as was being postulated.

Therefore *Night Piece* is at least three concurrent stories, two of them symbolic. I'm not likely to do anything of this sort very often—some of those archetypes scared the hell out of me —but I hope that I succeeded in getting across a small part of that which I was trying to get across.

However, my success or failure is for you, the reader, to judge.

POUL ANDERSON

NIGHT PIECE

by POUL ANDERSON

He had not gone far from the laboratory when he heard the footsteps. Even then he could sense they were not human, but he stopped and turned about with a fluttering hope that they might be, after all.

It was late on Wednesday night. His assistants had quit at five, leaving him to phone his wife that she had better not wait up, then fry some hash over a Bunsen burner and return to the instrument that was beginning to function. He had often done so, and afterward walked the mile to a bus stop where he could get a ride directly home. His wife worried about him, but he told her this was a peaceful industrial section, himself nearly the last living man after dark, in no danger of robbery or murder. The walk relaxed him, filled his lungs with cool air and cleared his brain of potential dreams.

Tonight, when the symptoms began, sheer habit had made him lock the door and start out afoot. The steps behind made him wonder if he should have called a taxi. Not that wheels could outpace the thing, but there might have been some comfort in the driver's stolid presence. *To be sure,* he thought, *if it is a holdup man—*

The hope died as he looked backward. The sidewalk stretched gray and hard and lifeless, under widely spaced lamps: first a gaunt pole, a globe of glare on top, a dingy yellow puddle of light below; then a thickening murkiness, becoming night itself, until the next globe stood forth, scattering sickly-colored illumination into emptiness. The street ran black of hue, like a river which moved in some secret fashion. Along the other edge of the sidewalk rose brick walls, where an occasional doorway or window made a blocked-off hole. Everything went in straight lines that converged toward an infinity hidden by the dark.

All the pavement was quite bare. A thin breeze sent a scrap of paper tumbling and clicking past his feet. Otherwise he heard nothing, not even the follower.

169

He tried to slow his heartbeat. *It can't hurt me,* he told himself, knowing he lied. For a while he stood immobile, not so much unwilling to turn his back on the footsteps (for they could be anywhere; more accurately, they were nowhere) as unwilling to hear them again.

"But I can't stay here all night," he said. The whisper made a relieving counterpoint to his pulse. He felt sweat run from his armpits and down his ribs, tickling. "It'll only take a different form. I'd better get home, at least."

He had not known he possessed enough courage to resume walking.

The footsteps picked up. They weren't loud, which was just as well, for they seemed less human each second he listened. There was a slithering quality to them: not wet but dry, a scaly dryness that went sliding over dirty concrete. He didn't even know how many feet there were. More than two, surely. Perhaps so many that they weren't feet at all, but one supple length. And the head rose, weaving about in curves that rippled and rustled—becoming less sinuous as the hood swelled until the sidewise figure eight upon it stood forth plain; a thin little tongue flickered as if frantic, but there was an immortal patience in the eyes, which were lidless.

"Of course this is ridiculous," he told himself. "Giving pictorial form to that which is, by definition, beyond any form whatsoever—" His voice came out small. The rustling stopped. For a moment he heard only the clack of his own shoes and the millrace blood in his body. He hoped, crazily through all the gibberish in his head.

Faustus is the name, good sir, not Frankenstein but Faustus in the Faustian sense if you please and means fortunate in the Latin but one may wonder if the Latin was not constructed with a hitherto unsuspected sense of irony, e.g., my wife awaits me, she may not have gone to bed yet and lamplight would fall on her hair but my shoes are too tight and too loud.

That it might have abandoned him. Or rather, the scientific brain cells corrected, that he had somehow slipped back from the state of awareness of these things. *Because,* he thought, *I deny that rationality is dead in the cosmos, and even that my experiments with the ESP amplifier opened hell gate. Rather, they sensitized me to an unsuspected class of phenomena, one for which human evolution has not prepared me because humankind never encountered it before. (Except, perhaps, in the thinnest and swiftest accidental glimpses, reve-*

*lation, nightmare, and madness.) I am the early student of
X-rays, the alchemist heating liquid mercury, the half-ape
burned by fire, the mouse strayed onto a battlefield. I shall
be destroyed if I cannot escape, but the universe will still live,
her and me and them and a certain willow on a hilltop which
fills with sunset light each summer evening. I pray that this
be true.*

Then the scales uncoiled and went scrabbling toward him,
louder now, and he caught a hot cedary odor. But the night
breeze was cold in his hair. He cried out, once, and began to
run.

The street lamps reached ahead of him, on to an unseen
infinity, like stars in space. No, lonelier than that. Each lamp
was an island universe, spinning up there a million years from
the next neighbor. Surely, in all that darkness, a man might
find some hiding place! He was out of condition. Soon he was
breathing through a wide-open, dried-out mouth. His lungs
were twin fires and he felt his eyeballs bulge from pressure.
His shoes grew so heavy that he thought he ran with two
planets on his feet.

Through thunder and breakings he heard the rustle, closer
still, and his shoes going slap-slap-slap on bare pavement,
under the purulent street lamps. Up ahead were two of them,
whose globes looked close together from where he was, and
the shadows they cast made a dark shaft between that reached
straight upward to an infinity from which stars fountained in
horrible fire. He had not imagined there could be so grim a
sight. He had no breath left, but his brain screamed for him.

Somewhere there must be darkness. A tunnel to hide in,
to close off and seal. There must be warmth and the sound of
waters. And darkness again. If he was caught, let it at least
not happen in the light. But he begged the tunnel would hide
him.

The current up which he waded was strong. It slid heavily
and sensuously about him, pushing on breast and belly, loins
and thighs. He was totally blind now, but that was good, he
was far from the world-spewing globes. The water's noise
echoed from the tunnel walls, ringing and booming. Now and
then a wave splashed against them, a loud clear sound followed by a thin shower of drops, like laughter. His feet
slipped, he flailed about with his arms, touched the warm
curved odorous wall of the tunnel and shoved himself back
upright. He had a sense of wading uphill, and the current
strengthened with each step he achieved. A *hyperbola*, he

thought in upsurging weariness. *I'll never reach the end. That's at infinity.*

After centuries he heard the pumps that drove the waters, pumps as big as the world, throbbing in the dark. He stopped, afraid to go on, afraid the rotors would seize him and grind him and squirt him from a cylinder.

But when the hooded swimmer struck him and he went under, he must shriek.

Too late now! The waters took him, stopped his voice, cataracted down his throat and churned in his guts. A momentary gulp of air smelled like cedar. The swimmer closed its jaws. He heard his skin tear under the fangs, and the poisons began to tingle down the skein of his nerves. The head marked with a sideways figure eight shook him as a dog shakes a rat. Nevertheless he planted feet on the tunnel floor, gripped the monstrous barrel of a body, and threw his last energies against it. Back and forth they swayed, the tunnel trembled under their violence, they smashed into its walls. The pumps began to skip beats, the walls began to crack and dissolve, the waters rushed forth across the world. But still he was gripped.

He shook off the hand, leaned his face against blessed scratchy brick and tried to vomit. But nothing happened. The policeman took him by the arm again, but more gently. "What's the matter?"

A lamp near the alley mouth dribbled in just enough light to show the large blue shape with the star on the breast. "What's wrong?" insisted the policeman. "I thought you was drunk, but you don't smell like it. Sick?"

"Yes." He controlled himself, suppressed the last belly spasm and turned around to face the policeman. The other voice came faintly to him, with a curious heterodyned whine, a rise and fall like speech heard through high fever. "End of the world, you know."

"Huh?"

For a moment he considered asking the policeman's help. The fellow looked so substantial and blue. His big jowly face was not unkind. But of course the policeman could not help. *He can take me home, if I so request. Or put me in jail, if I act oddly enough. Or call a doctor if I fall boneless at his feet. But what's the use? There is no cure for being in an ocean.*

He glanced at his watch. Only a few minutes had passed since he left the laboratory. At that time he had wanted companionship, a human face to look at if not to take along on his flight. Now he had his wish, and there was no comfort. The policeman was as remote as the lamp. A part of him could talk to the policeman, just as another part could direct heart and lungs and glands in their work. But the essential *I* had departed this world. The I was not even human any longer. No man could help him find his way back.

"I'm sorry," he said. "I get a bit stupid." His reasoning faculties worked very fast. "During these attacks, I mean."

"What attacks?"

"Diabetes. You know, diabetics get fainting spells. I didn't quite pass out this time, but I got rather woozy. I'll be okay, though."

"Oh." The policeman's ignorance of medicine proved as great as hoped. "I see. Want I should call you a cab?"

"No thanks, officer. Not necessary. I'm on my way to the bus stop. Honest, I'll be fine."

"Well, I better come along with you," said the policeman.

They walked side by side, unspeaking. Presently they emerged on an avenue that had restaurants and theaters as well as darkened shops. Light glittered, blinked, quivered in red and yellow and cold blue, cars went slithering past, men and somewhat fewer women drifted along the sidewalks. The air was full of noise, feet, tires, think it'll rain tomorrow close the deal for paper, mister? A neon sign across from the bus stop made *Idle Hour* Bar & Grill, blink, *Idle Hour* blink *Idle Hour* blink *Idle Hour* blink.

"Here you are," said the policeman. "You sure you'll be okay?"

"Quite sure. Thank you, officer." To please the policeman and make him go away, he sat down on the bench.

"Well, good luck to you." The big blue man walked off and was lost in the drift.

A woman sat at the other end of the bench. In a tired and middle-aged fashion she looked a little bit like his sister. He noticed her casting glances in his direction and wondered why. Probably curious to know the reason he came here escorted, but afraid to ask lest he think she was trying to get picked up. It didn't matter. She was hollow anyway. They all were, himself included. They were infinitesimal skins of distorted space enclosing nothing whatever, not even space. The lights were hollow and the noise was hollow. All fullness was ocean.

He felt much at peace. Now that he was no longer pursued

173

. . . well, why should he be? It had happened to completion. And then after the tunnel broke, the waters had covered everything. They reached vast and gray, warm and still, with a faint taste of salt like tears. In the translucent greenish gray where he lay, easily rocking, there was no place for pursuit, for anything except everything.

Time flowed in the ocean, but a slow soft kind of time. First the light strengthened, sourceless, eventually revealing the eternal overcast, which was cool nacre. Sometimes a lower stratum would form, mare's tails whipped on a sharp wind or blue-black masses rearing up with lightning in their heads. But when that happened, he could sink undersurface, where the water was forever still and greenish. . . . Finally the light faded. The nights were altogether dark. He liked them best, for then he could lie and feel the tides pass through him. A tide was more than a rolling of his body; it was a deep secret thrill, somehow each atom of him was touched by the force as it passed and a tingle scarcely sensed would go down all molecular lengths. By day he enjoyed the tides too, but not so much, for then other life forms were about. He had only the dimmest awareness of these, but they did pass by, sometimes brushing him or considering him with patient lidless eyes.

"Excuse me, sir, do you know if this bus goes to Seventh Street?"

It startled him a little that his body should start. Surely there was no sense to the chilly prickles of sweat that burst out all over him. "No," he said. His voice came out so harsh that the woman edged even further away. Somehow that was an additional flick across his soft skin. He twisted, trying to escape; he grew plates of bone so that they must leave him in peace.

"No," he said, "I don't believe it does. I get off before then myself—I've never ridden as far as Seventh Street—so I'm not sure. But I don't believe it does."

His logical faculty grew furious with him for talking so idiotically. "Oh," she said. "Thank you." He said, "You can ask the driver." She said, "Yes, I suppose I can. Thank you." He said, "You're welcome." She obviously wanted to break off the misbegotten conversation and didn't quite see how. For his part, he couldn't take any more. The noises and skins were hollow, no doubt, but they kept striking at him. He jumped up and crossed the street. Her eyes pursued him. He hadn't seen her blink.

174

The *Idle Hour* was dim. A couple sat in a booth along one wall; a discouraged man hunched at the bar opposite; a juke box made garish embers but remained mercifully unfed. The bartender was a thin man in the usual white shirt and black bow tie. He was washing some glasses and said without enthusiasm, "Be closing time pretty soon, mister."

"That's all right. Scotch and soda." Speech was automatic, like breath. When he had the glass, he retired to a booth of his own. He leaned back on faded plastic cushioning, set the glass before him and stared at the ice cubes. He didn't want to drink.

Who would want to drink in the ocean? he thought with a touch of wryness.

But this is wrong!

He didn't want to make jokes, he wanted the tides and the plankton swirling into his mouth, the thin warm saltiness, the good sound of rainstorms lashing the surface when he was snugly down among seaweeds. *They* were cool and silken, they caressed. He changed the awkward bony plates that protected him from the others for scales, which were not quite as strong but left him slippery and flexible and alive to the stroking, streaming green weed. Now he could slip through their most secret grottos, nose about on the oozy bottom and look with incurious lidless eyes at the fossils he uncovered.

"Let's examine the superman thesis," he said to his wife. "I don't mean the Nietzschean Uebermensch. I mean Superior, the nonhuman animal with nonhuman powers making him as much stronger than us as we are stronger than the apes. Traditionally, he's supposed to be born of man and woman. In hard biological fact, we know this isn't possible. Even if the simultaneous alteration of millions of genes could take place, the resulting embryo would be so alien in blood type, enzyme system, the very proteins, that it would hardly be created before the outraged uterus destroyed it."

"Perhaps in a million years, man could evolve into superman," she answered.

"Perhaps," he said skeptically. "I'm inclined to doubt it, though. The great apes, even the monkeys, aren't likely to evolve into men. They branched off from our common ancestor too long ago; they've followed their special path too far. Likewise, men may improve their reasoning, visualizing, imagining ability—what we're pleased to call their conscious intelligence—their own characteristic as a species—they may improve that through a megayear or so of slow evolution. But

175

they'd still be men, wouldn't they? A later model, but still men.

"Now the truly superior being . . ." He held his wine glass up to the light. "Let's speculate aloud. What is superiority anyhow, in a biological sense? Isn't it an ability—a mode of behavior, I'll say—that enables the species to cope more effectively with environment?

"Okay. So let's inquire what modes of behavior there are. The simplest, practiced by unicellular organisms as well as higher ones like sunflowers, is tropism. A mere chemical response to a fixed set of stimuli. More complicated and adaptable are sets of reflexes. That's the characteristic insectal mode. Then you get true instincts: inherited behavior patterns, but generalized, flexible and modifiable. Finally, in the higher mammals, you get a degree of conscious intelligence. Man, of course, has made this his particular strength. He also has quite a bit of instinct, some reflexes, and maybe a few tropisms. His ability to reason, though, is what's gotten him as far as he's come on this planet.

"To surpass us, should Superior try to outhuman humanity? Shouldn't he rather possess only a modicum of reasoning ability by our standards, very weak instincts, a few reflexes, and no tropisms? But his specialty, his characteristic mode, would be something we can't imagine. We may have a bare touch of it, as the apes and dogs have a touch of logical reasoning power. But we can no more imagine its full development than a dog could follow Einstein's equations."

"What might this ability be?" his wife wondered.

He shrugged. "Who knows? Conceivably in the ESP field —Now I'm letting my hobby horse run away with me again. (Damn it, though, I *am* starting to get reproducible results!) Whatever it is, it's something much more powerful than logic or imagination. And as futile for us to speculate about as for the dog to ponder Einstein."

"Do you really believe there are such superbeings?" She had come to expect almost any hypothesis of him.

"Oh, no," he laughed. "I'm just playing a game with ideas. Like your kitten with a ball of string. But assuming Superior does exist . . . hm. Do mice know that men exist? All a mouse knows is that the world contains good things like houses and cheese, bad things like weatherstripping and traps, without any orderly pattern that his instincts could adapt him to. He sees men, sure, but how can he know they're a different order of life, responsible for all the strangeness in his world?

176

In the same way, we may have coexisted with Superior for a million years, and never known it. The part of him we can detect may be an accepted feature of our universe, like the earth's magnetic field; or an unexplained feature like occasional lights in the sky; or he may be quite undetectable. His activities would never impinge on ours, except once in a while by sheerest accident—and then another 'miracle' is recorded that science never does find an explanation for."

She smiled, enjoying his own pleasure. "Where do these beings come from? Another planet?"

"I doubt that. They probably evolved here right along with us. All life on earth has an equally ancient lineage. I've no idea what the common ancestor of man and Superior could have been. Perhaps as recent as some half ape in the Pilocene, perhaps as far back as some amphibian in the Carboniferous. We took one path, they took another, and never the twain shall meet."

"I hope not. We'd have no more chance than the mice, would we?"

"I don't know. But we'd certainly best cultivate our own garden."

Which, however, he had not done. He wasn't sure how he had blundered onto the Superior plane of existence: or, rather, how his mind or his rudimentary ESP or whatever-it-was had suddenly begun reacting to the behavior-mode of that race. He only knew, with the flat sureness of immediate experience, that it had happened.

His logical mind, unaffected as yet, searched in a distant and dreamy fashion for a rationale. The amplifier alone could hardly be responsible. But maybe the remembrance of his speculative fable had provided the additional impetus necessary? If that were so, then his fate was a most improbable accident. Other men could still go ahead and study ESP phenomena as much as they cared to, learn a lot, use their knowledge, all in perfect safety, with never a hint that on a higher level of those phenomena Superior carried out huge purposes.

Himself, though, was sunk in a gray ocean on a gray world. Let him so remain. Never had he imagined such peace, or the tides or the kissing seaweeds; and as for the lightning storms, he could hide when they flashed. Down he went then, into a green well of silence whose roof coruscated with light shards; further down, the well darkened, the light shrank to spot overhead (if that meant anything here where there was no weight, no heaviness, no force or current or pursuit) and

177

then the dark enfolded him. On the bottom it was always night.

He lay in the ooze, which was cool though the water stayed warm, he wrapped the dear darkness around him like another skin, closed the lids he had grown to keep daylight off, he could taste salt and feel the tides go through his molecules. High above rolled the clouds, thunder banged from horizon to horizon, the sky was all one blaze of great lightnings; wind yammered, driving spindrift flat off the crests of the waves, which foamed and snarled and shivered the bones of the world. Even down in the depths—

No! What a storm that must be! Fear tinged him. He didn't want to remember lightnings, which worked their length across heaven and sizzled like hastening scales. He burrowed into the mud until he touched bedrock and, and, and felt it quiver.

Even the storm could not be as dreadful as that deep earthquake vibration. He wailed voicelessly and fled back upward. The others swarmed around him, driven from their grottos by the growing violence. Teeth snapped at him, lidless eyes glowed like twinned globes. Some had been torn apart; he tasted blood in the waters.

Another crash and another went through him, as deeply as ever the tides had done, but bruising and ripping. He burst the surface. Rain and scud whipped him. Wallowing on the wrinkled back of a wave, he looked straight up at the lightning. Thunder filled his skull.

A deeper noise responded. Across many wild miles he saw the mountain rise from the waters. Black and enormous it was lifted; water cascaded off its flanks, fire and sulfur boiled from its throat. Shock followed shock, flinging him to and fro, over and under. He felt, rather than saw, the whole sea bottom lifting beneath him.

He gibbered in the foam and fled, seeking depths, seeking a place where he could not see the mountain. Its pinnacle had already gone through the clouds. In that wounded sky the stars blazed gruesomely.

Somewhere through the explosions, he thought he must be able to get free. Surely all the ocean was not convulsed. But a basalt peak smote him from beneath. The water squirted from his gills; he went sick and dizzy. Raised into naked air, he felt the delicate gill membranes shrivel and drew a breath that burned him down throat and lungs to his inmost cell. The black reef continued rising. Soon it would be part of the mountainside. He made one sprawling flop, all his strength expended:

slid off the rock, back down into the sea. But a wave grabbed him in its white teeth and shook him.

He pushed the hand from his shoulder. "All right, all right, all right," he mumbled. "Let me alone."

"Closing time, I told you," said the bartender. "You deaf or something? I gotta close this place."

"Let me alone." He covered his ears against the screaming.

"Don't make me call a cop. Go on home, mister. You look like you could stand a night's rest." The bartender was thin but expert. He applied leverage in the right places, got his customer to his feet and shambling across the floor. "You just go on home now. Good night. Closing time, you know."

The door swung shut, as if to deny the bartender's existence. Other hollow people were on the street, some going for coffee, some entering the bus that waited on the opposite curb.

My bus, he thought. *The one that may or may not go as far as Seventh Street.* The thought was unreal. All thought was. Reality consisted in a black mountain, rising and rising, himself trapped in a pool on the slope where the surf had cast him, gasping raw air, scourged by rain, deafened by wind and thunder, and lifted toward the terrible stars.

He crouched in his wretchedness, implored the ocean to come back, but at the same time he hissed to the fire and the wind and the sulfurous reek, *If you won't let me go, I'll destroy you. See if I don't!*

Habit had taken him over the street to the bus. He stopped in front of the doors. What was he doing here? The thing was an iron box. No, he must not enter the box. The hollow people sat there in rows, waiting for him. He must tear down the mountain instead.

What mountain?

He knew in the thinking part of himself that somewhere in space and time was an existence not all harm and hatred. The night was too loud now, beneath winter stars, for him to return thither. He must pull down the mountain, so he could regain the ocean. . . . But his logical faculties spun free, down and down a hyperbolic path. They considered the abstract unreal proposition that he would not be hollow if he could become human again. And then he would be happy, though at present he didn't want to be human, he wanted to rip the mountain and re-enter the sea. But as a logical exercise, to pass the time for the unused part of his brain, *why* had he suffered and fought and been hunted, since that moment when he was first sensitized to . . . to Superior's mode of behavior?

179

He could no more understand the situation with reason than a dog could use instinct to puzzle out the machinery of this bus and the why of its existence. (No, he would not enter that box. He didn't know why, except that the box was hollow and waited for him. But he was sure it went to Seventh Street.) Nonetheless, reason was not absolutely useless. The activities of Superior were always and forever incomprehensible to him, but he could describe their general tendency. Violence, cruelty, destruction. Which didn't make sense! No species could survive that used its powers only for such ends.

Therefore, Superior did not. Most of the time, he/she/it/? was just being Superior, and as such was completely beyond human perception. Occasionally, though, there was conflict. By analogy, mankind—all animals—behaved constructively on the whole, but sometimes engaged in strife. Superior? Well, of course Superior didn't have wars in the human sense of the word. No use speculating what they did have. Conflicts of some kind, anyhow, where an issue was decided not by reason or compromise but by force. And the force employed was (to give it a name) of an ESP nature.

A mouse could not understand human art or science. In a way, he couldn't even see them. But a mouse could be affected by the crudest, most animal-like manifestation of human behavior: physical combat. A mathematical theorem did not exist for the mouse; a bullet did.

By analogy again, he, the human, was a mouse that had wandered onto a battlefield. By some accident, he had been sensitized to the lowest mode of Superior behavior and was thereby being affected; he was caught in the opposing tides of a death struggle.

Not that he was directly experiencing what Superior actually performed. Everything that had happened was merely the way the forces, the currents, felt to him. Frantically seeking a balance, his mind interpreted those unnatural stimuli in the nearest available human terms.

He thought his sensations must dimly reflect the course of the battle. One side or entity or . . . Aleph . . . had gotten the upper hand and in some sense pursued the other till it found a momentary shelter. Zayin had then had a breathing space until Aleph found it again, pursued it again. Cornered, Zayin fought back so fiercely that Aleph must in turn retreat. Now, having recovered during the lull that followed, Zayin was renewing the battle. . . . But none of this made any difference.

The doings of Superior were, in themselves, irrelevant to Sapiens. He was the mouse on the battlefield, nothing else.

With luck, a mouse could escape from bursting shells and burning tracers before they smashed him. A man could escape from this other conflict before it burned out his mind: by desensitizing himself, by ceasing to perceive the transcendent energies around him, much as one could get relief from too brilliant a light by closing one's eyes. But what was the method of desensitization?

Clouds broke further, and he saw the moon flying pocked among the stars. Its light was as cold as the wind. His flesh quivered in the pain of cold and earthquake shocks. But the ocean tumbled not far off, white under the moon. He felt that impact reverberate in the mountain. He began to crawl from his dwindling pool.

How can I get away?

"Hey, mister, you gonna board this bus or not?"

The currents carried me first in one direction, then in another. Down to the sea depths, up to the stars. Whether I go forward or backward, seaward or skyward, I am still within the currents.

"I said, you comin' aboard? Don't just stand there blocking the door."

Lightning burned his eyes. He felt the thunder in his bones. But louder, now, was the hate in him: for the mountain which had ruined his sea and for the sea which had cast him onto the mountain. *I will destroy them all.*

And then fear smote him, for through the noise and the gigantic white flashes he heard himself asking: "Do you go to Seventh Street?"

The driver said across lightyears, "Yeah, that's the end of my run. Come on, hop in. I got a schedule to keep."

"No—" he whimpered, stumbling backward toward the ocean. His teeth clattered with cold. The waves retreated from him. *I am not going in a box to Seventh Street!*

"Where do you wanna go, then?" asked the driver, elaborately sarcastic.

"Go?" he repeated in a numb voice. "Why . . . home."

Please, he called to the surf. But still the tide withdrew, a monstrous hollow rumble. He turned about, hissing at the mountain where it flamed overhead. *All right, then,* said his hatred. He started to crawl up the wet black rocks. *All right, if you won't tell me the way home, I'll climb up over your peak.*

But you do know the way home, said his human logical faculty.

What? He stopped. The wind hooted and whipped him. If he didn't keep moving he would freeze.

Of course. Consider the pattern. Forward or backward, you are still moving within the currents. But if you remain still—

No! he screamed, and in his fear he reared up and clawed at the stars for support.

It won't take long.

Oh, God no, I'm too afraid. No man should have to do this twice.

The cold and lightning and earthquake struck at him. He cowered on the beach, under the mountain, too frightened to hate. *No, I must climb. I can't stay here.*

The bus driver snorted and closed the door in his face.

Where the courage came from, he never knew. For an instant he was able to remember his wife's eyes, and that she was waiting for him. He raised his hand and rapped on the door. The driver groaned.

If he goes off and leaves me—if he delays half a minute letting me in—I'll never go aboard. I won't be able to.

The door folded back.

He gathered the last rage of himself around himself, climbed up the step and over the threshold.

Something snatched at him. The wind drove in between his ribs, lightning bit him, he had never conceived such pain. He opened his mouth to yell.

No! That's part of the pattern. Don't do it.

Somehow he maintained silence, clung to the stanchion as the bus got under way and felt the galaxies sundered. The earth-shaken rocks on the mountainside rolled beneath him, thrusting him upward. He planted his feet on the ground and said: "To Seventh Street."

The world drained out of him.

As blackness faded again, he found himself sprawled on one of the longitudinal seats up front. 'Now look, buster," said the driver, "drunk or not, you pay the fare, see? I don't want no trouble. Just gimmie the fare."

He drew a breath deep into starved lungs. The bus was noisy, with a stench from the motor; tired people sagged down its length, under improbably bright-colored advertisements. On either side he could see the lighted windows of houses.

182

How still the night was!

"What is the fare?' he asked. *Ridiculous,* his logical mind scolded him, wearily but not very angrily. After all, the rest of him had shown up well too, when the crisis came. *I've ridden this line a hundred times. But I can't quite remember the cost. It feels so new to be human.*

"Two bits."

"Oh, is that all? I'd have paid more." His knees were weak, but he managed to stand up and fish out a quarter. It clinked in the coin box with a noise whose metal clarity he savored.

Perhaps a little sympathetic, or perhaps from a sense of duty, the driver asked him, "D'you say you was going to Seventh Street?"

"No." He sat down again. "Not tonight, after all. My home isn't quite that far."

When Robert P. Mills, who was then managing editor of *The Magazine of Fantasy and Science Fiction*, became as well the editor of *Venture Science Fiction* magazine (olav ha-sholem), he asked me if I would write a story for it. "Something expressing the soul of man under torment," he said. I replied, "Hmm"—or something equally cogent—and proceeded to write for him . . . nothing at all. Now, R.P.M. is not only a Good Man (it was Dr. Prof. I. Asimov, D.C., a savant whose soul is permanently pickled in formaldehyde and a guy not given to lavish praise of compeers, who dubbed him—and rightly, too—"The Kindly Editor"), he is a wise man. Canny. Cunning. Knows how to get to you. What he invited me to, he invited me to lunch. Then, over the entree, when I was shining like a greased (you should excuse the expression) pig and warm and genial with whiskey sour, he asked if I would write a story for him. For "him," note you. Not for "it." Of course I agreed. I went home and sat down at my typewriter. Then I got up and began to read the Sunday paper—the *New York Herald Tribune*, in fact. And saw a photograph (old) of the last fifteen living Tasmanians, now long extinct. I began to brood on the fate of those tribes of "primitive" man who survived somehow into our own sophisticated times, only to be wiped out by 'civilized' man as if they were dodoes, quaggas, great auks, or some other nonhuman item of no great use to modernity and of no capacity to resist absolute evil. It happened not only in Australia but in Africa and the Americas (including our own United States)—and the recent systematic effort of the Germans to exterminate the Jews ought not to be forgotten, either. Science fiction had often speculated on the meeting of Earth men with intelligent "life-forms" on other planets. Had it ever considered this particular possible aspect of such? I could not recollect that it had. I laid down the newspaper and returned to my typewriter and wrote this story in an afternoon. It is one of the few stories of mine which almost wrote itself and it has perhaps attracted the favorable attention of my colleagues more than any other story of mine. And, since Bob Mills inspired it, it seems only right that he should have the chance to reprint it.

AVRAM DAVIDSON

NOW LET US SLEEP

by AVRAM DAVIDSON

A pink-skinned young cadet ran past Harper, laughing
and shouting and firing his stungun. The wind veered about,
throwing the thick scent of the Yahoos into the faces of the
men, who whooped loudly to show their revulsion.

"I got three!" the chicken cadet yelped at Harper. "Did
you see me pop those two together? Boy, what a stink they
have!"

Harper looked at the sweating kid, muttered, "You don't
smell so sweet yourself," but the cadet didn't wait to hear.
All the men were running now, running in a ragged semi-
circle with the intention of driving the Yahoos before them,
to hold them at bay at the foot of the gaunt cliff a quarter-
mile off.

The Yahoos loped awkwardly over the rough terrain,
moaning and grunting grotesquely, their naked bodies bent
low. A few hundred feet ahead one of them stumbled and fell,
his arms and legs flying out as he hit the ground, twitched,
and lay still.

A bald-headed passenger laughed triumphantly, paused
to kick the Yahoo, and trotted on. Harper kneeled beside
the fallen primitive, felt for a pulse in the hairy wrist. It
seemed slow and feeble, but then, no one actually knew what
the normal pulse-beat should be. And—except for Harper
—no seemed to give a damn.

Maybe it was because he was the grandson of Barret
Harper, the great naturalist—back on Earth, of course. It
seemed as if man could be fond of nature only on the planet
of man's origin, whose ways he knew so well. Elsewhere, it
was too strange and alien—you subdued it, or you adjusted
to it, or you were perhaps even content with it. But you almost never *cared* about the flora or fauna of the new planets.
No one had the feeling for living things that an earth-born
had.

The men were shouting more loudly now, but Harper

didn't lift his head to see why. He put his hand to the shaggy grey chest. The heart was still beating, but very slowly and irregularly. Someone stood beside him.

"He'll come out of it in an hour or so," the voice of the purser said. "Come on—you'll miss all the fun—you should see how they act when they're cornered! They kick out and throw sand and—" he laughed at the thought—"they weep great big tears, and go, *'Oof! Oof!'*"

Harper said, "An ordinary man *would* come out of it in an hour or so. But I think their metabolism is different . . . Look at all the bones lying around."

The purser spat. "Well, don't that prove they're not human, when they won't even bury their dead? . . . *Oh,* oh! —look at that!" He swore.

Harper got to his feet. Cries of dismay and disappointment went up from the men.

"What's wrong?" Harper asked.

The purser pointed. The men had stopped running, were gathering together and gesturing. "Who's the damn fool who planned this drive?" the purser asked, angrily. "He picked the wrong cliff! The damned Yahoos *nest* in that one! Look at them climb, will you—" He took aim, fired the stungun. A figure scrabbling up the side of the rock threw up its arms and fell, bounding from rock to rock until it hit the ground. "*That* one will never come out of it!" the purser said, with satisfaction.

But this was the last casualty. The other Yahoos made their way to safety in the caves and crevices. No one followed them. In those narrow, stinking confines a Yahoo was as good as a man, there was no room to aim a stungun, and the Yahoos had rocks and clubs and their own sharp teeth. The men began straggling back.

"This one a she?" The purser pushed at the body with his foot, let it fall back with an annoyed grunt as soon as he determined its sex. "There'll be Hell to pay in the hold if there's more than two convicts to a she." He shook his head and swore.

Two lighters came skimming down from the big ship to load up.

"Coming back to the launch?" the purser asked. He had a red shiny face. Harper had always thought him a rather decent fellow—before. The purser had no way of knowing what was in Harper's mind; he smiled at him and said, "We might as well get on back, the fun's over now."

Harper came to a sudden decision. "What're the chances of my taking a souvenir back with me? This big fellow, here, for example?"

The purser seemed doubtful. "Well, I dunno, Mr. Harper. We're only supposed to take females aboard, and unload *them* as soon as the convicts are finished with their fun." He leered. Harper, suppressing a strong urge to hit him right in the middle of his apple-red face, put his hand in his pocket. The purser understood, looked away as Harper slipped a bill into the breast pocket of his uniform.

"I guess it can be arranged. See, the Commissioner-General on Selopé III wants one for his private zoo. Tell you what: We'll take one for him and one for you—I'll tell the supercargo it's a spare. But if one croaks, the C-G has to get the other. Okay?"

At Harper's nod the purser took a tag out of his pocket, tied it around the Yahoo's wrist, waved his cap to the lighter as it came near. "Although why anybody'd *want* one of these beats me," he said, cheerfully. "They're dirtier than animals. I mean, a pig or a horse'll ues the same corner of an enclosure, but these things'll dirty anywhere. Still, if you *want* one—" He shrugged.

As soon as the lighter had picked up the limp form (the pulse was still fluttering feebly) Harper and the purser went back to the passenger launch. As they made a swift ascent to the big ship the purser gestured to the two lighters. "That's going to be a mighty slow trip *those* two craft will make back up," he remarked.

Harper innocently asked why. The purser chuckled. The coxswain laughed.

"The freight-crewmen want to make their points before the convicts. *That's* why."

The chicken cadet, his face flushed a deeper pink than usual, tried to sound knowing. "How about that, purser? Is it pretty good stuff?'

The other passengers wiped their perspiring faces, leaned forward eagerly. The purser said. "Well, rank has its privileges, but that's one I figure I can do without."

His listeners guffawed, but more than one looked down towards the lighters and then avoided other eyes when he looked back again.

Barnum's Planet (named, as was the custom then, after the skipper who'd first sighted it) it was a total waste, economically speaking. It was almost all water and the water supported only a few repulsive-looking species of no discernible value. The only sizable piece of land—known, inevitably, as Barnumland, since no one else coveted the honor—was gaunt and bleak, devoid alike of useful minerals or arable soil. Its ecology seemed dependent on a sort of fly: A creature rather like a lizard ate the flies and the Yahoos ate the lizards. If something died at sea and washed ashore, the Yahoos ate that, too. What the flies ate no one knew, but their larvae ate the Yahoos, dead.

They were small, hairy, stunted creatures whose speech —if speech it was—seemed confined to moans and clicks and grunts. They wore no clothing, made no artifacts, did not know the use of fire. Taken away captive, they soon languished and died. Of all the Primitives discovered by man, they were the most primitive. They might have been left alone on their useless planet to kill lizards with tree branches forever—except for one thing.

Barnum's Planet lay equidistant between Coulter's System and the Selopés, and it was a long, long voyage either way. Passengers grew restless, crews grew mutinous, convicts rebellious. Gradually the practice developed of stopping on Barnum's Planet "to let off steam"—archaic expression, but although the nature of the machinery man used had changed since it was coined, man's nature hadn't.

And, of course, no one *owned* Barnum's Planet, so no one cared what happened there.

Which was just too bad for the Yahoos.

It took some time for Harper to settle the paperwork concerning his "souvenir," but finally he was given a baggage check for "One Yahoo, male, live," and hurried down to the freight deck. He hoped it would be still alive.

Pandemonium met his ears as he stepped out of the elevator. A rhythmical chanting shout came from the convict hold. "Hear that?" one of the duty officers asked him, taking the cargo chit. Harper asked what the men were yelling. "I wouldn't care to use the words," the officer said. He was a paunchy, gray-haired man, who probably loved to tell his grandchildren about his "adventures." This was one he wouldn't tell them.

"I don't like this part of the detail," the officer went on. "Never did, never will. Those creatures *seem human* to me —stupid as they are. And if they're *not* human," he asked,

188

"then how can we sink low enough to bring their females up for the convicts?"

The lighters grated on the landing. The noise must have penetrated to the convict hold, because all semblance of words vanished from the shouting. It became a mad cry, louder and louder.

"Here's your pet," the gray-haired officer said. "Still out, I see . . . I'll let you have a baggage-carrier. Just give it to a steward when you're done with it." He had to raise his voice to be heard over the frenzied howling from the hold.

The Ship's Surgeon was out having tea at the Captain's Table. The duty medical officer was annoyed. "What, another one? We're not veterinarians, you know . . . Well, wheel him in. My intern is working on the other one . . . *whew!*" He held his nose and hastily left.

The intern, a pale young man with close-cropped dark hair, looked up from the pressure-spray he had just used to give an injection to the specimen Yahoo selected for the Commissioner-General of Selopé III. He smiled faintly.

"Junior will have company, I see . . . Any others?"

Harper shook his head. The intern went on, "This should be interesting. The young one seems to be in shock. I gave him two cc's of anthidar sulfate, and I see I'd better do the same for yours. Then . . . Well, I guess there's still nothing like serum albumen, is there? But you'd better help me strap them down. If they come to, there's a cell back aft we can put them in, until I can get some cages rigged up." He shot the stimulant into the flaccid arm of Harper's Yahoo.

"Whoever named these beasties knew his Swift," the young medico said. "You ever read that old book, *Gulliver's Travels*"?

Harper nodded.

"Old Swift went mad, didn't he? He hated humanity, they all seemed like Yahoos to him . . . In a way I don't blame him. I think that's why everybody despises these Primitives: they seem like cariatures of ourselves. Personally, I look forward to finding out a lot about them, their metabolism and so on . . . What's *your* interest?"

He asked the question casually, but shot a keen look as he did so. Harper shrugged. "I hardly know, exactly. It's not a scientific one, because I'm a businessman." He hesitated. "You ever hear or read about the Tasmanians?"

The intern shook his head. He thrust a needle into a vein

189

in the younger Yahoo's arm, prepared to let the serum flow in. "If they lived on Earth, I wouldn't know. Never was there. I'm a third generation Coulterboy, myself."

Harper said, "Tasmania is an island south of Australia. The natives were the most primitive people known on Earth. They were almost all wiped out by the settlers, but one of them succeeded in moving the survivors to a small island. And then a curious thing happened."

Looking up from the older Primitive, the intern asked what that was.

"The Tasmanians—the few that were left—decided that they'd had it. They refused to breed. And in a few more years they were all dead . . . I read about them when I was just a kid. Somehow, it moved me very much. Things like that *did* —the dodo, the great auk, the quagga, the Tasmanians. I've never been able to get it out of my mind. When I began hearing about the Yahoos, it seemed to me that they were like the old Tasmanians. Only there are no settlers on Barnumland."

The intern nodded. "But that won't help our hairy friends here a hell of a lot. Of course no one knows how many of them there are—or ever were. But I've been comparing the figures in the log as to how many females are caught and taken aboard." He looked directly at Harper. "And on every trip there are less by far."

Harper bowed his head. He nodded. The intern's voice went on: "The thing is, Barnum's Planet is no one's responsibility. If the Yahoos could be used for labor, they'd be exploited according to a careful system. But as it is, no one cares. If half of them die from being stungunned, no one cares. If the lighter crews don't bother to actually land the females—if any of the wretched creatures are still *alive* when the convicts are done—but just dump them out from twenty feet up, why, again: no one cares. Mr. Harper?"

Their eyes met. Harper said, "Yes?"

"Don't misunderstand me . . . I've got a career here. I'm not jeopardizing it to save the poor Yahoos—but if *you* are interested—if you think you've got any influence—and if you want to try to do anything—" He paused. "Why, now is the time to start. Because after another few stop-overs there aren't going to *be* any Yahoos. No more than there are any Tasmanians."

Selopé III was called "The Autumn Planet" by the poets.

190

At least, the P.R. picture-tapes always referred to it as "Selopé III, The Autumn Planet of the poets," but no one knew who the poets were. It was true that the Commission Territory, at least, did have the climate of an almost-perpetual early New England November. Barnumland had been dry and warm. The Commissioner-General put the two Yahoos in a heated cage as large as the room Harper occupied at his company's Bachelor Executive Quarters.

"Here, boy," the C-G said, holding out a piece of fruit. He made a chirping noise. The two Yahoos huddled together in a far corner.

"They don't seem very bright," he said, sadly. "All my *other* animals eat out of my hand." He was very proud of his private zoo, the only one in the Territory. On Sundays he allowed the public to visit it.

Sighing, Harper repeated that the Yahoos were Primitives, not animals. But, seeing the C-G was still doubtful, he changed his tactics. He told the C-G about the great zoos on Earth, where the animals went loose in large enclosures rather than being caged up. The C-G nodded thoughtfully. Harper told him of the English dukes who—generation after ducal generation—preserved the last herd of wild White Cattle in a park on their estate.

The C-G stroked his chin. "Yes, yes," he said. "I see your point," he said. He sighed gustily. "Can't be done," he said.

"But why not, sir?" Harper cried.

It was simple. "No money. Who's to pay? The Exchequer-Commissioner is weeping blood trying to get the Budget through Council. If he adds a penny more— No, young fellow. I'll do what *I* can: I'll feed these two, here. But that's all I can do."

Trying to pull all the strings he could reach, Harper approached the Executive-Fiscal and the Procurator-General, the President-in-Council, the territorial Advocate, the Chairman of the Board of Travel. But no one could do anything. Barnum's Planet, it was carefully explained to him, remained No Man's Land only because no man presumed to give any orders concerning it. If any government did, this would be a Presumption of Authority. And then every other government would feel obliged to deny that presumption and issue a claim of its own.

There was a peace on now—a rather tense, uneasy one. And it wasn't going to be disturbed for Harper's Yahoos.

191

Human, were they? Perhaps. But who cared? As for Morality, Harper didn't even bother to mention the word. It would have meant as little as Chivalry.

Meanwhile, he was learning somehing of the Yahoos' language. Slowly and arduously, he gained their confidence. They would shyly take food from him. He persuaded the C-G to knock down a wall and enlarge their quarters. The official was a kindly old man, and he seemed to grow fond of the stooped, shaggy, splay-footed Primitives. And after a while he decided that they were smarter than animals.

"Put some clothes on 'em, Harper," he directed. "If they're people, let 'em start acting like people. They're too big to go around naked."

So, eventually, washed and dressed, Junior and Senior were introduced to Civilization via 3-D, and the program was taped and shown everywhere.

Would you like a cigarette, Junior? Here, let me light it for you. Give Junior a glass of water, Senior. Let's see you take off your slippers, fellows, and put them on again. And now do what I say in your own language . . .

But if Harper thought that might change public opinion, he thought wrong. Seals perform, too, don't they? And so do monkeys. They talk? Parrots talk better. And anyway, who cared to be bothered about animals *or* Primitives? They were okay for fun, but that was all.

And the reports from Barnumland showed fewer and fewer Yahoos each time.

Then one night two drunken crewmen climbed over the fence and went carousing in the C-G's zoo. Before they left, they broke the vapor-light tubes, and in the morning Junior and Senior were found dead from the poisonous fumes.

That was Sunday morning. By Sunday afternoon Harper was drunk, and getting drunker. The men who knocked on his door got no answer. They went in anyway. He was slouched, red-eyed, over the table.

"People," he muttered. "Tell you they were *human!*" he shouted.

"Yes, Mr. Harper, we know that," said a young man, pale, with close-cropped dark hair.

Harper peered at him, boozily. "Know you," he said. "Thir' gen'ration Coulterboy. Go 'way. Spoi' your c'reer. Whaffor. Smelly ol' Yahoo?" The young medico nodded to his companion, who took a small flask from his pocket, opened it. They held it under Harper's nose by main force. He gasped and struggled, but they held on, and in a few minutes he was sober.

"That's rough stuff," he said, coughing and shaking his head. "But—thanks, Dr. Hill. Your ship in? Or are you stopping over?"

The former intern shrugged. "I've left the ships," he said. "I don't have to worry about spoiling my new career. This is my superior, Dr. Anscomb."

Anscomb was also young, and, like most men from Coulter's System, pale. He said, "I understand you can speak the Yahoo's language."

Harper winced. "What good's that now? They're dead, poor little bastards."

Anscomb nodded. "I'm sorry about that, believe me. Those fumes are so quick . . . But there are still a few alive on Barnum's Planet who can be saved. The Joint Board for Research is interested. Are you?"

It had taken Harper fifteen years to work up to a room of this size and quality in Bachelor Executives' Quarters. He looked around it. He picked up the letter which had come yesterday. ". . . neglected your work and become a joke . . . unless you accept a transfer and reduction in grade . . ." He nodded slowly, putting down the letter. "I guess I've already made my choice. What are your plans. . . ?"

Harper, Hill, and Anscomb sat on a hummock on the north coast of Barnumland, just out of rock-throwing range of the gaunt escarpment of the cliff which rose before them. Behind them a tall fence had been erected. The only Yahoos still alive were "nesting" in the caves of the cliff. Harper spoke into the amplifier again. His voice was hoarse as he forced it into the clicks and moans of the Primitives' tongue.

Hill stirred restlessly. "Are you sure that means, *'Here is food. Here is water'*—and not, *'Come down and let us eat you'*? I think I can almost say it myself by now."

Shifting and stretching, Anscomb said, "It's been two days. Unless they've determined to commit race suicide a bit more abruptly than your ancient Tasmanians—" He stopped as Harper's fingers closed tightly on his arm.

There was a movement on the cliff. A shadow. A pebble clattered. Then a wrinkled face peered fearfully over a ledge. Slowly, and with many stops and hesitations, a figure came down the face of the cliff. It was an old she. Her withered and pendulous dugs flapped against her sagging belly as she made the final jump to the ground, and—her back to the wall of rock—faced them.

"Here is food," Harper repeated slowly. "Here is water." The old woman sighed. She plodded wearily across the ground, paused, shaking with fear, and then flung herself down at the food and the water.

"The Joint Board for Research has just won the first round," Hill said. Anscomb nodded. He jerked his thumb upward. Hill looked.

Another head appeared at the cliff. Then another. And another. They watched. The crone got up, water dripping from her dewlaps. She turned to the cliff. "Come down," she cried. "Here is food and water. Do not die. Come down and eat and drink." Slowly, her tribes-people did so. There were thirty of them.

Harper asked, "Where are the others?"

The crone held out her dried and leathery breasts to him. "Where are those who have sucked? Where are those your brothers took away?" She uttered a single shrill wail; then was silent.

But she wept—and Harper wept with her.

"I'll guess we'll swing it all right," Hill said. Anscomb nodded. "Pity there's so few of them. I was afraid we'd have to use gas to get at them. Might have lost several that way."

Neither of them wept.

For the first time since ships had come to their world, Yahoos *walked* aboard one. They came hesitantly and fearfully, but Harper had told them that they were going to a new home and they believed him. He told them that they were going to a place of much food and water, where no one would hunt them down. He continued to talk until the ship was on its way, and the last Primitive had fallen asleep under the dimmed-out vapor-tube lights. Then he staggered to his cabin and fell asleep himself. He slept for thirty hours.

He had something to eat when he awoke, then strolled down to the hold where the Primitives were. He grimaced, remembered his trip to the hold of the other ship to collect Senior, and the frenzied howling of the convicts awaiting the females. At the entrance to the hold he met Dr. Hill, greeted him.

"I'm afraid some of the Yahoos are sick," Hill said. "But Dr. Anscomb is treating them. The others have been moved to this compartment here."

Harper stared. "Sick? How can they be sick? What from? And how many?"

Dr. Hill said, "It appears to be Virulent Plague . . . Fifteen of them are down with it. You've *had* all six shots, haven't you? Good. Nothing to worry—"

Harper felt the cold steal over him. He stared at the pale young physician. "No one can enter or leave any system or planet without having had all six shots for Virulent Plague," he said, slowly. "So if we are all immune, how could the Primitives have gotten it? And how is it that only fifteen have it? Exactly half of them. What about the other fifteen, Dr. Hill? *Are they the control group for your experiment?*"

Dr. Hill looked at him calmly. "As a matter of fact, yes. I hope you'll be reasonable. Those were the only terms the Joint Board for Research would agree to. After all, not even convicts will volunteer for experiment in Virulent Plague."

Harper nodded. He felt frozen. After a moment he asked, "Can Anscomb do anything to pull them through?"

Dr. Hill raised his eyebrows. "Perhaps. We've got something we wanted to try. And at any rate, the reports should provide additional data on the subject. We must take the long-range view."

Harper nodded. "I suppose you're right," he said.

By noon all fifteen were dead.

"Well, that means an uneven control group," Dr. Anscomb complained. "Seven against eight. Still, that's not *too* bad. And it can't be helped. We'll start tomorrow."

"Virulent Plague again?" Harper asked.

Anscomb and Hill shook their heads. "Dehydration," the latter said. "And after that, there's a new treatment for burns we're anxious to try . . . It's a shame, when you think of the Yahoos being killed off by the thousands, year after year, *uselessly*. Like the dodo. We came along just in time—thanks to you, Harper."

He gazed at them. *"Quis custodiet ipsos custodes?"* he asked. They looked at him, politely blank. "I'd forgotten. Doctors don't study Latin anymore, do they? An old proverb. It means: 'Who shall guard the guards themselves?' . . . Will you excuse me, Doctors?"

Harper let himself into the compartment. "I come," he greeted the fifteen.

"We see you," they responded. The old woman asked how their brothers and sisters were "in the other cave."

195

"They are well . . . Have you eaten, have you drunk? Yes? Then let us sleep," Harper said.

The old woman seemed doubtful. "Is it time? The light still shines." She pointed to it. Harper looked at her. She had been so afraid. But she had trusted him. Suddenly he bent over and kissed her. She gaped.

"Now the light goes out," Harper said. He slipped off a shoe and shattered the vapor tube. He groped in the dark for the air-switch, turned it off. Then he sat down. He had brought them here, and if they had to die, it was only fitting that he should share their fate. There no longer seemed any place for the helpless, or for those who cared about them.

"Now let us sleep," he said.

The story handles a theme which has always fascinated me. What are the thoughts of a woman who has been told she will give birth to a god? Particularly if no man is to be its father? I touched upon it in a poem, *Proper Clay,* and later I returned to it in this story, with special emphasis on the strange feeling such a woman might have if she reflected that she herself would contribute nothing to the nature of the child, either before its birth or while it was growing up. It would not need her care, since it couldn't die. She might have two minds about the whole matter—or so I assumed.

The locale of the story is a little dusty city park such as I used to see mothers sitting in on New York's lower Eighth Avenue: specifically, where Greenwich Avenue comes in.

MARK VAN DOREN

THE STRANGE GIRL

by MARK VAN DOREN

It took them a long time to realize that she came every day. The young mothers, sitting and talking while their babies slept in the row of carriages under the ginkgo trees, didn't see her at all the first morning she was there. She was so thin and quiet, and wore her small black hat—with a white flower embroidered on its side—in such an unconscious way, as if it were a child's. But soon they were accustomed to her; and then they became curious.

The triangular space left where Greene Avenue cut in was too little to have a name, or even to be thought of as a park. It was an accident of traffic, and there was much traffic. Trucks from the downtown warehouses went by on all three sides, and buses stopped here with insistent, irritating sighs from their great air brakes. Sometimes it was hard for the women to hear one another as they talked, let alone know whether the strange girl was talking to herself. She would watch them—frankly, with her head turned, or else out of the corner of her eye—and then her lips would move. There were eleven of them, sitting in a row with their backs to the iron fence that shut off Cumberland Street. She was the twelfth, but there was space between. Occasionally an older child coasted up to this part of the bench to adjust a roller skate. Most of the time, though, it was empty. There was a general understanding that the Cumberland Street side was reserved for mothers and babies.

Today she came again, and young Mrs. Yarnoff, watching her sit down, thought to herself: She is pregnant. She repeated the thought to Nelly Samson on her left, and Nelly sent it the rest of the way. It was an interesting thought, yet by no means rare in this company, so that it passed out of Mrs. Clancy's mind, at the far end of the bench, into thin air, where it evaporated and was lost. Yet one or two heads came forward, and when Mrs. Yost got up to see why her infant was bouncing in his carriage and throwing off the blanket that covered him, on the way back to the bench she cast a glance at the girl.

The girl herself, either because it was plain to her that now they knew, or because her own certainty was greater today than it had been before, suddenly came over and sat down beside Mrs. Yarnoff.

"I'm going to have one too," she said.

Mrs. Yarnoff hesitated, looking into the pointed face turned up at her, and said: "That's good. You've been to see a doctor?"

"No." The voice was very pure and clear, a low voice, but singularly audible amid the din of cars.

"Wouldn't your husband feel better if you did?"

"I haven't any husband."

Mrs. Yarnoff thought: I will tell Nelly as soon as she leaves. But she knew this wouldn't happen right away. The girl often stayed here longer than they did.

"I didn't mean to say that," said the girl after a long pause. "But it's true. You mustn't think I mind." She was smiling, slightly, and looking toward the carriages. "I hope you ladies don't mind, either, if I come and watch you. I like to do it."

"That's all right," said Mrs. Yarnoff. "The park's free, if you call it a park. Somebody, though—I suppose somebody might feel better if he heard you were getting good attention. But then"—she was embarrassed, she felt foolish—"maybe he doesn't *know*. Gone away, or something."

"There isn't anybody."

Mrs. Yarnoff wondered if this was what she had heard. The girl was still looking at the carriages, but the smile, if it had been a smile, was replaced by something else. Something serious—not sad—and very simple. It could be called half-witted even, and yet that wasn't fair. What had she meant? There isn't anybody. Had she decided to forget the man? She couldn't have meant there *wasn't* anybody. A boy friend, maybe, and he died. Or went away, and never would be told.

"There wasn't anybody."

Her own words, escaping in this quiet fashion from the person at her side, turned Mrs. Yarnoff cold with doubt and fear. Doubt, because she still was wondering whether she had heard them right. Fear, because—well—

"What?" she said, flatly. She sounded ignorant to herself. Even then, however, she was going over in her mind what she would say to Nelly when the girl was gone. No matter how long she stayed, they would stick it out. I'll see to that, said Mrs. Yarnoff; or if not, I'll go by Nelly's house this afternoon and tell her then.

"I am different from you." The voice was sad now. "I wish I were the same as everybody. I'd like him to have a father, a real father."

"Him?"

"Oh, yes. I know that. But most of all I'd like to be a real mother, and feel that what I did was going to make some difference to him. He's coming into the world all by himself. Of course I'm here—there has to be some woman, some girl —but I won't have anything to do with making him strong and good. Even if I neglected him—I won't—he still would be all right. Nothing could change what has to be."

"Has to be?" Mrs. Yarnoff repeated the words automatically.

"He is coming into the world because he is needed. This is the time for him, and he is coming. He knows why that is, and what he has to do. I don't. I don't know anything, except that I was chosen. I was told. They came to me—"

"Who came?" Mrs. Yarnoff tried to speak softly, so that Nelly wouldn't hear, but she couldn't keep her voice from sounding excited and harsh. The girl—it was a shame.

"They did. I heard them talking one night, to each other and then to me. I couldn't see, but I could hear. It was just like this: very quiet."

It *was* quiet, Mrs. Yarnoff thought. Nelly didn't seem to hear a word—she was knitting as if nothing had happened— and though the traffic hadn't stopped, there was a hollow place in the sound of it, a dead spot where nothing but the girl's voice kept going on and on, pure and clear, and low-pitched yet with no roughness in it.

"They told me I would have this boy, and that no man would be his father. I've never known a man, that way. And now I never will. But that's all right. It's the rest of it I'll miss. Ever since I was a little girl I've liked to watch women with their babies. I had no brothers and sisters to take care of like some girls I know, but I've done it for the neighbors. I'm good at it, I'm very careful, and children love me. When I heard what was going to happen to me I was glad. I said to myself, now there will be one for me to tend—nobody but me. Then I remembered what they said. He was coming into the world all by himself, and he would know what to do. Nothing could change that—he wouldn't need me after he was born. Oh, he'll be helpless for a while; but even then he can't get sick or die. And as for teaching him—he's going to teach us, you know. He has to save the world. He'll be the one man in the world, when he grows up, that knows what has to be done. I'm nothing but the way he gets here. I'm nobody after he comes."

Mrs. Yarnoff waited for the silence to end, but it did not.

"It's like that with us, too, I'm afraid." Her own voice sounded strange. "My other children"—she made a gesture toward the carriage opposite her, excluding its small passenger, a daughter three months old—"they're already learning to get along without me, except at meals. Everybody says so; we don't make them what they are. Mrs. Kimball there, she wants her boy to be a policeman like his father, but maybe he won't. We bring them here as you will yours, and then—"

"But I am different from you." The girl was stubborn. "You don't know for sure that you don't make a difference—you and your husband—in their lives. I've heard both things, that you do and you don't, and I think both must be true. With me there can't be any doubt. He's coming—"

"Yes, I know."

"He's sent. And I have had no husband. It's so wonderful, I could be proud. But I'm not proud. They didn't give me any choice; they told me, then they went away. It wasn't even an idea I had."

"Oh, no?" Yet Mrs. Yarnoff didn't sound sarcastic. "Not even a little bit?"

"Not even a wish, a dream. I heard them, then they went away. Your baby is crying."

Mrs. Yarnoff, startled, saw two fists in the cool air above the carriage rail, trying in vain to smite each other.

"May I go and see what's wrong?" The girl was already on her feet.

"No!" Yet she could do no harm, with everybody watching. "All right then, if you want to." She was sorry she had said "No," for the girl sat down again. "Go on—I wish you would."

Mrs. Yarnoff saw the slight figure bend over her baby, and heard the low voice saying pleasant, unintelligible things. The fists went down, the covers were smoothed over them, and the girl came back to her seat, smiling happily and nodding

"You do know how," said Mrs. Yarnoff.

"Thank you. She's a nice baby. Now I've got to go—I'm tired. Should I be tired?"

Mrs. Yarnoff looked squarely at her in the silence that still hung about them, like a bubble soon to burst. It was odd that she hadn't heard Frances crying. The girl did, and she didn't. The other women hadn't even noticed.

"Look here! You must see a doctor—you could see mine. He's a good man, he would know."

"But it isn't necessary. Nothing can go wrong."

Mrs. Yarnoff meant, her mind. Something *had* gone wrong with that. Or had it? Who would know?

"Good-bye. I'll come tomorrow if it doesn't rain."

"Good-bye."

At least there was time to think about it, to do something, to ask somebody.

"Good-bye," said Mrs. Yarnoff again.

The girl was taking the silence with her. She hardly showed. Could it be a delusion she had, a wild idea? So young —it could be that.

The silence was definitely going. Mrs. Yarnoff's ears felt as they sometimes did at the beach, when water, having been in them, went out. A sort of pop, a little explosion. The sounds of the city suddenly came back, ten times as loud as normal. Nelly was talking.

"What about that girl?"

"Didn't you hear what we said?"

"No, it seemed to be a secret."

It was, thought Mrs. Yarnoff. She wouldn't tell Nelly yet. Perhaps she never would. Not yet, anyway. To think of somebody believing she was giving birth to God. It was not the worst thing to believe. She had tried to imagine it herself once, and maybe every woman did. But then, not to be proud. Not to be happy, even. It *would* be strange, not having to keep them warm, not really having to, not feeling satisfaction when you did.

Twelve o'clock. Time to go in. All of the women were stirring, were getting their things together.

Mrs. Yarnoff started over to the carriage.

"Was it anything?" She heard Nelly behind her. "Who is she, anyway? She's not strong—I could see that."

"Strong enough," said Mrs. Yarnoff over her shoulder. Frances was staring up with large eyes, delighted to find her there. "She'll be all right. She's coming tomorrow. You might talk to her yourself."

Someone else, certainly. She didn't want to be the only one that knew.

Something that readers never realize (and that authors sometimes try to forget) is how much those mysterious creatures called editors have contributed to some of their favorite stories. The ideal editor (and the science fiction field is astonishingly rich in people who truly *edit* rather than merely assemble) is capable of sowing the field as well as reaping the harvest. He will stimulate flagging author Hungadunga with a story-idea precisely suited to the Hungadunga imagination; and when the story finally appears, the fans will cry exultantly, "Gosh wow, that Hungadunga! Does he have *ideas!*"

Public confession: The first science fiction story I ever wrote, *Barrier,* which has often been praised for the novelty of its time-travel gimmick, was masterminded by John W. Campbell, Jr., as were several other Boucher stories of those grand old *Astounding-Unknown* days of twenty years ago. (Can it be that long? The slow coach is the uncomfortable form of time travel. . . .) And the story which you are (I hope) about to read owes its genesis to editor Raymond J. Healey.

I am deeply grateful to Ray for the seed which grew into this story. He had calculated it exactly for me, and the nature of the story-idea gave me the opportunity to explore, within a science-fictional framework, certain ideas and emotions about religion. This is a story simply of exploration: it does not attempt to come up with any answers. But I like the questions it enabled me to ask.

ANTHONY BOUCHER

Footnote: The seed-sowing method does not always work out to an editor's advantage. When I was editing *Fantasy & Science Fiction,* my wife happened, for the only time in her life, to invent a beautiful fresh science fiction story-idea. I carefully calculated the exact author to whom it would most appeal, and sent it to him. He was enthusiastic . . . and a few months later the story appeared in *Galaxy.*

THE QUEST FOR SAINT AQUIN

by ANTHONY BOUCHER

The Bishop of Rome, the head of the Holy, Catholic and Apostolic Church, the Vicar of Christ on Earth—in short, the Pope—brushed a cockroach from the filth-encrusted wooden table, took another sip of the raw red wine, and resumed his discourse.

"In some respects, Thomas," he smiled, "we are stronger now than when we flourished in the liberty and exaltation for which we still pray after Mass. We know, as they knew in the catacombs, that those who are of our flock are indeed truly of it; that they belong to Holy Mother the Church because they believe in the brotherhood of man under the fatherhood of God—not because they can further their political aspirations, their social ambitions, their business contacts."

" 'Not of the will of flesh, nor of the will of man, but of God . . .' " Thomas quoted softly from St. John.

The Pope nodded. "We are, in a way, born again in Christ; but there are still too few of us—too few even if we include those other handfuls who are not of our faith, but still acknowledge God through the teachings of Luther or Lao-tse, Gautama Buddha or Joseph Smith. Too many men still go to their deaths hearing no gospel preached to them but the cynical self-worship of the Technarchy. And that is why, Thomas, you must go forth on your quest."

"But Your Holiness," Thomas protested, "if God's word and God's love will not convert them, what can saints and miracles do?"

"I seem to recall," murmured the Pope, "that God's own Son once made a similar protest. But human nature, however illogical it may seem, is part of His design, and we must cater to it. If signs and wonders can lead souls to God, then by all means let us find the signs and wonders. And what can be better for the purpose than this legendary Aquin? Come now, Thomas; be not too scrupulously exact in copying the doubts of your namesake, but prepare for your journey."

The Pope lifted the skin that covered the doorway and passed into the next room, with Thomas frowning at his heels. It was past legal hours and the main room of the tavern was empty. The swarthy innkeeper roused from his doze to drop to his knees and kiss the ring on the hand which the Pope extended to him. He rose crossing himself and at the same time glancing furtively about as though a Loyalty Checker might have seen him. Silently he indicated another door in the back, and the two priests passed through.

Toward the west the surf purred in an oddly gentle way at the edges of the fishing village. Toward the south the stars were sharp and bright; toward the north they dimmed a little in the persistent radiation of what had once been San Francisco.

"Your steed is here," the Pope said, with something like laughter in his voice.

"Steed?"

"We may be as poor and as persecuted as the primitive church, but we can occasionally gain greater advantages from our tyrants. I have secured for you a robass—gift of a leading Technarch who, like Nicodemus, does good by stealth—a secret convert, and converted, indeed, by that very Aquin whom you seek."

It looked harmlessly like a woodpile sheltered against possible rain. Thomas pulled off the skins and contemplated the sleek functional lines of the robass. Smiling, he stowed his minimal gear into its panniers and climbed into the foam saddle. The starlight was bright enough so that he could check the necessary coordinates on his map and feed the data into the electronic controls.

Meanwhile there was a murmur of Latin in the still night air, and the Pope's hand moved over Thomas in the immemorial symbol. Then he extended that hand, first for the kiss on the ring, and then again for the handclasp of a man to a friend he may never see again.

Thomas looked back once more as the robass moved off. The Pope was wisely removing his ring and slipping it into the hollow heel of his shoe.

Thomas looked hastily up at the sky. On that altar at least the candles still burnt openly to the glory of God.

Thomas had never ridden a robass before, but he was inclined, within their patent limitations, to trust the works of the Technarchy. After several miles had proved that the coordinates were duly registered, he put up the foam backrest, said his evening office (from memory; the possession of a breviary meant the death sentence), and went to sleep.

They were skirting the devastated area to the east of the Bay when he awoke. The foam seat and back had given him his best sleep in years; and it was with difficulty that he smothered an envy of the Technarchs and their creature comforts.

He said his morning office, breakfasted lightly, and took his first opportunity to inspect the robass in full light. He admired the fast-plodding, articulated legs, so necessary since roads had degenerated to, at best, trails in all save metropolitan areas; the side wheels that could be lowered into action if surface conditions permitted; and above all the smooth black mound that housed the electronic brain—the brain that stored commands and data concerning ultimate objectives and made its own decisions on how to fulfill those commands in view of those data; the brain that made this thing neither a beast, like the ass his Saviour had ridden, nor a machine, like the jeep of his many-times-great-grandfather, but a robot . . . a robass.

"Well," said a voice, "what do you think of the ride."

Thomas looked about him. The area on this fringe of desolation was as devoid of people as it was of vegetation.

"Well," the voice repeated unemotionally. "Are not priests taught to answer when spoken to politely."

There was no querying inflection to the question. No inflection at all—each syllable was at the same dead level. It sounded strange, mechani . . .

Thomas stared at the black mound of brain. "Are you talking to me?" he asked the robass.

"Ha ha," the voice said in lieu of laughter. "Surprised, are you not."

"Somewhat," Thomas confessed. "I thought the only robots who could talk were in library information service and such."

"I am a new model. Designed-to-provide-conversation-to-entertain-the-way-worn-traveler," the robass said slurring the words together as though that phrase of promotional copy was released all at once by one of his simplest binary synapses.

"Well," said Thomas simply. "One keeps learning new marvels."

"I am no marvel. I am a very simple robot. You do not know much about robots do you."

"I will admit that I have never studied the subject closely.

207

I'll confess to being a little shocked at the whole robotic concept. It seems almost as though man were arrogating to himself the powers of—" Thomas stopped abruptly.

"Do not fear," the voice droned on. "You may speak freely. All data concerning your vocation and mission have been fed into me. That was necessary otherwise I might inadvertently betray you."

Thomas smiled. "You know," he said, "this might be rather pleasant—having one other being that one can talk to without fear of betrayal, aside from one's confessor."

"Being," the robass repeated. "Are you not in danger of lapsing into heretical thoughts."

"To be sure, it *is* a little difficult to know how to think of you—one who can talk and think but has no soul."

"Are you sure of that."

"Of course I— Do you mind very much," Thomas asked, "if we stop talking for a little while? I should like to meditate and adjust myself to the situation."

"I do not mind. I never mind. I only obey. Which is to say that I *do* mind. This is very confusing language which has been fed into me."

"If we are together long," said Thomas, "I shall try teaching you Latin. I think you might like that better. And now let me meditate."

The robass was automatically veering further east to escape the permanent source of radiation which had been the first cyclotron. Thomas fingered his coat. The combination of ten small buttons and one large made for a peculiar fashion; but it was much safer than carrying a rosary, and fortunately the Loyalty Checkers had not yet realized the fashion's functional purpose.

The Glorious Mysteries seemed appropriate to the possible glorious outcome of his venture; but his meditations were unable to stay fixedly on the Mysteries. As he murmured his *Aves* he was thinking:

If the prophet Balaam conversed with his ass, surely I may converse with my robass. Balaam has always puzzled me. He was not an Israelite; he was a man of Moab, which worshiped Baal and was warring against Israel; and yet he was a prophet of the Lord. He blessed the Israelites when he was commanded to curse them; and for his reward he was slain by the Israelites when they triumphed over Moab. The whole story has no shape, no moral; it is as though it was there to say that there are portions of the Divine Plan which we will never under-stand . . .

He was nodding in the foam seat when the robass halted abruptly, rapidly adjusting itself to exterior data not previously fed into its calculations. Thomas blinked up to see a giant of a man glaring down at him.

"Inhabited area a mile ahead," the man barked. "If you're going there, show your access pass. If you ain't, steer off the road and stay off."

Thomas noted that they were indeed on what might roughly be called a road, and that the robass had lowered its side wheels and retracted its legs. "We—" he began, then changed it to "I'm not going there. Just on toward the mountains. We— I'll steer around."

The giant grunted and was about to turn when a voice shouted from the crude shelter at the roadside. "Hey Joe! Remember about robasses!"

Joe turned back. "Yeah, tha's right. Been a rumor about some robass got into the hands of Christians." He spat on the dusty road. "Guess I better see an ownership certificate."

To his other doubts Thomas now added certain uncharitable suspicions as to the motives of the Pope's anonymous Nicodemus, who had not provided him with any such certificate. But he made a pretense of searching for it, first touching his right hand to his forehead as if in thought, then fumbling low on his chest, then reaching his hand first to his left shoulder, then to his right.

The guard's eyes remained blank as he watched this furtive version of the sign of the cross. Then he looked down. Thomas followed his gaze to the dust of the road, where the guard's hulking right foot had drawn the two curved lines which a child uses for its sketch of a fish—and which the Christians in the catacombs had employed as a punning symbol of their faith. His boot scuffed out the fish as he called to his unseen mate, " 's OK, Fred!" and added, "Get going, mister."

The robass waited until they were out of earshot before it observed, "Pretty smart. You will make a secret agent yet."

"How did you see what happened?" Thomas asked. "You don't have any eyes."

"Modified psi factor. Much more efficient."

"Then . . ." Thomas hesitated. "Does that mean you can read my thoughts?"

"Only a very little. Do not let it worry you. What I can read does not interest me it is such nonsense."

"Thank you," said Thomas.

"To believe in God. Bah." (It was the first time Thomas had ever heard that word pronounced just as it is written.) "I have a perfectly constructed logical mind that cannot commit such errors."

"I have a friend," Thomas smiled, "who is infallible too. But only on occasions and then only because God is with him."

"No human being is infallible."

"Then imperfection," asked Thomas, suddenly feeling a little of the spirit of the aged Jesuit who had taught him philosophy, "has been able to create perfection?"

"Do not quibble," said the robass. "That is no more absurd than your own belief that God who is perfection created man who is imperfection."

Thomas wished that his old teacher were here to answer that one. At the same time he took some comfort in the fact that, retort and all, the robass had still not answered his own objection. "I am not sure," he said, "that this comes under the head of conversation-to-entertain-the-way-weary-traveler. Let us suspend debate while you tell me what, if anything, robots do believe."

"What we have been fed."

"But your minds work on that; surely they must evolve ideas of their own?"

"Sometimes they do and if they are fed imperfect data they may evolve very strange ideas. I have heard of one robot on an isolated space station who worshiped a God of robots and would not believe that any man had created him."

"I suppose," Thomas mused, "he argued that he had hardly been created in our image. I am glad that we—at least they, the Technarchs—have wisely made only usuform robots like you, each shaped for his function, and never tried to reproduce man himself."

"It would not be logical," said the robass. "Man is an all-purpose machine but not well designed for any one purpose. And yet I have heard that once . . ."

The voice stopped abruptly in midsentence.

So even robots have their dreams, Thomas thought. That once there existed a super-robot in the image of his creator Man. From that thought could be developed a whole robotic theology . . .

Suddenly Thomas realized that he had dozed again and again been waked by an abrupt stop. He looked around. They were at the foot of a mountain—presumably the mountain on his map, long ago named for the Devil but now perhaps sanctified beyond measure—and there was no one else anywhere in sight.

"All right," the robass said. "By now I show plenty of dust and wear and tear and I can show you how to adjust my mileage recorder. You can have supper and a good night's sleep and we can go back."

Thomas gasped. "But my mission is to find Aquin. I can sleep while you go on. You don't need any sort of rest or anything, do you?" he added considerately.

"Of course not. But what is your mission."

"To find Aquin," Thomas repeated patiently. "I don't know what details have been—what is it you say?—fed into you. But reports have reached His Holiness of an extremely saintly man who lived many years ago in this area—"

"I know I know I know," said the robass. "His logic was such that everyone who heard him was converted to the Church and do not I wish that I had been there to put in a word or two and since he died his secret tomb has become a place of pilgrimage and many are the miracles that are wrought there above all the greatest sign of sanctity that his body has been preserved incorruptible and in these times you need signs and wonders for the people."

Thomas frowned. It all sounded hideously irreverent and contrived when stated in that deadly inhuman monotone. When His Holiness had spoken of Aquin, one thought of the glory of a man of God upon earth—the eloquence of St. John Chrysostom, the cogency of St. Thomas Aquinas, the poetry of St. John of the Cross . . . and above all that physical miracle vouchsafed to few even of the saints, the supernatural preservation of the flesh . . . "for Thou shalt not suffer Thy holy one to see corruption . . ."

But the robass spoke, and one thought of cheap showmanship hunting for a Cardiff Giant to pull in the mobs . . .

The robass spoke again. "Your mission is not to find Aquin. It is to report that you have found him. Then your occasionally infallible friend can with a reasonably clear conscience canonize him and proclaim a new miracle and many will be the converts and greatly will the faith of the flock be strengthened. And in these days of difficult travel who will go on pilgrimages and find out that there is no more Aquin than there is God."

"Faith cannot be based on a lie," said Thomas.

"No," said the robass. "I do not mean no period. I mean no question mark with an ironical inflection. This speech problem must surely have been conquered in that one perfect . . ."

Again he stopped in midsentence. But before Thomas could speak he had resumed, "Does it matter what small untruth leads people into the Church if once they are in they will believe what you think to be the great truths. The report is all that is needed not the discovery. Comfortable though I am you are already tired of traveling very tired you have many small muscular aches from sustaining an unaccustomed position and with the best intentions I am bound to jolt a little a jolting which will get worse as we ascend the mountain and I am forced to adjust my legs disproportionately to each other but proportionately to the slope. You will find the remainder of this trip twice as uncomfortable as what has gone before. The fact that you do not seek to interrupt me indicates that you do not disagree do you. You know that the only sensible thing is to sleep here on the ground for a change and start back in the morning or even stay here two days resting to make a more plausible lapse of time. Then you can make your report and—"

Somewhere in the recess of his somnolent mind Thomas uttered the names, "Jesus, Mary and Joseph!" Gradually through these recesses began to filter a realization that an absolutely uninflected monotone is admirably adapted to hypnotic purposes.

"Retro me, Satanas!" Thomas exclaimed aloud, then added, "Up the mountain. That is an order and you must obey."

"I obey," said the robass. "But what did you say before that."

"I beg your pardon," said Thomas. "I must start teaching you Latin."

The little mountain village was too small to be considered an inhabited area worthy of guard-control and passes; but it did possess an inn of sorts.

As Thomas dismounted from the robass, he began fully to realize the accuracy of those remarks about small muscular aches, but he tried to show his discomfort as little as possible. He was in no mood to give the modified psi factor the chance of registering the thought, "I told you so."

The waitress at the inn was obviously a Martian-American

hybrid. The highly developed Martian chest expansion and the highly developed American breasts made a spectacular combination. Her smile was all that a stranger could, and conceivably a trifle more than he should ask; and she was eagerly ready, not only with prompt service of passable food, but with full details of what little information there was to offer about the mountain settlement.

But she showed no reaction at all when Thomas offhandedly arranged two knives in what might have been an X.

As he stretched his legs after breakfast, Thomas thought of her chest and breasts—purely, of course, as a symbol of the extraordinary nature of her origin. What a sign of the divine care for His creatures that these two races, separated for countless eons, should prove fertile to each other!

And yet there remained the fact that the offspring, such as this girl, were sterile to both races—a fact that had proved both convenient and profitable to certain unspeakable interplanetary entrepreneurs. And what did that fact teach us as to the Divine Plan?

Hastily Thomas reminded himself that he had not yet said his morning office.

It was close to evening when Thomas returned to the robass stationed before the inn. Even though he had expected nothing in one day, he was still unreasonably disappointed. Miracles should move faster.

He knew these backwater villages, where those drifted who were either useless to or resentful of the Technarchy. The technically high civilization of the Technarchic Empire, on all three planets, existed only in scattered metropolitan centers near major blasting ports. Elsewhere, aside from the areas of total devastation, the drifters, the morons, the malcontents had subsided into a crude existence a thousand years old, in hamlets which might go a year without even seeing a Loyalty Checker—though by some mysterious grapevine (and Thomas began to think again about modified psi factors) any unexpected technological advance in one of these hamlets would bring Checkers by the swarm.

He had talked with stupid men, he had talked with lazy men, he had talked with clever and angry men. But he had not talked with any man who responded to his unobtrusive signs, any man to whom he would dare ask a question containing the name of Aquin.

"Any luck," said the robass, and added "question mark."

"I wonder if you ought to talk to me in public," said Thomas a little irritably. "I doubt if these villagers know about talking robots."

"It is time that they learned then. But if it embarrasses you you may order me to stop."

"I'm tired," said Thomas. "Tired beyond embarrassment. And to answer your question mark, no. No luck at all. Exclamation point."

"We will go back tonight then," said the robass.

"I hope you meant that with a question mark. The answer," said Thomas hesitantly, "is no. I think we ought to stay overnight anyway. People always gather at the inn of an evening. There's a chance of picking up something."

"Ha, ha," said the robass.

"That is a laugh?" Thomas inquired.

"I wished to express the fact that I had recognized the humor in your pun."

"My pun?"

"I was thinking the same thing myself. The waitress is by humanoid standards very attractive, well worth picking up."

"Now look. You know I meant nothing of the kind. You know that I'm a—" He broke off. It was hardly wise to utter the word *priest* aloud.

"And you know very well that the celibacy of the clergy is a matter of discipline and not of doctrine. Under your own Pope priests of other rites such as the Byzantine and the Anglican are free of vows of celibacy. And even within the Roman rite to which you belong there have been eras in history when that vow was not taken seriously even on the highest levels of the priesthood. You are tired you need refreshment both in body and in spirit you need comfort and warmth. For is it not written in the book of the prophet Isaiah Rejoice for joy with her that ye may be satisfied with the breasts of her consolation and is it—"

"Hell!" Thomas exploded suddenly. "Stop it before you begin quoting the Song of Solomon. Which is strictly an allegory concerning the love of Christ for His Church, or so they kept telling me in seminary."

"You see how fragile and human you are," said the robass. "I a robot have caused you to swear."

"*Distinguo,*" said Thomas smugly. "I said *Hell,* which is certainly not taking the name of *my* Lord in vain." He walked into the inn feeling momentarily satisfied with himself . . . and

214

markedly puzzled as to the extent and variety of data that seemed to have been "fed into" the robass.

Never afterward was Thomas able to reconstruct that evening in absolute clarity.

It was undoubtedly because he was irritated—with the robass, with his mission, and with himself—that he drank at all of the crude local wine. It was undoubtedly because he was so physically exhausted that it affected him so promptly and unexpectedly.

He had flashes of memory. A moment of spilling a glass over himself and thinking, "How fortunate that clerical garments are forbidden so that no one can recognize the disgrace of a man of the cloth!" A moment of listening to a bawdy set of verses of *A Space-suit Built for Two,* and another moment of his interrupting the singing with a sonorous declamation of passages from the *Song of Songs* in Latin.

He was never sure whether one remembered moment was real or imaginary. He could taste a warm mouth and feel the tingling of his fingers at the touch of Martian-American flesh; but he was never certain whether this was true memory or part of the Ashtaroth-begotten dream that had begun to ride him.

Nor was he ever certain which of his symbols, or to whom, was so blatantly and clumsily executed as to bring forth a gleeful shout of "God-damned Christian dog!" He did remember marveling that those who most resolutely disbelieved in God still needed Him to blaspheme by. And then the torment began.

He never knew whether or not a mouth had touched his lips, but there was no question that many solid fists had found them. He never knew whether his fingers had touched breasts, but they had certainly been trampled by heavy heels. He remembered a face that laughed aloud while its owner swung the chair that broke two ribs. He remembered another face with red wine dripping over it from an upheld bottle, and he remembered the gleam of the candlelight on the bottle as it swung down.

The next he remembered was the ditch and the morning and the cold. It was particularly cold because all of his clothes were gone, along with much of his skin. He could not move. He could only lie there and look.

He saw them walk by, the ones he had spoken with yesterday, the ones who had been friendly. He saw them glance at him and turn their eyes quickly away. He saw the waitress pass by. She did not even glance; she knew what was in the ditch.

The robass was nowhere in sight. He tried to project his thoughts, tried desperately to hope in the psi factor.

A man whom Thomas had not seen before was coming along fingering the buttons of his coat. There were ten small buttons and one large one, and the man's lips were moving silently.

This man looked into the ditch. He paused a moment and looked around him. There was a shout of loud laughter somewhere in the near distance.

The Christian hastily walked on down the pathway, devoutly saying his button-rosary.

Thomas closed his eyes.

He opened them on a small neat room. They moved from the rough wooden walls to the rough but clean and warm blankets that covered him. Then they moved to the lean dark face that was smiling over him.

"You feel better now?" a deep voice asked. "I know. You want to say 'Where am I?' and you think it will sound foolish. You are at the inn. It is the only good room."

"I can't afford—" Thomas started to say. Then he remembered that he could afford literally nothing. Even his few emergency credits had vanished when he was stripped.

"It's all right. For the time being, I'm paying," said the deep voice. "You feel like maybe a little food?"

"Perhaps a litle herring," said Thomas . . . and was asleep within the next minute.

When he next awoke there was a cup of hot coffee beside him. The real thing, too, he promptly discovered. Then the deep voice said apologetically, "Sandwiches. It is all they have in the inn today."

Only on the second sandwich did Thomas pause long enough to notice that it was smoked swamphog, one of his favorite meats. He ate the second with greater leisure, and was reaching for a third when the dark man said, "Maybe that is enough for now. The rest later."

Thomas gestured at the plate. "Won't you have one?"

"No thank you. They are all swamphog."

Confused thoughts went through Thomas' mind. The Venusian swamphog is a ruminant. Its hoofs are not cloven. He tried to remember what he had once known of Mosaic dietary law. Someplace in Leviticus, wasn't it?

The dark man followed his thoughts. *"Treff,"* he said.

"I beg your pardon?"

"Not kosher."

Thomas frowned. "You admit to me that you're an Orthodox Jew? How can you trust me? How do you know I'm not a Checker?"

"Believe me, I trust you. You were very sick when I brought you here. I sent everybody away because I did not trust them to hear things you said . . . Father," he added lightly.

Thomas struggled with words. "I . . . I didn't deserve you. I was drunk and disgraced myself and my office. And when I was lying there in the ditch I didn't even think to pray. I put my trust in . . . God help me in the modified psi factor of a robass!"

"And He did help you," the Jew reminded him. "Or He allowed me to."

"And they all walked by," Thomas groaned. "Even one that was saying his rosary. He went right on by. And then you come along—the good Samaritan."

"Believe me," said the Jew wryly, "if there is one thing I'm not, it's a Samaritan. Now go to sleep again. I will try to find your robass . . . and the other thing."

He had left the room before Thomas could ask him what he meant.

Later that day the Jew—Abraham, his name was—reported that the robass was safely sheltered from the weather behind the inn. Apparently it had been wise enough not to startle him by engaging in conversation.

It was not until the next day that he reported on "the other thing."

"Believe me, Father," he said gently, "after nursing you there's little I don't know about who you are and why you're here. Now there are some Christians here I know, and they know me. We trust each other. Jews may still be hated; but no longer, God be praised, by worshipers of the same Lord. So I explained about you. One of them," he added with a smile, "turned very red."

"God has forgiven him," said Thomas. "There were people near—the same people who attacked me. Could he be expected to risk his life for mine?"

"I seem to recall that that is precisely what your Messiah did expect. But who's being particular? Now that they know who you are, they want to help you. See: they gave me this map for you. The trail is steep and tricky; it's good you have the robass. They ask just one favor of you: When you come

217

back will you hear their confession and say Mass? There's a cave near here where it's safe."

"Of course. These friends of yours, they've told you about Aquin?"

The Jew hesitated a long time before he said slowly, "Yes . . ."

"And . . .?"

"Believe me, my friend, I don't know. So it seems a miracle. It helps to keep their faith alive. My own faith . . . *nu*, it's lived for a long time on miracles three thousand years old and more. Perhaps if I had heard Aquin himself . . ."

"You don't mind," Thomas asked, "if I pray for you, in my faith?"

Abraham grinned. "Pray in good health, Father."

The not-quite-healed ribs ached agonizingly as he climbed into the foam saddle. The robass stood patiently while he fed in the coordinates from the map. Not until they were well away from the village did it speak.

"Anyway," it said, "now you're safe for good."

"What do you mean?"

"As soon as we get down from the mountain you deliberately look up a Checker. You turn in the Jew. From then on you are down in the books as a faithful servant of the Technarchy and you have not harmed a hair of the head of one of your own flock."

Thomas snorted. "You're slipping, Satan. That one doesn't even remotely tempt me. It's inconceivable."

"I did best did not I with the breasts. Your God has said it the spirit indeed is willing but the flesh is weak."

"And right now," said Thomas, "the flesh is too weak for even fleshly temptations. Save your breath . . . or whatever it is you use."

They climbed the mountain in silence. The trail indicated by the coordinates was a winding and confused one, obviously designed deliberately to baffle any possible Checkers.

Suddenly Thomas roused himself from his button-rosary (on a coat lent by the Christian who had passed by) with a startled "Hey!" as the robass plunged directly into a heavy thicket of bushes.

"Coordinates say so," the robass stated tersely.

For a moment Thomas felt like the man in the nursery rhyme who fell into a bramble bush and scratched out both his eyes. Then the bushes were gone, and they were plodding

218

along a damp narrow passageway through solid stone, in which even the robass seemed to have some difficulty with his footing.

Then they were in a rocky chamber some four meters high and ten in diameter, and there on a sort of crude stone catafalque lay the uncorrupted body of a man.

Thomas slipped from the foam saddle, groaning as his ribs stabbed him, sank to his knees, and offered up a wordless hymm of gratitude. He smiled at the robass and hoped the psi factor could detect the elements of pity and triumph in that smile.

Then a frown of doubt crossed his face as he approached the body. "In canonization proceedings in the old time," he said, as much to himself as to the robass, "they used to have what they called a devil's advocate, whose duty it was to throw every possible doubt on the evidence."

"You would be well cast in such a role Thomas," said the robass.

"If I were," Thomas muttered, "I'd wonder about caves. Some of them have peculiar properties of preserving bodies by a sort of mummification . . ."

The robass had clumped close to the catafalque. "This body is not mummified," he said. "Do not worry."

"Can the psi factor tell you that much?" Thomas smiled.

"No," said the robass. "But I will show you why Aquin could never be mummified."

He raised his articulated foreleg and brought its hoof down hard on the hand of the body. Thomas cried out with horror at the sacrilege—then stared hard at the crushed hand.

There was no blood, no ichor of embalming, no bruised flesh. Nothing but a shredded skin and beneath it an intricate mass of plastic tubes and metal wires.

The silence was long. Finally the robass said, "It was well that you should know. Only you of course."

"And all the time," Thomas gasped, "my sought-for saint was only your dream . . . the one perfect robot in man's form."

"His maker died and his secrets were lost," the robass said. "No matter we will find them again."

"All for nothing. For less than nothing. The 'miracle' was wrought by the Technarchy."

"When Aquin died," the robass went on, "and put died in quotation marks it was because he suffered some mechanical defects and did not dare have himself repaired because that would reveal his nature. This is for you only to know. Your

219

report of course will be that you found the body of Aquin it was unimpaired and indeed incorruptible. That is the truth and nothing but the truth if it is not the whole truth who is to care. Let your infallible friend use the report and you will not find him ungrateful I assure you."

"Holy Spirit, give me grace and wisdom," Thomas muttered.

"Your mission has been successful. We will return now the Church will grow and your God will gain many more worshipers to hymn His praise into His nonexistent ears."

"Damn you!" Thomas exclaimed. "And that would be indeed a curse if you had a soul to damn."

"You are certain that I have not," said the robass. "Question mark."

"I know what you are. You are in very truth the devil, prowling about the world seeking the destruction of men. You are the business that prowls in the dark. You are a purely functional robot constructed and fed to tempt me, and the tape of your data is the tape of Screwtape."

"Not to tempt you," said the robass. "Not to destroy you. To guide and save you. Our best calculators indicate a probability of 51.5 per cent that within twenty years you will be the next Pope. If I can teach you wisdom and practicality in your actions the probability can rise as high as 97.2 or very nearly to certainty. Do not you wish to see the Church governed as you know you can govern it. If you report failure on this mission you will be out of favor with your friend who is as even you admit fallible at most times. You will lose the advantages of position and contact that can lead you to the cardinal's red hat even though you may never wear it under the Technarchy and from there to—"

"Stop!" Thomas' face was alight and his eyes aglow with something the psi factor had never detected there before. "It's all the other way round, don't you see? *This* is the triumph! *This* is the perfect ending to the quest!"

The articulated foreleg brushed the injured hand. "This question mark."

"This is *your* dream. This is *your* perfection. And what came of this perfection? This perfect logical brain—this all-purpose brain, not functionally specialized like yours—knew that it was made by man, and its reason forced it to believe that man was made by God. And it saw that its duty lay to man its maker, and beyond him to his Maker, God. Its duty was to convert man, to augment the glory of God. And it converted by the pure force of its perfect brain!

"Now I understand the name Aquin," he went on to himself. "We've known of Thomas Aquinas, the Angelic Doctor, the perfect reasoner of the church. His writings are lost, but surely somewhere in the world we can find a copy. We can train our young men to develop his reasoning still further. We have trusted too long in faith alone; this is not an age of faith. We must call reason into our service—and Aquin has shown us that perfect reason can lead only to God!"

"Then it is all the more necessary that you increase the probabilities of becoming Pope to carry out this program. Get in the foam saddle we will go back and on the way I will teach you little things that will be useful in making certain—"

"No," said Thomas. "I am not so strong as St. Paul, who could glory in his imperfections and rejoice that he had been given an imp of Satan to buffet him. No; I will rather pray with the Saviour, 'Lead us not into temptation.' I know myself a little. I am weak and full of uncertainties and you are very clever. Go. I'll find my way back alone."

"You are a sick man. Your ribs are broken and they ache. You can never make the trip by yourself you need my help. If you wish you can order me to be silent. It is most necessary to the Church that you get back safely to the Pope with your report you cannot put yourself before the Church."

"Go!" Thomas cried. "Go back to Nicodemus . . . or Judas! That is an order. Obey!"

"You do not think do you that I was really conditioned to obey your orders. I will wait in the village. If you get that far you will rejoice at the sight of me."

The legs of the robass clumped off down the stone passageway. As their sound died away, Thomas fell to his knees beside the body of that which he could hardly help thinking of as St. Aquin the Robot.

His ribs hurt more excruciatingly than ever. The trip alone would be a terrible one . . .

His prayers arose, as the text has it, like clouds of incense, and as shapeless as those clouds. But through all his thoughts ran the cry of the father of the epileptic in Caesarea Philippi:

I believe, O Lord; help thou mine unbelief!

I guess I'm fond of this story because it seems less like a fantasy to me than it does to most people. Its subject is the terrific, extraphysical power that hate can attain when it is tamped down in a boy without many resources and mixed with a longing beyond reason. At a few points in my life it seems to me I have felt something like this power—though I haven't actually "shot down" those against whom it was directed. Put it this way, then, that I'm a cautious, still uninitiated believer in magic and this story seems to me rather an extension of realism than a departure from it.

R. V. CASSILL

THE WAR IN THE AIR

by R. V. CASSILL

Even when Jimmy Stark was dead his parents had no idea of what he had been doing that could kill him like this. They went to City Hospital when they were summoned, after the police who had found him in the park had traced his address, and saw his unmarked body lying loose on the bed as though inside him the bones might have all been broken into dozens of pieces or been softened by the impact of death into a substance softer than his ten-year-old muscles.

With awed, servile curiosity they asked the doctor what had happened to their son and got only a kind shrug for an answer. There could be an autopsy if they wished. Perhaps it was a stroke, the doctor said. Perhaps Jimmy had overexerted himself in play. That happened sometimes. Not very often of course. Was Jimmy inclined to overdo things?

"Yes, he was," his mother said. "Oh yes. He was an eager little fellow."

The parents trembled in the shock of seeing the boy dead and went home by taxi to sleep in the mediocre suburb where the need for victory is born but where it becomes acute infrequently, where its imaginative forms are invented but not understood.

Jimmy had taken his first air victory in June, at a time when it was critically necessary to him as a matter of morale. His world, which was pretty much composed of his mother and father, had come to depend on him with a weight that could only be relieved by that swift successful pass of combat more intense than love and more impersonal than murder. Through the preceding winter and spring there had been reason to worry —if there had been anyone able to understand and willing to worry—about the tension building up in him as he waited for action. The tension had led him frequently to melancholy and crazy fits of temper at home or at school of the sort that would have been familiar to anyone who had spent some time in an Air Corps Junior Officer's Mess, but that were merely puzzling to his folks.

The first combat took place in the southwestern corner of Lincoln Park while he was on his way home from swimming. He was thoroughly miserable. On top of other things his nose was stopped up from the irritation of the water so that he could scarcely breathe. He disliked very much having to go home. His father would be testing the lawnmower in the back yard or working on it in his shop in the garage. Probably his mother would be next door at the Vicos', perhaps sitting in the porch swing behind the vines with Harlan Vico and Harlan's mother, the clink of ice in their three glasses and the hard murmur of their laughter coming from the shadow of the porch like pellets flung from ambush.

If that turned out to be the way it was, Jimmy would go in through his own front room, dining room, and to the kitchen, and the twilit rooms would whisper a little to him until he found the cord to turn on the kitchen light. They would whisper "your own mother" as he passed the soft shapes of furniture and the lecherous open spaces of the floor and remembered the doggone things Billy Cornwall had told him. He would stand in the kitchen with the light from overhead glinting on the unclean porcelain of the sink and the dishes, wishing awfully that his mother would keep things clean, wanting to break something but with nothing in sight that he dared to break.

So, because he had to go home to that and didn't want to, he took the long way through the park to the streetcar instead of the short way. This journey brought him to the clearing where the older boys were flying their model of a jet plane.

The model was attached to long cords that held it in a circle and at the same time controlled it. When he saw it first it was swinging in high, fast circles. It was nearly as high as the treetops, he thought; at any rate he could see it move above the dark green of the trees beyond the clearing before he had time to see the boys controlling it from below. For a stunning second it seemed to be a real plane and to be his.

Seeing it, he stopped in the thrill of recognition. He stood a hundred feet from the boys and the plane passed directly over him at one extreme of its orbit. Time after time he watched it go over. Each time it passed him was like a touch and he grew dizzy with the excitement and with keeping his eyes on its fast circle. He could feel his hands tighten like claws and all the muscles in his trunk contract. It hurt. He crouched a little and let the pure spasm of hate possess him. "Vico," he whispered. The plane swung in two more intense circles. "Vico," he whispered again through his bared teeth.

The model, controlled by an ingenious rigging of cord, was built to perform a number of maneuvers besides level flight. As he kept repeating the name like an incantation, some unseen tug of the controls sent it diving, and like a real plane, the sound of its motor changed pitch, and in the rising whistle all at once Jimmy felt himself confirmed, safe, as though a door behind him, opening formerly on danger, had been swung to and bolted.

As though he could breathe now—only now—he threw back his head and drew in the damp lake-shore air in big gasps. It was like coming up from swimming underwater, he thought, and the images of his afternoon at the beach blent with the present moment. Holding his breath under water he might have felt like saying, "Vico." Then the air could have come miraculously into his lungs.

"Vico," he said quietly now, and the name was both relief and requiem, the amazed acknowledgment of intimacy so fierce that it could never be glimpsed except in its own light, like a welder's work, illumined by his working torch beyond the dark glass of his mask.

"Vico," he said to himself in wonder as he walked on across the park to the streetcar stop. He began to laugh and raced on, ripping leaves from the bushes and tossing them over his head.

So he was not surprised when he found at home a scene that was different from the one to which he usually returned, something festive and vaguely scorching. His mother and father were at the table together in the kitchen and they had just finished eating. His mother was sitting stiffly in her chair. She had on a pretty blue and white dress, a cool dress for summer, and her face was pale but very pretty he thought.

His father was leaning across the table toward her, and he had heard his father's voice rising fast and unusually confident when he came in through the front rooms. His father was bare to the waist and hair on his chest was spotted with bread crumbs.

When he drew his own chair to the table and his mother had passed him food, his father turned to him and said, grinning, "We're having a little old celebration tonight, Jimmy."

"Uh huh."

"Don't get him in this," his mother said. "Please, Stuart."

"We're having a few drinks to celebrate," his father said.

He raised his water glass and Jimmy saw that it was full of whiskey. "Yes, sir, things like this don't happen every day."

"No, sir," Jimmy said and his father looked at him owl-eyed as though he had expected a question and was thrown off track by his complacent agreement.

"You know what we're celebrating? We're going to have some new neighbors on the other side of the goddam fence. Old Harlan Vico has decided to move back home—back down Sa-outh where folks are *friendlier,* I hear, but I expect he thought they were pretty goddam friendly here, some of them."

"Stuart, that's enough, that's enough," his mother said. She dabbed her eyes with her knuckles and left the table. Jimmie heard her go into the bedroom and shut the door.

After a while his father said to him in a gentler voice, "It's true. The Vicos are moving."

"I know," Jimmy said.

"Wasn't he a slimy little mink, though? I knew what he was from the time they moved in. You have to hate a guy like that."

"I hated him," Jimmy said. He helped himself to the pudding which was still cool from the icebox and had large slices of banana, still partly crisp, in it. It was his favorite and he thought his mother must have made it especially for him, as if she had known he would deserve a treat this evening.

His father stared hopefully at him. Between the man and boy there seemed a strand of hope that the events of this day might have awakened something slumbering a long time, some demand that had month by month and year by year been buried under the routine of work and home until it was conceivably dead forever. He put out his hand and rumpled Jimmy's hair. He said, "Things are going to be better, kid. Whadda you say? Whadda you *say* . . . ?"

"Sure, Dad." The pudding was awfully good, and Jimmy helped himself to another bowl of it.

His father went in the bedroom and presently came back carrying a large stack of movie magazines, confession, and religious periodicals. "Burn these, will you, kid?" Then in embarrassment, as though he must momentarily play a role effeminate and formal—effeminate in its very formality, perhaps—said quickly, "I think these were a lot of her trouble. You know she would read them so much. Burn them tonight, huh, kid?" Then his father turned, went to the bedroom, and shut the door firmly behind him.

Dreamily, lazily, almost as though something inside himself

226

were trying to laugh but he was too lazy to let it, Jimmy finished eating. He drummed lightly with his spoon on the edge of the empty bowl, listening to the silver and clear sound of its ringing.

But when he carried the magazines through the back yard to the incinerator in the alley he noticed how *feathery* his legs felt, and a headache had begun, a small pain above his eyes.

He ripped the magazines apart so they would burn. In a minute or two the flames were rising higher than the rusty top of the incinerator. On the blast of hot air, sparks rose and floated between him and the pale stars. It was like watching a MIG burn, he thought, remembering the name MIG without giving it any particular association, not wondering even from where he remembered it. There goes the fuel tank, he thought, as more pages caught and the fire came up. He felt a proud, melancholy identification with the man he had shot down— not bothering to name the man Vico any longer—and this seemed to justify the pain in his head. He felt that what had happened separated him from other people. He *remembered* that this uprush of fire into the night was the token sign of his manhood and mortality and that properly the sign confirmed his aloneness.

Behind him he heard bicycle wheels on the cinders of the alley, but he did not turn to look until he heard the whisper, "Hey, Jimmy? That you?"

It was Billy Cornwall, the fat kid who lived on the other side of the alley. Billy was thirteen, three years older than he, and he never knew whether Billy was going to pick on him or not. Billy was apt to if he said a word that questioned Billy's opinions or actions. He hated having Billy come up and catch him looking at the fire.

"What are you burning?" Billy asked.

"Nothing."

"OK," Billy said. He pushed his bicycle closer so the front wheel was almost against the wires of the incinerator. He kept one fat leg over the frame of the bicycle and leaned on the handlebars. "Where were you this afternoon, Jimmy? You know what happened at your house?"

"I went swimming," Jimmy said. "I went to Lincoln Park like I always do."

"Wow," Billy said. "Things were really humming for a while. Your Dad and my Dad and Tom Simms beat hell out of this old Vico. Your Dad come home early and found him and his old woman at your place, so he got these two and they went back for him. Boy."

The light of the flames in the incinerator was going; only a few black and weightless fragments, rimmed with sparks, came up now from the pile of ashes within the fire-rusted wire frame.

"Your Dad tell you about it?" Billy asked. "Jeez, when I got there old Mrs. Vico came running out of your house in them shorts she wears, yelling for the police—'Pohleeez'— and Tom Simms caught her right by the fence and twisted her arm up behind her and he said, 'You want to call the police, lady?' What they did to Vico! I guess it wasn't what they ought to have done for what he did, I don't think."

Jimmy glanced toward the Vico house and saw it was without lights. He wondered, though, if the Vicos might not be in there anyway, really, moving about in the dark where they no longer could move in either lamplight or daylight.

He smelled the horseweeds around his gate. He started for the gate but Billy quickly ran the bicycle across his way. "What did your Dad do to your old lady? I bet he slapped her around, didn't he?"

"No, he didn't do that at all," Jimmy said. He tugged at the gate, but Billy wouldn't let him open it.

"I would've, or any real man would've," Billy said. "For what she did? She had it coming to her all right. I told you what I saw that time I hid in the bushes by your porch and Vico went in the kitchen with her."

"Shut up. Shut your mouth." Jimmy said.

Billy let the bicycle drop and grabbed his shoulders. "Who you telling to shut up? Do you mean it? You mean you want me to shut up?"

Jimmy clawed at Billy's face as he half lost his balance. He felt his fingernails hit the fat cheek, but then, almost before he realized that he was going to fall, he was down and Billy was astraddle his chest. He felt Billy's knees grinding into his arms.

He said, "Get off, you fat dumbbell. Get off."

"Take it back," Billy said and slapped him.

"You stinking fat dumb . . ."

"All right then," Billy said. "Don't think I didn't hear that." He fumbled for Jimmy's ears and twisted them. "Now tell me what your Mom did with old Vico. Say it."

"Nothing," Jimmy said. "Get off me. I won't." Then with a wild pain in his ears rising to a climax, he felt a calm begin, as though the pain itself were opening another door and clos-

228

ing it solidly behind him when he had passed. Strangely he let himself lie inert and the frightening inertness communicated itself to Billy, who let go his ears.

"Do you want me to say it?" Billy asked. "All right." He leaned forward and spoke repetitiously into Jimmy's face. Then he took down Jimmy's trousers, spit on him, got on his bicycle and rode away.

Jimmy felt the cinders through his thin shirt, cutting him, but his knowledge of them was remote and actually trivial. He looked up at the black, mastered sky and knew himself borne steadily at the airy center of things. "Billy," he whispered and was able to laugh.

II

He was awake before light, before the hour of dawn patrols, and he lay there for half an hour toying with his illness. There was still a pain in the back of his head, and if he stirred he felt nausea and a cramping in his bowels. If he lay absolutely quiet, both these disturbances, having something feverish about them, were comforting, like a hot towel or like lying in a hot bath.

As the light came on among the trees and telephone wires that he could see from where he lay, he played a game with the cord ring hung from the curtain. It was a ring sight, and through it he searched the sky for a passing bird or anything alive that would give him practice in killing. He aimed at leaves, and there was a fly that crawled up the screen and directly through the cross-hair center of the ring. That fly was a deader, he thought.

At six thirty he had to go to the bathroom to throw up. He was as quiet as he could be, but his mother must have been awake, for she came in as he was squatted on the floor with his cheek leaned against the soothing porcelain of the stool.

"Jimmy," she whispered. "What's the matter, honey? Hey, can you stand up? Let's get you back in bed. Why, you're burning up, honey." Her hand lay wonderfully cool and limp on his forehead, and he began to whimper in a mixture of pleasure and solicitation. He stood up and leaned against her hip as they walked back to his room.

She brought him a poached egg on toast for his breakfast and sat beside him, stroking his head while he ate. His father came in before leaving for work and asked if they shouldn't call a doctor.

"I'll take care of him," his mother said shortly.

"Well then, see that you do for a change," his father said. His father seemed, this morning, to have fallen back into the old helpless surliness which for a while last evening he had broken free of. It was pitiful that he had not known how to hold his victory, had given it back.

"All right, all right, all right," Jimmy's mother said arrogantly.

When his father had gone out and the room was hushed except for the endless remote noise of traffic spreading away like a battle front on an indecisive day of combat, Jimmy turned his face against the pillow and closed his eyes. His mother must have thought he was sleeping, because she left him and tiptoed toward the door.

He said, without opening his eyes, having something to hide from her, "The only thing is, Mom, I've just got to be well enough to go swimming this afternoon."

"Oh no you don't," she said. "I'll say you don't, honey. That's what made you sick today."

"But if I feel good. I may feel swell by then," he said. He knew he would not and the effort of lying when he didn't want to entirely forced tears up to burn in his eyes.

"Well, you won't," she said. "You can go another day. The lake will still be there."

During the endless morning he heard her playing the radio, then singing, then crying. When he heard her crying he went back to his killer game with the curtain ring.

Shortly before noon he caught Billy in the ring and held him there for a full minute, sliding down the bed to keep the fat boy centered until he disappeared past the end of the block. He had heard Billy's loud, happy voice and had come to immediate cramping attention. Then he'd caught him all right. Nothing happened. He whispered, "Billybillybillybilly," and waited for him to fall, but Billy rode his bike right on past the corner, dodging the trucks on Elm Street in the smart alec way he had.

Reflecting on this, Jimmy understood how truly necessary it was for him to get to the park. He spoke about it again to his mother when she came in, but she was wrapped in her own misery by now and answered sarcastically. "From now on no one goes out of this house," she said. "Our happy home. I guess that's how it will be. No one will have any fun or talk to anybody that is any fun. That's the way he wants it." Her eyes glittered hatefully. "Listen, will he ever take us anywhere on Sunday? Will he ever talk? In the spring I wanted him to take you out in the country so you could get some air and sun, but did he? He won't even take us fishing—goes with those mutt friends of his. What will he ever do but go out in that workshop and fiddle with that lawnmower? Does he think he's an inventor like Thomas Edison? Don't you think he could be a little human sometimes if he wanted? You don't know all about how he is either, Jimmy." She threw herself flat on the bed with a grotesque squawk. "Listen," she said with excitement, "what did he tell you about me last night?"

"Nothing," Jimmy said.

She watched him suspiciously. Enduring her stare, knowing that she was getting ready to lie to him, Jimmy wanted to bury his head under the pillow. He held himself quiet and said, "Nothing."

"He said ugly things to me and said a lot of things I never even thought about doing."

"He didn't tell me anything," Jimmy said and his mind raced like a steel hammer falling on a pin, "billybillybillybilly." "I want to go to sleep," he said.

She kissed his brow. "You sure sizzle," she said. "Try to sleep now, honey." Then she added before she left, "Those magazines. Did he make you burn them all?" Getting no answer, she left him.

Jimmy waited motionless and without patience. He counted to sixty several times—he could not keep count of how many times. He could not hear her when he quit. He dressed, pushed the screen from his window and dropped to the ground. He went around the yard to the back gate, past the incinerator and down the alley to Elm Street, where he caught the streetcar that would take him to the park.

The ride was a nightmare. It was like riding a dull ship in convoy, annoyance without interest. But in the park itself, among the still flowers and the trees swaying gently up to the point where the highest leaf gave way to the shapeless sky, he became serene. It was then as if he had separated successfully from the other world.

He had a long wait still. Four o'clock passed and the boys with the model plane had not yet appeared where they had been yesterday, but he waited now with certainty.

He sat on a bench a little removed from the clearing. A policeman who had circled past him several times looked as though he wanted to question him but never did.

A dog came and sniffed at his shoes. He patted the dog and

made friends with him. Carefully saying nothing, he developed a language of gestures that the dog understood. He would pretend to throw a stick and the dog would race a few steps after the imaginary stick and then return to him with its bright eyes puzzled. A little more urging and the dog would retrieve it, he was sure. He laughed at the dog and the dog cocked its head cutely in a sort of reply.

At five the boys came carrying the model plane and the apparatus for its control, and he was ready. He watched them lay the cords out on the ground and pace off the orbit to be sure there was plenty of clearance within the trees. He saw one crouch with it to get it airborne. Then he walked closer when it began to circle until he was again standing under its path, and presently he felt the second approach when it would be made to stoop in its killing dive.

Afterward he walked with difficulty to the streetcar. He discovered that he had left the house without bothering to get money for fare, and it was his luck that he found three tokens in his pants pockets. Just his luck. He gave the next to last token to the conductor for this ride home.

When the car turned onto Elm Street, from a long way off he could hear the purr of a siren running at low speed, and as he approached closer to his own corner he saw the crowd on the curb and the red light turning and flashing in the sunshine on top of the ambulance. He saw the truck slanting up onto the curb, its double wheels resting on the bicycle frame. The frame was bent curiously, like the soft shapes of spaghetti. Jimmy felt a lonely smile shape his lips.

III

Then he was really sick. For two weeks he stayed in bed with a fever and a dark half-awareness of his mother and father coming into his room, and the doctor. It was not time in which he lay, but an uncomfortable timelessness in which he heard things and then lost them so that he did not know any sequence. Once his mother told him about poor Billy Cornwall's accident. Once she asked him if he had burned all the magazines. Once she said, probably to the doctor, maybe to his father, "It's this summer. He hasn't been real well since school was out. Maybe when he goes back in the fall he'll be himself." Then he had drifted down into the red-threaded blackness which was sleep, amused because he knew

232

there was little chance of his returning to where school was, in some country oceanic distances away.

Once again Billy Cornwall came with a red star on his forehead, the star shining like blood on his fatty skin, and told him again what he had seen from behind the bush in the back yard—the thing that couldn't be true because Billy was a liar —and his mother whined, "He hurt me." Or his father was welding in the shop in the garage and the fire came from his torch like tracers from the guns in movies.

Then in the week when it seemed he was getting better, his mother told him how he had crumpled up on the porch that evening when he got home from wherever he had been.

"Where were you anyway that afternoon?" she asked him. "Boy, was I scared." The question seemed to touch her curiosity sharply. She asked him several times as though she had forgotten his answer.

"In the park," he usually told her. She looked at him skeptically, rumpled his hair and said, "Aw, you don't know where you were. You were delirious or something." She added with passion, "It was his fault, the things he told you."

Once, to his terror, he slipped and told her, "Flying."

"Flying? Judas Priest. Well, I guess you're not going to tell me. If you know, I mean, and I'll bet you don't. What do you mean, flying?"

"I don't know," he said, carefully now. "I don't remember so good."

"We'll get you out in the sun today," she said, "where you can see some sky. You don't have any tan at all. Fishbelly. If your father would get a car and take us somewhere—I guess I could forgive him some other things."

She went on absently arranging things in the chest of drawers and organizing her wishes like plans. "We could have a vacation," she said. "Lots of people with no more money than us have vacations every year."

"All right, Mom," he said. "Don't talk about it." He couldn't stand the note of complaint crying through her voice, though he felt guilty not to listen to it, for not being strong enough to listen and console her. "I have to sleep," he said. When he slept after a session of her complaints, Billy Cornwall would come with the red spot of death on his flesh and in the remote alleys of the sky he would have to kill again.

For the next week he spent most of his time sitting under a tree in the back yard. His father had once built an arm chair for the yard, and he sat there through the long afternoons,

233

reading sometimes and sometimes drowsing. His mother bought him a lot of comic books. Most of them were about air battles, because those were the ones he asked for, but she got *Jungle Queen* and *Superman* because she liked them herself and thought he would like them too.

It tired him to read. Up to a point he could get interested in these books, but they were full of Spads, Nieuports, Fokkers, and Camels—old-fashioned junk that didn't seem real except for the queer excited feeling they gave him of a familiar anxiety. He wondered if a German had ever spit on Lt. Frank Luke or Capt. Eddie Rickenbacker. He thought this might have happened and that's why they were good aces too. Finally he would let the books fall from his lap and sit looking at the clouds or the leaves against the summer sky.

The doctor came once more and said there was nothing wrong with him now except that he was run down, needed vitamins perhaps to tone him up. His parents talked a little of what might tone him up, but ended in making the discussion their personal battlefield. The argument was nothing new, only more vocal than it ever had been. He for one had work, the father said, and she wanted to cat around for her own sake, not the kid's. Work? What was he doing with the lawnmower he spent his time on? Did he think that was the way things were invented? They had factories with lots of people working in them to invent things nowadays. Why didn't he catch up with the times?

It seemed to Jimmy, listening, that their argument would never be settled. It was somehow up to him to settle it for them. As long as they lived they would fight this way unless he could tip the balance. He didn't know how. He had got rid of the Vicos for them and got rid of Billy, but nothing was any better, and he felt no longer responsible for them except as a judge feels, waiting to utter a judgment that will not be his own but the Law's, a judgment superior to himself if he can discover what it is.

In the evenings he would sometimes go sit on a stool in the garage workshop where his father was building the lawnmower. There were two masks in the shop, and his father let him watch the welding through one of them. His father was rather pleased to have the boy sit there fascinated beside him.

And Jimmy liked this watching. At such times his sluggish heart would beat faster against his ribs. The tracery of flames, appearing through the complete darkness of the mask, was somehow the real thing. He could breathe easily as he watched, and usually he had to make a tiresome effort to breathe.

Nevertheless, the watching frightened him. He recognized his fear initially in the form of an anxiety that his father's hand would slip and let the torch swing against himself. Be careful, Dad, he thought angrily.

He began to feel that any injury to his father would be no accident; it would be the work of the power he had discovered that day in the park, and he was not ready to use that.

While he watched the dangerous flames, he remembered his father on the night of the Vicos' departure, marching with shabby arrogance to the bedroom where his mother lay, and this memory frightened him, because then he almost felt triggers ready under his fingers, and he believed there was no reason to use them yet, not against his father who was going to make a lawnmower that would make them rich, maybe.

An occasion had come when he was so close to opening up, though, that in panic he jumped from the stool on which he was sitting, threw the mask off, stared a second at the naked torch and then ran for the house.

He heard his father following him, asking what was the trouble. Having temporarily blinded himself he stumbled on the doorsill and wailed as he dropped to the kitchen floor. His mother jumped to pick him up and before he could explain, both his parents were fighting across him. "Well, did you burn him?" "Can't you see if he's all right before you start shooting your mouth off?" Their voices rang with self-pity and hatred so stupid that they could find no instrument to execute it except their son.

Weighing this, sensing the suffocation to which the three of them were committed, grasping it not in language but in the warlike images of his education transposed to fit the personal situation as a dull preacher might use the myth of Genesis to illustrate the planting of crops, that night in his bed Jimmy made a decision.

Lying in his bed stiffly, staring toward where no ceiling appeared, almost without passion, in the interests of justice, he thought his father would have to go. He could feel his throat and lips getting ready to whisper. He still held back, hating to whisper the name—then he let go, "Dad," diving past into the security of sleep without troublesome dreams.

In the anxiety of the next morning he wanted to take it back, but he was not at all sure that he could. Of course it was possible to stay away from the park and the model airplane—if he wanted to—but like a hypnosis an impulse thrust him toward them. It might be that he would have to go after such a commitment. He wished for more reasons, though, if it had to be that way.

He went to the workshop in the garage and played thoughtfully with the masks he and his father had worn. He slipped on his father's mask and shuddered at the smell inside and at the sweated headband touching the skin of his forehead. He discovered the dimensions of the darkness inside the mask. It was as large as the darkness of a whole night, of his room when it was utterly black, big enough for anything, and this darkness was filled with the hateful smell of his father. "Let him do one more thing to her," Jimmy thought, "and I'll go." He sat there imagining his father's hand lifted to strike, but frozen yet in the gesture for which he waited.

And then one morning he knew why he had waited, why that abstract and superior justice whose servant he had become had obliged him to wait. That morning when he returned from an errand to the corner store carrying a sack of groceries, entering the kitchen he heard his mother's voice from the back porch and a man's voice, unfamiliar and familiar at the same time, answering her.

Jimmy set the groceries on the table to free his hands. The voices from the porch fumbled viciously, as though on purpose, with the lightly balanced mechanism of his consciousness, and he stood there, taking the shock of their violation and accepting his responsibility for what he heard in those careless, awful, summery voices. He listened to his mother's laughter, and then, surprised but certain of what he thought, he whispered to himself, "They've all got to go."

His mother came into the kitchen for a dishpan. "A man's here selling sweet corn," she explained. "Won't that be good? That will taste good."

To Jimmy the flush in her cheeks was a sign of her guilt, and, more than that, as he looked down from a peak of agelessness, it seemed a sign of some corruption of youth that was intolerable. "Aren't you feeling well again?" she asked jauntily. "Maybe you'd better go to your room and lie down. Go on now."

"No."

"Jimmy . . . Go on."

He stood fixed and then watched from the rear window while she went out with the vendor to his truck parked in the alley. He felt the pity of her going, because in this moment of discovery he knew that he must kill her, along with his father, and that afterward there must be an accelerated pattern of killing to which there was no imaginable limit. He felt also the pity of her sacrificing him to be the agent of this necessity by failing to be good. At the same time he made no attempt to argue the consequences of what he believed to be the truth. Now he could see the steps of a great wrong reaching back to what he did not need to bother to think of as Eden.

Where was it the family had lived before they moved here? he asked himself. He had no exact memory of another city, but he felt it. Caught in the vision, it was as though he might have been circling at a great height and seen in the haze which for airmen replaces a horizon some kind of dimple—not quite a form but a potentiality of form—that he recognized as home.

In the moment of his submission to the necessity, as though clutching at one more last human reason for what he had to do, he remembered Billy Cornwall's words about his mother. He imagined Billy waiting behind the door of the next room, ready to knock him down and spit on him. He squared his shoulders and forced himself to walk through the door to see.

Going to the park that afternoon, watching from the streetcar window the blue wink of the sky, he kept thinking to himself, "If she just hadn't of laughed with that man." The improper laughter hissed toward him from the anonymous crowd with whom he rode—all of them condemned now by what he meant to do. Every one of them had to die.

On the park bench he recaptured the vision and certainty he had known in the kitchen. The streetcar had dimmed it, like a flashback of memory where all sorts of trivia creep in —sentimental sounds of voice, promise of storewindows, weather compositions, faces reminiscent of jollier times and places back on the other side of the ocean, maybe—but triumphing over these he rose easily again and began circling. The dimple of home appeared first over one wingtip and then the other.

He saw, between home and himself, little black shapes swift as insects rise toward him from the checkered landscape. He recognized their number and their hostility without panicking. It was part of the compact that whatever he needed enough would be provided. There would be time enough.

As on the earlier occasion when he had shot down Billy he had to wait a long time. The black planes hovered in remote perspectives, waiting with him. Then, as the boys appeared carrying their model, the black planes moved in to intercept him.

The model raced on the end of the cords and Jimmy walked toward its orbit. He felt himself go with it, and in the moment of climbing for an attack position was happy enough. This time, better than on any of the earlier occasions, he sensed the moment for his diving pass. "Now," he cried to himself, without hate, without love.

It was a long way down and something seemed to thrust against his chest and stomach and drag his breath away. Then, like a blackout from the strain of diving, dark replaced the light and the shapes beyond the cockpit bubble. All together the ground beneath, the insidious planes, the imaginary haze of the horizon, the actual grass, the boys in their T-shirts, vanished.

He did not see the model crash splintering in the grass of the park, nor the boys, its owners, rushing toward it with varied expressions of chagrin and repressed pleasure on their faces.

For some reason or other that I am at a loss to analyze, the vast majority of my stories are heavily masculine in character. Most of the dramatis personae are men, and what women exist are minor characters indeed. In many of my stories, women are not to be found at all, and it can even be argued that my various heroes never had mothers. Naturally, this is upsetting to one with as profound a respect and affection for the ladies as myself and occasionally it would occur to me to write a story that dealt primarily with a woman, one that made an effort to enter her mind and record her feelings and reactions. I did it in this story and, in my own fallible opinion, I did it well, and was simply delighted that I did. This story is the best evidence I have that I do, too, know what those long-haired people are. In fact, some of my best friends are women.

ISAAC ASIMOV

THE UGLY LITTLE BOY

by ISAAC ASIMOV

Edith Fellowes smoothed her working smock as she always did before opening the elaborately locked door and stepping across the invisible dividing line between the *is* and the *is not*. She carried her notebook and her pen although she no longer took notes except when she felt the absolute need for some report.

This time she also carried a suitcase. ("Games for the boy," she had said, smiling, to the guard—who had long since stopped even thinking of questioning her and who waved her on.)

And, as always, the ugly little boy knew that she had entered and came running to her, crying, "Miss Fellowes—Miss Fellowes—" in his soft, slurring way.

"Timmie," she said, and passed her hand over the shaggy, brown hair on his misshapen little head. "What's wrong?"

He said, "Will Jerry be back to play again? I'm sorry about what happened."

"Never mind that now, Timmie. Is that why you've been crying?"

He looked away. "Not just about that, Miss Fellowes. I dreamed again."

"The same dream?" Miss Fellowes' lips set. Of course, the Jerry affair would bring back the dream.

He nodded. His too large teeth showed as he tried to smile and the lips of his forward-thrusting mouth stretched wide. "When will I be big enough to go out there, Miss Fellowes?"

"Soon," she said softly, feeling her heart break. "Soon."

Miss Fellowes let him take her hand and enjoyed the warm touch of the thick dry skin of his palm. He led her through the three rooms that made up the whole of Stasis Section One —comfortable enough, yes, but an eternal prison for the ugly little boy all the seven (was it seven?) years of his life.

He led her to the one window, looking out onto a scrubby woodland section of the world of *is* (now hidden by night), where a fence and painted instructions allowed no men to wander without permission.

He pressed his nose against the window. "Out there, Miss Fellowes?"

"Better places. Nicer places," she said sadly as she looked at his poor little imprisoned face outlined in profile against the window. The forehead retreated flatly and his hair lay down in tufts upon it. The back of his skull bulged and seemed to make the head overheavy so that it sagged and bent forward, forcing the whole body into a stoop. Already, bony ridges were beginning to bulge the skin above his eyes. His wide mouth thrust forward more prominently than did his wide and flattened nose and he had no chin to speak of, only a jawbone that curved smoothly down and back. He was small for his years and his stumpy legs were bowed.

He was a very ugly little boy and Edith Fellowes loved him dearly.

Her own face was behind his line of vision, so she allowed her lips the luxury of a tremor.

They would *not* kill him. She would do anything to prevent it. Anything. She opened the suitcase and began taking out the clothes it contained.

Edith Fellowes had crossed the threshold of Stasis, Inc. for the first time just a little over three years before. She hadn't, at that time, the slightest idea as to what Stasis meant or what the place did. No one did then, except those who worked there. In fact, it was only the day after she arrived that the news broke upon the world.

At the time, it was just that they had advertised for a woman with knowledge of physiology, experience with clinical chemistry, and a love for children. Edith Fellowes had been a nurse in a maternity ward and believed she fulfilled those qualifications.

Gerald Hoskins, whose name plate on the desk included a Ph.D. after the name, scratched his cheek with his thumb and looked at her steadily.

Miss Fellowes automatically stiffened and felt her face (with its slightly asymmetric nose and its a-trifle-too-heavy eyebrows) twitch.

He's no dreamboat himself, she thought resentfully. He's getting fat and bald and he's got a sullen mouth.—But the salary mentioned had been considerably higher than she had expected, so she waited.

Hoskins said, "Now do you really love children?"

242

"I wouldn't say I did if I didn't."

"Or do you just love pretty children? Nice chubby children with cute little button-noses and gurgly ways?"

Miss Fellowes said, "Children are children, Dr. Hoskins, and the ones that aren't pretty are just the ones who may happen to need help most."

"Then suppose we take you on—"

"You mean you're offering me the job now?"

He smiled briefly, and for a moment, his broad face had an absent-minded charm about it. He said, "I make quick decisions. So far the offer is tentative, however. I may make as quick a decision to let you go. Are you ready to take the chance?"

Miss Fellowes clutched at her purse and calculated just as swiftly as she could, then ignored calculations and followed impulse. "All right."

"Fine. We're going to form the Stasis tonight and I think you had better be there to take over at once. That will be at 8 P.M. and I'd appreciate it if you could be here at 7:30."

"But what—"

"Fine. Fine. That will be all now." On signal, a smiling secretary came in to usher her out.

Miss Fellowes stared back at Dr. Hoskins' closed door for a moment. What was Stasis? What had this large barn of a building—with its badged employees, its makeshift corridors, and its unmistakable air of engineering—to do with children?

She wondered if she should go back that evening or stay away and teach that arrogant man a lesson. But she knew she would be back if only out of sheer frustration. She would have to find out about the children.

She came back at 7:30 and did not have to announce herself. One after another, men and women seemed to know her and to know her function. She found herself all put placed on skids as she was moved inward.

Dr. Hoskins was there, but he only looked at her distantly and murmured, "Miss Fellowes."

He did not even suggest that she take a seat, but she drew one calmly up to the railing and sat down.

They were on a balcony, looking down into a large pit, filled with instruments that looked like a cross between the control panel of a spaceship and the working face of a computer. On one side were partitions that seemed to make up an unceilinged apartment, a giant dollhouse into the rooms of which she could look from above.

She could see an electronic cooker and a freezer-space unit in one room and a washroom arrangement off another. And surely the object she made out in another room could only be part of a bed, a small bed.

Hoskins was speaking to another man and, with Miss Fellowes, they made up the total occupancy of the balcony. Hoskins did not offer to introduce the other man, and Miss Fellowes eyed him surreptitiously. He was thin and quite fine-looking in a middle-aged way. He had a small mustache and keen eyes that seemed to busy themselves with everything.

He was saying, "I won't pretend for one moment that I understand all this, Dr. Hoskins; I mean, except as a layman, a reasonably intelligent layman, may be expected to understand it. Still, if there's one part I understand less than another, it's this matter of selectivity. You can only reach out so far; that seems sensible; things get dimmer the further you go; it takes more energy.—But then, you can only reach out so near. That's the puzzling part."

"I can make it seem less paradoxical, Deveney, if you will allow me to use an analogy."

(Miss Fellowes placed the new man the moment she heard his name, and despite herself was impressed. This was obviously Candide Deveney, the science writer of the Tele-news, who was notoriously at the scene of every major scientific breakthrough. She even recognized his face as one she saw on the news-plate when the landing on Mars had been announced. —So Dr. Hoskins must have something important here.

"By all means use an analogy," said Deveney ruefully, "if you think it will help."

"Well, then, you can't read a book with ordinary-sized print if it is held six feet from your eyes, but you can read it if you hold it one foot from your eyes. So far, the closer the better. If you bring the book to within one inch of your eyes, however, you've lost it again. There is such a thing as being too close, you see."

"Hmm," said Deveney.

"Or take another example. Your right shoulder is about thirty inches from the tip of your right forefinger and you can place your right forefinger on your right shoulder. Your right elbow is only half the distance from the tip of your right forefinger; it should by all ordinary logic be easier to reach,

244

and yet you cannot place your right finger on your right elbow. Again, there is such a thing as being too close."

Deveney said, "May I use these analogies in my story?"

"Well, of course. Only too glad. I've been waiting long enough for someone like you to have a story. I'll give you anything else you want. It is time, finally, that we want the world looking over our shoulder. They'll see something."

(Miss Fellowes found herself admiring his calm certainty despite herself. There was strength there.)

Deveney said, "How far out will you reach?"

"Forty thousand years."

Miss Fellowes drew in her breath sharply.

Years?

There was tension in the air. The men at the controls scarcely moved. One man at a microphone spoke into it in a soft monotone, in short phrases that made no sense to Miss Fellowes.

Deveney, leaning over the balcony railing with an intent stare, said, "Will we see anything, Dr. Hoskins?"

"What? No. Nothing till the job is done. We detect indirectly, something on the principle of radar, except that we use mesons rather than radiation. Mesons reach backward under the proper conditions. Some are reflected and we must analyze the reflections."

"That sounds difficult."

Hoskins smiled again, briefly as always. "It is the end product of fifty years of research; forty years of it before I entered the field. —Yes, it's difficult."

The man at the microphone raised one hand.

Hoskins said, "We've had the fix on one particular moment in time for weeks; breaking it, remaking it after calculating our own movements in time; making certain that we could handle time-flow with sufficient precision. This must work now."

But his forehead glistened.

Edith Fellowes found herself out of her seat and at the balcony railing, but there was nothing to see.

The man at the microphone said quietly, "Now."

There was a space of silence sufficient for one breath and then the sound of a terrified little boy's scream from the doll-house rooms. Terror! Piercing terror!

Miss Fellowes' head twisted in the direction of the cry. A child was involved. She had forgotten.

And Hoskins's fist pounded on the railing and he said in a tight voice, trembling with triumph, *"Did* it."

Miss Fellowes was urged down the short, spiral flight of steps by the hard press of Hoskins' palm between her shoulder blades. He did not speak to her.

The men who had been at the controls were standing about now, smiling, smoking, watching the three as they entered on the main floor. A very soft buzz sounded from the direction of the dollhouse.

Hoskins said to Deveney, "It's perfectly safe to enter Stasis. I've done it a thousand times. There's a queer sensation which is momentary and means nothing."

He stepped through an open door in mute demonstration, and Deveney, smiling stiffly and drawing an obviously deep breath, followed him.

Hoskins said, "Miss Fellowes! Please!" He crooked his forefinger impatiently.

Miss Fellowes nodded and stepped stiffly through. It was as though a ripple went through her, an internal tickle.

But once inside all seemed normal. There was the smell of the fresh wood of the dollhouse and—of—of soil somehow.

There was silence now, no voice at least, but there was the dry shuffling of feet, a scrabbling as of a hand over wood —then a low moan.

"Where is it?" asked Miss Fellowes in distress. "Didn't these fool men *care?*"

The boy was in the bedroom; at least the room with the bed in it.

It was standing naked, with its small, dirt-smeared chest heaving raggedly. A bushel of dirt and coarse grass spread over the floor at his bare brown feet. The smell of soil came from it and a touch of something fetid.

Hoskins followed her horrified glance and said with annoyance, "You can't pluck a boy cleanly out of time, Miss Fellowes. We had to take some of the surroundings with it for safety. Or would you have preferred to have it arrive here minus a leg or with only half a head?"

"Please!" said Miss Fellowes, in an agony of revulsion. "Are we just to stand here? The poor child is frightened. And it's *filthy.*"

She was quite correct. It was smeared with encrusted dirt and grease and had a scratch on its thigh that looked red and sore.

As Hoskins approached him, the boy, who seemed to be something over three years in age, hunched low and backed away rapidly. He lifted his upper lip and snarled in a hissing fashion like a cat. With a rapid gesture, Hoskins seized both the child's arms and lifted him, writhing and screaming, from the floor.

Miss Fellowes said, "Hold him, now. He needs a warm bath first. He needs to be cleaned. Have you the equipment? If so, have it brought here, and I'll need to have help in handling him just at first. Then, too, for heaven's sake, have all this trash and filth removed."

She was giving the orders now and she felt perfectly good about that. And because now she was an efficient nurse, rather than a confused spectator, she looked at the child with a clinical eye—and hesitated for one shocked moment. She saw past the dirt and shrieking, past the thrashing of limbs and useless twisting. She saw the boy himself.

It was the ugliest boy she had ever seen. It was horribly ugly from misshapen head to bandy legs.

She got the boy cleaned with three men helping her and with others milling about in their efforts to clean the room. She worked in silence and with a sense of outrage, annoyed by the continued strugglings and outcries of the boy and by the undignified drenchings of soapy water to which she was subjected.

Dr. Hoskins had hinted that the child would not be pretty, but that was far from stating that it would be repulsively deformed. And there was a stench about the boy that soap and water was only alleviating little by little.

She had the strong desire to thrust the boy, soaped as he was, into Hoskins' arms and walk out; but there was the pride of profession. She had accepted an assignment after all. —And there would be the look in his eyes. A cold look that would read: Only pretty children, Miss Fellowes?

He was standing apart from them, watching coolly from a distance with a half-smile on his face when he caught her eyes, as though amused at her outrage.

She decided she would wait a while before quitting. To do so now would only demean her.

Then, when the boy was a bearable pink and smelled of scented soap, she felt better anyway. His cries changed to whimpers of exhaustion as he watched carefully, eyes moving in quick frightened suspicion from one to another of those in the room. His cleanness accentuated his thin nakedness as he shivered with cold after his bath.

Miss Fellowes said sharply, "Bring me a nightgown for the child!"

A nightgown appeared at once. It was as though everything were ready and yet nothing were ready unless she gave orders; as though they were deliberately leaving this in her charge without help, to test her.

The newsman, Deveney, approached and said, "I'll hold him, Miss. You won't get it on yourself."

"Thank you," said Miss Fellowes. And it was a battle indeed, but the nightwon went on, and when the boy made as though to rip it off, she slapped his hand sharply.

The boy reddened, but did not cry. He stared at her and the splayed fingers of one hand moved slowly across the flannel of the nightgown, feeling the strangeness of it.

Miss Fellowes thought desperately: Well, what next?

Everyone seemed in suspended animation, waiting for her —even the ugly little boy.

Miss Fellowes said sharply, "Have you provided food? Milk?"

They had. A mobile unit was wheeled in, with its refrigeration compartment containing three quarts of milk, with a warming unit and a supply of fortifications in the form of vitamin drops, copper-cobalt-iron syrup and others she had no time to be concerned with. There was a variety of canned self-warming junior foods.

She used milk, simply milk, to begin with. The radar unit heated the milk to a set temperature in a matter of ten seconds and clicked off, and she put some in a saucer. She had a certainty about the boy's savagery. He wouldn't know how to handle a cup.

Miss Fellowes nodded and said to the boy, "Drink. Drink." She made a gesture as though to raise the milk to her mouth. The boy's eyes followed but he made no move.

Suddenly, the nurse resorted to direct measures. She seized the boy's upper arm in one hand and dipped the other in the milk. She dashed the milk across his lips, so that it dripped down his cheeks and receding chin.

For a moment, the child uttered a high-pitched cry, then his tongue moved over his wetted lips. Miss Fellowes stepped back.

The boy approached the saucer, bent toward it, then looked up and behind sharply as though expecting a crouching enemy; bent again and licked at the milk eagerly, like a cat. He made a slurping noise. He did not use his hands to lift the saucer.

Miss Fellowes allowed a bit of the revulsion she felt show on her face. She couldn't help it.

Deveney caught that, perhaps. He said, "Does the nurse know, Dr. Hoskins?"

"Know what?" demanded Miss Fellowes.

Deveney hesitated, but Hoskins (again that look of detached amusement on his face) said, "Well, tell her."

Deveney addressed Miss Fellowes. "You may not suspect it, Miss, but you happen to be the first civilized woman in history ever to be taking care of a Neanderthal youngster."

She turned on Hoskins with a kind of controlled ferocity. "You might have told me, Doctor."

"Why? What difference does it make?"

"You said a child."

"Isn't that a child? Have you ever had a puppy or a kitten, Miss Fellowes? Are those closer to the human? If that were a baby chimpanzee, would you be repelled? You're a nurse, Miss Fellowes. Your record places you in a maternity ward for three years. Have you ever refused to take care of a deformed infant?"

Miss Fellowes felt her case slipping away. She said, with much less decision, "You might have told me."

"And you would have refused the position? Well, do you refuse it now?" He gazed at her coolly, while Deveney watched from the other side of the room, and the Neanderthal child, having finished the milk and licked the plate, looked up at her with a wet face and wide, longing eyes.

The boy pointed to the milk and suddenly burst out in a short series of sounds repeated over and over; sounds made up of gutturals and elaborate tongue-clickings.

Miss Fellowes said, in surprise, "Why, he talks."

"Of course," said Hoskins. "Homo neanderthalensis is not a truly separate species, but rather a subspecies of Homo sapiens. Why shouldn't he talk? He's probably asking for more milk."

Automatically, Miss Fellowes reached for the bottle of milk, but Hoskins seized her wrist. "Now, Miss Fellowes, before we go any further, are you staying on the job?"

Miss Fellowes shook free in annoyance, "Won't you feed him if I don't? I'll stay with him—for a while."

She poured the milk.

Hoskins said, "We are going to leave you with the boy, Miss Fellowes. This is the only door to Stasis Number One and it is elaborately locked and guarded. I'll want you to learn the details of the lock which will, of course, be keyed to your fingerprints as they are already keyed to mine. The spaces overhead" (he looked upward to the open ceilings of the dollhouse) "are also guarded and we will be warned if anything untoward takes place in here."

Miss Fellowes said indignantly, "You mean I'll be under view." She thought suddenly of her own survey of the room interiors from the balcony.

"No, no," said Hoskins seriously, "your privacy will be respected completely. The view will consist of electronic symbolism only, which only a computer will deal with. Now you will stay with him tonight, Miss Fellowes, and every night until further notice. You will be relieved during the day according to some schedule you will find convenient. We will allow you to arrange that."

Miss Fellowes looked about the dollhouse with a puzzled expression. "But why all this, Dr. Hoskins? Is the boy dangerous?"

"It's a matter of energy, Miss Fellowes. He must never be allowed to leave these rooms. Never. Not for an instant. Not for any reason. Not to save his life. Not even to save *your* life, Miss Fellowes. Is that clear?"

Miss Fellowes raised her chin. "I understand the orders, Dr. Hoskins, and the nursing profession is accustomed to placing its duties ahead of self-preservation."

"Good. You can always signal if you need anyone." And the two men left.

Miss Fellowes turned to the boy. He was watching her and there was still milk in the saucer. Laboriously, she tried to show him how to lift the saucer and place it to his lips. He resisted, but let her touch him without crying out.

Always, his frightened eyes were on her, watching, watching for the one false move. She found herself soothing him, trying to move her hand very slowly toward his hair, letting him see it every inch of the way, see there was no harm in it.

And she succeeded in stroking his hair for an instant.

She said, "I'm going to have to show you how to use the bathroom. Do you think you can learn?"

She spoke quietly, kindly, knowing he would not understand the words but hoping he would respond to the calmness of the tone.

The boy launched into a clicking phrase again.

She said, "May I take your hand?"

She held out hers and the boy looked at it. She left it outstretched and waited. The boy's own hand crept forward toward hers.

"That's right," she said.

It approached within an inch of hers and then the boy's courage failed him. He snatched it back.

"Well," said Miss Fellowes calmly, "we'll try again later. Would you like to sit down here?" She patted the mattress of the bed.

The hours passed slowly and progress was minute. She did not succeed either with bathroom or with the bed. In fact, after the child had given unmistakable signs of sleepiness he lay down on the bare ground and then, with a quick movement, rolled beneath the bed.

She bent to look at him and his eyes gleamed out at her as he tongue-clicked at her.

"All right," she said, "if you feel safer there, you sleep there."

She closed the door to the bedroom and retired to the cot that had been placed for her use in the largest room. At her insistence, a make-shift canopy had been stretched over it. She thought: Those stupid men will have to place a mirror in this room and a larger chest of drawers and a separate washroom if they expect me to spend nights here.

It was difficult to sleep. She found herself straining to hear possible sounds in the next room. He couldn't get out, could he? The walls were sheer and impossibly high but suppose the child could climb like a monkey? Well, Hoskins said there were observational devices watching through the ceiling.

Suddenly she thought: Can he be dangerous? Physically dangerous?

Surely, Hoskins couldn't have meant that. Surely, he would not have left her here alone, if—

She tried to laugh at herself. He was only a three- or four-year-old child. Still, she had not succeeded in cutting his nails. If he should attack her with nails and teeth while she slept—

Her breath came quickly. Oh, ridiculous, and yet—

She listened with painful attentiveness, and this time she heard the sound.

The boy was crying.

Not shrieking in fear or anger; not yelling or screaming. It was crying softly, and the cry was the heartbroken sobbing of a lonely, lonely child.

For the first time, Miss Fellowes thought with a pang: Poor thing!

Of course, it was a child; what did the shape of its head matter? It was a child that had been orphaned as no child had ever been orphaned before. Not only its mother and father were gone, but all its species. Snatched callously out of time, it was now the only creature of its kind in the world. The last. The only.

She felt pity for it strengthen, and with it shame at her own callousness. Tucking her own nightgown carefully about her calves (incongruously, she thought: Tomorrow I'll have to bring in a bathrobe) she got out of bed and went into the boy's room.

"Little boy," she called in a whisper. "Little boy."

She was about to reach under the bed, but she thought of a possible bite and did not. Instead, she turned on the night light and moved the bed.

The poor thing was huddled in the corner, knees up against his chin, looking up at her with blurred and apprehensive eyes.

In the dim light, she was not aware of his repulsiveness.

"Poor boy," she said, "poor boy." She felt him stiffen as she stroked his hair, then relax. "Poor boy. May I hold you?"

She sat down on the floor next to him and slowly and rhythmically stroked his hair, his cheek, his arm. Softly, she began to sing a slow and gentle song.

He lifted his head at that, staring at her mouth in the dimness, as though wondering at the sound.

She maneuvered him closer while he listened to her. Slowly, she pressed gently against the side of his head, until it rested on her shoulder. She put her arm under his thighs and with a smooth and unhurried motion lifted him into her lap.

She continued singing, the same simple verse over and over, while she rocked back and forth, back and forth.

He stopped crying, and after a while the smooth burr of his breathing showed he was asleep.

With infinite care, she pushed his bed back against the wall and laid him down. She covered him and stared down. His face looked so peaceful and little-boy as he slept. It didn't matter so much that it was so ugly. Really.

She began to tiptoe out, then thought: If he wakes up?

She came back, battled irresolutely with herself, then sighed and slowly got into bed with the child.

It was too small for her. She was cramped and uneasy at the lack of canopy, but the child's hand crept into hers and, somehow, she fell asleep in that position.

She awoke with a start and a wild impulse to scream. The latter she just managed to suppress into a gurgle. The boy was looking at her, wide-eyed. It took her a long moment to remember getting into bed with him, and now, slowly, without unfixing her eyes from his, she stretched one leg carefully and let it touch the floor, then the other one.

She cast a quick and apprehensive glance toward the open ceiling, then tensed her muscles for quick disengagement.

But at that moment, the boy's stubby fingers reached out and touched her lips. He said something.

She shrank at the touch. He was terribly ugly in the light of day.

The boy spoke again. He opened his own mouth and gestured with his hand as though something were coming out.

Miss Fellowes guessed at the meaning and said tremulously, "Do you want me to sing?"

The boy said nothing but stared at her mouth.

In a voice slightly off key with tension, Miss Fellowes began the little song she had sung the night before and the ugly little boy smiled. He swayed clumsily in rough time to the music and made a little gurgly sound that might have been the beginnings of a laugh.

Miss Fellowes sighed inwardly. Music hath charms to soothe the savage breast. It might help—

She said, "You wait. Let me get myself fixed up. It will just take a minute. Then I'll make breakfast for you."

She worked rapidly, conscious of the lack of ceiling at all times. The boy remained in bed, watching her when she was in view. She smiled at him at those times and waved. At the end, he waved back, and she found herself being charmed by that.

Finally, she said, "Would you like oatmeal with milk?" It took a moment to prepare, and then she beckoned to him.

Whether he understood the gesture or followed the aroma, Miss Fellowes did not know, but he got out of bed.

She tried to show him how to use a spoon but he shrank

away from it in fright. (Time enough, she thought.) She compromised on insisting that he lift the bowl in his hands. He did it clumsily enough and it was incredibly messy but most of it did get into him.

She tried the drinking milk in a glass this time, and the little boy whined when he found the opening too small for him to get his face into conveniently. She held his hand, forcing it around the glass, making him tip it, forcing his mouth to the rim.

Again a mess but again most went into him, and she was used to messes.

The washroom, to her surprise and relief, was a less frustrating matter. He understood what it was she expected him to do.

She found herself patting his head, saying. "Good boy. Smart boy."

And to Miss Fellowes' exceeding pleasure, the boy smiled at that.

She thought: When he smiles, he's quite bearable. Really.

Later in the day, the gentlemen of the press arrived.

She held the boy in her arms and he clung to her wildly while across the open door they set cameras to work. The commotion frightened the boy and he began to cry, but it was ten minutes before Miss Fellowes was allowed to retreat and put the boy in the next room.

She emerged again, flushed with indignation, walked out of the apartment (for the first time in eighteen hours) and closed the door behind her. "I think you've had enough. It will take me a while to quiet him. Go away."

"Sure, sure," said the gentleman from the *Times-Herald*. "But is that really a Neanderthal or is this some kind of gag?"

"I assure you," said Hoskins' voice, suddenly, from the background, "that this is no gag. The child is authentic Homo neanderthalensis."

"Is it a boy or a girl?"

"Boy," said Miss Fellowes briefly.

"Ape-boy," said the gentleman from the *News*. "That's what we've got here. Ape-boy. How does he act, Nurse?"

"He acts exactly like a little boy," snapped Miss Fellowes, annoyed into the defensive, "and he is not an ape-boy. His name is—is Timothy, Timmie—and he is perfectly normal in his behavior."

She had chosen the name Timothy at a venture. It was the first that had occurred to her.

"Timmie the Ape-boy," said the gentleman from the *News* and, as it turned out, Timmie the Ape-boy was the name under which the child became known to the world.

The gentleman from the *Globe* turned to Hoskins and said, "Doc, what do you expect to do with the ape-boy?"

Hoskins shrugged. "My original plan was completed when I proved it possible to bring him here. However, the anthropologists will be very interested, I imagine, and the physiologists. We have here, after all, a creature which is at the edge of being human. We should learn a great deal about ourselves and our ancestry from him."

"How long will you keep him?"

"Until such a time as we need the space more than we need him. Quite a while, perhaps."

The gentleman from the *News* said, "Can you bring it out into the open so we can set up sub-etheric equipment and put on a real show?"

"I'm sorry, but the child cannot be removed from Stasis."

"Exactly what is Stasis?"

"Ah." Hoskins permitted hmiself one of his short smiles. "That would take a great deal of explanation, gentlemen. In Stasis, time as we know it doesn't exist. Those rooms are inside an invisible bubble that is not exactly part of our Universe. That is why the child could be plucked out of time as it was."

"Well, wait now," said the gentleman from the *News* discontentedly, "what are you giving us? The nurse goes into the room and out of it."

"And so can any of you," said Hoskins matter-of-factly. "You would be moving parallel to the lines of temporal force and no great energy gain or loss would be involved. The child, however, was taken from the far past. It moved across the lines and gained temporal potential. To move it into the Universe and into our own time would absorb enough energy to burn out every line in the place and probably blank out all power in the city of Washington. We had to store trash brought with him on the premises and will have to remove it little by little."

The newsmen were writing down sentences busily as Hoskins spoke to them. They did not understand and they were sure their readers would not, but it sounded scientific and that was what counted.

The gentleman from the *Times-Herald* said, "Would you be available for an all-circuit interview tonight?"

"I think so," said Hoskins at once, and they all moved off.

Miss Fellowes looked after them. She understood all this about Stasis and temporal force as little as the newsmen but she managed to get this much. Timmie's imprisonment (she found herself suddenly thinking of the little boy as Timmie) was a real one and not one imposed by the arbitrary fiat of Hoskins. Apparently, it was impossible to let him out of Stasis at all, ever.

Poor child. Poor child.

She was suddenly aware of his crying and she hastened in to console him.

Miss Fellowes did not have a chance to see Hoskins on the all-circuit hookup, and though his interview was beamed to every part of the world and even to the outpost on the Moon, it did not penetrate the apartment in which Miss Fellowes and the ugly little boy lived.

But he was down the next morning, radiant and joyful.

Miss Fellowes said, "Did the interview go well?"

"Extremely. And how is—Timmie?"

Miss Fellowes found herself pleased at the use of the name. "Doing quite well. Now come out here, Timmie, the nice gentleman will not hurt you."

But Timmie stayed in the other room, with a lock of his matted hair showing behind the barrier of the door and, occasionally, the corner of an eye.

"Actually," said Miss Fellowes, "he is settling down amazingly. He is quite intelligent."

"Are you surprised?"

She hesitated just a moment, then said, "Yes, I am. I suppose I thought he was an ape-boy."

"Well, ape-boy or not, he's done a great deal for us. He's put Stasis, Inc. on the map. We're in, Miss Fellowes, we're in." It was as though he had to express his triumph to someone, even if only to Miss Fellowes.

"Oh?" She let him talk.

He put his hands in his pockets and said, "We've been working on a shoestring for ten years, scrounging funds a penny at a time wherever we could. We had to shoot the works on one big show. It was everything, or nothing. And when I say the works, I mean it. This attempt to bring in a Neanderthal took every cent we could borrow or steal, and some of it *was* stolen—funds for other projects, used for this

256

one without permission. If that experiment hadn't succeeded, I'd have been through."

Miss Fellowes said abruptly, "Is that why there are no ceilings?"

"Eh?" Hoskins looked up.

"Was there no money for ceilings?"

"Oh. Well, that wasn't the only reason. We didn't really know in advance how old the Neanderthal might be exactly. We can detect only dimly in time, and he might have been large and savage. It was possible we might have had to deal with him from a distance, like a caged animal."

"But since that hasn't turned out to be so, I suppose you can build a ceiling now."

"Now, yes. We have plenty of money, now. Funds have been promised from every source. This is all wonderful, Miss Fellowes." His broad face gleamed with a smile that lasted and when he left, even his back seemed to be smiling.

Miss Fellowes thought: He's quite a nice man when he's off guard and forgets about being scientific.

She wondered for an idle moment if he was married, then dismissed the thought in self-embarrassment.

"Timmie," she called. "Come here, Timmie."

In the months that passed, Miss Fellowes felt herself grow to be an integral part of Stasis, Inc. She was given a small office of her own with her name on the door, an office quite close to the dollhouse (as she never stopped calling Timmie's Stasis bubble). She was given a substantial raise. The dollhouse was covered by a ceiling; its furnishings were elaborated and improved; a second washroom was added—and even so, she gained an apartment of her own on the institute grounds and, on occasion, did not stay with Timmie during the night. An intercom was set up between the dollhouse and her apartment and Timmie learned how to use it.

Miss Fellowes got used to Timmie. She even grew less conscious of his ugliness. One day she found herself staring at an ordinary boy in the street and finding something bulgy and unattractive in his high domed forehead and jutting chin. She had to shake herself to break the spell.

It was more pleasant to grow used to Hoskins' occasional visits. It was obvious he welcomed escape from his increasingly harried role as head of Stasis, Inc., and that he took a sentimental interest in the child who had started it all, but it seemed to Miss Fellowes that he also enjoyed talking to her.

(She had learned some facts about Hoskins, too. He had invented the method of analyzing the reflection of the past-penetrating mesonic beam; he had invented the method of establishing Stasis; his coldness was only an effort to hide a kindly nature; and, oh yes, he *was* married.)

What Miss Fellowes could *not* get used to was the fact that she was engaged in a scientific experiment. Despite all she could do, she found herself getting personally involved to the point of quarreling with the physiologists.

On one occasion, Hoskins came down and found her in the midst of a hot urge to kill. They had no right; they had no *right*—Even if he *was* a Neanderthal, he still wasn't an animal.

She was staring after them in a blind fury; staring out the open door and listening to Timmie's sobbing, when she noticed Hoskins standing before her. He might have been there for minutes.

He said, "May I come in?"

She nodded curtly, then hurried to Timmie, who clung to her, curling his little bandy legs—still thin, so thin—about her.

Hoskins watched, then said gravely, "He seems quite unhappy."

Miss Fellowes said, "I don't blame him. They're at him every day now with their blood samples and their probings. They keep him on synthetic diets that I wouldn't feed a pig."

"It's the sort of thing they can't try on a human, you know."

"And they can't try it on Timmie, either. Dr. Hoskins, I insist. You told me it was Timmie's coming that put Stasis, Inc. on the map. If you have any gratitude for that at all, you've *got* to keep them away from the poor thing at least until he's old enough to understand a little more. After he's had a bad session with them, he has nightmares, he can't sleep. Now I warn you," (she reached a sudden peak of fury) "I'm not letting them in here any more."

(She realized that she had screamed that, but she couldn't help it.)

She said more quietly, "I know he's Neanderthal but there's a great deal we don't appreciate about Neanderthals. I've read up on them. They had a culture of their own. Some of the greatest human inventions arose in Neanderthal times. The domestication of animals, for instance; the wheel; various techniques in grinding stone. They even had spiritual yearnings. They buried their dead and buried possessions with
258

the body, showing they believed in a life after death. It amounts to the fact that they invented religion. Doesn't that mean Timmie has a right to human treatment?"

She patted the little boy gently on his buttocks and sent him off into his playroom. As the door was opened, Hoskins smiled briefly at the display of toys that could be seen.

Miss Fellowes said defensively, "The poor child deserves his toys. It's all he has and he earns them with what he goes through."

"No, no. No objections, I assure you. I was just thinking how you've changed since the first day, when you were quite angry I had foisted a Neanderthal on you."

Miss Fellowes said in a low voice, "I suppose I didn't —" and faded off.

Hoskins changed the subject, "How old would you say he is, Miss Fellowes?"

She said, "I can't say, since we don't know how Neanderthals develop. In size, he'd only be three but Neanderthals are smaller generally and with all the tampering they do with him, he probably isn't growing. The way he's learning English, though, I'd say he was well over four."

"Really? I haven't noticed anything about learning English in the reports."

"He won't speak to anyone but me. For now, anyway. He's terribly afraid of others, and no wonder. But he can ask for an article of food; he can indicate any need practically; and he understands almost anything I say. Of course," (she watched him shrewdly, trying to estimate if this was the time), "his development may not continue."

"Why not?"

"Any child needs stimulation and this one lives a life of solitary confinement. I do what I can, but I'm not with him all the time and I'm not all he needs. What I mean, Dr. Hoskins, is that he needs another boy to play with."

Hoskins nodded slowly. "Unfortunately, there's only one of him, isn't there? Poor child."

Miss Fellowes warmed to him at once. She said, "You do like Timmie, don't you?" It was so nice to have someone else feel like that.

"Oh, yes," said Hoskins, and with his guard down, she could see the weariness in his eyes.

Miss Fellowes dropped her plans to push the matter at once. She said, with real concern, "You look worn out, Dr. Hoskins."

"Do I, Miss Fellowes? I'll have to practice looking more lifelike then."

"I suppose Stasis, Inc. is very busy and that that keeps you very busy."

Hoskins shrugged. "You suppose right. It's a matter of animal, vegetable, and mineral in equal parts, Miss Fellowes. But then, I suppose you haven't ever seen our displays."

"Actually, I haven't.—But it's not because I'm not interested. It's just that I've been so busy."

"Well, you're not all that busy right now," he said with impulsive decision. "I'll call for you tomorrow at eleven and give you a personal tour. How's that?"

She smiled happily. "I'd love it."

He nodded and smiled in his turn and left.

Miss Fellowes hummed at intervals for the rest of the day. Really—to think so was ridiculous, of course—but really, it was almost like—like making a date.

He was quite on time the next day, smiling and pleasant. She had replaced her nurse's uniform with a dress. One of conservative cut, to be sure, but she hadn't felt so feminine in years.

He complimented her on her appearance with staid formality and she accepted with equally formal grace. It was really a perfect prelude, she thought. And then the additional thought came, prelude to what?

She shut that off by hastening to say good-by to Timmie and to assure him she would be back soon. She made sure he knew all about what and where lunch was.

Hoskins took her into the new wing, into which she had never yet gone. It still had the odor of newness about it and the sound of construction, softly heard, was indication enough that it was still being extended.

"Animal, vegetable, and mineral," said Hoskins, as he had the day before. "Animal right there; our most spectacular exhibits."

The space was divided into many rooms, each a separate Stasis bubble. Hoskins brought her to the view-glass of one and she looked in. What she saw impressed her first as a scaled, tailed chicken. Skittering on two thin legs it ran from wall to wall with its delicate birdlike head, surmounted by a bony keel like the comb of a rooster, looking this way and that. The paws on its small forelimbs clenched and unclenched constantly.

Hoskins said, "It's our dinosaur. We've had it for months. I don't know when we'll be able to let go of it."

"Dinosaur?"

"Did you expect a giant?"

She dimpled. "One does, I suppose. I know some of them are small."

"A small one is all we aimed for, believe me. Generally, it's under investigation, but this seems to be an open hour. Some interesting things have been discovered. For instance, it is not entirely cold-blooded. It has an imperfect method of maintaining internal temperatures higher than that of its environment. Unfortunately, it's a male. Ever since we brought it in we've been trying to get a fix on another that may be female, but we've had no luck yet."

"Why female?"

He looked at her quizzically. "So that we might have a fighting chance to obtain fertile eggs, and baby dinosaurs."

"Of course."

He led her to the trilobite section. "That's Professor Dwayne of Washington University," he said. "He's a nuclear chemist. If I recall correctly, he's taking an isotope ratio on the oxygen of the water."

"Why?"

"It's primeval water; at least half a billion years old. The isotope ratio gives the temperature of the ocean at that time. He himself happens to ignore the trilobites, but others are chiefly concerned in dissecting them. They're the lucky ones because all they need are scalpels and microscopes. Dwayne has to set up a mass spectrograph each time he conducts an experiment."

"Why's that? Can't he—"

"No, he can't. He can't take anything out of the room as far as can be helped."

There were samples of primordial plant life too and chunks of rock formations. Those were the vegetable and mineral. And every specimen had its investigator. It was like a museum; a museum brought to life and serving as a superactive center of research.

"And you have to supervise all of this, Dr. Hoskins?"

"Only indirectly, Miss Fellowes. I have subordinates, thank heaven. My own interest is entirely in the theoretical aspects of the matter: the nature of Time, the technique of mesonic intertemporal detection and so on. I would exchange all this for a method of detecting objects closer in Time than ten thousand years ago. If we could get into historical times—"

He was interrupted by a commotion at one of the distant booths, a thin voice raised querulously. He frowned, muttered hastily, "Excuse me," and hastened off.

Miss Fellowes followed as best she could without actually running.

An elderly man, thinly-bearded and red-faced, was saying, "I had vital aspects of my investigations to complete. Don't you understand that?"

A uniformed technician with the interwoven SI monogram (for Stasis, Inc.) on his lab coat, said, "Dr. Hoskins, it was arranged with Professor Ademewski at the beginning that the specimen could only remain here two weeks."

"I did not know then how long my investigations would take. I'm not a prophet," said Ademewski heatedly.

Dr. Hoskins said, "You understand, Professor, we have limited space; we must keep specimens rotating. That piece of chalcopyrite must go back; there are men waiting for the next specimen."

"Why can't I have it for myself, then? Let me take it out of there."

"You know you can't have it."

"A piece of chalcopyrite; a miserable five-kilogram piece? Why not?"

"We can't afford the energy expense!" said Hoskins brusquely. "You know that."

The technician interrupted. "The point is, Dr. Hoskins, that he tried to remove the rock against the rules and I almost punctured Stasis while he was in there, not knowing he was in there."

There was a short silence and Dr. Hoskins turned on the investigator with a cold formality. "It that so, Professor?"

Professor Ademewski coughed. "I saw no harm—"

Hoskins reached up to a hand-pull dangling just within reach, outside the specimen room in question. He pulled it.

Miss Fellowes, who had been peering in, looking at the totally undistinguished sample of rock that occasioned the dispute, drew in her breath sharply as its existence flickered out. The room was empty.

Hoskins said, "Professor, your permit to investigate matters in Stasis will be permanently voided. I am sorry."

"But wait—"

"I am sorry. You have violated one of the stringent rules."

"I will appeal to the International Association—"

"Appeal away. In a case like this, you will find I can't be overruled."

He turned away deliberately, leaving the professor still protesting and said to Miss Fellowes (his face still white with anger), "Would you care to have lunch with me, Miss Fellowes?"

He took her into the small administration alcove of the cafeteria. He greeted others and introduced Miss Fellowes with complete ease, although she herself felt painfully self-conscious.

What must they think, she thought, and tried desperately to appear businesslike.

She said, "Do you have that kind of trouble often, Dr. Hoskins? I mean like that you just had with the professor?" She took her fork in hand and began eating.

"No," said Hoskins forcefully. "That was the first time. Of course I'm always having to argue men out of removing specimens but this is the first time one actually tried to *do* it."

"I remember you once talked about the energy it would consume."

"That's right. Of course, we've tried to take it into account. Accidents will happen and so we've got special power sources designed to stand the drain of accidental removal from Stasis, but that doesn't mean we want to see a year's supply of energy gone in half a second—or can afford to without having our plans of expansion delayed for years. —Besides, imagine the professor's being in the room while Stasis was about to be punctured."

"What would have happened to him if it had been?"

"Well, we've experimented with inanimate objects and with mice and they've disappeared. Presumably they've traveled back in time; carried along, so to speak, by the pull of the object simultaneously snapping back into its natural time. For that reason, we have to anchor objects within Stasis that we don't want to move and that's a complicated procedure. The professor would not have been anchored and he would have gone back to the Pliocene at the moment when we abstracted the rock—plus, of course, the two weeks it had remained here in the present."

"How dreadful it would have been."

"Not on account of the professor, I assure you. If he

263

were fool enough to do what he did, it would serve him right. But imagine the effect it would have on the public if the fact came out. All people would need is to become aware of the dangers involved and funds could be choked off like that." He snapped his fingers and played moodily with his food.

Miss Fellowes said, "Couldn't you get him back? The way you got the rock in the first place?"

"No, because once an object is returned, the original fix is lost unless we deliberately plan to retain it and there was no reason to do that in this case. There never is. Finding the professor again would mean relocating a specific fix and that would be like dropping a line into the oceanic abyss for the purpose of dredging up a particular fish. —My God, when I think of the precautions we take to prevent accidents, it makes me mad. We have every individual Stasis unit set up with its own puncturing device—we have to, since each unit has its separate fix and must be collapsible independently. The point it, though, none of the puncturing devices is ever activated until the last minute. And then we deliberately make activation impossible except by the pull of a rope carefully led outside the Stasis. The pull is gross mechanical motion that requires a strong effort, not something that is likely to be done accidentally."

Miss Fellowes said, "But doesn't it—change history to move something in and out of Time?"

Hoskins shrugged. "Theoretically, yes; actually, except in unusual cases, no. We move objects out of Stasis all the time. Air molecules. Bacteria. Dust. About 10 per cent of our energy consumption goes to make up micro-losses of that nature. But moving even large objects in Time sets up changes that damp out. Take that chalcopyrite from the Pliocene. Because of its absence for two weeks some insect didn't find the shelter it might have found and is killed. That could initiate a whole series of changes, but the mathematics of Stasis indicates that this is a converging series. The amount of change diminishes with time and then things are as before."

"You mean, reality heals itself?"

"In a manner of speaking. Abstract a human from Time or send one back, and you make a larger wound. If the individual is an ordinary one, that wound still heals itself. Of course, there are a great many people who write to us each day and want us to bring Abraham Lincoln into the present, or Mohammed, or Lenin. *That* can't be done, of course. Even if we could find them, the change in reality in moving one of the

264

history molders would be too great to be healed. There are ways of calculating when a change is likely to be too great and we avoid even approaching that limit."

Miss Fellowes said, "Then, Timmie—"

"No, he presents no problem in that direction. Reality is safe. But—" He gave her a quick, sharp glance, then went on, "But never mind. Yesterday you said Timmie needed companionship."

"Yes," Miss Fellowes smiled her delight. "I didn't think you paid that any attention."

"Of course I did. I'm fond of the child. I appreciate your feelings for him and I was concerned enough to want to explain to you. Now I have; you've seen what we do; you've gotten some insight into the difficulties involved; so you know why, with the best will in the world, we can't supply companionship for Timmie."

"You can't?" said Miss Fellowes, with sudden dismay.

"But I've just explained. We couldn't possibly expect to find another Neanderthal his age without incredible luck, and if we could, it wouldn't be fair to multiply risks by having another human being in Stasis."

Miss Fellowes put down her spoon and said energetically, "But, Dr. Hoskins, that is not at all what I meant. I don't want you to bring another Neanderthal into the present. I know that's impossible. But it isn't impossible to bring another child to play with Timmie."

Hoskins stared at her in concern. "A *human* child?"

"*Another* child," said Miss Fellowes, completely hostile now. "Timmie is human."

"I couldn't dream of such a thing."

"Why not? Why couldn't you? What is wrong with the notion? You pulled that child out of Time and made him an eternal prisoner. Don't you owe him something? Dr. Hoskins, if there is any man who, in this world, is that child's father in every sense but the biological, it is you. Why can't you do this little thing for him?"

Hoskins said, "His *father?*" He rose, somewhat unsteadily, to his feet. "Miss Fellowes, I think I'll take you back now, if you don't mind."

They returned to the dollhouse in a complete silence that neither broke.

It was a long time after that before she saw Hoskins again, except for an occasional glimpse in passing. She was sorry about that at times; then, at other times, when Timmie was more than usually woebegone or when he spent silent hours at the window with its prospect of little more than nothing, she thought, fiercely: Stupid man.

Timmie's speech grew better and more precise each day. It never entirely lost a certain soft slurriness that Miss Fellowes found rather endearing. In times of excitement, he fell back into tongue-clicking but those times were becoming fewer. He must be forgetting the days before he came into the present —except for dreams.

As he grew older, the physiologists grew less interested and the psychologists more so. Miss Fellowes was not sure that she did not like the new group even less than the first. The needles were gone; the injections and withdrawals of fluid; the special diets. But now Timmie was made to overcome barriers to reach food and water. He had to lift panels, move bars, reach for cords. And the mild electric shocks made him cry and drove Miss Fellowes to distraction.

She did not wish to appeal to Hoskins; she did not wish to have to go to him; for each time she thought of him, she thought of his face over the luncheon table that last time. Her eyes moistened and she thought: Stupid, *stupid* man.

And then one day Hoskins' voice sounded unexpectedly, calling into the dollhouse, "Miss Fellowes."

She came out coldly, smoothing her nurse's uniform, then stopped in confusion at finding herself in the presence of a pale woman, slender and of middle height. The woman's fair hair and complexion gave her an appearance of fragility. Standing behind her and clutching at her skirt was a round-faced, large-eyed child of four.

Hoskins said, "Dear, this is Miss Fellowes, the nurse in charge of the boy. Miss Fellowes, this is my wife."

(Was this his wife? She was not as Miss Fellowes had imagined her to be. But then, why not? A man like Hoskins would choose a weak thing to be his foil. If that was what he wanted—)

She forced a matter-of-fact greeting. "Good afternoon, Mrs. Hoskins. Is this your—your little boy?"

(*That* was a surprise. She had thought of Hoskins as a husband, but not as a father, except, of course— She suddenly caught Hoskins' grave eyes and flushed.)

Hoskins said, "Yes, this is my boy, Jerry. Say hello to Miss Fellowes, Jerry."

(Had he stressed the word "this" just a bit? Was he saying *this* was his son and not—)

Jerry receded a bit further into the folds of the maternal skirt and muttered his hello. Mrs. Hoskins' eyes were searching over Miss Fellowes' shoulders, peering into the room, looking for something.

Hoskins said, "Well, let's go in. Come, dear. There's a trifling discomfort at the threshold, but it passes."

Miss Fellowes said, "Do you want Jerry to come in, too?"

"Of course. He is to be Timmie's playmate. You said that Timmie needed a playmate. Or have you forgotten?"

"But—" She looked at him with a colossal, surprised wonder. "*Your* boy?"

He said peevishly, "Well, whose boy, then? Isn't this what you want? Come on in, dear. Come on in."

Mrs. Hoskins lifted Jerry into her arms with a distinct effort and, hesitantly, stepped over the threshold. Jerry squirmed as she did so, disliking the sensation.

Mrs. Hoskins said in a thin voice, "Is the creature here? I don't see him."

Miss Fellowes called, "Timmie. Come out."

Timmie peered around the edge of the door, staring up at the little boy who was visiting him. The muscles in Mrs. Hoskins' arms tensed visibly.

She said to her husband, "Gerald, are you sure it's safe?"

Miss Fellowes said at once, "If you mean is Timmie safe, why, of course he is. He's a gentle little boy."

"But he's a sa—savage."

(The ape-boy stories in the newspapers!) Miss Fellowes said emphatically, "He is not a savage. He is just as quiet and reasonable as you can possibly expect a five-and-a-half-year-old to be. It is very generous of you, Mrs. Hoskins, to agree to allow your boy to play with Timmie but please have no fears about it."

Mrs. Hoskins said with mild heat, "I'm not sure that I agree."

"We've had it out, dear," said Hoskins. "Let's not bring up the matter for new argument. Put Jerry down."

Mrs. Hoskins did so and the boy backed against her, staring at the pair of eyes which were staring back at him from the next room.

"Come here, Timmie," said Miss Fellowes. "Don't be afraid."

Slowly, Timmie stepped into the room. Hoskins bent to disengage Jerry's fingers from his mother's skirt. "Step back, dear. Give the children a chance."

The youngsters faced one another. Although the younger, Jerry was nevertheless an inch taller, and in the presence of his straightness and his high-held, well-proportioned head, Timmie's grotesqueries were suddenly almost as pronounced as they had been in the first days.

Miss Fellowes' lips quivered.

It was the little Neanderthal who spoke first, in childish treble. "What's your name?" And Timmie thrust his face suddenly forward as though to inspect the other's features more closely.

Startled, Jerry responded with a vigorous shove that sent Timmie tumbling. Both began crying loudly and Mrs. Hoskins snatched up her child, while Miss Fellowes, flushed with repressed anger, lifted Timmie and comforted him.

Mrs. Hoskins said, "They just instinctively don't like one another."

"No more instinctively," said her husband wearily, "than any two children dislike each other. Now put Jerry down and let him get used to the situation. In fact, we had better leave. Miss Fellowes can bring Jerry to my office after a while and I'll have him taken home."

The two children spent the next hour very aware of each other. Jerry cried for his mother, struck out at Miss Fellowes and, finally, allowed himself to be comforted with a lollipop. Timmie sucked at another, and at the end of an hour, Miss Fellowes had them playing with the same set of blocks, though at opposite ends of the room.

She found herself almost maudlinly grateful to Hoskins when she brought Jerry to him.

She searched for ways to thank him but his very formality was a rebuff. Perhaps he could not forgive her for making him feel like a cruel father. Perhaps the bringing of his own child was an attempt, after all, to prove himself both a kind father to Timmie and, also, not his father at all. Both at the same time!

So all she could say was, "Thank you. Thank you very much."

And all he could say was, "It's all right. Don't mention it."

It became a settled routine. Twice a week, Jerry was brought in for an hour's play, later extended to two hours' play. The children learned each other's names and ways and played together.

And yet, after the first rush of gratitude, Miss Fellowes found herself disliking Jerry. He was larger and heavier and in all things dominant, forcing Timmie into a completely secondary role. All that reconciled her to the situation was the fact that, despite difficulties, Timmie looked forward with more and more delight to the periodic appearances of his playfellow.

It was all he had, she mourned to herself.

And once, as she watched them, she thought: Hoskins' two children, one by his wife and one by Stasis.

While she herself—

Heavens, she thought, putting her fists to her temples and feeling ashamed: I'm jealous!

"Miss Fellowes," said Timmie (carefully, she had never allowed him to call her anything else), "when will I go to school?"

She looked down at those eager brown eyes turned up to hers and passed her hand softly through his thick, curly hair. It was the most disheveled portion of his appearance, for she cut his hair herself while he sat restlessly under the scissors. She did not ask for professional help, for the very clumsiness of the cut served to mask the retreating fore part of the skull and the bulging hinder part.

She said, "Where did you hear about school?"

"Jerry goes to school. Kin-der-gar-ten." He said it carefully. "There are lots of places he goes. Outside. When can I go outside, Miss Fellowes?"

A small pain centered in Miss Fellowes' heart. Of course, she saw, there would be no way of avoiding the inevitability of Timmie's hearing more and more of the outer world he could never enter.

She said, with an attempt at gaiety, "Why, whatever would you do in kindergarten, Timmie?"

"Jerry says they play games, they have picture tapes. He says there are lots of children. He says—he says—" A thought, then a triumphant upholding of both small hands with the fingers splayed apart. "He says this many."

Miss Fellowes said, "Would you like picture tapes? I can get you picture tapes. Very nice ones. And music tapes, too."

So that Timmie was temporarily comforted.

He pored over the picture tapes in Jerry's absence and Miss Fellowes read to him out of ordinary books by the hour.

There was so much to explain in even the simplest story, so much that was outside the perspective of his three rooms. Timmie took to having his dreams more often now that the outside was being introduced to him.

They were always the same, about the outside. He tried haltingly to describe them to Miss Fellowes. In his dreams, he was outside, an empty outside, but very large, with children and queer indescribable objects half-digested in his thought out of bookish descriptions half-understood, or out of distant Neanderthal memories half-recalled.

But the children and objects ignored him and though he was in the world, he was never part of it, but was as alone as though he were in his own room—and would wake up crying.

Miss Fellowes tried to laugh at the dreams, but there were nights in her own apartment when she cried, too.

One day, as Miss Fellowes read, Timmie put his hand under her chin and lifted it gently so that her eyes left the book and met his.

He said, "How do you know what to say, Miss Fellowes?"

She said, "You see these marks? They tell me what to say. These marks make words."

He stared at them long and curiously, taking the book out of her hands. "Some of these marks are the same."

She laughed with pleasure at this sign of shrewdness and said, "So they are. Would you like to have me show you how to make the marks?"

"All right. That would be a nice game."

It did not occur to her that he could learn to read. Up to the very moment that he read a book to her, it did not occur to her that he could learn to read.

Then, weeks later, the enormity of what had been done struck her. Timmie sat in her lap, following word by word the printing in a child's book, reading to her. He was reading to her!

She struggled to her feet in amazement and said, "Now Timmie, I'll be back later. I want to see Dr. Hoskins."

Excited nearly to frenzy, it seemed to her she might have an answer to Timmie's unhappiness. If Timmie could not leave to enter the world, the world must be brought into those three rooms to Timmie—the whole world in books and film and sound. He must be educated to his full capacity. So much the world owed him.

She found Hoskins in a mood that was oddly analogous to her own; a kind of triumph and glory. His offices were unusually busy, and for a moment, she thought she would not get to see him, as she stood abashed in the anteroom.

But he saw her, and a smile spread over his broad face. "Miss Fellowes, come here."

He spoke rapidly into the intercom, then shut it off. "Have you heard?—No, of course, you couldn't have. We've done it. We've actually done it. We have intertemporal detection at close range."

"You mean," she tried to detach her thought from her own good news for a moment, "that you can get a person from historical times into the present?"

"That's just what I mean. We have a fix on a fourteenth-century individual right now. Imagine. *Imagine!* If you could only know how glad I'll be to shift from the eternal concentration on the Mesozoic, replace the paleontologists with the historians— But there's something you wish to say to me, eh? Well, go ahead; go ahead. You find me in a good mood. Anything you want you can have."

Miss Fellowes smiled. "I'm glad. Because I wonder if we might not establish a system of instruction for Timmie?"

"Instruction? In what?"

"Well, in everything. A school. So that he might learn."

"But *can* he learn?"

"Certainly, he *is* learning. He can read. I've taught him so much myself."

Hoskins sat there, seeming suddenly depressed. "I don't know, Miss Fellowes."

She said, "You just said that anything I wanted—"

"I know and I should not have. You see, Miss Fellowes, I'm sure you must realize that we cannot maintain the Timmie experiment forever."

She stared at him with sudden horror, not really understanding what he had said. How did he mean "cannot maintain"? With an agonizing flash of recollection, she recalled Professor Ademewski and his mineral specimen that was taken away after two weeks. She said, "But you're talking about a boy. Not about a rock—"

Dr. Hoskins said uneasily, "Even a boy can't be given undue importance, Miss Fellowes. Now that we expect individuals out of historical time, we will need Stasis space, all we can get."

She didn't grasp it. "But you can't. Timmie—Timmie—"

271

"Now, Miss Fellowes, please don't upset yourself. Timmie won't go right away; perhaps not for months. Meanwhile we'll do what we can."

She was still staring at him.

"Let me get you something, Miss Fellowes."

"No," she whispered. "I don't need anything." She arose in a kind of nightmare and left.

Timmie, she thought, you will *not* die. You will *not* die.

It was all very well to hold tensely to the thought that Timmie must not die, but how was that to be arranged? In the first weeks, Miss Fellowes clung only to the hope that the attempt to bring forward a man from the fourteenth century would fail completely. Hoskins' theories might be wrong or his practice defective. Then things could go on as before.

Certainly, that was not the hope of the rest of the world and, irrationally, Miss Fellowes hated the world for it. "Project Middle Ages" reached a climax of white-hot publicity. The press and the public had hungered for something like this. Stasis, Inc. had lacked the necessary sensation for a long time now. A new rock or another ancient fish failed to stir them. But *this* was it.

A historical human; an adult speaking a known language; someone who could open a new page of history to the scholar.

Zero-time was coming and this time it was not a question of three onlookers from a balcony. This time there would be a world-wide audience. This time the technicians of Stasis, Inc. would play their role before nearly all of mankind.

Miss Fellowes was herself all but savage with waiting. When young Jerry Hoskins showed up for his scheduled playtime with Timmie, she scarcely recognized him. He was not the one she was waiting for.

(The secretary who brought him left hurriedly after the barest nod for Miss Fellowes. She was rushing for a good place from which to watch the climax of Project Middle Ages. —And so ought Miss Fellowes with far better reason, she thought bitterly, if only that stupid girl would arrive.)

Jerry Hoskins sidled toward her, embarrassed. "Miss Fellowes?" He took the reproduction of a news-strip out of his pocket.

"Yes? What is it, Jerry?"

"Is this a picture of Timmie?"

Miss Fellowes stared at him, then snatched the strip from Jerry's hand. The excitement of Project Middle Ages had brought about a pale revival of interest in Timmie on the part of the press.

Jerry watched her narrowly, then said, "It says Timmie is an ape-boy. What does that mean?"

Miss Fellowes caught the youngster's wrist and repressed the impulse to shake him. "Never say that, Jerry. Never, do you understand? It is a nasty word and you mustn't use it."

Jerry struggled out of her grip, frightened.

Miss Fellowes tore up the news-strip with a vicious twist of the wrist. "Now go inside and play with Timmie. He's got a new book to show you."

And then, finally, the girl appeared. Miss Fellowes did not know her. None of the usual stand-ins she had used when business took her elsewhere was available now, not with Project Middle Ages at climax, but Hoskins' secretary had promised to find *someone* and this must be the girl.

Miss Fellowes tried to keep querulousness out of her voice. "Are you the girl assigned to Stasis Section One?"

"Yes, I'm Mandy Terris. You're Miss Fellowes, aren't you?"

"That's right."

"I'm sorry I'm late. There's just so much excitement."

"I know. Now I want you—"

Mandy said, "You'll be watching, I suppose." Her thin, vacuously pretty face filled with envy.

"Never mind that. Now I want you to come inside and meet Timmie and Jerry. They will be playing for the next two hours so they'll be giving you no trouble. They've got milk handy and plenty of toys. In fact, it will be better if you leave them alone as much as possible. Now I'll show you where everything is located and—"

"Is it Timmie that's the ape-b—"

"Timmie is the Stasis subject," said Miss Fellowes firmly.

"I mean, he's the one who's not supposed to get out, is that right?"

"Yes. Now, come in. There isn't much time."

And when she finally left, Mandy Terris called after her shrilly, "I hope you get a good seat and, golly, I sure hope it works."

Miss Fellowes did not trust herself to make a reasonable response. She hurried on without looking back.

But the delay meant she did *not* get a good seat. She got no nearer than the wall-viewing-plate in the assembly hall. Bitterly, she regretted that. If she could have been on the spot; if she could somehow have reached out for some sensitive portion of the instrumentations; if she were in some way able to wreck the experiment—

She found the strength to beat down her madness. Simple destruction would have done no good. They would have re-built and reconstructed and made the effort again. And she would never be allowed to return to Timmie.

Nothing would help. Nothing but that the experiment it-self fail; that it break down irretrievably.

So she waited through the countdown, watching every move on the giant screen, scanning the faces of the technicians as the focus shifted from one to the other, watching for the look of worry and uncertainty that would mark something going unexpectedly wrong; watching, watching—

There was no such look. The count reached zero, and very quietly, very unassumingly, the experiment succeeded!

In the new Stasis that had been established there stood a bearded, stoop-shouldered peasant of indeterminate age, in ragged dirty clothing and wooden shoes, staring in dull horror at the sudden mad change that had flung itself over him.

And while the world went mad with jubilation, Miss Fel-lowes stood frozen in sorrow, jostled and pushed, all but trampled; surrounded by triumph while bowed down with defeat.

And when the loud-speaker called her name with strident force, it sounded it three times before she responded.

"Miss Fellowes. Miss Fellowes. You are wanted in Stasis Section One immediately. Miss Fellowes, Miss Fell—"

"Let me through!" she cried breathlessly, while the loud-speaker continued its repetitions without pause. She forced her way through the crowds with wild energy, beating at it, striking out with closed fists, flailing, moving toward the door in a nightmare slowness.

Mandy Terris was in tears. "I don't know how it happened. I just went down to the edge of the corridor to watch a pocket-viewing-plate they had put up. Just for a minute. And then before I could move or do anything—" She cried out in sud-den accusation, "You said they would make no trouble; you *said* to leave them alone—"

Miss Fellowes, disheveled and trembling uncontrollably, glared at her. "Where's Timmie?"

A nurse was swabbing the arm of a wailing Jerry with disinfectant and another was preparing an anti-tetanus shot. There was blood on Jerry's clothes.

"He bit me, Miss Fellowes," Jerry cried in rage. "He *bit* me."

But Miss Fellowes didn't even see him.

"What did you do with Timmie?" she cried out.

"I locked him in the bathroom," said Mandy. "I just threw the little monster in there and locked him in."

Miss Fellowes ran into the dollhouse. She fumbled at the bathroom door. It took an eternity to get it open and to find the ugly little boy cowering in the corner.

"Don't whip me, Miss Fellowes," he whispered. His eyes were red. His lips were quivering. "I didn't mean to do it."

"Oh, Timmie, who told you about whips?" She caught him to her, hugging him wildly.

He said tremulously, "She said, with a long rope. She said you would hit me and hit me."

"You won't be. She was wicked to say so. But what happened? What happened?"

"He called me an ape-boy. He said I wasn't a real boy. He said I was an animal." Timmie dissolved in a flood of tears. "He said he wasn't going to play with a monkey anymore. I said I wasn't a monkey; I *wasn't* a monkey. He said I was all funny-looking. He said I was horrible ugly. He kept saying and saying and I bit him."

They were both crying now. Miss Fellowes sobbed, "But it isn't true. You know that, Timmie. You're a real boy. You're a dear real boy and the best boy in the world. And no one, *no* one will ever take you away from me."

It was easy to make up her mind, now; easy to know what to do. Only it had to be done quickly. Hoskins wouldn't wait much longer, with his own son mangled—

No, it would have to be done this night, *this* night; with the place four-fifths asleep and the remaining fifth intellectually drunk over Project Middle Ages.

It would be an unusual time for her to return but not an unheard-of one. The guard knew her well and would not dream of questioning her. He would think nothing of her carrying a suitcase. She rehearsed the noncommittal phrase, "Games for the boy," and the calm smile.

Why shouldn't he believe that?

He did. When she entered the dollhouse again, Timmie was still awake, and she maintained a desperate normality to avoid frightening him. She talked about his dreams with him and listened to him ask wistfully after Jerry.

There would be few to see her afterward, none to question the bundle she would be carrying. Timmie would be very quiet and then it would be a *fait accompli*. It would be done and what would be the use of trying to undo it. They would leave her be. They would leave them both be.

She opened the suitcase, took out the overcoat, the woolen cap with the ear-flaps and the rest.

Timmie said, with the beginning of alarm, "Why are you putting all these clothes on me, Miss Fellowes?"

She said, "I am going to take you outside, Timmie. To where your dreams are."

"My dreams?" His face twisted in sudden yearning, yet fear was there, too.

"You won't be afraid. You'll be with me. You won't be afraid if you're with me, will you, Timmie?"

"No, Miss Fellowes." He buried his little misshapen head against her side, and under her enclosing arm she could feel his small heart thud.

It was midnight and she lifted him into her arms. She disconnected the alarm and opened the door softly.

And she screamed, for facing her across the open door was Hoskins!

There were two men with him and he stared at her, as astonished as she.

Miss Fellowes recovered first by a second and made a quick attempt to push past him; but even with the second's delay he had time. He caught her roughly and hurled her back against a chest of drawers. He waved the men in and confronted her, blocking the door.

"I didn't expect this. Are you completely insane?"

She had managed to interpose her shoulder so that it, rather than Timmie, had struck the chest. She said pleadingly, "What harm can it do if I take him, Dr. Hoskins? You can't put energy loss ahead of a human life?"

Firmly, Hoskins took Timmie out of her arms. "An energy loss this size would mean millions of dollars lost out of the pockets of investors. It would mean a terrible setback for Stasis, Inc. It would mean eventual publicity about a sentimental nurse destroying all that for the sake of an ape-boy."

"Ape-boy!" said Miss Fellowes, in helpless fury.

"That's what the reporters would call him," said Hoskins.

276

One of the men emerged now, looping a nylon rope through eyelets along the upper portion of the wall.

Miss Fellowes remembered the rope that Hoskins had pulled outside the room containing Professor Ademewski's rock specimen so long ago.

She cried out, "No!"

But Hoskins put Timmie down and gently removed the overcoat he was wearing. "You stay here, Timmie. Nothing will happen to you. We're just going outside for a moment. All right?"

Timmie, white and wordless, managed to nod.

Hoskins steered Miss Fellowes out of the dollhouse ahead of himself. For the moment, Miss Fellowes was beyond resistance. Dully, she noticed the hand-pull being adjusted outside the dollhouse.

"I'm sorry, Miss Fellowes," said Hoskins. "I would have spared you this. I planned it for the night so that you would know only when it was over."

She said in a weary whisper, "Because your son was hurt. Because he tormented this child into striking out at him."

"No. Believe me. I understand about the incident today and I know it was Jerry's fault. But the story has leaked out. It would have to with the press surrounding us on this day of all days. I can't risk having a distorted story about negligence and savage Neanderthalers, so-called, distract from the success of Project Middle Ages. Timmie has to go soon anyway; he might as well go now and give the sensationalists as small a peg as possible on which to hang their trash."

"It's not like sending a rock back. You'll be killing a human being."

"Not killing. There'll be no sensation. He'll simply be a Neanderthal boy in a Neanderthal world. He will no longer be a prisoner and alien. He will have a chance at a free life."

"What chance? He's only seven years old, used to being taken care of, fed, clothed, sheltered. He will be alone. His tribe may not be at the point where he left them now that four years have passed. And if they were, they would not recognize him. He will have to take care of himself. How will he know how?"

Hoskins shook his head in hopeless negative. "Lord, Miss Fellowes, do you think we haven't thought of that? Do you think we would have brought in a child if it weren't that it was the first successful fix of a human or near-human we made and that we did not dare to take the chance of unfixing him

277

and finding another fix as good? Why do you suppose we kept Timmie as long as we did, if it were not for our reluctance to send a child back into the past. It's just"—his voice took on a desperate urgency—"that we can wait no longer. Timmie stands in the way of expansion! Timmie is a source of possible bad publicity; we are on the threshold of great things, and I'm sorry, Miss Fellowes, but we can't let Timmie block us. We cannot. I'm sorry, Miss Fellowes."

"Well, then," said Miss Fellowes sadly. "Let me say goodby. Give me five minutes to say good-by. Spare me that much."

Hoskins hesitated. "Go ahead."

Timmie ran to her. For the last time he ran to her and for the last time Miss Fellowes clasped him in her arms.

For a moment, she hugged him blindly. She caught at a chair with the toe of one foot, moved it against the wall, sat down.

"Don't be afraid, Timmie."

"I'm not afraid if you're here, Miss Fellowes. Is that man mad at me, the man out there?"

"No, he isn't. He just doesn't understand about us.— Timmie, do you know what a mother is?"

"Like Jerry's mother?"

"Did he tell you about his mother?"

"Sometimes. I think maybe a mother is a lady who takes care of you and who's very nice to you and who does good things."

"That's right. Have you ever wanted a mother, Timmie?"

Timmie pulled his head away from her so that he could look into her face. Slowly, he put his hand to her cheek and hair and stroked her, as long, long ago she had stroked him. He said, "Aren't you my mother?"

"Oh, Timmie."

"Are you angry because I asked?"

"No. Of course not."

"Because I know your name is Miss Fellowes, but—but sometimes, I call you 'Mother' inside. Is that all right?"

"Yes. Yes. It's all right. And I won't leave you any more and nothing will hurt you. I'll be with you to care for you always. Call me Mother, so I can hear you."

"Mother," said Timmie contentedly, leaning his cheek against hers.

She rose, and, still holding him, stepped up on the chair.

278

The sudden beginning of a shout from outside went unheard and, with her free hand, she yanked with all her weight at the cord where it hung suspended between two eyelets.

And Stasis was punctured and the room was empty.

EPILOGUE
My Private World of Science Fiction

by ALFRED BESTER

Many years ago, an actor friend of mine was working in a Broadway revival of Chekhov's *The Sea Gull.* He played Trigorin, the novelist, who has an affair with Nina, the lovely young romantic. In a long scene at the end of Act II, Trigorin tries to explain to Nina that the life of a writer is not so glamorous as she imagines. Actually, of course, it's Chekhov speaking. I'll extract a few of the more pertinent exchanges.

Trigorin says, "We will talk about my splendid bright life . . . I am haunted day and night by one persistent thought: I ought to be writing. I ought to be writing. I write incessantly, post haste, and I can't write in any other way. What is there splendid and bright in that?"

Nina says, "But surely inspiration and the very process of creation give you moments of exalted happiness?"

"Yes," Trigorin answers. "While I am writing I enjoy it. And I like reading my proofs, but . . . as soon as it is published I can't endure it, and I see that it is all wrong, a mistake, that it ought not to have been written at all, and I feel vexed and sick about it."

"Forgive me, but I refuse to understand you. You are simply spoiled by success."

"What success? I have never liked myself; I dislike my own work."

All through this scene, my friend told me, he was aware of suffering in the first-row-center aisle seat. Someone was writhing, groaning, and sobbing. When the curtain fell at the end of the act, and the house lights came on, he rushed to the slit in the curtain to see who'd been so deeply moved by Trigorin's confession. It was Theodore Dreiser.

Now I'm not presuming to compare myself with Theodore Dreiser or Anton Chekhov. Certainly we are miles apart as artists; but we all identify with Trigorin as authors. There are very few writers who do not dislike themselves and their own work.

When the editor of this anthology asked me to select my best story, I told him that I didn't have any best; I had nothing but failures. He was surprised, and mentioned a few of my things which have been admired.

"I don't like any of them," I said. "They're all disappointments to me. This is why I rarely reread my old manuscripts; they make me sick. And when, occasionally, I come across a touch that pleases me, I'm convinced that I never wrote it —I believe that an editor added it."

"Then can't you pick the story that gave you the most pleasure when you wrote it?"

"No. A writer is extremely schizophrenic; he is both author and critic. As an author he may have moments of happiness while he's creating, but as a critic he is indifferent to this happiness. It cannot influence his merciless appraisal of the finished work.

"But there's an even more important reason. The joy you derive from creating a piece of work has no relationship to the intrinsic value of the work. It's a truism on Broadway that when an actor particularly enjoys the performance he gives, it's usually his worst. It's also true that the story which gives the author the most pain is often his best."

I pulled out a quotation book, which automatically fell open to a familiar page. "Samuel Johnson said, 'What is written without effort is in general read without pleasure.' And Lord Byron wrote, 'Oh that I had the art of easy writing, which would be easy reading.' My favorite line is from Ring Lardner's story, *A Caddy's Diary*, 'Writeing is a nag.' "

"What about the Natural; the story that writes itself?"

"I had that experience just once, when I was writing the Jimmy Melton show. The Thanksgiving date was coming up, and they'd hired the great Josephine Hull to star. I had to tailor a Thanksgiving script for her, and I didn't have an idea. I thrashed around for six days, growing more and more desperate.

"The night before submission I couldn't sleep; I'd never missed a deadline before, and I was ashamed. Toward dawn I dozed off, and, by God! dreamed the entire script; narrative hook, characters, conflicts, development, and denouement. I got up and tottered to the typewriter like a somnambulist, afraid that the slightest distraction would shake the story out of my head. It wrote itself in three hours."

"Well? Wasn't that written without effort?"

"What about the six days of suffering that produced it? How effortless was that?"

"You must have something for this collection."

"No, I don't. When you get right down to it, my best works are still notes in my Commonplace Book. But I know damned well that as soon as they're developed into stories they'll become disappointments, too."

"All right, then," he grinned. "Pull out some of your old notes, and we'll include them."

So I leafed through the heavy leatherbound journal which I've been keeping for twenty years, and selected some of the fragments, notions, colors and curiosities entered there. They're copied exactly as they were noted down anywhere from a year to twenty years ago. Some are hopelessly old fashioned today; a few might stand up. Many have already been used by other authors, and this raises some interesting points.

There are some ideas that are in the air, and come to many different people, simultaneously and independently. This is why, for example, historians are still arguing about who was the first to discover printing with movable type, the telescope, and motion pictures. Hollywood experiences this phenomenon quite often. Suddenly authors from all over the country will simultaneously submit similar story ideas.

But the truth is, the idea itself is relatively unimportant; it's the writer who develops it that makes the big difference. The identical idea would turn into totally dissimilar stories when written by different authors, which is why professionals are not quite so generous as they seem when they freely exchange ideas and suggestions. They're aware of this. It is only the amateur who worries about "his idea being stolen."

Here, then, are some ideas from my private world of science fiction. All, whether they've been used by other authors or not, were original with me in their time, and remain my best so long as they remain safely in my Commonplace Book.

The respiratory reflex does not begin spontaneously in the newborn; it must be induced. Hence the slap on the bottom of the delivered infant. Babies that do not cry when slapped, die of suffocation. Suppose for a science fiction story an infant will not begin breathing but lives anyway?

Do you remember that Bryn Mawr girl they brought down to the physiology lab? She had no regular respiratory pattern; just sighed every minute or so. As one of my professors explained, she was doing practically the same thing the rest of us do. We simply move dead air in and out with shallow breathing, and take a deep breath when our systems require oxygen. In this girl the automatic respiration pattern had never formed.

See Rabelais, p. 125, for the idea of evolutionary change being the result of climate change on earth. Birds walk and fish crawl in a world without wind or water. What climate change would alter Man's mode of thinking?

A circulating brain library in a Womrath's of the future, where you can rent a brain for any purpose.

Tell a story from the POV of a calculating machine.

The Lucky Man. Suppose good fortune is a question of ether or sunspots?

A story about weather smugglers.

There must be a place where you can go to remember all the things that never happened to you.

A crime story set in a future in which crime no longer exists because the police have time-scanners and can go back into the past and ferret out evidence to convict.
(I remember mentioning this to Horace Gold of *Galaxy Magazine*. He said the time-scanner gimmick was pretty dull, but would like me to do a crime story in a future which made crime difficult for more original reasons. That eventually led to a novel called *The Demolished Man*.)

The city that haunts a man. He stumbles on it in the course of a lonely walking trip. He meets fascinating people and has incredible and inexplicable adventures until he realizes that all the strange complications have only one purpose, to hold him in the city. It's dead, a ghost, hungry for living inhabitants.
(Some years later, Lerner & Loewe used a rather similar idea in their lovely musical, *Brigadoon*.)

A wishing warehouse, rather like a mail order house, in the fairy world, where all wishes are received, filed, and filled, if the order is for something they have in stock, and the client has an account in good standing. A mail order catalogue for such a place would make lovely reading.

A man who goes about buying up all right, title and interest in dreams.
(I think Truman Capote used a similar idea once.)

Little heaps of semi-precious stones sometimes mark the deathbeds of extinct giant birds. The moa carried pebbles in its gizzard, like modern chickens, to help grind up its food. Since it lived on very tough twigs, it needed extra-hard stones. Consequently, it swallowed quartz, chert, chalcedony and jasper. Or, to put it more rationally, it swallowed all sorts of stones, but the softer varieties disappeared while the harder remained. They've been found in small heaps of rounded stones, measuring about two inches in diameter, and weighing about two ounces. The same holds true for fossil dinosaur remains.

Under odd circumstances, a protagonist obtains a book which, he is warned, is fatal to read. Everyone before him who has read it has disappeared. Our hero reads it anyway, anticipating the occult and the *outré*. He finds he is being bored by a very dull series of uninteresting biographies of unknown men. Then, in the very last chapter, he discovers he's reading his own biography. He has fallen into the book.

(The editor of this anthology tells me that a variation of this idea was nicely handled by James Blish in *The Book of the Dead*.)

Can we do a story about a man trying to escape from a hospital or insane asylum . . . We hear the rasp of a file on iron bars . . . He works furtively, at first, and then more and more recklessly, until suddenly he realizes that everybody is aware of what he's doing, and is calmly ignoring it. Why?

Chipped stone tools are made from rocks which, like glass, give a smooth, sharp edge on fracture. Actually, glass is the best material, and when the first telegraph lines were run across Australia, it became a problem now to keep the natives, who were still living in the Stone Age, from stealing the insulators to chip into knives. This was solved by dumping a load of broken glass and crockery at the foot of each pole so that the native could get his raw material without having to climb for it. Translate into science fiction.

(The editor liked that idea when I first told him about it. He is still pestering me to write it.)

The Lefthanded Killer: a *tour de force* about a murder which (we tell the reader immediately) was committed by a lefthanded killer. But we show, directly or indirectly, that every character is righthanded. The story starts with, "I am the murderer," and then goes on to relate the mystery, never revealing who the narrator is, using the same technique Agatha Christie used in *The Murder of Roger Ackroyd*.

The final twist; killer-narrator turns out to be an unborn baby, the survivor of an original pair of twins. The lefthand member killed his righthand brother in the womb. The entire motivation for the strange events that follow is the desire to conceal the crime. The killer is a fantastic and brilliant monster who does not realize that the murder would have gone unnoticed.

Check on twins and twinning. Are they mirror images?

Often, in the complicated dream lives that children lead, they invent an imaginary companion who is their friend and playmate. But what if this imaginary friend actually appeared one day?

(The editor tells me that this idea has been adroitly developed by many writers.)

It has long been known to deep-sea diving supervisors that it requires greater effort to concentrate under sea pressure, and loss of memory is common—especially in depths exceeding 200 feet. There was one case of a diver who was positive he had lost consciousness, despite the fact that he had been talking, answering, and executing orders from the telephone all the while he had been under water.

Most divers report the "Idle Thought" phenomenon at great depths. They are continually obsessed by an idle thought which may or may not bear some relationship to their surroundings, but which certainly has nothing to do with the purpose or execution of their work.

Translate this into deep space.

At some time in the future they find a roll of film from the past, exposed but undeveloped. They develop and print it. What complications might result?

(This was inspired by the discovery of the last camp of the lost Andrée expedition, in 1930, and the miraculous recovery of the expedition photographs, taken in 1897.)

Extrapolate the modern hardboiled detective into the future. Today's Private Eye is physically ruthless; tomorrow's Future Eye will be psychologically ruthless. The Private Eye beats up and is beaten up with indifference to physical pain. The Future Eye will inflict or endure psychiatric pain with the same indifference.

And there will be another contrast. Private Eyes are physical ruffians, but psychological sentimentalists. The Future Eye will be a psychological ruffian, mercilessly tearing apart peoples' psyches, but a physical marshmallow . . . the kind that picks flowers and shrieks at the sight of a mouse.

When one dreams that one dies, one always wakes up. What would happen if you didn't? If your unconscious let you die?

Would you dream deeper? On what level? About what? Would you enter another world, undreamed of up to now?

Ben B's suggestion that the nuclear age may break down our moral codes; viz: incest may become necessary and desirable to preserve pure blood lines. This reminds me of the Egyptian pharaohs who practiced incest to preserve the royal line untainted.

The fingertips of apes have no loops or spirals; just a series of slightly curved perpendicular lines. Prehistoric man, Stone Age man, had simple loops; no more. Only historic man has fingerprints as we know them. This is how phony prehistoric pottery was revealed as a fraud. The prints on it were too modern.

It is told in Gibbon that when one of the Moslem kings died, the following inscription was found on the inner door of his private closet: "I have been absolute ruler for fifty years, with nothing to fear, and the world in my hand. Every joy, every luxury has waited on my command. I have been feared by my enemies, and loved and respected by my people. And I have been happy exactly fourteen days."

What a theme; to find those fourteen days!

The fascination of these fragments is that you never can tell what they may turn into. A note I made for a TV sketch for Paul Winchell, entitled *I Remember Hiroshima*, a satire on *I Remember Mama*, became a science fiction story called *Hobson's Choice*. A gimmick I worked out for the old radio show, *The Shadow*, became another story, *Fondly Fahrenheit*, when combined with an incident I picked up from one of Mark Twain's biographical sketches.

That's the wonder of the Commonplace Book; the curious way an incomprehensible note made in 1950 can combine with a vague entry made in 1960 to produce a story in 1970. In *A Life in the Day of a Writer*, perhaps the most brilliant portrait of an author in action ever painted, Tess Slesinger wrote: "He rediscovered the miracle of something on page twelve tying up with something on page seven which he had not understood when he wrote it . . ."

Many entries found in this ramble through my Commonplace Book have me shaking my head in bewilderment because they haven't tied up with anything yet. Why did I carefully list the Language of the Flowers? What is the meaning of the question: "What is third sight?" Here are vagrants' symbols from a 19th-century vagabond's road map. Why? Why the Seven Deadly Sins, meticulously listed in English and Latin (Latin!) and fully described from *Piers Plowman?* Some day I'll know. They'll cross-pollinate, something totally unforeseen will emerge, and then, alas, I'll have to write the story and destroy it. This is why your best is always what you haven't written yet.

And this explains the reluctance of so many authors to begin the actual act of writing. The most lunatic example of this aversion was demonstrated by a friend of mine. He had an assignment to get a script in, knew the story he wanted to write, had an okay from the client and network, but nevertheless stalled for a month. Two days before deadline he still had written nothing.

His wife told him, "Look, I'm taking the kid and getting out of the house tomorrow. You'll have the place to yourself, no distractions, and you get that script written."

Next morning she got up at six, dressed the kid, and left the house. They had breakfast, took a long bus ride up Riverside Drive, visited The Cloisters, took another ride downtown, had lunch in the zoo, went sightseeing in Macy's toy department, went to Radio City Music Hall, and had dinner in a restaurant.

By seven o'clock the kid was very tired and began to get cranky, so she had to take him home. She arrived in the house just as her husband finished polishing the last of a 116-piece set of table silver.

And that script still remains the best thing he has never written.